THE VELIERI UPRISING

BOOK THREE

POWER UNLEASHED

TESSA VAN WADE

ISBN: 979-8-9878741-6-5 (hardcover)
ISBN: 979-8-9878741-7-2 (paperback)
ISBN: 979-8-9878741-8-9 (ebook)

HARLOW & KITT PUBLISHING

Printed in the United States of America
1st Edition 2024

For the world.

It's time we clean house and take our Power back.

PROLOGUE

I stare across the street at two women, one light haired and the other dark. In an instant, I become a mother with very little memory of it. The joy of my newfound freedom falls to the wayside, as this revelation sinks to the pit of my belly. Not a criminal anymore, but a mother who abandoned her children at their youngest and most impressionable ages. Tears begin to build within my eyes.

Arek watches me. I'm sure he's grateful to not carry this secret alone anymore, yet it is obvious by his face that he fears my response.

"Remy," he says softly.

I look at him but say nothing. There is so much confusion. How could he have not told me? My children. Our children.

My feet are planted on the dirty sidewalk along the cityscape of San Francisco. This hustling metropolis, where my life as an Epheme took place, still holds a rich, but suddenly strange nostalgia over me. The air smells of spices and herbs from nearby restaurants that I would go to in my past life as a teacher. That world, that experience— DeSean, the other students, Ian, my apartment—seems so long ago.

I barely notice the high-pitched hum of electricity, the click-clack of street cars, and, like most days, the rushing wind through corridors and alleys that forces everyone to wrap their thin sweaters a bit tighter. Today, I just let my skin turn to ice.

The last time I was here, I was single, empty of hope, lost after my mother's cancer, and afraid of everything. So much has happened since my name was Willow, that I do not recognize her anymore. I have laid that name to rest with the old and lonely life that used to be mine.

However, this existence continues to prove that it will not be easy. Maybe it's not life if you aren't having to prove to yourself and to others that you can dig deep and make it through. I'm angry with myself at this moment as my eyes follow the perfect curvature of their cheeks. These women are so clearly a combination of Arek and me. My chest feels hollow and, although it should be a moment of great joy, it is by far the opposite.

I step closer to the curb, my shoulders tight. One of the women resembles Holona—Arek's mother: her long, dark hair drapes her back and her green eyes are the exact hue of Arek's. The other could be my sister: blue eyes and dark blonde hair framing high cheekbones. My toes teeter dangerously close to the edge, as the blonde one extends a hand and gives a faint smile. I desperately want to run to them, but Arek gently stops me by holding my arm.

"We can't," Arek whispers.

"What?" I turn to him, horrified.

"We can't, not yet," he says again, his eyes surveying every corner of this block as if we are still running. I turn away from him and take a bold step off the curb and onto the street.

"Remy," Arek says. He does nothing to stop me, yet there's wisdom in his voice that I catch. Defiantly, I continue anyway. Just as I reach the yellow line in the middle of the road, I hear his voice again. "Remona," he says calmly. "Please. Trust me for once in your damn life."

The women look on with opposing expressions. The blonde smiles with excitement, while the one with dark hair has pursed lips and a tight jaw. Eventually she crosses her arms in front of her.

Cars pass and honk as I stand on the traffic lines. It is obvious from the look on Arek's face that he doesn't wish to tell me no, however, he hopes that I will recognize the danger that I'm placing us in. My chest rises, then after a moment, falls with surrender.

"Remy," Arek says, his voice enveloping me with compassion. "I spent years keeping them safe, making sure that no one, not even Sassi and Kilon, knew about them. Please . . ."

A memory returns—two beautiful daughters, one dark haired, the other light, barely able to walk on their own, waddling along the Spanish hills near our cottage. I grab them in my arms and spin around as the sun hits their faces. If my memory serves, this is only a small bit of time before my execution.

So much time lost, I think to myself. A wave of sadness unlike anything I've ever felt before crashes over me—a mother's instant love. *Yet, how can that be, I've never really been a mother.*

Unexpectedly, Arek's voice is right next to me as I emerge from this memory. "You are a mother. You carried them, gave birth to them, loved them."

Without force or expectation, Arek's hand gently takes mine as I invest one last look toward the women across the street.

He looks at his daughters, lifts his phone in the air to tell them that he will call, then winks. One responds with a nod, and the other with a wave, but then together, they go back to their day. It is obvious they know the extensive lengths Arek has taken to make sure they are safe and, as usual, I am the only one who wants to break the rules.

He laughs, "No, you're not."

"Get out of my head," I whisper as he wraps his arm over my shoulder, but I pull away. Most of the time I say this casually, but today I am angry.

"As if I had the choice," he whispers in my ear, so close that his lips touch my skin. When he studies our surroundings again, I can't help but ask, "Is there some kind of danger that I should know about?"

"Until Navin is dead, there will always be danger."

"How could you not tell me?!" There is no reason to hold back anymore, and it explodes.

He moves us into the shadow of an overhang and cocks his head to the side as he runs his hand through his hair. "Do you think it was easy to keep them safe? It was the hardest thing I've ever done. Anybody could be watching, especially after the mess we just made by sending Covey to the Cellar. You'll meet your daughters at the Gianda tonight. But until then, trust me."

I glare at him, so he steps closer and runs his hands down my face. "Trust me."

I close my eyes. "How did I not remember?" Tears finally fall down my cheeks and the cold air hits the streaks. "My own children. How could I do that?"

"It was the best way, Remy." He waits until I look up at him. "It was the best way. Had you known when you were weak, Navin would know about them."

I lean against the brick building as he comes closer. "It was the best way. Do you trust me?"

Through sheer stubbornness I don't want to respond, but ultimately I do, "Yes."

He grins playfully. "Are you sure?"

I look away, trying not to smile. "Yes."

He places an arm around my shoulders as we move down the sidewalk and pass a woman wearing yoga clothes while carrying her mat and a roofer who is taking pictures of his next job. Arek stops walking for a moment and looks at me, his green eyes complimenting the blue sky as I look up. There is a new longing within me that I've never felt before and it's drawing me back to my daughters. "Tell me their names?"

4

He smiles. "Lya . . . our Lioness. She is everything that word means and more. Her dark hair will be gray before yours."

"And Daye. She is full of brightness and sunshine just like her hair."

"Lya and Daye," I whisper. I rest my hands on my head as my cheeks continue to burn and a battle wages within me of whether to hold on to my anger, to run back to them, or to accept how difficult this must have been for him. "I missed everything." The words wrestle their way out of my mouth.

Arek slides a hand under my hair and against the side of my face as he says, "I'm sorry."

"I just always thought I would be a good mother."

"You were."

"What do I say to them? What do I do?"

He pulls me to his chest as I fantasize about what it would have been like to be with them as they grew up—instead, Arek watched his wife reach every milestone at the same time as his children.

A loud clang makes both of us jump, until we notice a store owner has thrown his security gate open. "Life never slows down," I breathe out.

He lifts me into his arms until my feet dangle. "I'll make it slow down for a bit. For the first time in a long time, I have you to myself for a few hours."

I touch his strong jaw and cheek, then trace his lips with my thumb. He kisses me, sending the natural healing aloe through my skin that only my Yovu can, then it swiftly turns to electricity that travels through my lips. "Come on," he says.

A few minutes later we step inside the grand foyer of the Palace Hotel near Union Square. I look around with wide eyes, having never had the money to experience this place before. Several people walk by, looking at me strangely. One of them can't help herself and reaches us before we leave the lobby.

"Excuse me, Miss Landolin . . . or maybe Rykor?" She looks

at Arek, then at me with confusion, but neither of us knows the answer so we say nothing. Her tall red hair is perfectly quaffed and hair-sprayed, and her southern accent drips heavily from her painted red lips. "I can't believe we are running into you. I knew it all along. I never believed what they tried to tell us about you."

"Thank you." I smile at her as Arek leads me away by the hand.

"It's a true honor to meet you," she says as her husband pulls her elbow, whispering to leave us alone. "This world is going to be better for it."

As they walk away, she speaks loudly to her husband, "I told you it was her."

In just a few minutes we enter a beautiful hotel room and before I can even turn around, Arek leans in, grabbing my lips with his own. It starts gently, but rises in intensity until I'm desperate for breath. His mouth parts my fervent lips as he takes my face in his hands, letting his wallet and keys fall to the floor. I follow suit and our bags scatter about. Every kiss from Arek is just as vibrant, just as wanting, just as perfect as the one before. There is no greater comfort than his large frame wrapping around my own, and after so many years of loving the same woman, it still makes my stomach flip how much he so clearly needs me and wants me—a constant convincing that I am whom he desires.

Before we can go any further, as if his kiss has reminded me that he, too, has his own story, I pull away just slightly. "Will we ever talk about what we just experienced? In Tri Planum?"

He stares at me for a moment. Then for the first time, Arek's pain comes to the surface. "I watched the last breath of the love of my life, the mother of my children, stolen from me before her time . . . there will never be words horrible enough. But now you're here."

"Holona's death, Sassi and Kilon's daughter?" I hesitantly broach what we haven't spoken of that showed itself within his unconscious. "Holona was found to be a witch?"

"Many Velieri women were," he says, as I watch his jaw clench.

"My mother was no exception."

"It is no wonder why Navin hates Ephemes."

Arek stands taller at just the mention of his brother. "We have all lost parts of ourselves, and no more than Ephemes. That is war."

"It's no wonder that moment stayed within you."

"I was young. Her trial was propagated with stories of Satanic rituals and spells—but I always knew they were just rumors and gossip from men who claimed to know God better than most."

My hand is on his chest and I feel the rapid beating of his heart under my palm. "The women in your life bring you a lot of trouble."

"The women in my life are exactly who I want them to be. They are strong and ready for anything." He narrows his focus to stare into my eyes. "It was after your death that things were different. I had work to do and little girls who needed protection. Briston, Elizabeth, and Prophet Jenner helped me raise them to be the strong women that they are, but not once did I ever believe we were coming close to how you would have raised them."

I lean in and kiss his bottom lip. When he lifts me into his arms, I wrap myself around him, my strong legs finding this easy. I've now experienced Tri Planum and before long, as he kisses my neck down to my belly button, we pass from one level to the next. He kisses each hip bone, while gliding his own body over mine as he makes his way up. All the while, he pulls my shirt over my head. His large hands caress every inch of my body until my breath shakes. A small groan escapes my lips, which makes him smile.

CHAPTER ONE

Within the city, there are three blocks that look to be several buildings nearly seven hundred feet high—fifty stories. The idea is the same as the Niemeyer classics in Rio de Janeiro, except for the architecture, which is a mix between Victorian and modern. From the outside it appears to be separate buildings, but on the inside, Arek and I walk into the urban sprawl, passing several guards along the way who know us both.

Even though it's grand and people are staring, I have no other focus but meeting Lya and Daye. *What will I do? What will I say?*

The many Fidelis that walk about the open space, going about their business, comfortable and protected within these walls that Hok and I conjured up, recognize me immediately. In Brazil, perhaps due to the impending threat, the people were timid and careful not to come too close, but it is different here. Kids run up to me with large smiles on their faces and groups of people leave their businesses to gather around us. We shake hands and touch their shoulders—there is a sense of peace.

"It is because of you," a middle-aged woman with an unusual

shade of black hair and desperately pale skin says, "that I have been able to raise my sons in a world where they aren't declared criminals for the acts of their grandfather." Running around her legs are two little boys with bluish black hair and several more boys of different ages standing behind her. The eldest is near twenty.

Arek and I catch eyes as people tell us their stories, and he grins. Soon, a short woman with gray hair, a tattooed neck, and wrinkled skin, who stands only at the height of my elbow, comes to my side. Arek notices her immediately and chuckles. "Good evening, Tam," he says.

"Good evening, sir. I can take you to Lya and Daye if you'd like?" she says with a voice that matches her size.

"We'd like that. Thank you." He turns to the throng and lifts a hand. "You all have done an amazing job here. Thank you for welcoming us. We will meet with Lya and Daye, then later we will say our goodbyes before we leave."

As everyone disperses, Tam leads us past the crowd, into an elevator, and up several stories. "It's good to see you, sir. And can I say, Remy, it is a pleasure to finally have you back." Just then the elevators open to reveal an expansive and white hallway that I've seen before. We take a few paces, until something occurs to me, and I stop.

"Oooooh, Arek . . ." Before I say anything, he already knows what's on my mind. I continue anyway, "This is it. This is the white, marble hall . . . in your unconscious." I whisper to make sure that Tam does not hear.

Arek nods, "Yeah, I guess it is . . . just a truncated version really."

As Tam walks a few steps ahead, I grin, "How hard did you have to work to keep Lya and Daye out of your unconscious?"

"Well, remember when we first practiced . . . the first time that I failed taking you in with me?"

"—the water. That's why it was so difficult, and Navin was there. You were trying to keep us from knowing about them." I shake my head with the realization.

"Their entire lives. It was my mission to give them the freedom that you so desperately wanted for them."

Our eyes connect for just a second before Tam stops in front of a door and sweeps her hand toward it. "They're ready for you."

"Thanks, Tam." Arek nods and Tam leaves from the direction we just came. "You ready?" The question is rhetorical, since he opens the door before I answer.

Behind this door are several rooms, split by glass walls—very modern, very open. Many people sit at desks, talk on phones, and tap on computers. The glass walls that divide do nothing to hide Lya and Daye in the very back room with a group of people sitting around a table.

Arek doesn't wait and quickly heads there, passing each desk while saying hello to all, who are intrigued by his presence. Finally, he reaches the conference room and the moment he opens the glass door, our daughters smile.

One of them clears her throat. "Can you leave us with Commander Rykor, please?"

The group exits, except for one man who has a soft belly, scraggly beard, and shy eyes that give no command to his presence at all. Using a remote control, the blonde quickly presses a button that turns the glass wall black so that no one can see in or out. The moment this happens, both hurry toward Arek and wrap their arms around him. After they release, Arek turns to the man at the end of the table and shakes his hand, "Adam. It's good to see you."

Arek looks at his daughters with a kind face, clearly understanding the gravity of the situation. "I know you thought it would never happen. Daye," he touches the shoulder of the blonde woman who looks very much like me, "this is Remy."

"Remy, this is Daye."

For a moment, there is hesitation on her face, until it is replaced with a large smile. Instantly she brings her hands together in front of her and shakes her head. "I have been waiting all my life." She hurries forward and hugs me until I can hardly breathe. When she pulls away, she clicks her tongue. "It's weird that you're younger than us, but I'll take it."

"I have enough memories at this point to have lived hundreds of years, so not exactly," I say with a grin.

Daye looks at me a bit more. "I guess you're right. Welcome back, Mom." The sound of this is shocking. I breathe in heavily and smile.

Arek clears his throat, then looks at the other woman in the room. "This is Lya."

Lya's presence is different. She does not run to me, and she's careful to not smile too big. Instead, her eyes remain serious, and her response is reserved. I can't help but notice how much she takes after Arek and strangely even a bit of her uncle Navin. "Welcome to the Gianda. You built it, so you should be proud," Lya says without much emotion at all.

"Thank you," I respond.

The guy at the end of the table uncomfortably clears his throat. Lya rolls her eyes toward him. "This is Adam. He's my husband."

My breath catches. They've lived a full life without me. Everything is new. I know nothing of their lives on this earth, except that they have lived here, hidden from everyone. "So, he knows?" I ask quickly.

Arek nods. "Yeah," he says reluctantly. "I made it clear that if he betrayed my trust, I would kill him."

Adam awkwardly hurries forward, nodding his head. "Yeah, he did say that. But Remy, I want to promise you that you can trust me." Just as he's about to reach out his hand to take mine, he knocks over a pencil holder and spills pencils all over the table and floor. Out of surprise, he pulls back and hits Arek in the chest with his elbow, to which Arek glares at him—not helping his nerves. "Sorry!" He drops to his knees and picks them up quickly. "It's just so good to meet you."

Daye has not stopped smiling and she takes my arm in hers. "It's so good to have you here."

I breathe out a long forgiving breath, feeling the relief extend through my limbs. "It's unbelievable," I say quietly as I look into her eyes. More memories instantly rush back of them as babies. "Your eyes haven't changed."

"You remember?" Her excitement shows itself by the pitch of her voice.

I nod.

Lya nearly turns her back to me, while smiling at her father. Her beautiful long black hair is all that I see. Daye notices and gives me an "I'm sorry" look.

Lya picks up her keys from the table and wraps her arm in Arek's. "I want to show you what we've been working on."

Arek nods, "Okay."

Moments later, we're wandering through the Gianda with Lya at the lead. "I heard you used Tri Planum against Alfonzo's men. No one can do that."

Arek chuckles then with a rise of his shoulders says, "Well I guess that's not exactly true, is it?"

"You know what I mean." She refuses to look at me. There is a strength and stubbornness within Lya that makes her seem indifferent. Whether I am there, or I never returned, it appears to mean very little to her. She continues, "We built out the wing that you, Hok, and I talked about . . . just like we said we would." We pass the main square, pass several businesses on the main floor, then walk through several halls. We reach a door with intense safety measures. Lya stands on one side of the door and Daye stands on the other. There are what look to be long and thin mirrors that they stand in front of. A bright red line begins above their heads, then quickly scans their bodies all the way down. Both women state their names, then lastly reach their hand and place it on the mirror where the red line has turned into a red circle. Finally, the thick metal doors open.

We enter a room with black shiny floors. Along the walls from floor to ceiling are weapons of all kinds behind glass. Arek looks around with a smile as Lya waits for his approval.

"What do you think?" Lya asks him.

"It's exactly how we discussed." Arek smiles with a nod. "Hok would be proud."

"He was," Lya says with a grin. "He was here last week and gave his seal of approval."

"What have you prepared for an emergency? Can you get to them quickly?" he asks.

"The room knows who is allowed. We've installed all leaders' information and the computer can tell who you are by heat sensor, eye sensor, and anything else that it needs. It's been calculating since we entered. Call out what you want, even if you don't see it," Daye explains.

Arek spins around. "Saiga 12."

Within moments, we watch as the weapons behind the glass shuffle about, revealing that what we see is just the surface of what is actually behind these walls. Finally, a section of the glass casing shoots out into the middle of the room. Twenty-five Saiga 12 shotguns hang on metal pegs behind the glass.

"Touch the glass with just your five fingerprints," Lya explains.

"Where?"

"Anywhere."

Arek reaches out. The moment his fingerprints touch the glass, it slides away, letting him grab any of the guns. "M7A3 CS gas grenade," Arek says again. The wall juts out from across the room, this time carrying grenades. "Amazing. I'm proud of you." He turns to me, "Even though we didn't have the technology when you died, this was your idea."

"Mine?" I ask with surprise.

"Yep. All of this was you and Hok. Your vision was seen through because we saw value in it," Arek explains. I notice disappointment in Lya's eyes and feel it with her energy.

"Let's keep going," Lya says. We reach the thick metal door on the other side of this room and it slides open when she steps toward it.

Beyond this large weapons armory, we enter a massive open room with hanging lights every few feet. "We managed to get our architect to construct this space. It has more than one hundred thousand square feet."

Rows of Fidelis in dark gray uniforms with weapons on their belts stand shoulder to shoulder within these cement walls. Their hands are linked behind their backs and their chins remain high as a woman with curly brown hair tied up under a hat walks through them. She is the most decorated of them all.

Her deep and resonant voice yells, "We stand, we fall!" Then, the soldiers in unison return the command with, "Fidelis!"

"Next drill . . ." she yells. "Eight to one. Do not think! Do not question! Pass their guard. Spread out for eight to one!" They adjust their weapons at their sides in perfect unison then move into equal groups.

"Impressive," I say.

Daye stands nearby. Despite her thirty-five years, there is an innocence to her smile, and she nods. "It's all due to her. Commander Wakefield. Since she's come in everything has been different. Don't know what we'd do without her."

Adam, Arek, and Lya take a few more steps.

"You've been busy," Arek mentions.

"The amount of sign-ups increase every day." Lya's intensity is consistent. "Especially with what I have been finding. I have something to show you."

Daye leans forward, "I'm pretty sure she means WE have something to show you. But you should watch this first." She points to the rows of soldiers.

Commander Wakefield calls out. "Prepare!"

The groups of eight, without hesitation or confusion, place one person in the middle of each circle. "Go!" Commander Wakefield hollers. I watch in awe as the soldier in the middle of the circle must fend off all eight attackers. Some are able, while others are seized and must start again. We watch for a moment, intrigued by the process until Lya makes it clear that we must move on.

"Just wait," Daye suggests.

"No. We don't have the time. Come on." Lya steps into an office nearby, as Daye rolls her eyes. We follow Lya into a round room that gives a 360-degree view of the training hall with windows all the way around, from the waist up. Several people are working on computers. Only one portion of the wall does not have windows, rather it is a screen with live information constantly being updated. What the numbers are, I don't know.

"What is all of this?" Arek asks as he walks to the nearest picture.

Lya clasps her hands behind her back. "These are hundreds of people we have found in our research that continue to be a part of some underground group called the GENOS."

"GENOS," he repeats as though he knows the name. Arek looks at her. "I've only heard that once . . . don't know what to make of it."

Lya shakes her head. "Honestly, neither do we . . . but what we do know is that everyone on this wall has some connection to either Covey or Hawking." She raises her eyebrows at Arek, knowing this is important information. "The strange thing about them is that we don't know why they are all connected, but I've never seen so many Black Hats in all my life."

"Black Hat?" Arek rubs his jaw as he always does when he's uncomfortable. "How do you know they're Black Hats?"

"What's a Black Hat?" I ask.

"Criminals who can hack into anything," Arek explains.

Lya crosses her arms in front of her. "We started noticing a lot of traffic . . . not just a lot . . . ridiculous amounts of traffic on these sites that were all set up for Velieri. We wouldn't have thought twice about them, except we got a strange call a few months ago. It gave us no reason, but told us to look into these groups. So, we did. Regular and ordinary Velieri are a part of these groups called the GENOS. However, it's the leaders of each site that have us concerned. They are all ex-criminals from the Cellar, all known for their prolific ability to hack into anything and everything. Black Hats usually don't like to work together . . . but apparently now, they do. Not only that . . . we can't get into these websites. I've had every hacker of mine try and it's almost on an invite basis. I don't really know how to get in. But we need to. Something's going on and it's not good. I can tell you that."

"Did you try Beck?" Arek asks.

"No." Lya admits. "He won't answer to anyone."

"Yeah, that sounds about right." Arek looks at the picture for a moment. "What do you think is going on?"

Lya breathes in heavily. "Well . . . one time we managed to get a little bit deeper, but the web was so large and so intricate that it felt like the amount of these groups far outnumbered anything we've ever seen before."

Daye sits in a chair near me and taps her fingers. "We're sure Navin is a part of this. Whatever it is."

"Why do you say that?" I ask.

Lya turns to me with a furrowed brow. "Are you serious? You of all people should know that Navin, right now, is a part of everything. Especially when it comes to Hawking and Covey."

"But Covey's in the Cellar," I say. "There must be more reason than that. Sure, they've worked together before, but how do we know these GENOS have anything to do with Navin?"

Lya's temper is obvious. It reminds me very much of Arek . . . the constant burden of the world on his shoulders. I can see that I will have to earn her respect.

"There is one way we know Navin is a part of this. Look." Lya takes a piece of paper posted to the nearby wall and hands it to Arek.

Arek reads the paper. "This is the date of Remy's execution."

Lya nods.

Something comes to Arek and it shows on his face. He looks at me and lifts the paper. "Navin has used the date of your execution as a declaration, a code, what he has put as a stamp of the rebellion on anything and everything for many years. The day he proved to the world that the Prophecy wasn't real."

Lya continues, "And for only a moment, just one branch we followed used this code. They might have found that we were getting close and they stopped using it. Which is why I'm sure that Navin is heading this."

Arek nods. "Okay, well, keep people on it. Have you told Leigh?"

Lya smiles for the first time since I met her. "Grandpa? Are you kidding? He's supposed to be searching for Navin himself, but do you know where he was last week?"

Arek looks at her. "Where?"

"He was with Hawking. They had some sort of meeting in the Courts in Switzerland."

"By themselves?" Arek asks.

"Yeah."

"How do you know all of this?" I ask Lya.

Daye answers instead, "She never sleeps."

"Shut up," Lya says to her sister. "I feel like it's my job to make sure we keep an eye on our uncle."

A knock sounds on the door and Commander Wakefield comes in. "Will you come watch this?"

Lya and Daye hurry outside, where the commander has spread all the soldiers into a large circle. Only one person waits in the middle, although he doesn't seem to be sure why the commander has him waiting.

"I need you to see this," the commander explains. Then she calls out several names and more than eight very large men head into the middle too. "Clutch!" she yells, as though it is the name of the lone man in the middle. He is no more than eighteen. He is short with dark skin, hair, and eyes, but his body is stocky and curved with muscle. Staying there in the middle, the large men surround him.

Wakefield nods at them, and instantly they crouch down in fighters' position and circle one another. Arek stands close to me as we wait for what's next. Then suddenly the men lunge forward. They do not separate for Clutch's ease, but Clutch begins to strategically and calculatingly take them down. He jumps out of the way when needed, attacks strategic body parts to immobilize, uses one to confuse the other, and after a few minutes, he is out of breath, but the only one standing. The large men are sweating as they lie on the floor.

Arek whistles, then calls out, "Well done!"

The commander looks at her stopwatch. "It took five minutes and twenty-seven seconds."

Both Lya and Daye smile. "We've been working hard around here." Lya says with pride.

I turn to Commander Wakefield. "Are they Tracing while they fight, Commander?"

She clears her throat. "We teach Tracing after they've been taught strategy for the fight."

Lya sarcastically laughs. "You want us to flood their brains with that right away?"

Something occurs as I stand there—she's not someone who will back down unless I make her. "I think that Tracing is the first thing we need to teach."

Arek waits a moment, knowing his daughter's possible reaction before responding. "You're doing a great job here, but yes, I do think that you should be teaching this first."

The commander gives Lya the side eye as if to say *I told you so,* then smiles in agreement. "I'll start working with them on it. They know Tracing, but are they capable of truly affecting someone with it, while they fight? I don't know." She asks, "Why don't you give it a try?"

I look at Arek as though he will respond but realize quickly that she is speaking to me. "No, no, no. I don't think so."

"You suggest Tracing as though what we're doing is wrong, then you won't show us why?" Lya says. "That's convenient."

I glare at Lya, but she refuses to care. So, I reluctantly agree. "Sure."

The walk is silent and slow. Soon, I stand in the middle of eight men, larger than me by at least fifty pounds and six inches of height. Before the commander yells for us to drop into ready stance, I begin Tracing. Searching through their minds with a fine-tooth comb. Riding the wave of their energy is more important than how I physically move anyway. There's a difference between those who are skilled enough to remain invisible and those who climb haphazardly within someone's brain or into their psyche one at a time trying to dissect their rhythms. With this, they can't move as quickly or succinctly. It doesn't matter if they are even trying to Trace me, I can feel nothing but their emotion and hear nothing but their specific cadences. Gliding into the Void—where all things become clear and precise, where calculations can be made in only seconds—is like breathing now. While these men are Velieri, it is obvious as I slide right in that they know the basics, but lack the greater understanding of our psyche in fight mode. I close my eyes, draw in my breath, and begin my assault. They are waiting for the commander to say go, but I've already begun. The best I can describe it is throwing a lasso around their fear and pulling it to the surface.

Just as the commander yells, "Go," I've lassoed my last man. "Go!" she yells again, but nothing is happening. There are no footsteps running toward me as I slowly open my eyes, while never letting go of their most sensitive secrets. One of them lost his parents, another battles the demons of his own anger daily, and how easy it is to wrap myself within these moments to steal from them mentally and physically. Just as when Kilon was comatose on the floor in Tri Planum, none of these men are moving a muscle. Carefully, without losing my hold, I walk to each of them. It is unexpected when just our energy alone clashes midair and their feet are pushed back along the cement floors. This reminds me of the first fight I witnessed within the Union School when Navin's feet scuffed the floors from

Arek's energy alone.

One by one, I lay a hand on their chest and they fall to the ground. They instantly wake with intense confusion. Not only that, but they breathe as if they've run a marathon. Their fatigued bodies lay flat on the ground as their chests rise and fall.

Well, that's the first time I've ever done that, I think to myself.

Somewhere behind me I hear the air conditioning fan click on. Arek's wide eyes are the first that I see. He grins, but covers it up with his hand when Lya looks at him.

The commander shakes her head and comes to my side. "Perfect example. Thank you, Remy. It's time to work."

When I pass Clutch, he sticks his hand out to shake mine. "Amazing. Thank you, Miss Landolin."

"If you're capable of fighting like that, then you're capable of this. I know I'll see more of you." His dark eyes and skin shine under the lights as he nods his head.

"Thanks," Clutch says, then walks back to the group of soldiers.

When I get back to the group, I look at Lya. Like acid to her tongue, she says quietly, "You proved your point."

"Yeah, because that's what she was trying to do," Daye says with sarcasm while rolling her eyes. Then she looks at Arek, "When are we leaving?"

"Leaving?" I ask with surprise.

"Yeah, the Prophets and Powers have called together a meeting in New Orleans," Daye says with a beautifully large smile. "We're going with you to meet the others. Our bags are packed and clearly my sister needs some down time."

Lya gives Daye an angry glare, but Daye passes by without a thought. "Get your bags, sister," is all she says.

Arek walks me around the Gianda a bit more as Lya and Daye prepare their last things to leave. While both Giandas have everything that the other has, there are small differences, particularly in design. "Are all of the Giandas different?" I ask Arek.

He nods. "Yeah, you wanted it that way. You wanted to make sure that each one of them felt like a different world."

"Lya doesn't seem to be too excited that I'm here," I finally mention, after debating whether I should say anything at all.

"Listen, Lya is our fire. She lives and breathes justice . . . and sometimes with that, she's bound so tight that I wonder if she'll someday unravel. Unfortunately, she needed her mother the most, and with you being gone, she created armor that is hard to break. She'll come around."

A few minutes later we stand at the entrance as the crowds gather about to see us off. With one final wave of her hand, Lya addresses the crowd. "Adam is staying behind. Be strong, be safe, and we'll see you all soon."

Lya walks to Adam, and for the first time, for just a moment, I recognize that there is a softness there as she kisses him. And just like that, the power of the Yovu is in full display.

CHAPTER TWO

The jet lands softly and I smile when I see Kilon and Sassi waiting on the tarmac for us. Kilon leans against Sassi's beautiful white Rolls-Royce Cullinan with a slick black suit, while she's standing not too far away looking like a six-foot-tall model in a pure white, fitted suit. This is the longest we have been apart since this all began and as Lya sits across the jet, either ignoring me or giving me the side eye, I want nothing more than to be with them again. When they drop the airstairs, I take them two at a time and jump into Sassi's arms.

"We missed you," Sassi says as she kisses my cheek, then Kilon grabs me until my feet are dangling from his massive frame.

"So, you can stay alive without us there?" Kilon quips.

"It's not as fun though," I say, to which Arek responds with an insulted, "Hey."

Lya and Daye follow with their bags. It is easy to forget that Sassi and Kilon do not know the truth. To them, Lya and Daye are no different than Hok—chosen to oversee San Francisco's Gianda.

Sassi takes one of Daye's bags over her shoulder. "Welcome, Lya and Daye. I was glad to hear you were coming."

"Good to see you, Sassi," the women respond.

It feels strange to keep such a massive secret from Sassi and Kilon, even though Arek's reasons are valid.

After climbing into Sassi's expensive Cullinan we soon find ourselves driving through the deep green, overgrown backroads of Louisiana's bayou. "This place hasn't changed," I say of the Spanish moss hanging loosely and the sounds of crickets, running water, and croaking frogs. Everyone looks at me with intrigue.

"Have you remembered more?" Kilon asks from the passenger seat.

"It keeps coming, little by little. Holes are starting to fill in," I mention with a soft glance toward Lya and Daye, who sit behind Arek and me.

"After all that we lost during your execution, this was the only place we found comfort. We needed to recalibrate and figure out how to live without you," Sassi says as she pulls the vehicle onto a lush green drive.

"So instead of figuring that out, you thought . . . nah let's just go watch her for a while. That'll be interesting enough." My words drip with sarcasm.

"Are you kidding? I think Arek called us the second he found out that the Fellows found a baby with the same DNA as Remona Landolin," Kilon breathes. "I knew then that we couldn't run off to the Bahamas like I had planned."

I crack the window to listen to the bayou. "Yet even with all of that . . . here we are: I'm back and we're free."

Lya chuckles, "You are not technically a criminal anymore, but Remy, we are not free. And the damage that has been done since you came back is irreparable."

Arek takes my hand and sets it on his thigh.

Sassi looks in the rearview mirror with a furrowed brow toward Lya, but I can see that she thinks better of saying anything. "I'm going to stop for a second." Sassi pulls beside some old-timey gas pumps in front of an out-of-the-way store. The lime green tin of the roof is practically swallowed by a massive weeping tree that hangs over its rusted metal.

The humidity thickly moves down my lungs as I take my first breath upon exiting the car, then follow Sassi up the stairs. The clerk inside, a young girl with a kind smile, says good morning. This store is old and small with the barest of shelves. I walk through the cracker aisle as Sassi grabs coffee, and Arek talks on the phone just outside the front door.

Two middle-aged men, dressed in dirty clothes, their hair long and scraggy, enter after a few minutes. Their unlaced boots hang from their feet, so they make a lot of noise when the rubber of their soles squeals against the floorboards. They subtly take glances at Sassi and me while snatching items to buy.

It doesn't take long to find what we need. We stand at the counter, when I can feel an energy behind me that makes my skin crawl.

"Haven't seen you two around here." His voice is raspy and deep from smoking. The sour smell of old cigarette breath passes my nose and I cringe. "I would remember you two if I'd seen you here before." His grin shows grayish yellow teeth behind his unkempt beard. "Where you from?"

Neither of us say anything.

"It's rude not to answer," his friend, who stands beside him, says.

The clerk, a young girl, looks around our shoulders. "I don't want none of this in here today. Please, Joe. Not today."

"What?" Joe shrugs. "I'm being nothing but friendly."

When we turn to leave, the men block our way to the door. "We don't live far; you wanna come to our house?"

Sassi steps toward him as she hands me her items. "I'd suggest you move."

"Come on, we won't hurt ya. Just wanna get to know you is all." The man steps closer to Sassi until he's within inches of her. The other comes closer to me. Just then Lya and Daye enter the front door but stop when they feel the uncomfortable energy.

"You know what?" Sassi asks him.

"What?"

With fast hands, Sassi takes Joe to the floor by slapping her arm across his chest and sweeping his feet out from under him with her leg behind his ankle. The crack of his head against the tile is angry and loud and she quickly places her knee on his chest while he struggles to catch his breath.

The second man shouts at Sassi, "Hey!" and lunges toward her, but I quickly block the way. I decide to have a bit more fun.

"Hey yourself," I grin. He doesn't realize what I'm doing, but I've Traced him in seconds. Every time I Trace him—his name is Al—a bit of his filth and wreckage is revealed. The hairs stand tall on the back of my neck, from even the smallest glimpse of his darkness through which I sift. Something sits quite shallow within his subconscious, a memory . . . I suddenly walk along a dark road in the country, the only light from an old 1967 Chevy truck coming toward me. It has rusted parts and broken windows and I hear yelling from within its cab. As I walk toward it along the beam of headlights, the passenger door opens, and something—someone—falls to the ground. In seconds the engine revs and Al, sitting in the driver's seat, races away. The woman on the ground is silent and beaten, her face no longer looks normal. While I see this full memory, knowing of the crimes this man has so easily committed, it takes me only a moment before I become his worst nightmare. I can make him see anything. So, I study her face as I use this memory against him. When I lean toward him, my eyes are red with broken blood vessels. Within his mind, I've turned myself from Remy to this woman he left for dead. However, it's my choice, my power, and I use it. Not only do I have her face, bloody and swollen beyond measure, but his mind creates a monster. Her eyes are no longer human, her teeth are now daggered and drip dark liquid. He steps back with wide and terrified eyes as my face distorts.

"What's wrong?" I allow very little space between us. Every time he steps back, I close the distance. "What do you see?"

He trips over one of the displays, sending cups all over the floor. "No!" he cries out. He trips on the cups and falls to his back.

From under Sassi's knee, Joe calls out. "Al?"

I dig a bit deeper and bend down closer to Al's face, which makes him crawl more aggressively until his fingernails bleed, when she turns the red eyes toward him and a low growl replaces my whisper. "What do you see?"

"No!" He covers his face.

"Look at me," I whisper. He shakes his head and yelps in fear. "Look at me!" Finally, through slitted eyes he tries to, as sweat pours from his forehead and his eyes gloss over. "You see, it's not forgotten. She's always there."

"Joe!" Al yells as he now pulls both arms over his face to block himself from the monster.

I clear my throat. "You're gonna take your friend home and neither of you are coming back through here. You understand? Ever."

"Yeah . . . yes! Yes! We understand!" he yells.

Finally, I back away and let him clamber to his feet. It doesn't take him long to tear out the door, refusing to wait for Joe. After Sassi lets him go, he also runs out as Kilon salutes him with a sarcastic, "Bye."

Sassi addresses the clerk as she grabs our things. "Hopefully they won't come back."

"Thank you. They give me trouble every week," the young girl says, and appears truly relieved.

As we walk to the car Sassi looks at me with a shake of her head. "You're getting dangerous."

"Dangerous? Me?" I chuckle.

She gives me the side eye and lifts a brow as she climbs into the car. "That was fast. Scary fast."

Arek walks by me and leans in close to my ear. "Scary . . . and sexy."

"They've called a meeting," Kilon says from the front as he looks at his phone.

"Why?" Lya asks from the back seat.

"They want to discuss the empty seat since Covey is gone," Sassi tells her. "But the meeting is not for a couple of days."

"What could they possibly want from any of us?" Lya shakes her head and looks out the window at the passing foliage. "Just find Navin and let us do our jobs."

Arek clears his throat. "Prophet Jenner has asked that we come. She doesn't wish for her and Prophet Mannon to be alone in their quest for time."

"Time for what?" Daye asks.

"Time to find another crooked Prophet," Kilon growls.

I speak up, "What are these cottages ahead?"

Kilon looks back at me, "This land is ultimately owned by Landolin Enterprises. Your grandfather owned the deed and passed it to your father. Briston has been kind enough to house plenty of us over the years. Conferences between the Reds and the Powers have been had here, gatherings before declarations of war, even housing famous actors and musicians." We drive down a tree-lined road that ends with a circle drive and a large white-pillared home with a wrap-around porch. Deep in the woods surrounding this home and along the property, puffs of smoke waft in the air from small chimneys hidden within the trees. "Those are the small cottages where each one of us will stay."

When we come to a stop, I step out of the car, and just as I do, a heavy breeze brushes past me reminding me instantly of moments throughout the years when we stayed here; visions of President Kennedy, Babe Ruth, Aretha Franklin, Sarah Vaughan, and even Bobby Jones, the golfer from the '40s. The more I am visited by these visions, the less they feel like they once happened—but rather,

Bobby Jones smiles as he passes me. I watch him walk up the stairs, then his body slowly dissolves into thin air, until I am looking at, once again, an empty porch. Arek notices my stare and comes close. "What's going on?"

"President Kennedy was Velieri?" I ask.

He understands suddenly. "No, he wasn't. We wish he was. He was holding meetings for years, between the Reds and the Powers, in order to find a solution. If he had lived, we might have found a way for Velieri to stop hiding."

"Wait, I remember now." I see him standing there beside me, my pill box hat sitting demurely on my head.

"Yeah, that's why the Epheme world has so much mystery about his death."

"Wow," I whisper.

Briston rushes out when he sees that we are there and quickly hugs us all. I watch him as he greets Lya and Daye—while he is careful, there is an obvious connection from granddaughters to grandfather. A part of me wants to break the secrecy immediately.

"Soon," Arek whispers.

We quickly drop our things in individual cottages, while slowly the group starts to arrive. First is Gal and Diem, they screech their car to a halt on the cement circle drive and jump out. "Cheeee!!!!" Diem yells. He runs to Arek and lifts him in his arms for a hug. Gal dances around Briston, then sweeps him into her body.

"Aye, the party is here," Gal laughs.

A bit later, a beautiful dark blue Lexus LC 500 pulls into the drive as we have gathered for tea on the porch. When Mak steps out of the car—his handsome face sharing with me a sweet smile—I am tempted to run to him, but I stop quickly when Aita emerges from the backseat. Kenichi slowly collects himself as he arises from the passenger side.

With a grin, Arek says, "Aita wanted to come. I told him it wouldn't be a good idea but apparently, she was adamant."

"This should be fun," I whisper back.

He runs his hand down my arm and walks away as Mak comes to the bottom of the porch stairs. "Hi, my friend," he says to me.

"Hi," I answer back.

"It's good to see you and I promise, she will be on her best behavior," Mak says and winks, so I simply grin.

An hour later, a new car drives down the tree-lined road and parks behind the others. A driver emerges that I don't recognize, then he walks to the back and opens the door. All of us stand when we realize who has come. Prophet Jenner exits the car in all her beautiful glory. Her bright dress flows behind her, accentuating her curves. Everyone looks on with surprise.

"Prophet Jenner," Kilon smiles, running down the stairs and greeting her with a hug.

"Kilon." She bows her head, then takes his arm as she walks up the stairs. "Don't be so surprised everyone. We have work to do."

By evening, we sit around the large table in a grand dining room. The table is covered with hot and delicious food, while the chatter has reached an intense decibel.

Everyone quiets when Elizabeth—who has been recovering here—descends the stairs aided by Briston. The color has returned to her face, and her eyes don't look as lost as they once did.

"Everybody eat," Briston commands.

Elizabeth sits just across from me. "It's good to see you, Aunt Elizabeth."

"It's good to be seen." She untucks her napkin and sets it properly on her lap in preparation.

"How are you?" Sassi asks from the other side of me, as the rest of the guests default to their own conversations.

She hesitates uncomfortably, then nods. "I'm okay . . . thank you. It's taking me a while to feel like myself again." Briston runs his hand along her back. After so many years and so much devastation in their relationship, they can now be together. I watch their lingering eyes and his tender touch.

After tapping her wine glass, Prophet Jenner clears her throat when people quiet down. "You all have probably wondered why I called you all back together so quickly. I need you here."

Arek shifts uncomfortably in his seat as he can tell something has happened. "Prophet Jenner, it's not a time for secrets. What has happened?"

"They know something. And I don't know what." Prophet Jenner is tense, even though her pursed lips indicate she's desperately trying to keep it together.

"Well, that's nothing new," Sassi states.

"No, you're right. And I do think it's important for everyone to just enjoy themselves tonight. Let's give ourselves fully to the freedom we feel at this moment." Prophet Jenner reaches for her glass of wine, but Peter stands and tops it off before she can reach it.

"Looks like you could use it." Peter nods as he sets the bottle down.

"Yes, honey, thank you." She takes in a large sip of the local wine. "Let's bless each other with laughter, song, and dance . . . maybe in hopes that this will someday be our normal."

"Cheers!" Everyone beams.

"Then tomorrow we work," she says, more as a command than a suggestion.

We all know that Arek will never be able to let his guard down with such vague information. "Prophet Jenner, we have to be prepared for what is happening. What have they said?"

She breathes out, but then looks over at Elizabeth. "Elizabeth, why don't you—" But Elizabeth interrupts her.

"Prophet Jenner, I'm okay, thank you. I can handle it. Besides, I'm better than ever and I want to see this end. No more Navin, no more rebellion, but also no more corruption and hiding. I will do anything to make that happen."

Briston runs his hand along her arm with a smile.

"I don't know who, but they're trying to fill Covey's seat quickly.

I need you all there to vote. We need to make it impossible for them to choose another Prophet without knowing who is truly corrupt."

Lya speaks up, "I have proof that Hawking is just as corrupt as Covey."

Daye chimes in as she sits beside Geo. "We have proof."

Lya rolls her eyes. "They get what I mean. What do we do? Do you need me to be able to share this?"

Arek and Kilon both shake their heads at once, as though they've spoken about it. Arek speaks first. "No. Until we know who we can trust, it's best to keep our cards close."

Lya nods.

Peter suddenly speaks up, his eyes serious and reprimanding, "We're going to keep it quiet, Aita, right?"

Her deep red lips part slightly with surprise and her eyebrows furrow. "Why are you pointing at me?"

Peter adjusts his look to say, *Are you kidding?*

Mak stays quiet, clearly not wanting to speak for his wife, and soon she takes in a breath. "I am here to apologize to Remy. I told Mak that I want to be a part of the team and hope that you will allow me." Even Kenichi turns a side eye to Aita, to which she replies, "What? It's true!"

Instead of challenging her more, I nod. "I think that's great, Aita. Welcome."

Our eyes meet and although it is not a perfect connection, we understand each other.

"Well, with that said," Prophet Jenner breathes out, "I do not want to ruin our night. It's been too long since we've enjoyed ourselves. Let's make sure that we do."

Just after dinner, the lights are dimmed as we head into the grand room. Wine and champagne fill our glasses all night. Music covers the room, while some dance and others laugh. For the first time since this began, everyone lets themselves go. Sweat covers our skin as we move to the rhythm.

Aita comes to me, her perfect red lips thin and surrounded by brilliantly porcelain skin. "It has always been difficult for me."

I can barely hear her over the beat, yet her eyes are genuine. I touch her arm with my hand. "Let's go outside . . . get away from the music."

We walk out onto the wraparound porch. I wait for her to speak first. "He loves you still," she whispers.

"No, Aita."

She lays a calm hand on my arm with surrender in her eyes. "It's okay. I know why. I hated you because of it, but I see . . . I see that you are Arek's. But Mak loves you and will always. I cannot compete."

"Aita, I . . ."

"It's okay, Remy. I have done everything I can to break that bond, but I realize now, it is impossible. But I don't blame you. Not anymore."

"Why? Can I ask? Why don't you blame me anymore?"

Aita leans on the railing and looks out over the land, so I follow. Then her soft voice speaks gently, "I see you with Arek. It is how I look at my husband."

There is so much vulnerability in Aita that I place my hand on hers. "Mak loves you."

She smiles and looks at me with a sideways glance. "You are kind to say so."

Someone clears their throat behind us. When we turn, Arek is smiling. "Come with me."

"I—" I begin to protest because of Aita.

She nudges my shoulder with her own. "You should go. We'll talk later."

"Are you sure?"

"Yes. Thank you."

I start to walk away and take Arek's hand, but I stop and turn back, "Aita . . ." she looks at me. "It's good to have you here."

Arek leads me through the people, never saying where we are going. I stop at Mak as we pass, "Go find your wife," I tell him. It is obvious that Mak is surprised by what I've just commanded. Yet he smiles as I point to Aita through the double doors.

When we step out under the night stars, I pull on Arek's hand. "Where are you taking me?"

He stops just as we've begun the small trail toward our cottage and comes so close that I can feel his chest on mine. "It's time."

"Time for what?"

"You'll see."

The cool breeze kisses our shiny skin. Soon, we step into the cottage, and his eyes stare into mine for a moment. "Marry me."

My heart races. The way he looks at me catches my breath. "Aren't we already married?"

"Your execution makes that a bit tricky. No one really knows the answer to that."

As he runs his hands through my hair, then traces his fingertips along my neck, I nod.

"Here . . ." he says as he hands me a simple dress that I've never seen before. I slip it on and catch myself in the mirror. So much more than my appearance has changed. For the first time, there is a woman looking back at me, feeling only little remnants of darkness. After the Cellar, there were moments that I never believed I would recover, but here I am.

When Arek reenters the room with a white button-up shirt and dark pants, the nerves rise within my body. At times I forget the force that he is.

He looks at me for a moment, clearly enjoying my appearance. Then he reaches out his hand, "Let's go."

Along a wooden path through the heavily forested bayou, we duck beneath hanging branches and moss, following lanterns that light both sides of the lazy river. A soft ethereal music plays somewhere in the distance. "What is that?"

He doesn't say anything, but his green eyes tell me a story—one of love and loss on the greatest of scales. Others might have given up through the tough moments, but we managed to find each other again.

As we walk, the earth talks to us, from the drops of soft dew in my hair, to the chirping and croaking, and the passing water. The vibration within my skin where he has left his mark is impossible to ignore. I danced with many tonight at the party, but there were none that left me with lines of heat and electricity on my skin like him.

Finally, we reach an old moss-covered dock on the edge of the bayou, where trees are growing out of the enclosed space. Small lights are wrapped about each tree, and fireflies bounce around from here to there. The outside of this covered dock is in shambles but as we enter the small woodshed where lanterns line the ground, the orange glow erupts and dances on the walls. Everyone is there with smiles as we enter—even Mak and Aita. Just ahead Prophet Jenner waits while Daye and Lya stand on each side of the room.

She begins the ceremony. It is unlike an Ephemeral wedding. She takes my hand, then sets his on mine as she speaks beautiful verses from somewhere in the Manchester Books. "Yovu need no one, and nothing except the sacred tie held only by their match." She interlaces a red ribbon through our fingers, then around our hands and wrists and lets the end of the ribbon hang down nearly to the floor. After she speaks, Arek says quietly, "I need you and no other."

An image comes to me of the man who watched me outside my apartment in San Francisco. So much time has passed, yet it also feels like so little.

"I need you and no other," I whisper, then smile.

Finally, he kisses me as applause fills the quiet bayou.

He pulls me into him, then drops his lips to my ear as he whispers, "Forever my wife."

CHAPTER THREE

My heart pounds in my ears as I run through the thick rainforest. With each heavy step, branches and twigs break beneath my feet as large elephant-size leaves slap my face, forcing me to use my sleeve to wipe the drops of dew away. It doesn't really matter anyway as the humidity has mixed with my sweat and it cascades down my temples, chest, arms, and even on the small of my back.

Arek also weaves in and out of the trees to my right. I see a flash of color just beside him and yell, "Arek!" as he is overtaken by someone and they crash to the ground. He wrestles with the stranger, growing dirtier with each roll and turn. I've been told to continue no matter what happens, so I keep racing through the bayou.

Who is around? I can feel something or someone, yet I can't see them in the lush trees near the bayou. My legs burn with every hill, yet my newly developed muscle helps me cut in and out. On my back I carry a bag with several weapons, but the faster I go, the more it bounces so I yank its leather strap tighter across my chest to hold it in place. My lungs are on fire, but I am used to it now.

A dock appears between the trees, which only makes me push harder, however beyond sight or sound, I can feel that someone is tracking my movements. I search to my right and catch the slight difference between the green leaves on a nearby tree compared to the shuffle of camouflaged clothing. My eyes stay fixed to this spot in the trees, until it moves and instantly my body alerts to the pursuer. But he's far enough away that I'm not worried . . . not yet. Only then, directly behind me, my skin rises, and my spirit is aware of someone. I count to three. Then I dive forward, headfirst, into a long jump, curling at the very last minute into a forward roll. Just as a figure in black flies above me, missing me by just an inch. This surprises him when he nearly hits the tree ahead. His face is covered by a black mask.

He runs directly at me, but within five moves I have him down, and my Benchmade Adamas knife is tight against his neck within my fist. Before I pull his mask off, two more men appear from the thicket. I roll onto my back as they come near just so that I can see their ankles and take control. I find one and wrap my arms around his ankle while climbing his thigh with my legs, then squeeze like a boa constrictor. My pressure on his hip counters against his ankle and takes him off balance, sending him to the ground, then I wrench his ankle and knee until he cries out in pain. The other attacker is trying to stop me, but my constant movement makes it difficult. I trip him with a swipe of my heel and point my weapon at his skin.

This frees me, so instead of dealing with them anymore, I choose to run. Three more men come from all around. Yet it is the thumping shoes to my right that I am more interested in. I turn my eyes for just a moment and catch my father's sweaty face. He has no shirt on and for his many years, and just coming back from near death, he looks fit and healthy. In fact, he says this is the fittest he's been in centuries. Navin's injection was harder to recover from than expected. Briston runs to me, as the men set an ambush from every side. They outnumber us; however, my father and I take every one of them down. Our chests rise with deep writhing breaths, ready to be done.

Briston takes control of the man I am kneeling on and yells, "Go, Remy!"

I am learning. Instead of arguing with the Electi, or choosing to do something else, I leap from the ground and race through the trees. Bullets hit the trees beside me, but I dip in and out of line. Finally, just out of the corner of my eye, there is an abandoned home. Moss covers every inch, as ivy hangs from the roof to the trees and untamed shrubbery. I hide behind one of the trees, then beeline my way within the abandoned place. After finding a dark back room with multiple exits, I pull my bag from my back and start shuffling through the weapons.

My hair stands on end. Lately, my intuition has surpassed any of my other senses. I grab my gun, pressing myself up against the wall as my skin dances with the energy of someone in the next room. Slowly and methodically, a man with a mask comes out of the room next to me. Keeping my feet light, I take him down before he even knows that I'm there, yet this only brings five more men to the fight. In less than a minute, I have them all on the ground, every one of their weapons safely in my possession.

"Okay! Enough!" someone yells from outside. "We're done for the morning."

"Oh, thank god!" I yell.

The men on the ground groan and pull their masks off. Systematically I add insult to injury and offer my hand to help them to their feet. "Good job, Remy," one of them says as he rubs his ribs.

"Thanks." I smile and pat him on the shoulder.

Geo appears through the front door and puts his hand out to high five me as he walks up. "Even better than before," he says.

We exit the abandoned building to see the others heading our way. Diem cheers from the distance as Arek walks to me with a smile and a bloody lip. Gal and Diem make their way to us. "I told ya my men would give ya hell," Diem says.

"Your men, you oaf?" Gal asks Diem as she hits his chest with her hand.

"Aye, my men." Her eyes dig into his and it's clear when Diem changes his mind, "Our men."

"Be quiet, you nit," Gal growls.

Geo lifts an eyebrow as my father appears with a towel already around his neck, "And you're doing pretty good, old man."

Briston says fiercely, "Just wait until you get three hundred years older and see if you look as good as this."

Geo chuckles, "I believe I have Gyre's fate upon me."

"You're going to look like Gyre?" I ask as we step out into the woods.

"That is the apparent possibility if I make it as long as they have."

"But I thought we are the Electi blood. We're the longest lasting." I nudge my father's shoulder.

Briston raises an eyebrow and his shoulders. "Sure, if we are ever allowed to live that long."

"Showers," Sassi calls from the top of the nearest hill. "Then a bit of meditation and a meeting with Prophet Jenner tonight."

⌇⌇⌇

We gather deep in the swamp where plenty of large-bottomed cypress with feathered foliage stand tall above the dark and mossy waters of the bayou. The air is thick with humidity, which makes my skin glow and my hair thick. Egrets and pelicans stay for a moment, cocking their heads to figure out whether we are safe. They soon flee to the air while their cries warn that an enemy is near. Just ahead, a long wood-slatted bridge juts out into the water, then curves slightly to the left until it disappears into the massive wall of trees, water, and foliage. Where the end of this bridge leads, I don't know. However, the mystery of the bayou and the echo of all its inhabitants is magical, so wherever the bridge goes, I am convinced it is a perfect place.

The boardwalk is barely wide enough to allow us to pass each other, so we head out across the swamp, one by one, and take a seat on the wooden bridge. One step too far on either side and I will fall into the murky waters and possibly hit a couple of trees on the way down. There are no railings, and it feels so shaky, that I wonder if Geo has made sure this bridge can carry all of us.

Our team keeps growing, and even so, they've become family. Sassi, Kilon, Peter, Geo, Gal, Diem, Lya, Daye, Arek, Briston, and I take our places. Soon we all listen to the natural chime of the bayou. Lying with my hands palm up in order to feel the vibration of my blood pumping through my veins helps calm my mind. At first, I fall into the Void where everything feels weightless and at peace. In all my training now, Kenichi and Geo have done well to teach me that the Void is only the beginning of this Velieri Meditative state. As long as I reach the Void, empty of thoughts and negativity, accepting all the light that God is, the Sui—a word the Velieri use for Spirit—delivers what can only be described as complete peace. It feels a bit like falling, but also floating. As the afternoon descends, I hear a whisper, "Open your eyes."

At first, I test that it is not my own thoughts and wait. Yet again, the whisper fills the space within and outside of my body, "Open your eyes."

Slowly, I look up to the darkening sky that is not yet full of stars, but no longer daylight. Spanish moss blows back and forth from the large monstrous oak above and I watch it for a moment. Yet the feeling that I have is nothing like I've felt before. The air becomes rich as though I am breathing in speckles of gold. Something divine has filled the air with its perfect nature until it passes through every molecule of everything. A mist has rolled in along the water and the sky has turned shades of purple. Yet there's something more in the space around us. At first it appears that within the purple sky are misshapen and jagged lines of shadow. It is difficult to understand, yet I study it, trying to delve deeper. Everyone else still lies along the bridge with their eyes closed—I am the only one sitting up and looking around. They seem to be unaware of this voice that I hear, and what I am seeing at this moment.

Are these shadows a part of the clouds or mist?

The longer I watch the more I see—these shadows—they move like we move. They pass each other, dance about, walk from here to there.

The longer I gaze at the always-changing shadows, movement becomes clearer. The same voice whispers again, "Look beyond." My breath catches as I try to understand what it is that I'm seeing. Then it becomes clear. I am being shown what is happening when we think we are alone, when we think there is nothing beyond what we see. The movement of the souls and the ones—whatever they are called—that exist with us. It isn't like human existence; it is the same as when two photographs develop one on top of the other.

Then, in the quiet of the murky water and the rustling trees, a faint chorus of beautiful song and chatter envelops me, and I stand to my feet as the awareness opens up even bigger; these spirits, souls, or whatever name they go by pass around me and the others. This other world seems just as dedicated to their own work—or whatever it is that they are doing. And somehow, I know they are always aware of us, unlike us to them. I cannot see them fully, rather the best that I can describe it is a shadow or an apparition that leaves a trail of its luminance.

A bright flash happens suddenly, and I am alone with the apparitions. Gal, Sassi, and the others are gone. Only Holona stands there.

"Holona," I whisper. "Does this always exist?"

She looks at the apparitions about us and nods. "There's always more than you can imagine petitioning for you." She sighs, but not in a profoundly good way. "Remy, you will have very little time to rest. The world can't wait any longer. This is a harsh place and only getting worse."

"Can't wait for what?" I look at her with question, but it's like she doesn't hear me.

"It's time," she says. "You're trained now and you will see things that others won't. Don't be afraid of it." Her eyes are calm as usual, but her tone is cautious.

"Holona, is everything okay?"

It takes her a moment to respond. "It will be."

The soft smell of moss, evergreen, and cypress fills my nose with a bit of smoke from the main house. The air is a perfect mixture between cool and warmth. I listen to the frogs, bubbling water, hooting owls, and even swipe my hand at the buzzing mosquitos that pass my face.

When I swipe my hand by my face, I notice it looks different. So, I take a better look. My breath sticks in my lungs as I notice the deathly gray of my fingers up to my wrist. Places of deteriorating flesh plague every inch of my hand and it starts to shake with adrenaline. My skin begins to fall away from the bone and I gasp just before pulling my decaying hand to my chest. When I look up again, I am no longer on the bridge in the bayou with Holona. I am somewhere near a man-made ditch nearly half the width of the river. Men, women, and children stare at me from inside the ditch with longing in their eyes. I walk closer to the edge of it.

What is this?

Something touches my thigh and I look down. A little girl with gray skin and sunken eyes stands next to me. "Help," she whispers and moves closer. She reaches out her hand. Her skin is dying in places just like mine and I gasp.

"Remy?" Arek's voice wakes me.

By the time I blink, once again I am back with the others in the bayou. They are all sitting up and staring in my direction.

"What happened?" Arek asks.

I shake my head. "I wish I knew."

CHAPTER FOUR

After an early morning run, a hot shower, and a small breakfast, I meet everyone within the main house. Together we drive through New Orleans and venture out into the countryside of Louisiana. After miles and miles of vast open fields, I see the rounded top of a very large building. Signs pass along the road that say, "Restin Power Plant." Just these signs alone flood my mind with memories. It is not a power plant, rather this large building in the middle of nowhere is this territory's Cellar. I'd come here many times in my life for many reasons, but the main reason is that the Elite Bloodline of the Landolins has always taken its place at proceedings. It is our job and our duty. Or at least it was, until I brought shame upon the Landolins and died as a criminal. My execution did not happen here, rather in Switzerland, but it doesn't seem to matter within my body. My heart begins to pump heavily as the automatic gates take my father's code and begin to open for our caravan.

This building has clearly seen many renovations over the years and is now surrounded by the best security money can buy. Guards stand along every ten feet with their dangerous weapons held at their sides. Sassi drives up to two large doors and they squeal as they open, letting us continue on to the underground parking lot.

"I can't seem to escape this place," I whisper.

Sassi clears her throat. "The difference is that you aren't a criminal anymore. That changes a lot."

"I hope so." I still find myself rubbing my hands together until they're sweaty.

Once we've parked, we take a modern elevator up several floors and it opens to a grand hall where a large crowd has gathered. Everyone turns to see that it is us, and they stare with surprise. Or perhaps anger. We know that Navin is never without his spies, wherever we are.

On my right within this large hall are the four effigies—these are the Velieri statues made to represent every reason the Ephemerals cannot win. These statues are double the size of an actual man and beautifully hand carved out of a green marble. To ignore those who are unable to look away from me, I walk to the statues to study them. I remember every inch of these in particular. My grandfather walked hand in hand with me, explaining the reason for each of them. This was long before these green marble statues were brought to the Louisiana Cellar, but rather they sat within the walls of an old 14th century church that has since been torn down. "An old man by the name of Henry de Marte carved these beautiful statues. It only took him twelve years to complete all four. This one with no neck declares that the Ephemes cannot and will not look behind them to learn from their history. This one was my favorite." My grandfather smiles at me with his kind and rugged eyes. "This statue with two heads shows that Ephemes notoriously cannot and will not work together. It is always said that if this head could turn toward this head, it would bite it off completely, never realizing that it would kill itself by doing so. And this statue with the necklace of gold so heavy it cannot live a normal life . . . it cannot even raise its head." My grandfather clicks his tongue, showing disgust. "And last, a statue with no eyes."

Strangely, as I study these creatures, it occurs to me now that I've lived both sides, that neither side lives in peace well. The tribal nature of humanity is just that—hellbent on blame and judgment while turning a blind eye to their own sins. It seems apropos as I stand in wait to watch this spectacle that is about to happen within the courtroom.

When the doors open to the courthouse, we begin to make our way in. Just as I'm passing the doors, I hear faint but eerie voices from somewhere down the hall toward the doors that lead to the Cellar. Even here, when I am not standing directly within the Cellar, I can feel the evil seeping through any cracks. Somewhere deep down, below our feet, are men and women alone in their cells pulsing with a darkness that we will never understand.

There are rows and rows of seats, with varying differences to the courtroom in Switzerland. Five chairs are lined up in front of box seats and stairs. Once we sit, the doors to the wings of the stage open up and many of the Powers take their places within the box seats. My father climbs the stage, then up some stairs and into his own box seat, the same as Kenichi and Mak.

"If my father is here, he will be on the stage with the Powers in that seat," Arek says as he points to the right where Leigh always stands. "But if he is not, I will take his place. It is expected."

"Of course." I nod.

As the Powers file in, the courtroom audience chatters away. Only when one of the guard steps forward and announces the Prophets does the courtroom get quiet. One door opens and Hawking, with her red-braided hair, dressed in the white robe that nearly matches her skin, enters first. She is followed by Zelner, then Mannon, and last but certainly never least, Jenner. One high-backed chair has no occupant since Covey is hopefully rotting away in his cell in Switzerland.

Arek begins to stand, until Leigh finally enters. His stiff body stomps across the stage to take his place in a lone seat on the right. Prophet Mannon, being the oldest prophet left now that Covey is gone, sits with the gavel in his hand. Prophet Jenner peers through the crowd.

Prophet Mannon hits the gavel against the wooden sound block to gather everyone's attention. "Good morning. It's eleven o'clock a.m. and I'd like to call this meeting to order. Roll call, please."

One by one, starting with the main representative from each territory of Power, each person stands, says their name, and to what territory they belong. My father stands, introduces the other two representatives with him, and then himself. "Briston Landolin, Switzerland." The Prophets then declare themselves and finally Leigh stands, "Leigh Rykor, First in Command of the Protectors."

Mannon continues once the roll call has ended. "We come here on this day to discuss freely the next step we as a Velieri Government must take in order to swear in the next Prophet. I leave open the floor. You will request to be heard."

Prophet Jenner presses a button on her desk, one that every desk carries, and a blue light shines from her seat. Mannon grins as though he knew Prophet Jenner would be the first. "You have the floor, Prophet Jenner."

"Thank you, Prophet Mannon. After many discussions with the Prophets and Powers, as well as civilians, I believe it is in our best interest to choose to leave Covey's seat undeclared until we can do our due diligence in providing the people their best option for leadership. A great deal has happened in a short amount of time and I just don't think—"

She is interrupted by Prophet Hawking, who now carries a foul expression. "We cannot drag our feet on this, Prophet Jenner. One Prophet was stolen from us and it is of dire need that we fill his position immediately."

Mannon clears his throat. "Prophet Hawking, please refrain from speaking until you take the floor."

Prophet Hawking shakes her head. "Of course."

Prophet Jenner continues, "I understand that we have many things to discuss. However, a Prophet cannot be chosen without due diligence."

Prophet Hawking begins to speak, but Mannon gives her the eye, to which she reaches out and presses her button. A blue light shines beside her seat. "I am afraid to say that we do not have the time. Events are happening every day and it is of the utmost importance that we are able to come to agreements. Let me give you an example. Prophets, let us take a vote on who believes we should replace Prophet Covey with another as soon as possible?"

Hawking and Zelner raise their hands. To which Hawking continues, "And which prophets believe we should keep the seat empty?"

Prophet Jenner and Mannon raise their hands.

"You see. It is impossible. This is the very reason that five are necessary. Now, many of us have nominated who we believe will be able to bring us back into reality and offers this seat something it has lost."

The audience grows louder upon hearing that they might know who the next Prophet could be. Prophet Jenner has begun to sweat, and it obvious from her face that she is beyond concerned.

Prophet Mannon's facial expression changes as he looks at Hawking sideways. "You have nominated someone?"

"That's right. I have."

"Who is that?" Prophet Mannon asks.

"We've thought long and hard and we believe Isaiah Aldo will be a fine Prophet."

The name alone constricts my chest, although I can't attest to why. Pictures of rooms and a man with no face fill my mind. Just the memories alone make my head pound. It isn't just this, but the moment his name is broached, Sassi and Kilon show immediate rage. Arek, and even Mak, cast quick glances in my direction. I don't understand why, but my body is telling me there is a reason that I don't wish to know.

"Prophet Hawking, we are not at a place to be nominating anyone. If you have someone then surely others will need time to provide a secondary." Prophet Jenner's voice is deeper than usual, as though she hasn't slept.

"I believe we are. Can you give me any reason why we cannot accept his nomination?" Prophet Hawking asks.

"We need time," Prophet Jenner says.

"You have time. But as of now, I request a motion for Isaiah Aldo to be our next Prophet." Just then, the doors to the courtroom open and the faceless body I've been seeing in my memories saunters into the room and onto the stage. Isaiah has dark eyes and dark hair. He looks to be of Spanish descent, with a short stature and muscular forearms under his white button-up shirt. I stare at his face, willing it to tell me something. *Why do I know him? Why do I fear him?* Every muscle is tense until my headache worsens. But it is Kilon's reaction that surprises me the most. Kilon leaps over the pony wall in the courthouse, enraged, but Arek stops him before he can rush the stage.

"Silence!" Hawking yells. "Arek, get hold of him!"

Arek whispers something in Kilon's ear as his chest rises and falls. Kilon's body is shaking with hate that appears to be directed at Isaiah. Arek's words seem to calm Kilon enough for him to begrudgingly go back to his place.

"Let us take a vote." Hawking touches her braided hair, but quickly lets it go as though reminding herself to not fidget. "He is a man of great stature. He worked for Alfonzo Geretzima and graduated from his time within the Umbramanes." While she explains his massive accomplishments, I can see that everyone on my team is tense. Arek's jaw clenches and unclenches, while there is no denying the hate emanating from Sassi and Kilon. When I look over at Gal and Diem, their wild behavior never tamed, they are both flipping Isaiah the bird, until he looks at them. He quickly pretends that he doesn't see them by sending his eyes in the opposite direction.

Hawking notices the crazy couple and leans in close to her microphone. "Diem and Gal, you will be removed if you don't refrain."

This only adds to the smiles on their faces. "Oh sure, Prophet Hawking, throw out the Irish, would ya."

However, Arek shakes his head at them and they reluctantly quiet themselves so that Hawking continues with her praise about Isaiah. "Why'd you do that?" I ask Arek.

"We need their vote if it comes to one," he explains.

"Prophet Hawking, we need to take our time," Prophet Mannon says in agreement with Prophet Jenner.

"We don't have time." For some reason Prophet Hawking draws back as though she's flustered, then reneges, "What I mean is that there are decisions, important ones, that need to be made."

"And they will. We can make them. That is no excuse to hurry and compromise our position." Prophet Jenner's beautiful lips move with such grace, I find it hard to look away.

"Leigh," Hawking calls out. "What say you?"

Leigh looks around dully with no expression, then stands to his feet with a nod. "It is best we fill the seat immediately."

The audience erupts when Hawking smiles and finally Mannon stands. He turns to the Powers behind him. "It is of no service to us to bring in another compromised prospect."

The courtroom erupts with people arguing on both sides. Just then, the doors to my right open and Andrew Vincent, three-feet-high, is nothing more than purely and wonderfully confident. For a small man, he owns every room he's in. Before he says anything, he catches my eye with a wink and I smile. Just behind him, three people—two women and a man—enter. Immediately, I gasp. One of the women is the president of the United States—President Maria Alamay. I voted for her and have loved her for the three years that she has been president. My Ephemeral self merges with my Velieri self and I feel the eruption of excitement in my chest. Never would I have believed that I would someday be within feet of President Alamay. Her fashionable blue suit fits perfectly to her six-foot-tall frame. Strangely, even though Andrew is beside these women, he still draws our eye. That is the reason that he is Andrew Vincent, a television journalist for both the Velieri and the Ephemes.

There's another woman with them, with dark brown eyes and blonde hair that falls just above her shoulders. She has a long scar from her ear to her chin, and another from her eyebrow to her temple.

Andrew steps up to the middle platform and pulls the microphone down to his mouth, careless of whether he has been asked.

"Andrew Vincent? We are in a meeting; might it wait?" Prophet Hawking asks.

Andrew laughs. "You know what, my darling, it really can't." Every word toward Hawking is sour. "Prophets and Powers, I come before you with the Reds after some new information has been brought to my attention."

"Yes, Andrew?" Prophet Mannon lets him stay; in fact, he almost seems grateful for the interruption.

"It seems we may have a crisis on our hands."

"How so?" Prophet Jenner asks.

"Well, I have been with the Reds all morning. They've been supplying information for the last several months that has been gravely ignored. And I fear that I might have no choice but to threaten a story if something is not done. I mean, you know, I don't wish to do so," he says practically through a grin, knowing that what he is saying is not believable since it is coming from him. "Perhaps my presence and the artful and excruciatingly brutal way I can so eloquently put words together, might give weight to their voices?"

Hawking slams her fists on the table as she stands. "Is this truly necessary as we have just lost one of our own and are in no way capable of any decision-making until his chair is filled?"

Andrew grins as he glares at Hawking. "Oh, Covey. The man with no real interest but his own. Hmmmm, a fool will never make wise decisions. Isn't that right, Prophet Hawking?"

"Andrew . . . I—" she begins, but Mannon stops her mid-sentence.

"Andrew, let's hear what needs to be said."

"You all should know Kinnie Brown, leader of the Reds." Andrew turns to Kinnie, the woman with the scars, as she steps up to the microphone.

"Good morning, Prophets, Powers, and Velieri members. For nearly eight months we have been providing your government with information regarding those who have gone missing."

Prophets Jenner and Mannon are both confused by her information. "Missing?"

"Yes. More than a year ago we started noticing that men, women, and children were disappearing in the middle of the night. Gone. Vanishing into thin air. So, we began sending you notices, letting you know of the strange phenomenon. Yet here I am. Nothing has been done, and there still continues to be more and more disappearing as we speak. You've done nothing, said nothing, and we are left to wonder: Is there a reason that those who have needed our help for so many years are staying silent? Is there something we should know?"

Jenner stands to her feet and turns to look at Leigh. "Leigh, what say you here?"

Leigh shakes his head. "We have received no such information."

Andrew pushes his way back to the microphone all the while unfolding a piece of paper, then he begins to read. "Thank you for your information. There is no proof or evidence that would suggest Velieri are involved with the disappearances. We suggest that you search in-house. If you prefer to make accusations, you may do so, however we will take action accordingly. Be it at your own risk. Our legal team is aware of your false statements and believe we have a case should you choose to defame the Velieri name. All other manners of communication about this subject will be forwarded directly to our lawyers. Leader of the Protectors, Leigh Rykor." Andrew finishes, clicks the side of his cheek and shrugs, with a faint hint of righteousness within his grin.

"What say you, Leigh?" Prophet Jenner says, her chest rising and falling with anger.

Leigh stands with his fists tight at his sides, his body looking more and more withered and aged than ever before. His stubble is white while his hair and eyebrows are salt and pepper. "We did what was necessary with the threatening letters that were sent by the Reds. There is no evidence that Velieri have anything to do with this."

Andrew does not back down. "It is our duty to help those who have helped us over the years. And besides, the only evidence that we do have is regarding your son. Does that surprise you, Protector Rykor? I think not." He chuckles. "But I also understand your predicament completely. Either you stand against your son, or you stand against us. Not an easy decision, I'm sure, even though he's a mass murderer. If only you had another son, one who is a hero." He turns with a raised eyebrow to look at Arek. Arek tries to hide his smile by looking away. "Yeah, that decision is tough." Andrew Vincent's sarcasm can be read by the lift of the left side of his mouth. I've seen it again and again. I have a memory glide through my mind of sitting across the table as Andrew lays his cards down, showing a full house, while playing poker.

Prophet Mannon pounds his gavel. "Madam President and Madam Brown, I assure you that I will look into this immediately. Leigh, you will send me everything you have received from the Reds. Meet me in my office directly after this session, Leigh."

"Yes, your Honor." Leigh bows his head and walks back to his chair.

"Madam President and Madam Brown, I promise you, you will be taken care of. Thank you, Andrew, for bringing this to our attention."

"Of course, Your Honor," Andrew says.

Kinnie Brown leans in to the microphone just before they are about to leave. "We do not wish this to affect our contracts with you, but we are losing men, women, and children at an outrageous rate. If nothing is done, a change will be necessary."

"We understand," Prophet Jenner assures them. "Andrew, would you please meet me in my chambers to discuss the next steps."

"Of course, Prophet Jenner."

"Thank you."

With that, Andrew leads the Ephemeral women out of the courtroom and the meeting resumes. Before long, Prophet Hawking once again requests a vote, this time the majority, if only by a small concession, chooses to vote. Within the next five minutes, Isaiah Aldo is chosen as the next prospect to take Covey's place.

CHAPTER FIVE

After the meeting and just before sunset, I quickly pull my messy hair back in a ponytail as I walk along the path near the bayou. On the other side of the water there is a quick splash as an alligator drags his heavy and scaly body into the water from the cool mud. I stop for a moment and look around. I've stood here many times in many years. Flies zip about my ears, but swatting at them is of no use in the bayou. When the lowering sun suddenly blasts through two branches and lands on my shoulder, the heat brings with it memories of this place. The crack of breaking twigs turns my head. Sassi, with her head wrapped in a white scarf, is wandering the path.

"Are you ready?" she asks.

"Yeah." But instead of turning toward the main house, we stand together, looking out over the water. There's something just so beautiful about the rich greenery as the day nears its end.

"It truly is peaceful out here. Our daughter always loved it." These words don't come easily, and her voice constricts as though her chest can't bear them. She doesn't look at me but stares out into the water as I watch her beautiful profile.

I'm hesitant, but I finally ask, "Was that your daughter? In the halls during Tri Planum? She was yours, wasn't she?"

Finally, Sassi's nearly golden eyes turn to me. "Her name was Nayo. And she was my world . . . my everything. When she died, I thought that I had. And you know, it's different when you're Velieri. It just means it's longer before you'll ever be together again."

"I didn't think about that," I whisper.

"Really? I think about it every damn day."

"I'm sorry, Sassi."

"You were the best of friends. She loved you like a sister." Sassi takes my hand in hers.

I'm caught off guard at first, but when I allow myself to drift with this thought, Nayo's face comes back to me. Moments of laughter and joy. Moments of strength and fighting beside each other. The sadness drags through me like sludge through my veins until I close my eyes. "I remember her," I whisper.

"I would give my life to see her again." As Sassi's words are full of hope, I turn my eyes back to the water.

"How do we win, if this is what sits in our unconscious? There's no way to forget Nayo. Sadness or anger can just be manipulated."

"No, but it's my work—my work to release her. She's somewhere . . . I feel her quite often. And I need to just let her live there . . . and not steal her essence and shackle it within my pain. But you see . . ." She turns to me with wise eyes. "I want to. I wanted so badly to forget about everything else and just stay there in those white halls in Tri Planum, just to be with her. But I know that's not her. She's somewhere beyond . . . living free."

After a moment of silence, we look at each other. "I'm going to do my work," Sassi says, "so no one else can ever use Nayo's death against me. She'd never want to be my weakness . . . only my strength." Sassi reaches out and moves my hair from my shoulder. "Are you ready for dinner?"

I nod.

Sassi is a strong woman. I've only seen her eyes reveal such sadness when it comes to her daughter. Her choice to turn away from Nayo while in Tri Planum is burned in my memory. As we walk, arm in arm, I hear a faint sound behind us, yet Sassi does not. Within the foliage just off the path, I see something moving slowly. When I stop and turn Sassi looks at me with concern.

"You all right?"

I say nothing for just a moment, then cock my head to the side with surprise. It is too fast to be sure, but it appears to be Nayo's sweet smile and eyes that peek out from a cypress tree, then swiftly disappear. Almost as though she had been walking with us. *Is it memory? Is it spirit? I suppose I'll never know.*

"Yeah. I'm fine."

✓∿✓

Prophet Jenner brings her perfectly manicured hand up to her curly hair while sitting at the head of the table, as she prepares for our meeting. "Okay all, it's time to address some things." The chatter dies down. She takes a moment to think, then clears her throat and jumps in. "Obviously, as you saw, the Powers are divided—more than I've ever seen them. This vote places us in a bind. Within the Manchester Books it states simply that we must find a candidate or, within a month, Isaiah Aldo will be able to take his place within the Prophets."

"It's a strange phenomenon," Kilon says with a growl while comforting himself with strong arms wrapped around his chest.

"What's that, Kilon?" Prophet Jenner asks.

He chuckles, "Did you know that people used to believe cotton came from a vegetable attached to a lamb by an umbilical cord? Some even believed that the Earth was the center of our universe and flat, mind you. Hell, our founding fathers believed that, to end war, an entire group of humans should deny their longevity and hide themselves to the point of near slavery to the government."

"Your point?" Sassi encourages him to hurry with a grin.

"My point is why do we continue to abide by words and laws created thousands of years ago. We do not evolve with our knowledge and that is ridiculous. That is my point."

Briston rubs his neck, then cheek as he clears his throat—the usual sign that he is about to speak. "Prophet Jenner is aware and she has been working tirelessly to change this. At risk of losing her position and her wealth, she is giving relentlessly to this cause. Prophet Jenner, your thoughts on where to go next? Do you have someone in mind?"

Prophet Jenner and her deep and rich voice stay steady, however, I notice the slight shake in her hands just as she continues to speak. "There is a large number of us who believe we might be ready for something different. The original Prophets believed in something bigger for our world, something greater. That is why they put very specific rules and regulations on how things are run. Kilon, you are correct that we are caught in a whirlpool of two sides, neither letting the other breathe. We all know that the loftier the power the more apt we are to be corrupted, and unfortunately, I have met greater prophets on the street than the ones that sit in those chairs today. I'm trying to push for the Powers to wait, but it's been damn near impossible. Besides we all know that Hawking has just as much hate toward the Ephemes as Covey did. They want Isaiah because they know where his loyalty resides."

"Who is Isaiah Aldo?" I ask. Suddenly it is as if I have dropped a bomb on the room. Their faces cloud over, sending a hush over the room that immediately causes an uncomfortable ball in my chest. "What?"

"You do not remember him?" Sassi asks me carefully.

"Should I?"

Arek clears his throat and stands. "Isaiah is not our biggest problem at the moment."

"What about Zelner? On what side does he land?" Briston asks as he scratches his gray beard.

"I don't know. I even wonder where Leigh's loyalty belongs." Prophet Jenner wipes the sweat from her lip with a purple handkerchief, then shakes her head. "I'm going to make sure my voice is heard."

"How can we help you?" Arek asks sincerely.

"Find Navin. How do we fight anything when we don't know to what extent we are fighting?" she admits. "But also, I've emailed every one of you the list." We grab our phones and instantly begin to scroll. "This is the list of the missing people. I was able to speak with Andrew, Kinnie, and President Alamay just after court today. It is more than I expected."

"How many?" Sassi asks as she scrolls through the list on her phone.

"Thousands." She lets that rest on the ground for just a moment before continuing. "Thousands of people that the Reds are warning us if we don't find, then they will pull out of every contract with us. Now you know me, I do not need their money, but I do want their continued support and friendship," Prophet Jenner explains.

Peter pipes in, "Why does this only matter to the Reds? Are there no Velieri missing?"

"Only Ephemes are missing. There are no large amounts of Velieri where their trackers simply went silent in the middle of the night."

Peter, who has only learned history and not lived it, nods. "Sounds like the Red Summit."

Jenner nods, "That's right. It sounds exactly like the Red Summit. However, this is larger . . . by far."

Kilon swipes up with his finger again and again until he furrows his brow. "All of these people are missing?"

The weight of it shows in Prophet Jenner's eyes. "Yes. All of them. Men, women, and . . . children. So here is what I need—while

I keep the Powers and Prophets from adding another ego to the seat, I need you to research how we find out who these people are, where they are, and who did this."

Peter chuckles sarcastically. "I'll give you one guess *who* did this."

Jenner nods, "I'm sure. Maybe if you find Navin, you find them. Also, with the amount of people who went missing within a short period of time, the questions are many: How? Where are they? Are they alive? If we can't figure this out, the Reds may never trust us again." She stops and looks away. Her heavy eyes tell of the empathetic soul that is her greatest gift, and most expensive weakness, for it sells her out again and again to anyone watching. Briston reaches out and touches her hand, which makes her turn back to the table all the while clearing her throat, most likely to swallow the lump within it. "Over the last six months, nine thousand, nine hundred and thirty-eight men, women, and children have just disappeared, and the only way we know is that their trackers went dead. Every month more go quiet."

"How do thousands of people just disappear? Wouldn't this be on every news station?" Kilon asks. "And how do we know they aren't just freeing themselves of the tracker and disappearing?"

"First of all, that theory would mean that the Ephemes have somehow caught on to the tracker. It's possible though, and I would suggest going into it with that idea as well. And in regard to the media, the Reds and CTA have worked tirelessly to keep that from happening. But they are nearly done covering this up. They've given us a month to figure it out and are threatening drastic measures if we don't do everything in our power."

Suddenly, I understand why Holona warned me that we would not be able to rest. Arek takes my hand from under the table as we both scroll through the names of the missing. A bit of the world's burdens come back to his eyes as he stares into mine, so I squeeze his fingers.

Gal claps her hands together, startling everyone to attention.

"Oh get on, folks. This ain't nothin' fer us. We'll do it, we'll find 'em."

Diem gives a powerful nod. "Aye, I say we split. Some of us continue lookin' fer Navin, and some of us go after the missin'. Aye? Never know—it may lead us to the same place."

Briston leans back in his chair with a long breath. "Not without a plan."

Kilon speaks up, "We have a few things to look up. We'll go into the city tomorrow and meet Caynan at the base."

Arek nods. "Let's get some rest. Prophet Jenner, we are here for you. Whatever you need, we will do."

She stands up, lifts her hands in the air, closes her eyes, and breathes. "May we end this, finally."

CHAPTER SIX

The steam from the shower covers the mirror as my fingers pull my towel tightly around me then tuck it under the other side. For a moment, while staring at the foggy glass, my mind wanders, falling inevitably down a black hole wondering where the missing Ephemes have gone. Mindlessly, I wipe the mirror. A gasp escapes my lips from what I see and I nearly fall back, hitting the wall behind me. Just like my hand the day before, my eyes are gray, my skin is rotting, and my hair has nearly all fallen out. Mud falls from my chin, while the rest of my decaying skin is wet and covered in layers of dirt and leaves. I turn away from the mirror and, standing in the shower, the little girl from the dock—her hair straight and brown, her eyes sunken and skin gray—looks up at me with harsh eyes. "Help," she breathes out in a barely there voice.

I trip over the rug as I step back and hit the door with my fist. Seconds later, Arek calls from the hall, "Remy?" and rushes in. The little girl has disappeared in the blink of an eye. "What happened? You okay?"

"Yeah. I think so." He watches me for a second with concern, so

I reach out and touch his face with my hand. "I'm good. Just felt off for a second."

I step out into the hall, but once again feel off kilter. The world starts to spin so I use the wall to keep myself upright and try to breathe. Stars pass before my eyes and I wait while pressing my palm to my heart. Its fast beat taps against my fingers, yet there is something different—something that makes the hair on my neck stand up.

"Remy?" Arek says again.

Then, unexpectedly, someone passes by me followed by a gentle breeze. I open my eyes, but I'm not in our cottage, I'm now in a large hallway. My feet stand on white marble, my hand rests against red brick covered in a thin layer of creamy plaster. The back of a tall man is visible as he walks away from me. He looks slightly like Arek, yet I know it's not.

When he disappears into another room, I follow, but just as soon as I round the corner, the man turns and sees me. It is Navin. He looks at me and smiles. "You're here." He walks toward me until I back away from him. "Do you know why you are here?" He steps so close that I reach out and touch his shirt to find out that the material is cotton and, yes, I can truly feel it. He angrily grabs my hand until the squeeze hurts. "I figured you wanted to play games, so let's play games. Expect to be drawn to me," his grin changes to serious thin lips, "at any moment and anywhere."

With two hands he pushes me so hard that I fly back and land against a wall, then fall to the wooden floorboards. My head slams against the drywall, leaving a small hole.

"Remy?" I hear Arek's voice while my eyes are closed. "Remy?"

When I open my eyes, my body feels depleted—my muscles worn out as though I've run a marathon. *What just happened?* I am back in the cottage and Arek is kneeling in front of me. In an awkward position on the floor with my back against the wall, I am somehow on the other side of the room from where I started. My arm is still burning where Navin grabbed it, and when I lift it between Arek and I, we notice the red skin with his handprint. "What is that?" Arek asks.

"I don't know. I have no idea what just happened."

⌁⌁⌁

Geo stares at me with concern. "What do you mean?" he asks.

"I mean, I met him where he was . . . I think?"

"Explain it to me, again," Geo repeats for the third time.

"I was walking through my hallway after taking a shower and suddenly it just felt like my equilibrium was off. A bit like the room was spinning, so I used the wall to rest . . . closed my eyes . . . and when I opened them, I was somewhere that I haven't been. Navin walks past me in a hall. He disappears around the corner ahead of me, so, I follow him into an unfamiliar room. But when he turns around, it's like he expected me there."

"It didn't feel like a memory? Or a . . . manipulation?" Geo asks.

"No. It doesn't feel like Tracing. Or even that I'm within my subconscious or unconscious levels. He was there. Or actually I should say . . . I was there. There was a very specific feeling to it. Like it was taxing my body more than usual. I hate to say this, but like my molecules were expanding and shrinking all at the same time."

A group of us are in the living room of the main house. Geo turns to Arek, "What was she doing while you were watching this?"

Arek clears his throat and looks at me with concern. "She started to seize. Her body was convulsing and she almost went to the ground, until she flew back and hit the wall."

"I did?" My soft voice emerges with surprise.

Finally, Geo looks at Briston. "We need the Manchester Books."

"Why?"

"There's something that I seem to remember from a long time ago . . . something that only one or two Velieri have been able to do. But I'll need the books to figure it out," Geo says.

However, Kenichi shakes his head. "No need for those books," he says as he pulls his phone out of his pocket. For a moment he types something then hands it to Briston. "Read."

Briston looks down and before long his deep voice begins, "There have been those that exist freely, without the confines that most of us endure in this life. It is not known whether it be spiritual, or simply interdimensional, but these humans facilitate the gift of existing in multiple realms. It is not often done for long periods of time, rather small moments. We do not have the knowledge of how or why someone would be gifted with this. The first known instance was Shea Courtier, who was eventually accused of evil doings and beheaded by King Henry XIII."

Kenichi nods. "You see."

"Is it like Tri Planum? Am I in his subconscious or unconscious?" I ask carefully, trying to understand.

Briston shakes his head. "I didn't think this would awaken so quickly."

"But you knew it would?" I ask him.

"Yes. Remy was just finding her ability to do this. Just before she died, she came to me. It was the first time I saw her afraid. This is how she knew about your mother, and about Navin. She had had moments, seconds really of . . . she called it Traveling. It's not like Tri Planum. Many people over the years have learned to ride someone's unconscious or subconscious levels at the same time as their conscious levels, but Tri Planum is always done when you are close to someone and it is within your mind. Within a certain distance. But Traveling felt different for her. Traveling was an ability to actually be in a different country, in a different place, with no connection to why or how. Remy was having trouble before she died because she said it was happening more and more, but she had no way to control it. And she also said . . ." It seems he doesn't want to continue.

"What? What did I say?"

"You said that the only place you ever ended up was with Navin or Japha."

The look on Arek's face does not go unnoticed. Sassi touches his arm, "Arek, did you know this was happening with Remy?"

Briston interrupts before Arek can respond, "He didn't. Remy was afraid to tell anyone out of fear. The Powers and Prophets had already turned against her and there were people following her everywhere after the Prophecy was released. The last thing she wanted at that moment was more attention."

"I knew," Arek says quietly. Briston is now the one surprised. "She told me just before she died after she had a seizure in front of me."

Prophet Jenner taps the table with her red fingernails. "There is no denying you are one of a kind, Remona Landolin."

"Rykor." I try to add humor even though it is obvious by my forced grin that I do not feel capable.

Sassi smiles and breathes in heavily. "Just one more reason that I believe in the Prophecy."

CHAPTER SEVEN

The morning sun, filtered by yellow curtains in the small cottage, sprinkles across our faces. Arek is still asleep next to me with his arm over my chest. A perfect breeze that feels so familiar blows across my hot skin. It drifts over my body, with the smell of grass and summer, allowing a distant memory to return. *Arek and our two babies are sleeping soundly next to me. Just as the morning sun rises, I listen to the bleating sheep, while smelling the fresh grass, then Arek's hand crosses over the girls and rests on mine. We smile.*

This moment needs to last forever—I'm desperate for it. Every day the memories extend, widen, fill in, and produce intense feelings for this man across from me. I'm beginning to understand what he meant so long ago when he explained love that stood the test of time. Just like the line across my skin that excites from his touch, the power of the Yovu inhabits a place within my soul that I didn't know existed.

A bit of trickling water is heard, along with the bayou's morning chorus. "I could lie here forever." I feel the rumble in his chest when Arek whispers. He digs and burrows closer, hiding his face in my pillow until I wonder if he can breathe.

As I stare into space, he rolls over onto me and waits for me to finally look at him. My palm feels the heat of his skin as it slides down his temple and cheek and across his jaw. He smells like soap and he is freshly shaved. He reaches his lips up to kiss mine. Once again, the memory of thousands of moments when he has looked at me the way he is now, shift from dormant to instant nostalgia, and it makes my stomach flip. He kisses down my neck and my chest, then pulls my shirt over my head. "My wife," he says as he kisses and licks down my stomach. Finally, he stops right before my panty line and looks up at me with a smile. "Make another baby?"

"Will I get to see this one grow up?"

"I promise."

Suddenly, just next to us on the table our phones buzz at the same time. Arek doesn't jump to grab his, so I don't either. It stops for a moment, until Arek's phone nearly falls off the table from vibration. He reluctantly reaches behind him to grab his phone and places it on speaker.

"Yeah?" He wipes his eyes.

"Arek, get up," Sassi warns. The gravity of her voice tells us there's something wrong, and it makes both of us sit up.

"Sassi? What's wrong?" he asks.

"Meet us at the main house. Five minutes."

"Yeah, five minutes," Arek says.

✕✕✕

We gather at the main house, my heart beating fast when I see the looks on the faces of Sassi and Prophet Jenner. Something is wrong . . . really wrong. The air in the room pulses with nervous energy, and yet all I can hope is that they say it quick and get this wait over with. Everyone is there, but Lya. Daye looks at the doorway as if she expects her sister to enter.

"What's going on?" Arek asks.

Prophet Jenner presses a button to lower a TV from the ceiling. Sassi stands next to the TV and begins quietly, "I'm going to show you the videos first. Andrew Vincent sent me some . . ."

"Have you seen all of this?" Peter asks. Peter, while veering toward adult, still holds on to his baby face. He often spends most of his days on Facetime with his girlfriend, Lily, with whom he reconnected at the Gianda many months ago.

"Some," Sassi responds.

Footage of buildings from all over the world, smoke billowing from their windows, begins to play. SWAT teams stand ready along multiple streets in multiple cities, with reporters, news vans, and yellow caution tape.

Even Gal and Diem stop eating and watch the grave new beginnings.

"It's begun." Sassi's voice is heavy. "The war we have always tried to avoid is here. I think our time as peacemakers has ended and we will now have to pick a side or create our own. They set it up . . . all of it . . ." Sassi explains. "They've taken over many government buildings."

"How?" I ask in disbelief.

"We think they embedded people for years and years in the system and around the building. This wasn't just planned in a week." Prophet Jenner places her hand to her mouth while Sassi explains. "This has to have been going on since before your death."

"Oh my god," I whisper.

"They've killed seven governors: California, Colorado, Virginia, New York, Illinois . . . and Texas."

"All in one night?" I ask.

"It's still going on out there. We won't be safe for long here."

Arek takes both of his large hands and rubs his forehead, then runs them through his hair. His skin is red with emotion and the anvil is back on his shoulders. "There's no way he can have an army in every state. There's no way that Navin has built this up alone."

Prophet Jenner speaks up. "You're right. Navin certainly hasn't done it alone. This was not just the Rebellion. If we think that the Rebellion is working without the help of certain Powers and Prophets, then we need to think again."

Just then, Lya explodes in the room with her phone in her hand. Arek stands with concern, "What's going on?"

"Adam just called me. Those groups I was telling you about the other day, the Black Hats . . . every group was sent the same message."

"Arek?" Prophet Jenner asks.

Arek nods, "Lya, show them what you've found."

Lya shares her phone screen with the main computer. "Several of my team found this. This is a website. At first it looks okay, until you dive further in. When you search . . . my team found groups upon groups upon groups that were formed years ago—made up of anyone who hates the Ephemes. They are calling themselves the GENOS and each group is led by Black Hats . . . the top Velieri hackers. We've watched them grow in numbers, even in the small amount of time we've been watching them. All we know is that they were told for years to wait. If they waited patiently, one day, they would get a message. That message was sent out yesterday at nine in the evening."

"Message?" Kilon asks.

Briston reaches out to Elizabeth, who is clearly having a hard time hearing this information.

Lya continues, "A text was received from one of our people. Navin sent a text telling everyone to do as they've been told. In the text he said, 'The time has come. Refuse to back down and Rise.'"

"Do we know what they're supposed to do?" I ask with a dry mouth.

Lya hesitates, as though saying it will make it true. "We believe GENOS stands for genocide. They are to kill any Epheme within their territory and any Velieri that gets in the way."

Silence punctures the room, wounding every one of us until we find it difficult to breathe. Navin has done his work.

"How did we not know this was coming?" Briston says angrily.

The room grows with a bit of chatter until Arek speaks up. "We did know. Maybe what we didn't see was the slipknot he'd been tying for us and the ladder he was building for them. He has forced us to live on defense for so many years that we fell for his mirage. He outplayed, outmaneuvered, and now we are here . . . living in a world of very angry but invisible enemies."

Everyone is silent as we let his words sink in, so he continues.

"People need no proof to believe hate anymore. The world wants a side. They want to believe in a doctrine that vilifies difference and allows them to punish it. That's how he did it. Navin is no fool."

Prophet Jenner wipes her eyes of tears as Lya continues. "Navin sent this to many of the Powers and Prophets." She turns on a new video. Navin stands in front of the camera and as he begins to speak, he takes a moment to clear his throat. "We've been asking for years for justice and freedom. Yet all of us know, with Ephemes, it is useless to request any such thing. You'll understand now, what I've been doing. After today, things will never be the same. But hear me out . . . we've been waiting. The GENOS have been waiting in the shadows. Sitting in plain sight at an Epheme's dinner table, laughing at their neighbors' jokes, joining groups all with the knowledge that one day, I would say *Go*. The Ephemes would never know that the neighbor sitting at their table for dinner was there for one purpose . . . to make sure we can someday be free. So welcome to the new world. My new world."

Kilon rushes forward when he sees Prophet Jenner needing to sit down and helps her to a chair. Her emotions are evident and after a moment, her words flow out, "It doesn't have to be like this. Yet here we are: riots, fear, hiding—across the nation and beyond. For the first time there is not even a thought of war between countries, rather we are at war between neighbors and friends. No one can trust anyone."

Suddenly Lya's phone rings. When she sees the name, she quickly leaves the room to take the call. After a few minutes, she returns and I can see that something is not right. "I just got a call from Adam. San Francisco is being torn apart. A civil war is taking over the city . . ." Daye stands and the sisters share a moment, "We have to go."

CHAPTER EIGHT

Lya's knee bounces fervently as she stares at her phone or out her window while our procession of cars travels through the quiet bayou. "Is there any way you can hurry?"

Sassi looks into the rearview mirror at Lya with kind but direct eyes. "Lya, for the millionth time, I am already twenty miles per hour over the speed limit."

"Yes, but the speed limit is ridiculous around here. I mean for god's sake, there's no one out here anyway," Lya growls.

"Honey, you are on my last nerve . . ." Sassi smiles at Kilon. "We will get there when we get there. Just calm down and breathe."

Arek leans over to her and whispers something in her ear. These are the things that I wonder if I would be doing had I been around. She seems to calm just a bit from his attention.

"Lya," I say from the other side of the car. She turns to me with heavy eyes. "Did Adam say he's okay?"

"For now." And that was it. Lya turns away from me.

On our right, the small gas station where we stopped on the way in is passing by, and out of nowhere a man runs out in front of the car. Sassi slams on the brakes just in time and his hands pound the hood. He looks up into our eyes through the windshield, as Sassi opens her door and jumps out. Immediately he begins backing away, sweat rolling down his face. "They're attacking her!" he yells as he starts to run in the opposite direction.

"Who?!" Sassi calls out.

"I don't know." His voice is panicked, as though he's seen more than he can handle. Finally, he turns fully away from us and runs . . . fast.

Sassi reaches in the car and grabs her gun. Without thinking twice, I also reach for mine.

"What are you doing?" Lya yells from the back seat. "We have to go!"

The shop doors are standing wide open, with newspapers and magazines strewn about the driveway.

"I'm behind you, Sassi!" I call quickly.

I fly out of the car. Arek is soon behind me, as the other cars pull up. I hear Diem as he gets out of the car, "Playtime already?"

Inside the vintage store, there is obvious disarray. Food is smashed all over the floor, the refrigerator doors are open with bottled drinks broken, and dark liquids have traveled along the cracks of the foundation. No one is manning the front counter, but it doesn't take long to hear loud yelling and screaming coming from the back room. I make sure that my mind is protected. This is when I feel powerful . . . the most like Remy.

I pass the front counter, and then turn to look at Arek. "Can you feel him?"

He nods.

Deep down, we recognize that Velieri energy is within the place. Sassi joins after checking a back room on the other side and she instantly shakes her head. "This energy is new. It wasn't here the other day."

There's a closed door that leads to another room behind the store and as I get closer voices leak out from under it. I make sure to hide my energy and rhythm so that whoever is here cannot feel it. When I peek through, a man on the other side is banging on a locked door.

He's angry, covered in blood, and yelling at the top of his lungs. "There's no hiding in there, girl. I will get to you." Finally, he pulls his gun from his belt and shoots the handle, then he kicks open the door. Inside, the clerk who was there just the other day screams and falls back into the bathroom, where she has tried to hide from him.

I burst through the door, taking several shots and hitting him in the back just as he is about to grab her. He cries out and turns, shooting at me and forcing us to get out of the way. Within seconds I jump toward him. He can fight but it is nothing compared to me. In seconds, I kick his feet out from under him and slam my knee to his chest.

"What are you doing?" I yell at him.

Suddenly, as though a veil is lifted, he notices who I am. His eyes grow wide and the split on his lip separates as he speaks. "It's you."

"Tell me what you are doing." I press my palm against his forehead.

"It's time," he says.

"Time for what?"

"Time to be free." He is out of breath and angry, but the sight of me is so powerful that he stops thrashing. "There's enough of us to make it happen."

"Make what happen?"

"The Uprising. To change the world as we know it." This is not a crazy man, his eyes are not empty of sanity; rather this is a man who believes what he is saying is doctrine.

Kilon comes to my side and reaches for him. "Let me take care of him."

As Kilon pulls him to his feet, he yells, "What are you going to do with me?"

"Take care of her," Kilon says and nods toward the scared

Ephemeral girl who has pushed herself against the wall. She is crying and beaten.

"It's okay," I tell her as I kneel before her and reach out my hand. "We are going to help you."

"Thank you," she whispers.

After a few minutes, she sits on the couch in the break room, and we've locked the door to the outside. As I hand her some water, I ask, "What do you know about what's going on?"

"Not much," she says between tears. "Just before he came in my brother called, telling me to be careful . . . that the world was going crazy or something like that . . . Some kind of terrorists were killin' a bunch of people. That's when I saw a regular customer coming in that I've seen many times before and he's never given me trouble. Today, it was different, he was different."

"Did he say anything before he attacked you?" I hand her some tissues for her tears.

"All he said was, it's time. Oh . . . and that he hated my kind and had just been waiting to get rid of all of us." She cries a bit more and shakes her head. "He'd always been so normal . . . a friend even."

Arek steps toward her and kneels. "Do you have any family nearby?"

"Yes. I walk here from my mom's house every mornin'."

"I need you to listen to me carefully," Arek says with kind eyes. "You're going to grab every ounce of food you can from here and you are going to take the back roads to your mom's house with that food. Then together you are going to lock the doors."

"For how long?" She sniffles; her black mascara has run all the way down her cheeks.

He shakes his head. "I don't know. Make sure you have access to the news. You'll be able to watch things, but I don't know how this is all going to turn out. Are there any weapons here or at your mom's house?"

"We keep a gun . . . in that drawer." She points to the counter behind Arek. He sifts through the drawer and preps the weapon for her. "Have you ever shot a gun?"

"Yeah."

"Okay good." He smiles as he tenderly places the weapon in her hands. "You aim every time for right here." He presses his finger to the back of her ear. "Every time."

"Okay."

"What you are dealing with is not what you're used to. Do you understand that?"

"I guess," she says.

"Do you have your phone?"

She nods and shakily pulls it out of her ripped pocket. Minutes later Arek taps his against hers to pass information. He shows her the screen—the one that I stared at the very first time in Switzerland—where bright flashes of red dance from one side to the next. "If anyone else comes near you or your mom, you take your weapon and your phone, and you hide while you concentrate hard on these lights. Do you get that? This is the only way to protect yourself against the others."

"Okay." A tear lands on the phone.

Within ten minutes we have her packed up with food and her weapon. Behind the store is a thick forest and, terrified out of her mind, she thanks us, then disappears within it.

"Do you think she'll make it?" I ask Arek.

He runs his hand down my hair. "I hope so. Come on, we gotta go."

We jump back in the cars where Lya is still beside herself. Sassi presses her foot heavily on the gas until billowing dirt flies behind the procession of cars.

"Oh my god," Sassi whispers.

Just outside the window on our right there is an old graveyard that those within New Orleans call Cities of the Dead. Sun-bleached tombs sit above ground and rusty old iron fencing give an eerie aura as a man and a woman run through the cemetery with terrified expressions. We soon see that several people are chasing them.

"What do we do?!" I ask.

"Nothing!" Lya yells. "We have to go!"

Just then, the chasers in the graveyard lift their weapons in the air and shoot. The man falls first, to which the woman screams at the top of her lungs. Instead of continuing to run, she stops in surrender. Her eyes, filled with tears, turn to us as our cars drive by and somehow I watch her as the bullets ricochet through her body.

"We've got to stop!" I yell.

"It's already done," Lya says.

"No!" I cry as the woman drops to her knees while blood drips from her mouth. Without questioning what I'm doing, I open my door while the car is still moving. Sassi slams on the brakes just as my feet drop to the broken blacktop road. "Hey!" I yell.

The group looks up. I lift my gun in the air and let the bullets fly. A few of them are hit, but the rest run away before I can do much else. The woman looks at me as I kneel at her side and touch her neck. She takes her last couple of painful breaths as her lungs fill with blood. I remember that feeling. I remember drowning in my own Ephemeral body as Arek carried me to the hospital just after the attack. The pain and panic of that will never leave me.

"Two Ephemes," Geo says after checking the dead man.

"I can't believe what this has come to," I whisper. "How did he do this?"

"Because nobody said enough is enough. Too many years with the wrong people in charge with the wrong intentions," Sassi whispers.

"Enough is enough," I say as I close the woman's eyes with my palm.

CHAPTER NINE

"You're not going to believe this." Kilon's shoulders are stooped and his fists are tight as he enters the belly of the plane with his computer under his arm.

"What's wrong?" Sassi asks quickly. Together, she and I have wrapped ourselves in a blanket since the plane is especially cold. It's been several hours since leaving Louisiana and none of us can sleep knowing there is so much chaos on the ground.

Kilon sets up his computer on a tabletop and each of us stands to look over his shoulder while he navigates through news channels. Every journalist is anxious to be the first to break this story. Kilon stops on a Velieri news channel with Andrew Vincent, whom we always trust will be the voice of truth.

"A disturbing video has emerged within the last few hours," Andrew explains, with his hands crossed on the table in front of him. "We all know him as Navin Rykor, leader of the Rebellion. Just a few hours ago, he released a video. Just a warning, this is not for the faint of heart." The news channel cuts from Andrew to a warehouse where several men and women with black bags over their heads are ushered in by men with the same black masks I have seen repeatedly, with red Xs on their eyes and mouth. These masks form to their skin, looking nearly like skin itself.

"Oh my god," Sassi whispers. "Who is it?"

"Keep watching," Kilon answers with frustration.

The video continues as one of the Rebellion's guards pulls the black bag from the head of one of the prisoners. Kinnie Brown, the leader of the Reds, with puffy red eyes and messy hair, her face red from crying, struggles to open her eyes under the bright lights.

"Kinnie." Sassi shakes her head. "Do we know who the others are?"

"No, but they have the vice president and the attorney general," Kilon explains since we can't see the faces of the others. "It seems they did their job at keeping the president safe. President Alamay is in hiding."

"This is unbelievable," Peter whispers while leaning on Arek's shoulder. It seems that he grows an inch every day.

Kilon pauses the video and turns to all of us. "Navin's not hiding anymore. He doesn't really give a damn, does he?"

Arek's chest is wide and tense. His jaw clenches. "He's never given a damn, he was just waiting for the right time."

Peter's shocked voice resonates in the jet. "One of my friends . . ." He stops, shakes his head, then tries again. "One of my friends said that he was at a barbecue with his neighbors. One of the people there got a call on his phone. He went into the house and when he came back out he had guns . . . and he started shooting. He killed three people, but stopped at my friend, who is also Velieri . . . my friend asked him what he was doing, and the guy just answered: *'Doing what I have to.'* He said, *'I'm making it so that none of us have to hide anymore.'*"

For several minutes, we sit in silence, letting the danger of the world permeate our beings.

Lya's phone rings, so she steps away. In just moments, she returns in panic.

Daye stands next to her sister. "What's happened?"

Arek reaches back and places a hand on Lya's knee. *"Te meta misseu penavasete?"*

Lya sucks in a strangled breath. "It seems that they created factions of GENOS within the military." She hesitates, "GENOS everywhere have taken hostages. And there's no way to say how many. Adam says the streets of San Francisco are overwhelmed."

⋁⋀⋁

As the jet flies over San Francisco, all of us are horrified by the smoke billowing from the city.

Briston speaks to the pilots. "Don't land at the airport. Head to the Jasper ranch just outside of the city."

Sassi shakes her head, "Isn't that too far from where we need to be? We will be hours from the Gianda . . . the traffic will be horrible, especially since people are fleeing."

"I just spoke with Ryan and he'll let us use his helicopter. The hospital is not far from the Gianda and they have a helipad," Briston explains, until he's distracted by Lya checking her guns four times, so he places a hand on hers. "We'll get there," he assures her. Ryan Jasper, a billionaire who has given insane amounts of money to both the Reds and Velieri, has remained close friends with Briston throughout the years. I remember him, somewhere deep in my memory bank.

Lya nods nervously at her grandfather. "Not soon enough." I can tell that Arek has been watching the others, trying to see whether they've caught on to Lya and Daye's significance, but thankfully, the secret remains.

Within the hour, we land on Ryan Jasper's five-hundred-acre property just outside San Francisco. We duck beneath whirring helicopter blades and jump into two of three helicopters—two to fit our party, and the third for Ryan Jasper. He, too, has an arsenal and quickly updates Briston on his plans as he runs beside his comrade. They are about the same age, though Ryan doesn't have the charisma and handsome features that my father does. He's balding with plain features, and a dad bod. Just as Briston steps into the helicopter, he turns to Ryan and yells, "Keep safe, my friend and thank you!" Ryan raises his hand, just as he steps into his own helicopter.

"Where's he going?" I ask, as we all place headphones on.

"Just before Kinnie Brown was taken, she asked him to help keep the Reds together and safe. He has a history in combat and a strong relationship with the Reds." Briston reaches back to me and grabs my hand, "You okay?"

"Yeah. Let's go."

Thirty minutes later, we land on the hospital helipad. Our group takes the back halls through the hospital and then we exit into an alley between the buildings. That's when the reality hits us. Our senses are overwhelmed by the smell of gas, smoke, and fire. The city is no longer a paradox of hustle and ease, it's overwhelmed by loud explosions, yelling, screaming, and guns . . . lots of guns. Sirens are blaring, the roads are in chaos with damaged cars. Very few people walk the streets, so we keep hidden in the shadows as we hurry toward the Gianda.

"What is happening?" Peter cries out as he tries to text Lily. Finally, she returns his call and he quickly makes sure she is okay.

A group of men and women with baseball bats, shovels, and anything else that can do damage are smashing windows of every storefront and apartment building on the other side of the street.

"Hey!" Kilon yells at them and races toward them. They run away on swift feet.

"Why don't you just put 'em to sleep or something, damn it." Peter places both hands on the top of his head, still holding his gun in one hand.

Kilon turns and lays a calming hand on Peter's shoulder. "I would if I could. It's all right Peter. We'll get her." Kilon's intuition is correct as the teenager can't help but worry about his girlfriend.

"Come on!" Lya yells impatiently.

The restaurant across the street is burning and large billowing black clouds worsen our vision. My heart races as I turn to Arek. "I used to eat there all the time."

"I know."

When we reach the Gianda, we enter through a back door and descend the steps into a large underground parking lot. There's an elevator on the other side, a hundred feet away, and just beside that are stairs. Suddenly a large van races through the parking structure, but when they see us, they screech to a halt and several people jump out, instantly shooting.

"Get upstairs!" Lya yells as she races toward the stairs.

"Lya, wait!" Arek yells angrily. I hear the father in his voice. She pays no attention, which makes him growl just before he hurries after her.

Kilon follows quickly, "Come on!"

Every one of us keeps low as we run up the stairs, while taking shots at the people from the van. It is difficult to get through the labyrinth of the Gianda stairways, passing level one, then two—all urine-scented corners. However, it helps us lose those from the van. When we reach the third level, we've caught up to Arek and he is placing his ear up against a metal door, but Lya is nowhere to be seen. After listening for a moment, he grabs the handle and throws it open, instantly sending his gun out in front of him. The Gianda is eerily quiet and completely thrashed.

Arek and I press ourselves against one wall to hide in the shadows. Sassi and Kilon, Diem and Gal, Geo and Peter find their own places to hide. Everyone else finds cover as well. Everything has been demolished, so paper and debris fly about. There are no signs of the Fidelis that lived here just hours before. The park in the middle of the Gianda is empty, as are the stores and cafes.

We hear a noise directly behind the park ahead, then three men scatter. "Hey!" Kilon yells and gives chase.

I'm not sure who shoots first, but the barrage seems to come from every direction until the air turns gray from wall dust.

As usual, Arek and Kilon work together like a well-oiled machine. Their eyes bounce back and forth, as they speak in near riddle, yet manage to strategize with very little communication. Somehow, they stay out of harm's way and trap the vigilantes in corners.

"What are you doing in here?" Arek yells at one of them, making the young man drop his gun and raise his hands in surrender.

"I just—" he begins, but stutters.

"Are you GENOS?" Arek steps closer with his gun pointed straight at his eyes.

The man looks around with obvious confusion. "GENOS? What's that?"

Arek waits a moment then looks at Geo, and Geo nods. "He's telling the truth."

"Then why are you in here?" Arek asks again.

"I just didn't know what else to do." He appears to be in his twenties, obviously just out for an experience. It doesn't take him long to recognize that our large group is together. "Hey," he says, suddenly curious. "Who are you guys? You know what this is all about, don't you? I'll join you."

Arek shakes his head, drops his gun, and pushes the man's shoulder away from him. "Get out of here. Go home."

"I'm telling you, I can fight, man. Whatever it is, I can do it."

"Go!" Arek yells.

He doesn't back down. Finally, Arek hands me his gun and shows his irritation. He turns back around, and in seconds he has twisted the stranger in knots, until he's begging to be let go.

"I just want to help . . . that's all!" the man cries as his friends watch on, unsure about whether to step in. Kilon places himself between them and Arek with his eyebrows lifted.

"I wouldn't think about it," Kilon warns.

"Let him go!" one of them yells.

Arek leans over him with serious eyes. "Do what I tell you to do. Go home."

"I just want to help," he says with a groan as he grows uncomfortable in his twisted position.

"Look at you right now . . . do you really think you would be of any help?" Arek looks up at the other men as well. "It is best that you go home and take care of your families. Trust me. Now go."

Finally, Arek lets go and the man climbs to his feet. And with that, he runs out, followed by the others.

"Up!" Arek yells as he heads to the fourth floor, where we have to handle another group of Velieri. They are no match for us and flee after only moments.

We watch them run away. Sassi wipes dirt from her shirt as she speaks, "GENOS are clearly just civilians with no training."

"Not always," Briston warns.

Arek bangs his fist against the fourth-floor metal door and it shakes on its hinges. Daye comes forward and presses her hand against the biometric door lock and instantly we hear a whirring sound. "We installed an emergency door on the other side of this one, so that in case of something like this, people can be safe on the fourth floor." Finally, the whirring stops and Daye is able to open it.

Several men wait on the other side and are happy to see Daye as she walks in. "It's good to see you back," one of the main men says as he walks beside her. The others quickly close the door and lock it carefully. A second large metal door, half a foot thick, slides down in front of the main one just as Daye mentioned. "You see," she says to Arek. "No one is getting through this." Daye turns her attention back to the man at her side. "Where's Lya, Jude?" Jude hurries to keep up next to Daye as she walks swiftly through the hall.

As soon as we enter the common space, most of us stop with surprise. Many Fidelis line the walls, leaving barely any room to walk through. Their tired eyes peer up as we enter, and I immediately notice they're intrigued by our presence. The mother with all the sons, whom I met when I first came, nods at me as I pass. Only her eldest sons remain by her side.

Soon, we see Adam passing out water bottles to the crowd.

"Adam!" Arek calls out.

"Sir!" He hurries and shakes Arek's hand. "Welcome back. It's been . . ." Adam doesn't have the words to describe what they've just gone through.

"Where's Lya?" Daye asks with obvious frustration.

"Where do you think?" Adam grins. "She's on the phone in the office."

Adam walks us through the crowd to the glass doors. "We were able to get most everybody out quickly. These people are just the leftovers who couldn't get out fast enough before the GENOS made it in. You know Lya and Daye, they've been prepping everyone for years, so they all grabbed their things and knew what to do. We have a rendezvous point for everyone. Hopefully everyone will make it. I suppose these are all the people who wish to stay around to fight."

Arek shakes his head, letting a long breath out as he passes Adam to open the door. "Fight what? We don't even know what we're fighting yet. Let's just keep everybody safe. Adam, get everybody ready to leave on a moment's notice."

"Yes, sir."

Once inside, we find Lya on the phone pacing the floors behind the glass walls of the conference room. Daye passes by me and nudges her shoulder against mine. "Lya doesn't know how to do anything calmly," she whispers. She races into the office. "What do you think you are doing, Lya? Do you want to compromise the safety of everyone here?"

Lya places a hand in the air telling her sister to be quiet.

Suddenly, the door to the office flies open and an attractive woman with curly dark hair rushes through and into Arek's arms. His hands fly up, but never come back down to rest comfortably on her, even though her hands are very much at ease on his body. His eyes search for me quickly and when they meet, it is obvious he's uncomfortable.

"Arek," she sighs. "I'm so glad that you're okay. I just flew in this morning."

"Masey," he says uncomfortably.

He takes her hands off him, but then her manicured fingers reach up to rest on his face. Her attention is intimate and familiar as she looks at him with sincere eyes. He whispers something to her that I cannot hear, which makes her nod and my body tense. Not long after, her eyes survey the new group of us, and she notices me. It is not difficult to recognize the brutal look of someone in love. Her glare is vicious.

The uncomfortable moment is broken by Lya's yell as she throws her phone across the room. She throws her hands over her head as several other people ignore her while working on computers nearby.

"No one is answering!" She sees Arek and stops speaking. "They've all just conveniently lost their phones when I call."

Daye rolls her eyes. "Conveniently . . ." Her sarcasm brings a hidden grin to everyone's lips. Lya scowls at her sister, until Daye slinks away.

Arek cautiously walks toward her and takes her shoulders in his hands. I watch their exchange with interest as her hard shell seems to melt. "Lya, we need to get out of here and not worry about the other Giandas. They've all been trained for this and know what to do."

"Everybody just needs to do what they've frickin' been told to do and answer the phone!" Lya growls.

Daye shakes her head.

Again, the energy between the sisters clashes mid-air.

Through the glass walls I find myself drawn to the people waiting on the fourth floor, stuck, and without any plan. "Most important thing to do is get these people to the rendezvous point, right?" I pull out my phone in order to look at the maps. "Groups . . . I think groups are key."

Lya turns to me. "You'll have a voice when you've earned a voice in here."

Instantly, Arek steps toward his daughter. "I got you . . . I got this. But Lya?" When he speaks her name, something shifts in her body as though she knows she's gone too far. He continues, "How's this? You treat her like that again, and you will have to deal with me. She is your leader . . . and my wife." This sound rolls off his tongue so beautifully and I feel the relief that this is no longer a question. I am his wife once again.

Lya calms down, never lifting her eyes again to look at me. "Sorry. It's been a long morning."

Sassi speaks, "We'll get these people out of here."

Adam lays his hand gently on Lya's shoulder as she whispers something in his ear. Suddenly the building shakes with a thunderous crash. "What was that?" Lya yells.

Geo runs to the window and looks down. "A truck has run into the side of the building."

Arek pulls out his phone and puts it on speaker. Soon, Leigh answers. "Leigh, what do we know? What's the plan?"

Leigh's voice is intense. It seems he is on the move, from the other sounds we hear on the phone. "I have no time to talk now. We are doing our best to gather those who need our help. Find a place where you can hide, and we'll meet with everyone in a day or two. Right now, there is nothing to do but get out of the cities and protect our leaders."

Arek hangs up the phone. Suddenly, Hok calls on the other end of the line. "Yeah, Hok?" Arek says as he places it on speaker, "How are things?"

"We're all okay. No one has breached our walls. And you?"

"San Francisco has been breached. We're figuring out how to get everyone out at the moment."

"Keep me updated, Arek. And Arek . . ."

"Yeah?" Arek says.

"Tell Lya I wasn't ignoring her call."

Arek smiles, and finally, for the first time in a while, so does Lya.

Adam finally speaks as Arek ends the conversation with Hok. "I honestly don't know whether we were attacked this morning because Navin knew about us, or whether Navin's men and women are simply turning the city inside out. I'm hoping it's the latter. What I do know, is the moment they scaled our walls, they saw what we had built here . . . who knows whether they can figure it out."

Sassi crosses her arms in front of her. "Where is everything of importance . . . all paperwork, anything confidential—"

Daye nods, "—safe. Everything is safe."

Lya chimes in, "I had Adam hide everything."

Daye shakes her head. "Should I use my invisibility for good . . . or evil?"

"Sorry," Lya rolls her eyes. "We . . . We had Adam hide everything." She looks at her phone. "We have twenty hours to meet the rest of the Fidelis at our safety point. I've heard from some that it's been dangerous and taken an unexpected amount of time to just get out of the city. Adam sent the commander and our army to protect the Fidelis who have already left."

We hear a crash above our heads that is so piercing that most of us duck for fear of the roof caving in.

Lya immediately runs to her desk and pulls out several guns. "They're in!"

Kilon grabs his guns from his backpack, Diem and Gal check theirs, and everyone else follows.

Lya continues, "We can get out one of two ways . . . up or down."

"Down," Daye says calmly.

As everyone prepares their weapons, Arek thinks for a moment. "Do we have a map of the building?"

Adam jumps onto the nearest computer and has it up in seconds. "Here."

"I'm telling you down is the way to go," Daye says again, this time a bit louder.

Arek and Lya hurry over to study the map. After a moment, Lya points at the roof then to the fire escapes. "There might be less to deal with if we go up. Use the fire escapes."

Suddenly a loud pounding fills the halls of the fourth floor. Adam runs out of the room to see what is happening, then runs back in, pointing behind him. "They're trying to bust down the door."

"Is that possible?" Briston asks.

"Only if they can hack into the building's computer system," Lya explains. "I think this is our best chance."

Next to me, Daye shakes her head. Geo comes to her side, "Daye, what are you thinking?" She smiles at him softly, their eyes lingering just a bit longer than normal. From beside them, their energy is infectious and I am within the crossfire as his eyes stare into hers, carefully. "You think down is better?"

Daye nods, "I know down is better. The fire escapes have been under construction for the last several months, and obviously the roof is already compromised. I've been planning this escape, in case anything happened. Besides, I can get us to cars. I made sure that every Fidelis parked their cars in a specific place."

There is no air of righteousness or conceit when she speaks, just facts and truth. It is obvious she would rather stay quiet than make Lya upset. Geo leans in and whispers something that I can't hear, then she steps toward Arek and lays a hand on his shoulder. "The fire escape is not safe and I've secured several cars in a nearby parking structure that will fit all of us. Down is the only way to go."

Lya begins to argue, but Arek places a hand on hers and nods at her sister. The pounding in the hall has increased until we hear an alarm.

"What is that?" Briston asks.

"Adam!" Lya says as he jumps to the computer. "They've hacked into the system."

Arek grabs his guns and warns everyone else to do the same, then looks at Daye, "Get us out of here, Daye."

Daye and Lya look at each other for a moment until Lya nods in approval. Daye runs out of the office and addresses the Fidelis still left behind.

"Everyone, stay quiet and follow me. We're going to take the back way."

Just as we are about to head down, the locks clang and the doors to the fourth floor disappear into the walls. Several men from the Rebellion immediately rush in from upstairs, causing the young Fidelis to cry out in fear. Arek and Kilon rush to defend everyone. It is obvious now that these men are different than the ones from the first floor who knew nothing of the GENOS; they fight well and are dressed in full regalia. One of them crashes into Daye, sending her to the ground, but Geo is there in seconds, taking care of them quicker than I've ever seen him move. There is no doubt in my mind that visions of Beckah still run through his head. But just as Geo saves Daye, she stops an attacker from behind him and in turn saves him.

Soon, we descend the stairway while Kilon and Sassi stay behind to make sure no one from the roof surprises us. Geo and Daye lead the way past the second floor, then to the first. Instantly, bullets pass our eyes and shoulders, so we must hide in any corner for protection.

"We don't know whether we're dealing with Velieri or Ephemes now," I whisper to Arek as we hide.

"Yeah we do. We know."

As soon as he said it, I knew he was right. I could feel that we were surrounded by Velieri. The Tracing in the air, which I so instinctively protect myself from now, swirls around so thick and penetrating that my old self would have fallen apart. However, just like the man in the mini-mart in Louisiana, there was something less obtrusive here— less skilled. They are not a part of the Elite, the political, the royalty of Velieri, rather just common . . . civilians.

Again, as though Arek reads my mind, just as a bullet passes and

Daye jumps out of her hiding space with two guns at the ready, he shakes his head, "I'm sure Navin's kept his most trained vigilantes around him."

Suddenly we hear screaming as we pass the second floor. Just beside us, someone has lunged toward Masey. She falls, unable to defend herself, as the man wraps his arms around her neck with a gun pointed to her temple. She whimpers as he pulls her to her feet and presses the barrel of the gun heavily against her skin.

"Arek!" she cries out.

Arek steps toward them, but the man jerks back.

"What do you want?" Arek asks as sweat drips down his forehead.

"I want out of here. Let me go," the man growls.

"Gladly. Get the hell out of here." Kilon steps closer, but this bothers the attacker.

"Are you a part of the GENOS?" Peter asks.

Suddenly I notice Arek's hand behind his back. He's making a sign to Geo that I don't understand.

"Yeah, so what?" the man says with increasing agitation. "I let her go once you let me through."

"Arek," Masey cries out. She's a beautiful woman and even in the midst of chaos, I can't help but recognize the familiarity between them. It makes my stomach turn. She expects his protection just as I would, and instantly, I want to know their story.

After watching Arek's signing, Geo quietly moves to the back of the group, trying to be invisible. He keeps himself short behind everyone else, but tries to get closer.

Unexpectedly, the man holding Masey begins to act confused. His eyes start to twitch and the veins in his hand thicken as though he's working extra hard to keep the gun at her temple. "Who's doing that!" he yells.

No one says a word, but I suddenly recognize what Arek is communicating with his hand signals. Kilon's eyes are focused, as well as Sassi's and Geo's. The attacker is fighting to keep his hand from moving, but he's losing the battle. "I'll kill her! I swear I'll kill her!"

"You don't have a chance," Arek warns him.

I watch as his finger tries to pull the trigger, but between Geo, Arek, Kilon, and Sassi, he's unable to do so, which only frustrates him. Finally, he can't fight anymore and with the power that Geo and the others are using, Masey runs out of his arms and into Arek's. The man twists his gun around and takes a shot, hitting Sassi in the shoulder. She cries out, and Kilon ends his life in seconds.

Masey melts into Arek as tears flow down her face. Soon, we can hear pounding of boots racing down the stairwell and we hurry on. Sassi's bleeding, but she holds on to her arm and grimaces as we make our way out of the building.

The air outside is full of dust from the ravaged surroundings. Papers waft from the sky and have landed on the streets. I grab one. My feet stop as I stare at the paper. "Oh my god."

Arek leaves Masey, and instantly I notice the strange look that comes over her face when he returns to my side. His chest rises then falls as others begin to surround us. Navin's picture is on this paper.

"It's a political poster. He's taken the Velieri symbol and slapped it on the corner," I say.

Sassi reads the sentence at the top out loud, "Fight for your freedom under the true Prophet."

Another one of the papers that Peter picks up has the same horrible and ancient picture that I saw in the history book that Arek showed me in Switzerland. Under it reads, "The Ephemes hunted the Methos until they were forced into hiding."

I look at my father, who stands so near to me that I feel his arm against mine. "Dad?" I whisper. "Only Velieri will know what this means, right?"

My father nods. "Navin's relying on that. He'll take every advantage he can."

Sassi shakes her head, "This is insane! What's he doing?"

Just then we see a group of men and women running down

the street, one block from where we are, and they are angry, waving weapons and yelling obscenities. "Come on!" Daye yells at us to continue, so we do. She leads us underneath a building and down several flights of stairs into a parking garage. I've not realized until this moment how large our group has become, including the Fidelis who have stayed behind.

"Are there enough cars for everyone?" I yell at Daye, who runs ahead.

"There are three vans! The Fidelis go in there. The others take the cars!" Daye yells back without looking.

We see them, parked in a line across the back wall of the parking structure. It was clear and obvious that Daye had prepared for all of this. Deep within me, I wanted to smile. Lya and Daye had become everything we'd hoped, and here it was . . . paying off.

"You ten go in that van and you over there!" Daye directs everyone.

Something in the corner catches my eye. A slinking shadow hidden within the corner of the parking structure.

"Hey!" I yell as Arek jumps into a nearby car.

It's no bigger than a child, although I can't see her face. As though she's right next to me, I hear her whisper, *"Help."* And it stops me dead in my tracks.

"What?" I call out.

"Come on!" Arek yells at me, but I can't help but draw nearer the whisper.

"Help." I hear it again. The closer I come, the more I see under the garage lights, the same little girl who stood in the shower and in my room in New Orleans. Her skin is gray, her eyes are sunken in, her hair is thin and balding. Just the sight of her tortures my soul. A tear falls down her cheek. *"Help,"* she says again, only this time she lifts her hand as if to draw me near.

"Remy!" Arek yells as he revs the engine of a white truck.

"Wait!" I yell back at him.

"What do you need?" I ask as I draw closer. Only now, more people are entering the parking structure as the rest of our team screeches out of the parking spaces. She reaches out, holding something in her hand. I come near enough to accept whatever it is that she has, and as I reach out to take it, once again I find that my skin is gray and decaying. My hand shakes with adrenaline, but this time I do not pull it away. Her small fingers drop a soft object in my hand.

"Remy! Let's go!" Arek begs. A mob descends the stairs.

"There they are!" One of the mob yells as they reach our level within the parking structure. Instantly they run faster and barrage the cement walls with bullets. Kilon and Sassi are the first ones on the move as they choose a large yellow Jeep to hotwire. Sassi zips around the parking lot screeching the SUV between the mob and Arek and me.

"Remy, let's go!" Arek yells again. "Remy, now!"

I turn on my heels and run toward the truck, but before I can reach it, a man grabs my arm. Within three moves, I send him to the ground as though he has no weight to his large frame. This immediately makes the rest of the mob step back with wide eyes when I look up at them. They've clearly not seen anything like this before as the man groans with the wind knocked out of him. I raise my gun in the air and point it in their direction. "Get back!"

With my gun still raised, I race to the passenger side and jump in. Just as we are driving away, I look to see if the little girl is still standing in the darkness, but there is no one. Within my hand is a flower.

"What is that?" Arek asks.

"Did you see her?" I ask.

"See who?"

"She gave me this. Do you know what it is?"

"Yeah, it's a yellow Kowhai," he answers. "It's a native tree in New Zealand."

"Yeah, well that's where we need to go."

"Why?" he asks as he pulls out of the parking structure and onto the San Francisco streets just behind the large van with the Fidelis.

"I think that's where we're going to find Navin."

CHAPTER TEN

The city is a combination of eerily empty streets and those that are swarmed with looters and gangs of Velieri ready to find every Epheme. Sirens seem to be coming from every direction. Stores have no glass and doors are beat to hell. A lamppost has fallen across the street blocking everything but one small section, which doesn't allow us to move very fast. "Come on!" Arek hits the steering wheel as the crowds grow more out of hand. Sassi and the others are ahead. As we pass a liquor store, a man runs out of it with a bottle in his hand. Material hangs from the end of it. Strangely our eyes meet, this man with the bottle and me. He exudes a rage so thick that my chest tightens. He lifts a lighter to the material in the liquor bottle and it instantly catches fire.

"Arek!" I yell just as the man throws the bottle directly at my slightly open window.

Arek reaches out as glass sprays my body and face from my now shattered window, but the fire follows by only seconds. I scream and duck toward Arek's side. The flames don't last long, but when it's over I can feel and smell my singed skin and clothes.

"Are you okay?!" Arek cries out, even though the only thing he can do is continue to drive and get us out of this neighborhood.

"Yeah, yes . . . I'm okay." But my arm and neck feel scorched.

Near the end of the street is an apartment building, and a woman, with blood in her hair and down her shirt, races out of the entrance. Arek is forced to slam on his brakes and comes within inches of her. Her eyes are filled with fear, but not because she was nearly hit, rather a man with a gun in his hands exits the building directly behind her. She screams and tries to run, but trips as her attacker steps closer and raises his gun. Arek throws the car in park and jumps out with his Glock instantly pointing at her attacker. It's a standoff. When the man doesn't back down, I jump out with my gun ready. My seared skin stings when the wind blows against it.

"Don't do it!" Arek yells at him. He speaks to the whimpering woman, who still lies on the ground, without looking at her, "Go!" She looks at Arek in terror. "It's okay, get up and run!" he assures her.

For just a second, I allow myself to Trace this woman. I can sense her fear, but another thing that I read is her confusion. She doesn't know why any of this has happened, and her Ephemeral mind is so easy to Trace by using her emotion. She nods at Arek and jumps to her feet, running in the opposite direction of her attacker. She passes in front of Sassi's car as well as Daye's as everyone has stepped from their vehicles, except the Fidelis, who stay inside the vans. The man sees that he is outnumbered and starts backing away.

"Okay, fine man. It's fine . . . but she'll die on the next corner anyway. There's enough of us . . . this will be over before you know it." He continues to back away, but Arek shakes his head.

"Don't move!" Arek yells at him. "Tell me what you know!" Arek demands as he steps around the car toward him.

"Can't," he says, as he backs up just a bit faster.

"Stop!" Arek growls.

The man shrugs and then turns to run. Arek shoots his knee, and he falls to the ground in severe pain as his gun flies out of his hand

and across the sidewalk. Kilon hurries to watch Arek's back as they close in on the writhing man.

Arek turns to the rest of our group. "Make a circle and watch our backs." Arek kneels beside him. "I gave you a chance. I won't give you another one. What is the plan?"

Between cries, as he holds on to his knee that shouldn't take too long to heal, he grunts, "This! This is the plan. It's been long enough . . ." he grimaces. "Ephemes don't care about us, man. If they knew who we were, they'd want us dead, so we do it first."

"How did Navin do it?"

"Who is Navin?" the man asks. His pain seems to be subsiding just a bit, so Arek warns him with his gun on his thigh.

"Who do you work for?"

"We work for ourselves."

Finally, Arek loses his patience and places the gun to the man's head, which makes him flinch and cry out. "Wait!!! Wait! Whoa man, just wait!"

"How did you know to do this?"

Arek looks back at Geo, who has now come closer. Geo nods, then speaks, "Who sent you the text to kill the Ephemes? How did you get involved with the GENOS?"

The man finally realizes when the pain has died down that he isn't leaving without answers. As the city explodes into chaos, he is quiet for a minute before finally dropping his head to the ground. "Several years ago, my sister told me about the mass killings that have been happening. Yet we don't know about it, you know . . . we don't know about these mass killings because the Ephemeral government and the Reds keep covering it up. Masses of Velieri herded away in the night, killed by Ephemes . . . so someone created the GENOS. My sister showed me a website that had a private group attached. I joined. I'm just standing for what's right. Here . . ." He lifts a hand to warn us that he will be digging in his pocket, then he pulls out his phone. After swiping for just a few seconds he turns his phone toward us and shows us pictures of mass graves. The last picture is a grotesque sight of bodies piled on top of the other. "See?" he says. "Velieri are being massacred in the thousands. The GENOS are doing this world a favor."

Before the man can stop him, Arek grabs his hand and presses his own phone against his. Instantly Arek's phone dings, signifying that the information is now on his device.

"Get out of here," Arek tells the man.

Painfully, the man clambers to his feet and limps off.

Peter squints under the sun and runs a few yards down the sidewalk. "You let him go? Why!?"

"Peter!" Arek warns. "Let him go."

"Is it true what he said?" Peter asks. "Are the Ephemes killing Velieri?"

Arek looks at his younger brother. "No," he says with confidence. "In order for that to be true there would have to be enough Ephemes that know about us."

Peter shrugs, "Who's to say there aren't?"

Everyone looks at one another but stays quiet. Finally, Lya speaks before anyone else has a chance, "We have to go! The rest of the Fidelis are waiting."

We notice several mobs making their way toward us, so we quickly jump back into our cars.

As Arek races through the streets, I stare at his serious profile. "You don't know if it's true, do you?"

An angry grin spreads across his face. "You see? That's how easy it is. It takes only one lie to infiltrate your mind." He picks up his phone and hands it to me. "Look at the pictures I took from him."

I scroll through his phone and find them. For a moment I stare at the grotesque scenes. "What am I looking for?"

While still watching the road, he scrolls to one of them specifically. "You see the man in the corner of this one? Look at the symbol on his uniform."

There's a man who faces away from the camera. I zoom in with two fingers to see the symbol and instantly recognize it. When I do, I turn to Arek with concern. He nods. "Those aren't pictures of Ephemes killing Velieri—those are pictures of Velieri killing Ephemes."

"They look recent."

"Yeah." His chest rises and falls with a deep breath. "I think these are pictures of our missing Ephemes."

One perfectly planted lie . . . among many.

CHAPTER ELEVEN

We drive through the night. The stars are beyond beautiful and it seems quite a paradox set against the angst of the world. Our procession of cars stays out of the city and within areas that feel untouched to the point of "normal." Yet as I watch a falling star cross my window and I feel the car's air conditioning make my feet slightly cold, nothing keeps the sight of San Francisco on fire from wrecking my peace.

"This is life," I whisper.

"What?" Arek's voice is scratchy due to the fact that we haven't spoken in nearly two hours.

I look at him, my singed face still red. "This is life. Never being able to have peace and keep peace."

He looks at me for a moment under the blue light of the moon. When he says nothing, I continue, "My mom was always bringing home boyfriends, some that were okay, others that were mean. She was lonely, but her quest for companionship only made me lonely. I couldn't figure out who I was. Nothing felt right, or made sense, but I suppose that's because my mother was always searching and never finding. After she died, I ran from my relationship with Ian, and my friendships. Then . . ." I breathe out as I look back to the stars. "You came. And we've been running ever since. All of my memories before my trial, everything that I've gotten back since I was a child, it's always in and out of fear and peace." I raise my finger to draw a circle on the foggy glass as we enter the cold desert.

"Maybe peace isn't what you thought. Maybe it's not about one or the other, fear or peace, but recognizing that we must have peace through times of fear or sadness."

I nod, but say nothing. The moon has not moved, no matter how far we go.

"When do we tell everyone about Lya and Daye?" I finally ask.

"I don't know. I'm afraid the moment one person knows, everyone will."

"And is that bad?"

He grins, "Is that bad? I don't know."

"Perhaps you need to let go. They're grown women and this world is on fire, we may as well let them conquer it all." I smile, but only for a second. "Who is she?" The question is weighted, but we've had enough silence that I'm willing to take the chance.

"Who?"

"Masey."

He takes in a deep breath and just about the time he's ready to tell me the story, the vans veer off into the parking lot of a gas station. It's untouched by the attacks as it sits in the desert.

"We have only an hour before we reach the rendezvous point." Arek changes the subject as he pulls to a stop behind the others. Everyone exits the vehicles, stretching and tired, ready to be with the other Fidelis who have hopefully already made it.

I stand against the car while Arek fills up the tank. Kilon throws me a protein bar as he passes, so I pat his shoulder. However, what catches my eye is Daye stepping toward Geo with a smile. They've been driving together for the last several hours, and I can't help but feel a warmth in my chest as I watch them. Subtly I turn until I can lean over the trunk toward Arek.

"Hey, husband," I call Arek.

He turns around, then leans across the other side of the trunk until our faces are close, "Yes, wife."

"Take a look over there." I lean my head in their direction, so he looks over my shoulder. Instantly, he shows his curiosity with a raise of his eyebrow.

"She could do a lot worse," Arek grins. Geo touches the small of her back as he passes.

"True. Beckah told me before she died that she knew she wasn't the one for him."

"Did she mention it was our daughter?"

"That would have been weird considering she didn't know we had one." I stand tall and walk around the car to his side, kiss his cheek, and then head toward the station. "I'm going to get some water."

"Okay, don't take too long."

"I won't."

I enter quietly, noticing the clerk's eyes are glued to the television. Every news channel is showing the worst of what's out there—every explosion, every killing, and anything that makes us all fearful to NOT watch. I walk down the line of refrigerators toward the ten various options for bottled water and suddenly the clerk's voice fills the place. "Have you been in the city?"

When I look around, no one else is there, so it's obvious he's talking to me. "Yeah."

"They're showing footage of it over and over . . . I can't believe it. Have you heard what they're saying?" he says, still spending very little time looking at anything but the screen.

"No." I reach in to grab some water, feeling the cold air hit my skin. Then I walk to the counter, setting it down loud enough so that he'll know I'm ready. Still, he does not turn. The man, whose nametag says *John,* is scratching his head nervously.

"I live down the street from here and my mom called me this morning. She's all the way in Des Moines with her boyfriend, Chuck. They saw on their cameras last night that their neighbor tried to get in their house. At one or two in the morning he's at their front door, then he goes to their back door . . . even their garage he tried. But, she said, he didn't knock, he didn't yell. But now I haven't heard from her." Finally, he looks at me with fearful eyes. "I don't know what to do. Do I just leave work . . . try and get to her any way that I can? What do I do? Some say they don't know who this group is or why they're doing it. Others say that it has something to do with terrorists. What do you think?"

I hesitate, desperately wanting to help him but not knowing what answer will do that. "I don't know. I think maybe you should . . . you should go and be with her."

"But I own this. This station's mine. My employee just didn't show up today."

Unexpectedly, my head begins to spin, and I press my fingers to my temples. I look up at the man behind the counter, but quickly realize the way I'm feeling is not because of him. I am too protected, too strong when it comes to Tracing and somehow this doesn't feel the same. My skin tightens, but my insides expand. It grows until the room begins to waver in and out.

"Are you okay?" John asks.

"Just a second . . . I need some fresh air." I step outside, sucking in a big breath, hoping that it will help, but it doesn't. Across the way I catch sight of Masey and Arek talking to each other. It's heated and intimate, but my body's telling me that there's no time to care. Masey touches his arm, and he leans into her with a hard expression.

"Remy?" Kilon has now seen the look on my face and begins to walk to me. Every limb tingles, my chest is tight. It's hard to breathe, and my knees are beyond weak. Suddenly my body is too heavy to keep upright. "Arek!" Kilon yells as he runs to my side just in time, as I fall helplessly into his arms. "Remy!" I look up into the stars, then

I blink . . . and the stars are gone.

v∿v

When I wake up, I'm staring at a fresco painting on the ceiling. I've never seen it before, but it's beautiful. My body no longer feels the in and out or the dizziness, yet it still takes me a moment for my brain to catch up. My fingers squeeze the material beneath me, which turns out to be a thick bathroom mat. This bathroom belongs in a mansion. I sit up, taking in the décor around me. *How have I gotten here? Where is here?*

Every inch of my body screams in agony as I carefully use the nearby countertop to stand. There is no light but for the moon and stars outside, which leaves everything in shadow. With hesitant fingertips, I push a nearby door open. It creaks just slightly. Peering into the next room, there are two people asleep in a bed. For a second, I don't move. My eyes squint, trying to see better in the dark, but it's not easy to pick out details. If I stay in the bathroom, I am trapped with only one door. Yet if I search for an exit, where am I trying to go? I don't even know where I am.

The woman rolls over in the bed, and it's obvious that I don't know who she is. Her long hair sticks to the pillow and I can't help but think about how comfortable she is. I've not slept in more than a day.

Slowly and methodically, I head to the door to exit the room, but stop. *Who is with her?* On the balls of my feet, I head to the other side of the bed and look closely. His upturned nose, his pasty skin, and jet-black hair . . . *Navin.* My heart races. *Why again?*

Something catches my eye near his desk. A wall of information, papers strewn about, pinned to a board, but it's almost impossible to see in the darkness. On his bedside table, close to Navin's head, is his phone. I sigh, try one more time to see the papers on the wall, then realize I need some light. Once again, I carefully make my way toward him. Just as I am reaching out for his phone, he lifts his head to adjust it for comfort. My heart stops. After a moment he settles. I wait a few moments, then reach for the phone. Before long, I stand in front of his desk and swipe down for the flashlight. As soon as it comes on, the room awakens with light and I slap my hand on it. A small bit of light is able to get through my fingers, so I place it to the papers on the wall.

There is a map. At first it is difficult to understand what any of it means, but soon, I recognize a name. *Bryer.* I think back to the old, dilapidated castle . . . the area of land where no one has jurisdiction. On this map are three colors of pins. Black pins sit on several places all over the world, but the one nearest my eyes says *Bryer* in New Zealand. *New Zealand.* I think back to the flower the little girl placed in my hand. I check every inch of the board.

"Find anything interesting?" I jump as the phone flies out of my hands. Navin stands over me, his tall frame more terrifying than I remember. His phone sprays interrupted light here and there, just as he grabs my neck with strong hands and my windpipe gets pinched.

I look around and just to bother him, I reach out my hand and let my fingers glide down the information tacked along his wall. "You're coming for me?" I grin. "I'm coming for you." He squeezes my throat harder. "So, this is what you've been up to?" I whisper.

He stands in front of the map before I can read anymore and clenches his jaw. "There's nothing you can do to stop it."

"Navin," I say directly. "If you keep going, you will force everyone into the fight and we will stop you."

He comes so close that our bodies collide. "It won't be enough. Whatever you do won't be enough for everything that I have planned. It's too late, Remy."

Once again, the same feeling washes over me, and I know it's happening again. I press my hands to my head and feel my stomach twist and turn. I close my eyes for a second, but then, when they open again, I am back at the gas station. Everyone is there, kneeling over me. Arek takes my face in his hands, "What happened? Where'd you go?"

"Navin." I sit up as everyone looks at me with wide eyes. "He's in New Zealand."

Geo bends down in front of me. "How do you know?"

"I was just with him."

"Just like before?" Geo asks.

I nod. "How am I doing this? How am I Traveling? And why only to him?"

Arek sees the red on my neck and runs his finger along it. "What is this?"

"He didn't like that I was there."

"How can this be? She was with us—no one touched her neck," Arek asks.

Everyone waits for Geo to give his understanding of it and even Kenichi is standing quietly to the side. Finally, Kenichi steps forward. "We know so little. But we do know our brains are powerful. Whether he is physically touching her, or she can simply feel it is a question that we may never know."

"Unless he kills me on the other side . . . then we'll know. I had no control over it at all." I climb to my feet. "How can I be there and here at the same time? But I could not experience both at once like Tri Planum. I have no understanding of how long I was gone."

Kenichi nods with his arms crossed in front of him. "They both happened. You were here and you were there."

Arek helps me to my feet as I ask. "So, what did I do here? My body feels wrecked."

I can tell from the looks on their faces that it wasn't good. Sassi touches my arm with her hand, "You had a seizure."

Peter, young and without control, says, "She's screwed if that ever happens at the wrong time."

Lya comes to the crowd. "We have to go."

As we walk back to the cars, Arek runs his hand down my face.

"Are you okay?"

"Yeah. What do we do about Navin? I know where he is."

Arek thinks for a moment as many of the cars start to pull away and make a precession once again down the highway. "We have one hour to reach the Fidelis that are waiting. Once there, we make a plan for them, and we make a plan for us. And we go."

"Okay." We jump in the car, but just as he's about to speed away, I notice the clerk from the station standing on the sidewalk watching us with his wide, uncomfortable eyes. "Arek."

Arek notices and pulls the car around to John. I roll down the window to speak. "Hey, John," I keep my voice calm, as his hands twist uncomfortably around each other. "Find a safe place. Prepare a weapon . . . or prepare many of them and don't trust anyone. It's okay to go find your mom but trust me . . . don't listen to anyone."

"Okay, okay." John's eyes look about as though he's only half way paying attention. "Thank you. Thank you."

"Hey, John," Arek calls from the other side of the car. "Come here." John walks to Arek's window and as he does, Arek reaches out to shake his hand. John hesitates for a moment, then takes it. In only a moment, John's body clearly calms and a small smile comes to his lips. "John, you can trust us." Arek winks at the man.

"Yeah, okay. Yeah," John says with a gentle nod as he steps away.

I nod. "You'll be okay."

With that, Arek zooms out of the gas station and down the street, speeding in order to catch up with the rest of our group.

"What did you just do?" I ask Arek.

"I let him know we weren't anything to fear."

"How?"

"People never realize what is passed from human to human, no matter Velieri or Epheme. To concentrate on all that is good in the seconds before you connect, our energy passes from one being to the next." He smiles, his thick lips revealing his perfect teeth. "Now, come on, let's get out of here."

CHAPTER TWELVE

L ate in the night, our caravan rolls into the arid temps of the Nevada desert, which gives a new understanding of darkness. There are no lights and no civilization, so the stars are vast with perfect purple halos around the brightest. A ghost town of many rustic parcels comes into view. When we finally pull to a stop, Lya jumps from her car and races to the site.

As she approaches, though, no one appears, so she holds back and quickly pulls her gun. Many of us follow suit. With the pursing of her lips, she makes a bird call that is surprisingly good. After a few moments, several people emerge under the night sky, followed by more, until finally, hundreds of Fidelis from the San Francisco Gianda are greeting us. Commander Wakefield leads the crowd—her soldiers taking up the sides and rear around the civilians.

"Commander," I say as I take her hand and shake it.

She looks at Lya and Daye. "We managed to get everyone here safely. There are only a couple of injured."

"That's great, Commander Wakefield. Thank you," Lya says.

I am surprised to find that Hok is there, and I smile when he hands me a water—which reminds me that mine is still on the counter in the gas station. "Hok!"

"I felt I needed to be with them," he says. "They are young and although Lya believes she always knows what's best . . . you and I both know she does not. There are plenty of my people to watch over the Gianda in Brazil. I have made sure of it. Besides, they have not seen the worst of it yet, unlike San Francisco." He points behind us, and that's when we see people emerging from one of the structures. Soon, I am hugging everyone and listening to what has happened to them so far.

Briston comes to our side. "We need to meet. All of us. Figure out the next step. Is there a place, Commander Wakefield? A place where the leaders can gather?" he asks.

"There is." She points to the last cabin on the main street of the ghost town. It takes but moments to gather everyone. I look around once we enter the old saloon. There are still a few chairs and tables, along with a bar and an old piano that haunts the corner covered in spider webs. Briston, Kenichi, Mak, Aita, Arek, Kilon, Sassi, Geo, Lya, Daye, Gal, Diem, Hok, and I find places to sit or stand. Arek stands behind me, so I lean lightly against his chest. Finally, Briston clears his throat and the small chatter in the room stops.

"I had hoped that we would never be in this position. But here we are. Navin has left us no choice but to fight. Here's what we know . . ." He pulls out his phone and surfs through saved messages. Then his bright blue eyes look up and I can read that my father has not slept. In fact, none of us truly have since Louisiana. "I received a message from Prophet Jenner. It is possible they have decided, due to all that has happened, to confirm Isaiah Aldo. Prophet Jenner is protesting with the other Powers and Mannon at this very moment."

Although I've only just heard the name during court in the days prior, the energy in the room shifts uncomfortably, making the air hot and sticky. Sweat pours down my temple even though it is not hot outside and I recognize that what I have become—what I have experienced—has affected me in ways that I don't understand. Like the moment on the bridge, it's as though space around me takes on color and emotion, so my body reacts to the invisible. The most obvious shift are all of the eyes from around the room that are now afraid to look at me.

Sassi shakes her head. "I knew it. I knew Isaiah would do everything he could to make his way to the podium."

Peter pipes in, "They knew if they made enough trouble, it would look as though they had no choice but to elect him quickly."

Even though my body is nervous to ask, there are too many people staring at me. Something is wrong. "Tell me who he is," I finally demand.

Briston breathes out as though he's been holding it in anticipation of my question. Arek is behind me, and his chest rises as he speaks. "Isaiah Aldo was Covey's wingman. When Covey needed him to cover things up, Aldo did."

Diem speaks out with curled Irish words, "He hated ye."

"Me?"

"Diem!" Mak hollers from the other side of the room.

"The woman is stronger than I am at this point and the moment she sees him again, she's gonna know. You'd rather her be surprised when she remembers?" Diem nods as he scratches his curly hair just above his pointed ears, then he looks back at me.

Just as he's about to speak, Arek interrupts. "I'll tell her." Diem wants to continue, so Arek says it again, but more forcefully. "Stop Diem. I'll tell her." After a sigh, he continues. "He was in line many, many years ago to become a Prophet. The man does seem to know things . . . and he is connected to something beyond this world—"

Before he can continue, Gal calls out over Arek's voice, "It ain't good, whatever it is."

Arek continues anyway. "Although the closer he came to being accepted as Prophet, the more we stood against him. But the man knows business and he knows money. So, other Prophets and Powers have fought to have him. He nearly made it in the last time, but Briston and Kenichi managed to use their influence to get Prophet Jenner in instead."

I can tell without anyone saying a word that there is more to the story. My chest warms and my right hand begins to shake, so I make a fist in and out to see if I can stop it. I step away from Arek so that I can see him.

He clears his throat once our eyes meet. "We have assumed he was helping Navin all this time. So, if they manage to get Isaiah in, it is no different than having Covey."

Again, Gal raises her voice. "It is different, it's worse. The man took ye, Remy. Ye don't remember?"

The bomb drops. "What?" I ask, then look at my father, then Arek. "What are you talking about, Gal?"

Diem is touching Gal's arm, but she feistily pulls it away. "No!" she yells at her husband. "The woman has a right to know. Because she's a woman she can't handle it? Buggar off. Remy, you need to understand because of who ye are, you've been runnin' your entire life. Maybe it was a gift that you died and don't remember. I don't know, Mother Mary does mysterious things. But here it is: Isaiah Aldo did everything for Japha. One day, in the sixteenth century, ye go missin'. The prophets had tried for years to keep it quiet that you were the One, but small inklings were getting out about ye. So, all of a sudden, one day you're gone. Poof, like a ghost."

As she's speaking, feelings are starting to return. Visions of the 16th century come to my mind. There is a darkness to everything that returns to me. The same feeling I had with Japha as a little girl is the same evil that surrounds me now.

"No one knows what happened while you were gone, but ye. Arek . . . come on. Tell her. She was gone for more than two years." Gal raises her eyebrows in expectation.

I look at Arek and my father, who has come toward me. "It's true. You disappeared and when you were gone, no one could find

Isaiah either. We looked everywhere for you. It seemed insane since you were at the top of your game, the best at Tracing, the best at strategy, the best at fighting. Yet for nearly two years, we just couldn't find you. One day, I got wind of where you were from someone who had worked for Japha and Covey. When I found you, you had been—a lot had happened to you, for I don't know how long. They tried to ruin you . . . but you were so strong they couldn't do it. Had we not found you when we did, they might have. Yet they were all gone. Someone had tipped them off, and you were the only one we found. It was too difficult with who the Prophets and Powers were at the time to get a conviction on Japha, Covey, or Isaiah. But we believe, since Japha and Covey never disappeared, that it had been Isaiah Aldo who had you the entire time."

Suddenly memories, bits and pieces, come flooding back to me. I picture Isaiah's face and the hours he spent doing his best to change me through hostile and inhumane ways. It all comes rushing back, until I look around the room and see the sympathy in people's eyes through small bits of tears hanging on my bottom lashes. Without another word, I rush out. Cool air hits my face and I just walk. Away from everyone, away from the ghosts of this town. The desert is long and vast, and I am very aware that there is no end to how far I can go. It feels as though I could walk into the stars if I wished.

"Remy!" Arek's voice calls out to me. We are now a hundred yards from the dilapidated town, with only the flat earth to see. I stop walking and wait for him to catch up. He looks at me like no other person can. "Remy, I thought we could go forever without reliving that."

"It never ends, Arek," I say quietly. "We're all living in our own individual Cellars . . . every one of us. So many memories that return to me, tell me what I don't want to know about this world. The way that people can abuse each other, the way that people will do any-thing to get what they want. This one Prophecy hanging over my life . . . it gave others free reign over me and what I was to become." I turn away and look out to the flat horizon. "Words written and said by someone else made my life hell. These memories of what Isaiah tried to do and take from me . . . and it was my job to heal from it. It was my job to forget. He chose that for my life. And now look at the world. Arek, look at the world and the way people hate each other. What are we doing? What does this Prophecy mean? If I'm it, I don't know how to be. How do you do what you're on this earth for, if you don't know how?"

Arek stays quiet for a moment, then finally speaks, his deep voice wrapping around me with comfort. "I fell in love with a woman because of her laughter . . . it's what I think about when I see the hate. I fell in love with a woman because when she saw something in the world that needed to be fixed, she fixed it. It's what I think about when the world is trying to turn me into something I'm not. And I fell in love with a woman because she recognized what something could be and never lost hope for it. It's what I thought about when she was taken from me too early, and my daughters needed to know how to see the world. I would give anything to keep you from getting hurt."

I turn to him, just as the sun begins to rise. He takes my face in his hands and we look at each other for a moment. Every time we do, more memories return, lightly covering the bad. He kisses my lips softly, until we notice that someone is coming our way in the dawn. Daye is moving hesitantly, so Arek calls her over with his hand. She quickens her pace. I wipe away my tears.

Daye looks at me with sensitive eyes. "I'm sorry you just learned that. I didn't know either." She waits a moment, then reaches out and touches my arm. "I want you to know that as I was growing up and learning about my mom, all anyone ever told me was how strong, how brave, and how amazing you were. And all I remember thinking was how that would be me. I would be just like you."

Arek grins. "And you are. You are just like your mother."

"And I'm ready," she says. "I'm ready to fight this . . . with you."

I shake my head. "What if I'm not?"

Together, we walk back to the saloon where everyone still waits.

"What did we miss?" Arek asks.

Sassi speaks up first. "Caynan is already trying to help Prophet Jenner. Briston, Kenichi, Mak, and Aita are going to see how they can help. They're going to try and contact as many Powers as they can to see where we stand. We need to figure out who's getting bad information and, frankly, who's on our side."

Diem speaks up. "We are headin' with ye . . . to try and find Navin."

"So am I," Hok agrees.

"And I'm in," Geo calls out from the corner of the room where he leans on the door frame.

Lya steps forward. "And that leaves Commander Wakefield to stay here with the Fidelis?"

Adam speaks out from his place behind Lya. "I'll stay."

Lya turns around with surprise. "What? No."

Adam chuckles, "You don't trust me?"

"It's not that."

The room is quiet before Adam shrugs his shoulders. "I'll do it. I can help Commander Wakefield keep everyone safe and when you need us to fight, I'll make sure everyone's ready."

Sassi looks over at Briston. "How do we get them weapons without anyone knowing they're here?"

Mak speaks up. "I have a way. I'll work on it."

"Okay." Sassi looks around the room. "We have our work cut out for us. We're being told from everywhere . . . the War is here. It isn't tomorrow . . . it's now. The only way to figure this out and know what we have to do is to find Navin."

A woman's voice echoes from the entrance, turning everyone's heads toward her. "I'll go with you." When I look over, it's difficult not to roll my eyes. Masey steps to the forefront of the group. I catch the look in Arek's eyes and I can see that he's uncomfortable.

Peter speaks up, "What about the missing Ephemes?"

Sassi shakes her head. "Briston?"

Briston nods. "I think the only way to find them is to find Navin, but I've also rounded up our own Black Hat. Arek and the others will meet him before they search for Navin."

My skin crawls thinking about the fight ahead. Yet the further this goes, the more I am ready to be done . . . to end this War.

CHAPTER THIRTEEN

"Where are we?" I ask as towering mountains pass outside the SUV's window. It's a beautiful and quiet place that doesn't seem familiar.

"Banff, Canada." Arek turns to me and his green eyes are bright under the intense light of day. Sometimes I wonder how I ever existed without him.

"Why is it so quiet here?" I ask as Sassi drives a massive van with all of us hunkered inside.

Kilon shakes his head. "'Cause it isn't America. Drama runs through America's DNA. America was created after killing the natives, after running from the rules of the king, only to have its leaders take the place of tyrannical leadership. Drama is America's love language."

"Well, you're quite opinionated," Sassi chuckles.

"Canadians are probably locked in their homes waiting for order." Kilon shrugs.

"What's here though?" I ask.

"It's not what, but who. Briston set up a meeting with an old friend. He's a hacker . . . one of the best," Arek explains as he reaches out and moves a hair from in front of my eyes.

Sassi speaks up from the front seat, "There's a reason for that . . . he does nothing else."

"True." Arek grins.

"He's better with computers than he is with people," Kilon quips.

"That he is," Gal says as she and Diem sit in the back seat.

"So, you all know him?" I ask.

"Know him?" Gal laughs. "It's not really possible to know him. But we've all heard of the dangers of him."

"How do we know that Navin hasn't gotten to him first?" I ask. Everyone laughs. "What?"

Arek shakes his head. "The only person who might hate Navin more than you or me is Beck."

"Why?"

"Let's just say, Navin is the reason Beck spent twenty years in the Cellar . . ."

My mind wanders and heat flushes my cheeks. Instantly I wonder what Beck looks like and what he sounds like. Why? I don't really know . . . except I want to feel an instant connection with someone who has experienced that place. The halls, the nightmares, the smells, the dripping water, the mind games of the darkest evil piercing you through. These thoughts cover me with an overwhelming sense that Beck might be the only one to understand . . . me. I do not question the very reason Beck lives as a hermit.

We pass through town and pull into a parking space at the end of the street. Arek is the first to jump out of the vehicle, then helps the rest of us. Just as my foot touches the sidewalk, a large bang carries within the slight wind, forcing all of us to duck. Within seconds Arek has his gun. Nearly a hundred feet away, one man runs across the street while looking behind him in fear at an angry mob chasing after him. This has become the new normal. They are gone before they even notice us and leave the rest of the tiny town quiet. "Let's get off the street," I say quickly. "He's meeting us in a public place?"

Arek shakes his head and turns back around. "No. He rents out an apartment above here." He points to the shops just behind us, and just above those are several windows that overlook this main street. From the corner of one window, I see a figure looking down on us. It disappears the moment I look up.

We enter through a small door between a seamstress and a café that leads into a tiny hallway with mailboxes on one wall, while the brown interior paint is chipping until there are large patches missing. It occurs to me that this looks similar to cow print. The stairs we climb shift and moan with every step, so much so, that Peter laughs. "Can't sneak up on Beck."

At the end of the hall on the second story is a black door with stickers all over it. It takes me a moment but I soon realize that each sticker is the same word, just in different languages. *Danger.*

Arek knocks and then we stand there for several moments while we hear someone scurrying about inside. "Beck!" Arek yells.

"Yeah, yeah." We hear the growl.

Finally, the sound of four or five locks and then the whoosh of the door opening makes us step back. Standing on the other side is a harsh-looking man, shorter than six feet, but built with muscular shoulders. He's attractive in a lumberjack kind of way, which I didn't expect. He has thick-rimmed glasses, a short beard, wild eyebrows, and hair pulled back in a ponytail. One ear is pierced all the way up. "Oh god," is all that he says.

Arek smiles and then pulls him in for a hug. "It's good to see you, Beck."

"It's never good to see you. It always means something." He has a severe cockney accent and it fits every inch of his tough exterior. He turns around and sits on the computer desk, then spins to us while everyone crams into the small studio. The amount of people instantly makes him fidget. "Hello all."

Diem does a dance toward the man and as soon as Beck sees him, he jumps up and backs away yelling, "No, no, no, no, no!" Although he's cowering from Diem's bear hug, there's a small grin underneath his dark eyes. "I didn't know you would be here, you wanker."

"Of course! A chance to bother the hermit? Would I miss that?" Diem is still holding him tightly, then finally lets go and messes up Beck's hair.

Beck looks around as he pulls his hair neatly back once again. It's obvious when he tries not to engage, until his eyes stop on me. "Well, well, well. It's like you brought the world's reckoning when you returned."

I nod. "I suppose I did."

Arek speaks up, "The storm has been brewing for our lifetime, Beck. How have you been doing here?"

"Doors are locked. I haven't seen anyone for two days. It's been good." He smiles. He breathes out with hesitation. "What did I do to deserve this visit?"

"We need your help," Arek says. It takes Arek only a few minutes to tell Beck everything about what Lya and Daye discovered from other Black Hats. He rubs his face until he leaves red marks and stays quiet even when Arek is finished.

"So, Navin's turned the world through the web. I can bet I know who he's using." Beck spins on his chair and turns away from us. He moves his head from side to side as if to crack his neck.

Lya steps forward. "I've had my best people on this and they haven't been able to get around his spyware."

Beck says nothing but opens one of his many computers. With fast fingers, he types for two minutes. When he's done, he turns his computer toward us. There's a long list of codes and then a snapshot of Navin's underground website. "Were they able to get these?"

"What's that?" Lya asks.

"It's every site under his protection *and* this tells you every Black Hat he's using. I know them all. They're good . . . really good."

"Better than you?" I ask.

This makes him turn to look directly into my eyes. "No one's better than me, love."

"Oh god," Lya says with irritation.

Beck looks at Lya with one eye closed and a raised eyebrow on the other side as an exaggeration of his own agitation. "Who's she?" he asks Arek.

Arek clears his throat. "This is Lya, she's been running the San Francisco Gianda. She's smart . . . a pain in the ass sometimes, but smart."

"Listen," Beck says, "you don't have enough money to use me. I'm over this. Nobody's gonna touch me here and why would I try to get involved in this mess? I didn't create it."

"This is the guy?" Lya says to Arek. "We don't need him."

"Lya, go out in the hallway," Arek commands.

"What?"

"In fact, everybody go . . ." Arek tells them.

Gal and Diem don't care about leaving. Diem steals a kiss on Beck's neck while Beck growls and pushes him away, just before they exit. As I'm walking out, I hear Beck's voice: "Not you." When I turn, Beck is staring at me.

"Me?"

"You stay. Arek, you can go."

"Beck, come on." Arek is irritated and breathes out heavily. "No games this time. We don't have time."

"Do you want me?" Beck dares him with his eyes and when Arek says nothing he nods. "If you want me . . . there's time."

Arek breathes heavily, looks out the window, then at me. "Don't try anything," Arek says, then he walks out into the hall and closes the door.

The small room stays silent for a moment, until the screech of his swivel chair as he stands up, opens a cupboard, and pulls out a bottle of whiskey. He pours himself one and a second one, then hands me the small shot glass. "For old times' sake," he says.

"Did we used to do this?" I say as I take the glass.

"Ahhhh, you don't remember. The way you'd sit on my lap and we'd drink whiskey. Anytime you wanted something, you did that."

I furrow my brows and give him a questioning look. "I did?"

He chuckles, "Maybe that was a fantasy. I guess you'll never know."

"Why am I standing here, Beck?"

"It's good to look at you . . . the woman behind all of the madness."

"Beck." My voice is serious, which flips the switch and suddenly Beck changes his tone.

"Navin got you sent to the Cellar?" He comes close and clinks our glasses together, then waits for me to down his whiskey. I relent and together we take a shot. He takes a step toward me until we are so close—and he smells good, like a mixture of musk and pine. "Did it change you?"

I don't know Beck and there's very little coming to my memory of him, but his eyes are sincere as he asks a question that whittles down to the aching part of my soul. "Yeah."

He stays close but silent for a moment, then he reaches his forefinger to mine and touches it. "Me too." Finally, he continues, "Don't tell anyone but I'll do whatever you want to kill him . . . Navin. If it's the last thing I do, I'll kill him."

"We think he's behind thousands of missing Ephemes and we don't know what he's done with all of them."

"Hmmm. If they've said anything about it online . . . I'll find it on one condition." He comes so close to me that his shoulder touches mine.

"What's that?"

"I come with you when it's time to see him off." He pulls a book from his shelf and shows it to me. "Look at the front page."

I open the book to the front page and see my handwriting. A small note telling him how much I care about him and how I'm sorry for his loss. "What's this?"

"Before you died, I often wondered how you cared so much about everything and everyone. It looked exhausting. After my wife died, I got to be on the giving end of your empathy. You earned my loyalty. None of them did . . . just you." He's staying close but it doesn't feel pushy or inappropriate. His charisma is consuming and enigmatic. Something begins to feel familiar.

He walks toward the whiskey again and pours another for himself, then another for me. I happily suck it down after feeling the quick numbing effect of the first one. "Beck, how did you get over the Cellar after being there for so long?"

"Remy, you don't. I didn't and I won't, which is why I would give my life to take Navin down."

"I think there's many of us," I say. He sits on the edge of his desk. "You think you can beat all of his hackers?"

"I can destroy them. There's not a firewall I can't infiltrate."

"Is that a promise?" I ask with a grin.

"It's a threat."

I come closer until I can see his computer. "Enough said. Welcome to the team, Beck."

"Is it weird?" he grins.

"What?"

"To not remember what relationship you've had with people you've known all your life?"

"Beck, there was only one relationship that was strong enough for him to follow me for thirty years without any guarantee of whether I'd ever come back to him. And I felt it before I even knew it."

"Damn Arek." Beck breathes out a boozy breath. "It was always the monogamy thing that got in the way for me."

"You had a wife?"

Beck nods, "Yeah, I did. And for three years I was able to give her all the devotion she deserved."

"Three years? Oh Beck, I'm starting to remember you." I shake my head as he leisurely sits on the desk next to me. "Come with us."

"That's a lot of time with people."

"You don't like people."

"Not so much, no." He looks around and grabs his phone. "Look, send me a pin of where you want me to go, and I'll get there."

Suddenly I feel the expansion and retraction of my being and the shakes that come with Traveling. "Oh no," I say suddenly and grab my head. Beck looks at me with concern.

"Remy? What's wrong?"

He reaches out as my equilibrium betrays me and the ground gets closer and closer. He catches me in his arms, but all goes black.

When I open my eyes, I remember what Navin told me and I sit up, swiftly checking for him. Strangely I'm in the corner of a massive gymnasium with a pool on the left. There are many people walking about, setting up computer systems, laughing as they work. Suddenly the doors to the gymnasium open and the laughing instantly stops. Navin walks in. I don't think he can see me, so I hurriedly scoot behind the bleachers. The door behind me opens and two men walk in with extension cords over their shoulders—one carries a monitor. They see me on the floor and stop. Then they yell. With one foul kick, I debilitate one of the men by taking out his knee, but the other drops the things he's holding to grab me. I don't allow him. With fast hands, I block him, then use one leg to sweep his right ankle and jump to my feet. He's trying to balance on the one foot while I hold his other over my shoulder. He yells again to grab everyone's attention, so I hold tightly to his ankle and twist my body until he can no longer balance, and he slides across the floor. With my boot, I stomp on his head and his eyes roll back. By this time the entire gymnasium, including Navin, are racing toward me. I grab a nearby rolling table and yank it in front of me. Those who are closest run directly into it, and one of them flies over it.

"Remy!" Navin yells, as I slam the doors open and race outside.

However, my feet come to a sliding stop when I see several of Navin's men outside and a long line of Ephemes—their heads down and forlorn, some with tears and others with injuries. Navin's men are leading these people into a small room on the outside of the Gymnasium. Navin nearly crashes into me and traps me with his arms.

"What are you doing with them?" I yell out.

Just as he's about to answer, I feel the same pull of Travel. In moments, I'm back on the floor with Beck beside me, but now Arek and the others are there as well. "Where'd you go?" Arek asks.

"He has them . . . they're prisoners . . . at least several of them . . . and I don't know what he's going to do," I explain.

Geo steps forward from beside Daye. "Where is he?"

"I don't know. I wasn't there long enough to see anything or know what they're doing." Again, I can feel that my body is tired from convulsing.

"What the hell is this?" Beck seems a combination of curious and concerned. "What just happened? And what the hell are you talking about?"

"She Travels."

"Travels?" Beck laughs. "Seriously, what kind of black magic are you throwing around here."

"Come on," Arek says as he pulls me to my feet, while ignoring Beck. "Beck, are you in?"

"Are you actually going to get him this time?" Beck gives a sideways glance to Arek.

"Yes," Arek says with a growl.

Beck looks around at everyone. "Okay. I'll find you . . . in a few days."

Arek grins. "Don't get lost."

"It's what I'm best at. Where are you off to now?"

"New Zealand. We have reason to believe Navin is there," Arek says.

Beck turns to me and nods. "Don't forget what I said."

"Of course."

Everyone begins to exit the room, but Beck grabs my hand and leans into my ear. "For you and me . . . I'll kill him."

CHAPTER FOURTEEN

We land in New Zealand. Whether Navin is actually here or he isn't permeates all of us till we find it difficult to speak. Except for Masey. She seems ambivalent to the danger ahead, but it's quite possible that she's just preoccupied with Arek. There are many responsibilities that keep him busy and able to stay clear of her, but I watch her eyes. He was a major love of her life. I have to keep myself from falling into the trap. *What were they like together? Did he love her?*

We'd all like to believe that our lovers would love only us forever, but I knew nothing of him. He was just in the shadows as I grew up this second time around. A man trained to disappear until he wants to be seen and yet, all along, he hadn't the assurance that I would ever fully return to Velieri. I watch as Masey's hand sweeps across his arm as she passes . . . the way they speak as though they know each other deeply . . . or as she refills his drink as we fly to the next destination. I do everything I can to ignore the obvious familiarity, but deep down I am watching—becoming more afraid of the years Arek was alone.

From the airplane, to the car, to the hotel where we check in with our group and the weapons, questions rush through my mind. *If Navin is here, can we end this now?*

"There is so much to fix," I whisper to Arek as he sets our things down in the hotel room.

He stops, breathes out, and nods. "One step at a time."

"If we see him today?" I ask. "How do we stop him?"

"I don't know." Arek comes close and moves my hair out of my eyes.

"Have you thought about what you're going to have to do?"

"Many times. He's my brother, but when someone's as dangerous as he is, there's nothing else to do."

After a moment's hesitation, I ask, "Who is Masey?"

Arek doesn't need me to elaborate. It's surprising when he walks away and takes a seat on the corner of the desk in the room. "Masey was in love with me . . . *is* in love with me. She came into my life nearly fifteen years ago."

"But you knew about me fifteen years ago."

"I know. I never pursued anything with her."

"You said that you never moved on."

"I very obviously didn't, Remy. You are my wife and always have been. There was never a chance that I would marry again, even if you turned out to never come back to the Velieri side. But Masey has a way of taking what she wants."

"I see that. She still wants you."

He stands, towering over me, and comes so close that I have to look straight up. "I am yours always. You are the only woman I want."

✓✓✓

An hour later, we hike along the mountain ridge where the fog is so thick it is difficult to see just a few feet ahead. We maneuver in and out of trees, dodging swinging branches as people pass. The ominous gray affects my mood and with each step, the moisture in the air feels weighted like anvils instead of watery drops. Every giant tree has branches that look like witch's fingers and her cranky old extremities reach out for us as we pass. The one thing I can say is that the green is so rich—when the fog parts at all, I am mesmerized by the beauty of this land.

Arek walks steadily beside me, followed by Diem, Gal, Hok, Daye, Lya, Kilon, Sassi, and Masey. Our jackets are cold and wet, but they do their jobs to keep us warm. Within the eerie forest, suddenly I feel lightning bolts shoot through my skin from head to toe as a breeze breathes across my neck, lifting my hair ever so slightly. My body feels like it has sprung to life in an instant, but I'm unsure why. I stop walking and take a look around. I half expect ominous ghosts to be riding our backs like hitchhikers, but the only thing people carry are weapons. My skin crawls when I feel someone's breath on my ear.

I swiftly look to my right, but there is no one.

"What?" Arek's deep voice cuts through my inauspicious thoughts, but I say nothing, when the sound of many voices fills the air. I spin around, but no one in my group has said a word. "Remy?"

"You don't hear that?" I ask.

Everyone else shakes their head, except Sassi. She nods, "I do."

"What do ye hear?" Gal asks, lifting her weapon to her chest.

Sassi and I lock eyes but stay silent a bit longer. Finally, she speaks, "Voices . . . many, many voices."

The sound of wailing, crying, moaning, gasping as if layered fills the air. Sassi comes so close that she touches my hand. It is an awful sound, forcing my heart to pound against my chest. "What is this?" I ask her.

She can only shake her head.

"Let's keep moving," Arek suggests.

As we do, the horrible moans increase. Then I begin to feel that the air has thickened, almost as though I am trying to push through a wall of brush, yet it is just fog. It sweeps across me, one rush here, another there. One at a time, as though things are running through me and by me.

My lungs are sore, as if I've run miles uphill. Again and again, something brushes my body, and Sassi shifts uncomfortably when she feels the same.

"Something has happened here," Sassi whispers. "You feel that?"

"It feels like the Cellar."

Sassi nods. "Let's keep moving. I don't know what Navin has done here . . . but something is wrong."

We continue. Again and again, the deep breaths of spirits blow through the trees as though they are searching for something. I'm not sure what death is like . . . even though I myself died. In a short time since this all began, I have been gifted with sensitivities to a world that blurs the line between the living and dead. I get the feeling that we are all more connected than any of us choose to understand. *Once again,* I wonder, *could it be that being Velieri is the curse, not the gift? Anchored to this world—shackled even, forced to experience any separation from what is beyond here.*

Arek comes to my side and softly whispers, "A curse or a blessing is decided by us."

"Stay out of my head," I warn.

"That's impossible . . ." he grins.

With each small step is a larger feeling that not just one presence is surrounding me, but many. I close my eyes and it is as though I can feel the brush of their wings on my cheeks as they fly about me. My cheeks turn rosy and my heart is heavy when I soak in their torture. *Yes.* There is sadness soaking deep within my soul. And fear—like a child within a dark room. My hands begin to shake, and my arms and legs weigh more than I can carry.

"Do you feel this?" I ask Sassi.

Sassi nods. She bends at the waist just to breathe. "There is so much death here."

It is as though our feet are strangled of their circulation and the chains of whomever, or whatever, is sweeping about us, until it's a heavy burden to walk.

Arek moves us along. "Come on, we need to move."

Another two hundred yards and we come upon a ditch. I recognize where I am and stop walking. "Wait!" I say, feeling as though I need a moment.

"What's going on?" Kilon asks with concern.

"They're up there." I'm having trouble breathing, and I feel like retching. Coming through the fog is the little girl; her pink coat wraps her bruised body and her long hair is messy and full of leaves. Her eyes connect with mine. She passes each of the others as though she doesn't see them and they don't see her. Her gray skin and sunken eyes look me over as I struggle to breathe. When she is close enough, she reaches out her hand, her skin rotting as it was before, but it is her eyes that make me take her tiny fingers in mine.

Without a word she turns and leads me toward the ditch ahead. As we get closer, the bodies stacked one upon the other come into view. Sassi can't help herself, and I can hear her soft cries next to me.

The air has frozen my fingers, but they are nothing next to the little girl's icy skin. The colorful sprays of clothes dampened by weather and dirt, the different shades of dying skin, and the many faces of men, women, and children that are lying on top of one another in the ditch.

All of us stand before the grotesque sight.

"Oh my god," Diem says. "Are these them?"

"Not all of them," Arek says.

"He has to be stopped," Sassi says. "The lengths that he will go . . . there is no end. This isn't about coming out of hiding anymore—this is more than that. This is about power."

Daye and Lya stand by each other, their arms around each other's waists.

"I was wrong," I say. "Navin isn't here. This was the marker on the map." I am drawn to the other side of the ditch, but the only way down is a steep embankment which also means walking near the dead. Whatever it is keeps calling me from the other side, so I proceed ahead, even when the others look at me with concern.

"Remy?" Sassi asks.

I hear Arek's footsteps following me closely while I slide down the embankment, scratching my hands along the rocks on the way down. At the bottom of the dry riverbed, I walk within a small tunnel through the pile of Ephemes, taller than Arek by a few feet. "There's something over here."

The sounds of the forest are resonant as I try to keep my eyes looking forward, unable or unwilling to think about how any of these people died. A small hand lays out on the dirt path and instantly I recognize her hair. The little girl with sunken eyes . . . yet she is no longer here.

For a moment, the other side doesn't look like a possible exit, until I see a couple of rocks sticking out of the wall, and I test them for safety. They are solid to the touch and soon I heave myself one rock at a time up the small rocky steps of the mountain. When I finally climb over the other side, Arek is already at the top and lends a hand to help me up.

"Show off," I whisper.

He grins.

"Come on." A small path winds through the trees. Arek hacks at the thick brush so that we can make it through. After a few moments, I stop him with a hand on his arm. "Wait," I say quietly. "You hear that?"

Somewhere ahead of us, there is a small buzzing sound—not that of an insect, but rather something closer to a phone line. Both of us know there are no phone lines around here. The rest of our group quietly emerges through the path we've created from behind us, but this doesn't seem to be connected to the buzzing.

Arek and I continue now that everyone is following, until he unexpectedly stops. "Wait," he whispers. "Stay here," he says to the others.

He and I continue through the trees until I finally see something ahead. It is out of focus at first, until two branches part and we run into a fence, double Arek's height. I start to reach out to touch it, but Arek grabs my hand and stops me.

"What?"

He points up to the lines stretched all the way across the fencing. "It's charged . . . this'll give you a good shock." Just then Kilon comes from behind us and his jaw drops.

"What in the world are we looking at?" he asks.

"I don't know." Arek shakes his head then begins to walk the fence line hidden by the trees. We follow. Within the chain-link fence are cabins, some big and some small. They are simple and without cold or heat; without the normal luxuries of today. We hide as a few people walk the property holding guns, dressed in matching uniforms that look eerily familiar. My eyes travel from their heavy black boots up to their black shirts, a red X over the left breast. Something hangs around their necks and I squint my eyes to see better. One of the soldiers turns away from us and the thing that hangs around his neck is laid out flat across his shoulder blades. A noise of surprise escapes my lips, enough to make Kilon and Arek turn to me. Each guard wears a black mask with red Xs over the eyes and mouth.

"What?" Kilon asks.

"When Meryl, Davi, and the other men attacked me in the Cellar, they wore those masks. The ones hanging around their necks."

Arek raises his phone and takes a picture.

Kilon hits Arek on the shoulder. "Look there," he says. Together we walk around the fence, keeping well hidden within the trees. The dusk is aiding in our quest to remain invisible, but I also get hit in the cheek with some painful pine needles. We hide as one of the guards slowly and methodically walks the boundary lines, holding his rifle to his chest. As we wait there for him to pass, a truck—built to withstand the elements—drives up to the gate a hundred feet ahead. Guards run out to open the chain-link fence and let them in.

"What do we do?" I ask.

"We can't do anything," Kilon answers solemnly, "not until we know what we're looking at. We should go and get the others. Go back to the hotel and figure out a plan. It's getting dark."

"Wait," Arek says. A strange horn blasts through the camp and on every building, doors open up, as people emerge. Yet there's a strange tinkering sound and I squint to see clearer. Men, women, and children emerge, their feet tethered together so that they have to move slowly and methodically. They walk out in lines, perfect, straight, long lines, from the building, almost to the fence. Their clothes are just rags, their faces dirty and sad. Twenty lines with about eighty people in each, standing perfectly straight.

Suddenly another blast is heard and this time a guard emerges from the building where the truck just entered. He walks confidently, stoically across the grass and dirt; his chest rises nearly above his eyes; his face is menacing. As he walks toward the south side of these twenty lines, several guards follow him, but he is the leader to watch. Raising two fingers to his mouth, he whistles, and instantly the prisoners turn as though they have done this millions of times. Arek feels the need to get closer, but before he does, he warns me with a hand on my back. I say nothing but I nod as the light grows dim.

He nearly crawls toward the fence, making his way to a large boulder that he can hide behind.

Saying very little, the intimidating guard walks to the prisoners and looks them over—their nails and hands, their feet, he even places two hands on their cheeks to look into their eyes. Even the children seem used to this, and make as few moves as possible.

He passes three people, then directs the fourth to step out of line—while one of the guards disconnects the chains on their ankles. Then he passes two more and pulls another. This continues until he yells at some of the guards to help him with the other lines. They do the same.

On the last line, the guard removes an elderly woman, but the elderly man next to her cries out and nearly trips as they undo her chains while his are still intact. "No! Please!" he cries. "Don't separate us . . . please."

The guards push him down. "Be quiet. Get back in line."

He tries again, but they kick him down before he can stand and the elderly woman cries out, "Don't, please. Leave him . . . leave him!"

The head guard whistles again, and this time the remaining prisoners—with the chains still around their ankles—turn away and head back to the barracks. While they maintain as much composure as possible, it is obvious that loved ones have been separated. The elderly woman cries, but a young girl comes to her side and comforts her with a hand around her slumped back.

Several guards appear by the fence and open the door to let these separated prisoners out of the fenced-in area. Arek and Kilon look at each other with concern. "We know where they're going," Kilon whispers.

"We do?" I ask.

Arek hurries back to our side and points a different direction. "We need to go fast and get to the others before they do."

In seconds we are running through the trees, pine needles sticking to our pants and poking our skin. Kilon leads, Arek follows, and I am doing everything in my power to keep up with their pace. Up and down hills, weaving in and out of trees, our legs scream in defiance. All I can hear is the pounding of my heart, the burn of my lungs, while the light of the sun draws to a close.

Soon we are back at the ditch where the others wait. They stand at attention when they see us rushing. Kilon throws his hand in the air and waves them to hide from across the mass grave. Sassi knows instantly and makes sure everyone does as they're told. The rustle of trees is the first giveaway that they're here, the guards commanding movements from the group of prisoners. Arek, Kilon, and I push ourselves back into the thicket of trees and look out between the small spaces of the branches.

It isn't until the prisoners see the ditch that they know what's coming and the wailing and screaming, the clawing and running begins. Yet at some point, the guards had managed to hook them back together before they reached this disturbing scene.

"Oh my god," I whisper.

"Your weapon," Arek says to me. I pull my gun out and make sure it is ready. We can only see Sassi's eyes between the branches across the ditch, but that's enough to tell her to prepare her gun. "We need to try and not use them," Arek says. "It's too loud. We don't want to attract any other guards."

They line the prisoners up, one by one and side by side. The weapon in my hand feels like a brick that I'm tired of using. If only there was a world that didn't believe guns were ever the solution. The atrocities seem to never end. Do you fight death with more death? Or violence with more violence? Do you give your life without a fair fight?

"Arek," I say, "control them." I point to my temple. "Control them."

He nods, as does Kilon.

The prisoners are terrified. They are obviously Ephemes, as I listen and feel their thoughts and emotions. Children, women, men—no one is spared in this group.

Lifting his gun in the air and telling the other guards to follow, the leader points his weapon directly at the Ephemes.

"Ready?!" the main guard yells.

Arek and Kilon rush out with their weapons pointed at the guards. "Set your weapons down." Arek's voice is aggressive and commanding.

"I wouldn't do that, brother," Kilon says to one of the guards.

Sassi and the others jump out of hiding. Their weapons face the prisoners, and ours face them.

As I delve deep, my Trace within their minds, I can feel that Sassi and the others are there as well. These guards are trained and block us immediately.

"Dual Planum," Arek whispers. "They're strong enough to battle the immediate Trace, but they're weak enough that Dual Planum should be enough."

"Can we get them all at once?" I ask.

"Yep," Arek says confidently.

The guards point their guns at us, as we point our guns at them. They yell a barrage of profanities, yet it is obvious they are shocked that we are there, and they haven't a clue as to how we found them. The tears fall down the cheeks of the prisoners standing helplessly without weapons, without their loved ones, and obviously confused by the standoff.

"You must leave this forest now!" the main guard yells.

"We don't leave without those people behind you." Kilon's voice seems to vibrate the earth when everything within him—all the anger and rage over injustice—emerges from deep in his belly.

"There is no chance of that." The main guard takes a step toward Kilon but thinks twice about it when Kilon cocks his head to the side and raises an eyebrow.

Yet as we stand there, they don't even know, I've already made it in. In fact, Arek glances at me with surprise when I'm the first one to slide into their subconscious. The only way to describe this slide—this slip—into existing within our conscious and multiple subconsciouses, is that two dimensions exist at once. The conscious is where our bodies, minds, and souls exist all at once, reacting to the present. However, our subconscious, when never healed or cleaned, is the darkness beneath a child's bed, or the basement with the light-bulb broken. None of us want to be there if it is the dimension that distorts and spins. And our unconscious is the graveyard out back, where all our real and true darkness is buried.

When the split happens, it is just a blink, and when I open my eyes, I am in an actual graveyard. I hear a clearing of his throat and turn around to find Arek there, just behind me. He's looking around, as we both know we only have moments until an experienced Velieri figures out how to block us.

"Let's hope they haven't been trained," I say.

He shakes his head, "They haven't."

Several newly dug graves sit just ahead and I have an idea. I've never been in this graveyard before, so I know it isn't from my memory bank. "Is this yours?" I ask Arek.

"No, it's definitely one of theirs."

Suddenly Sassi appears, walking from the opposite direction toward the open graves. "Where are they?" she asks about the guards.

"Coming," I say.

I blink on purpose and through my mind's control, I drive the idea deep within the stranger's memory, and suddenly there are the exact amount of open graves for each guard. From the sky at the end of strong whips of lightning, specks of black fall from the stormy clouds. Arek touches my arm as though to move me out of the way, but I know where the black specks will land and I place my calm hand on his.

In our conscious, I can see that the guards have no idea anything is happening with them. Instead, the main guard continues to warn us, but we counter with each step he takes. The tension is building until the cries of the prisoners grow uncontrollably.

Meanwhile, in the subconscious, the black specks grow bigger as they near the ground and finally we can see that they are bodies. One thud happens after another, sending clouds of dirt billowing from the earth of the open graves. Sassi, Arek, and I look at one another, then Kilon suddenly appears from a nearby tree. "You made it," I say.

"Just in time, apparently," he says.

We walk to the graves and peer down. We have stolen each of Navin's guards' subconscious, until they now lie in the open graves, covered in dirt, and panicked at the tight squeeze. In the darkness of night, only the moon gives a slight glow, and as we peer over, each one of them looks up at us with surprise.

"What is this?" the main guard yells to us from his six-foot tomb. Specks of black dirt cover his nose, lips, and eyes and he quickly begins to claw at the wall to get out.

"Well," I say as I kneel next to the hole, "I believe this is some-one's experience. Maybe they don't remember it, maybe they do, but it was easy to grab hold of, so whatever this place is, it's dangerous."

All I have to do is look at the dirt of the shoveled walls, which causes a big enough landslide within his grave to knock him down. He cries out as the dirt covers him. When it's over, he has to nearly dig his way out. I look around at all of the other graves and most of the guards are searching for a way out. "Don't let them get out," I say, but Sassi looks at me with a cockeyed glare.

"Are you serious? Of course I won't let them out."

Kilon kneels on the other side of the grave of the main guard, who has just gotten himself free of the dirt.

"You need to stop what you are doing out there," I say.

He shakes his head at me with angry eyes. I can tell he's still trying to figure a way out of this.

Strategically, I set my hand down on the grass and feel the energy swell within my body. Kilon and Arek are both watching me with suspicion. After just a moment, every insect and burrowed critter from within the fresh earth starts to emerge from the walls of the graves. As the ground turns to a slithering, crawling fortress of rats and insects, the man panics.

"Stop!" he yells, as rats and spiders crawl up his legs, under his shirt, and up his neck. "Please stop!"

"Whatever makes you stop. That's when I'll stop."

Sassi yells at the other guards to stay within the graves as they clamor for relief from the nightlife. Then suddenly, without my help, the ground begins to shake. A gravestone crumbles and falls just next to us.

"What is happening?" Sassi asks.

"I don't know," I tell her quickly.

Then, from the ground, an apparition emerges, sucking all light around her. She crawls across the ground, unable to use her legs. A horrible sound emerges from her that makes all of us cringe. It is obvious after a moment that she knows where she is going, and soon she slithers over the edge of the main guard's hole. When he sees her from below, he cries out with a deeply anguished plea. "No!"

We walk to the edge and see that she has pressed him down into the dirt, as the earth starts to fall on top of them.

"I get the feeling you know her," I mention.

His scared eyes look up at me, although his body is paralyzed by this apparition. "Help me."

Sassi comes over to see. "Don't you feel it?" She nods. "He knew her for sure. Her wrath is his very nightmare." Sassi kneels down as the ground continues to cover him—he will soon be buried alive. She calls out to him, "She's haunted you before . . . hasn't she?"

"Help!" he says, just as large clods of dirt fall into his open mouth.

Soon there is no need for our subconscious as the main guard falls like a tree in the forest, paralyzed in our conscious. With the prisoners in panic, two more of the guards fall, completely frozen. We bring ourselves fully back from our subconscious, and suddenly there is no fight. The remaining guards drop their weapons out of fear and back away.

"No!" Kilon yells at them. "Come here and put your hands out."

Soon we have them tied to the trees just beyond the ditch and, using the keys from one of the guards, we hurriedly let the prisoners go one at a time.

"Thank you!" the old lady says with tears running down her face.

"We need to get you out of here," Sassi says to them all.

As quickly as we can, we lead them back through the forest. Arek comes to my side and lays a hand on my neck. "All of the others that we couldn't get to. What do we do?" I ask.

"I don't know yet. We'll take these people with us, including the guards. It's our only choice. But we'll figure out the others later. They aren't the only ones, if I know Navin," he says. Arek looks me deep in the eyes. "There will always be more, until we end this."

"Why do I sometimes feel like this is just the beginning?" I whisper.

CHAPTER FIFTEEN

As a large caravan, we race across the southern island of New Zealand where the terrain is some of the most beautiful in the world. A part of me wonders whether I was right to bring us here. We pass fields of purple and pink flowers wrapped around each other under the blue sky, but it isn't long until this colorful display turns into the glassy mirror of a calm body of water that holds the reflection of massive mountains.

I'm tired, but my brain won't settle down, so when Arek reaches his hand out and gently caresses my neck, it snaps me back.

"Are you there?" he says quietly, trying not to wake Lya and Daye as they sleep in the back seat.

"Not really. I'm everywhere."

He nods, but remains quiet.

I lean my head against the headrest and take in a deep breath. "Where do we stop?"

"Up here, just a ways."

Twenty minutes later we pull down a steep embankment, past several fields of sheep—there doesn't seem to be any civilization for miles. I watch as a massive mansion comes into view just ahead. It looks no different than an extravagant country castle, old and rustic, but beautifully maintained.

"What is this?" I ask.

"This is the South Newy Gianda."

"Newy?"

"Carol Newy. She was one of the benefactors who believed in you and offered to turn this place into a Gianda." Just from his description, a woman's face returns to me with purple hair, far too tanned and leathery skin, with brown eyes. Her smile lit the room. "Yeah, I remember her. Will she be there?"

Arek takes a haunted breath . . . "No. She was found murdered soon after your death."

I rub my face with my palms. "How many did that happen to?" I ask.

"You don't need to worry about that."

"In other words, too many."

Still, he remains steadfast in giving no answer.

From the back seat, Lya's deep voice cuts in. "Of course it was too many." I look back at her hard eyes. "Carol Newy died because of you. Too many people died because they helped you." Unexpectedly, Arek screeches off the road, tosses the car into park, and jumps out of the driver's seat. Sassi's car pulls to a stop and she rolls down her window.

"What's going on?" The others are asleep in the back.

"Keep going, we'll be there." Arek gives no explanation, but his face is enough. She nods then her car sends dust billowing as she continues.

Arek opens Lya's door. "Get out."

"What? We're almost there." Lya rolls her eyes then steps out.

He pulls her into the field by the arm and out of hearing distance. Daye and I watch as he addresses her sternly, and it isn't long before she's yelling.

142

My eyes must show my concern because Daye breaks the silence. "Listen, I know how she can seem. We spent years listening to many people blame you for so many things . . . I was able to write it off because I trust my father. He said that you believe truth is all anyone ever has and sometimes that means dying for it. I don't know about you . . . but that sounds pretty noble to me. And the funny thing is, Lya's the same way. She either doesn't know it, or she's just chosen to deny it." She takes a pregnant pause, then continues, "But Lya is good to have on your side. She'd give her life for anyone, if it meant justice."

"Just maybe not me," I whisper.

"Don't be fooled. I think in her own way . . . *especially* for you she'd give her life." Daye reaches out and squeezes my hand.

Arek and Lya finally return, but neither say a word. Before long, we pull into the grounds of South Newy Gianda. We drive through gardens, greenhouses, and orchards that provide sustainability for the Fidelis.

"It's a ghost town," Arek whispers as his eyes survey the vegetable gardens.

The Newy Gianda is a Jacobethan style of architecture and faced with Bath stone. The gorgeous home is so grand that every gaudy detail is mesmerizing. When I step out of the car, I lean back to study its entirety.

In minutes, we stand in the entrance, looking at a foyer fit for a king and queen. Arek leads us to two large double doors and when he throws them open, the true essence of a Gianda returns. Ornate railings on curved stairways come from at least eight unique hallways. This Gianda isn't as open as Brazil's or San Francisco's, but I can tell that there is so much more, far beyond what we can see.

"This is like Downton Abbey Gianda," I whisper to Daye.

She laughs and nods. "Totally. You should see the Gianda in Dubai. I've never seen anything like it. Walls made of glass so you can see the city lights from every angle at night. Sleek and modern furniture, powerful technology, and the installation art is massive and beautiful."

For a place that's usually bustling, the fact that we can hear our toes tap the tile is unnerving. Soon, a large woman with big hands and a wide jaw enters through two heavily carved wooden doors. As they swing open and close behind her, I notice the makings of a commercial kitchen.

"Sam," Sassi reaches her long sinewy hand out and Sam's hand swallows it.

"Sassi, Arek, Kilon . . . it's good to have you."

"Sam," Arek says her name like someone has just died, but she puts her hand up. "It's okay. We're all fine." She turns to me, "Remy, it is so good to see you again. My husband and I run this place for you. It's been our pleasure for the last forty years." Her beautiful accent twists and turns almost as much as the nearby spindles and the staircases.

"I remember." Her husband more than her, but she doesn't need to know that. "Where is everyone?"

"They're glued to the media center. We have multiple televisions watching the devastation." She seems resilient . . . steadfast. "We're lucky to be so secluded out here."

The prisoners, who have followed quietly without much to say at all, look around inquisitively. "Who do we have here?" Sam asks.

Arek pulls her to the side so as not to discuss everything that just happened in front of the prisoners. Soon Sam addresses them with kindness. "We'll get you back with your families soon enough. Until then, can I get you some food or clothing?"

One of the women steps forward, "I have to go back for my son."

Arek nods, "We understand. We'll do our best . . . until then, follow Sam."

Hesitantly, they do as they're told. Moments later, the rest of us meet in an office with a large computer on which Briston's worn out face appears. "Tell me."

"We found some of the prisoners. I'm starting to believe he's using the Bryers. It's a mess, Briston. Many taken, caged, poorly treated."

Sassi steps beside Briston, "That's not all, Briston. Many have been killed. We found piles."

Briston's eyebrows furrow as he scratches his head with his rough fingertips. "And Navin?"

Arek shrugs, "Not there as far as we know. But plans changed and we couldn't search the place."

"So how many are still being held?" Briston taps his pen on the table where he sits. It appears he's back in his office in Switzerland. The last I heard he was trying to gather alliances.

"Hundreds . . . just in this one alone," Sassi answers.

"Why not just kill them? Why would he hold them?"

Kilon interrupts, "Why kill your bargaining chip?"

Briston nods, "Good point, Kilon."

"Briston, that's not all." Arek explains, "We have ten of the prisoners."

Just then, Gal and Diem come in from outside. "We got the guards secured in the backhouse. We checked them for weapons, tracking devices, and anything else that they could use against us." Gal sees Briston and waves, "Heyo, Mr. Elite."

"You have the guards from the Bryer?"

Arek brings the attention back to him. "We had to. If they stayed, they'd tell everyone what we did and who we are. We couldn't take the chance."

Briston rubs his scratchy chin with his palm. "Okay. What a mess. You did the right thing . . ."

I clear my throat. "What do we do with the prisoners?"

"I don't know . . . yet." Briston stops, drops his elbows onto the desk, then rubs his face.

"Have you been sleeping?" I come closer to the screen as I ask.

"I'm not sure anyone is. How are you?" He looks at me with care.

However, suddenly the air changes. My body turns rigid, and I can feel the unique pull of Travel.

"Arek!" I say, knowing that I only have moments.

"Remy?" He leaps to his feet and rushes over. He wraps his arms around me as I fall off the chair and it feels like everything is moving in slow motion. Then they're gone.

CHAPTER SIXTEEN

The cement floors are cracked and I can feel the sharp edges dig into my skin. Navin is kneeling near me, rolling a wooden coin back and forth in his hand as he waits for my senses to return. Each time I Travel, the place I land is different, and I take note of this. This time there is nothing but cement floors, cinder block walls, and a ceiling fan above us that casts a revolving light on his white skin.

"How are you doing this?" I say with little emotion, but disdain behind my glare.

"We are doing this. You, me, and Dr. Karine."

A man enters with dark, wide rimmed glasses. "Forget all this . . . ask her now."

Somehow, I know this is Dr. Karine. Now that I'm able to see his face, I have remnants of memory with him in it. "That's why you were looking for him when he was in the Cellar. When you nearly killed my father."

Navin pushes the wood piece deep into his pocket, then looks up at me. "So, he made it?" Navin looks at Dr. Karine with irritation.

"That man just won't die." Then he turns back to me. "I can't keep you here. I know that, but I need to know where you are . . ." He leans so close to me that I can see the growing lines of age around his eyes, extending down his cheeks. "Did you know that you are weaker when you Travel?"

That's when I become aware of him. Not the Navin kneeling in front of me, but the familiar rustling about in my brain that I have been so good at fighting. I begin to panic.

"So, you're going to tell me where you are."

"I'm stronger than that, Navin."

"Not right now and not in this." My head has increasingly ached since arriving here. I had nearly forgotten what this feels like. His pupils grow large and his eyes are like stone. There is nothing more horrible than the grating sound of Navin picking and clawing.

"Stop!" I yell.

"New Zealand," he says.

"Stop!" I cry out. My head feels like it will split in two. I bring my hands to my temples and press my chin to my chest.

After a few seconds the air changes and I hear Arek's voice. "Remy."

My body is stiff with tension and feels as though I have just run a full marathon. I sit up in a panic, despite my weakness. "He knows."

"Knows what?" Sassi asks.

"Where we are. New Zealand."

"At the Gianda?" Geo asks.

"I don't know."

"How?" Arek asks.

"I have no way to stop him when I'm there. I'm weak when I Travel both here and there."

Sassi shakes her head.

Geo kneels down beside me, "You saw Dr. Karine."

I nod. "A man with wide rimmed glasses, dark hair, dark eyes?"

Geo nods. "That's him. She didn't start Traveling again until he found Dr. Karine. When was Dr. Karine put in the Cellar, because she was starting to Travel at the end of her life, right?"

"Karine pled guilty to several things a few years after Remy died," Arek answers.

"We have to go," I say.

Geo stands up and looks around with concern.

"What is it, Geo?" Arek asks.

"When someone Travels . . . Time isn't the same. It doesn't exist between travels."

"What are you saying?"

"I'm saying, she could have met him hours ago, weeks ago. We just don't know. Travelers can get better at Traveling to the right times, but not when they're forced by someone else."

Everyone jumps to their feet. "Let's go," Sassi says.

"What about everyone here?" Daye asks.

But just before anyone answers, the lights flicker and then go out.

CHAPTER SEVENTEEN

People are running about, dodging furniture, and checking the halls. Many use their phones for light, yet this place is so large that this gives us just a fraction of sight. My eyes have not adjusted and my arms and legs are so tense that my muscles feel like rocks beneath the touch.

"Kilon?" Arek's voice is directly beside me. "Check the house."

Kilon's voice emerges from somewhere in the room. "Already done. The lights are out everywhere—"

Geo interrupts, "Someone's here. I can feel it."

It isn't long within this eerie black that we hear screaming from down the hall.

"Oh my god," Sassi says as she pulls her gun.

Everyone else follows.

"Can you stand?" Arek asks me. He carefully pulls me to my feet, but my knees shake. Gunshots pop closer and closer. Diem and Gal, Kilon and Sassi rush out of the room.

"Lya and Daye!" Arek calls out in the dark. "Get to the car."

When we enter the pitch-black hallway, we are met with screams.

I'm able to see down one hall and catch the orange glow of several blasts.

"Come on!" Arek yells.

The front door is just feet away when a dark outline emerges from the corner. It cuts off our exit. Daye flashes her light. Navin's sharp features are pronounced under the harsh light. Lya and Daye slide to a stop. Then, Arek pushes them behind him.

"Don't think about it," Arek warns his brother.

Navin lunges toward Arek. Their bodies crash, and it knocks Daye's phone across the room. It's easier to hear them than to see them—their deep grunts and the crash of fists against bone.

Suddenly the lights above us flicker. Arek throws a punch that sends Navin flying. Before he can gather himself to stand, Arek is able to get atop him and continue to smash fist after fist into Navin's cheeks until he's bloody. Arek seems to always be one step ahead, his movements are more precise and less chaotic, but neither brother is going to give up without knowing that the other is dead.

Despite my exhaustion, I try to help but several of Navin's men rush in from the other end of the hall. One of them grabs Daye and two others attack Lya. However, it isn't as easy as these men expect. The sisters work together. Every move they make is like a dance. Their strategy and technique are great enough to leave no need for brute strength or power.

A deep guttural sound turns my attention back to Arek and Navin. The look in Arek's eyes is shock as he looks down. A syringe hangs from his chest and with shaking hands he pulls it out.

"Arek!" I yell. He looks at me and that's when I see the dark line running from his chest up toward his neck.

As I step to Arek, Lya cries out. When I turn, both girls are stumbling with black veins crawling up their bodies.

"Daye!" I call out. "Lya!"

Both of them weaken and reach out for the other, but they eventually fall to their knees. The dark spidery veins reach in every direction, reminding me of my father's skin after Navin injected him.

The sweat rolls down Arek's brow and his large body is losing its power. His eyes squeeze shut in pain as his knees buckle beneath him. He fights, but is unsuccessful.

"*Grati kimen!*" Navin yells at his men, who rush toward me.

"Kilon!" I yell, just as they grab me.

My strength is coming back, but not entirely. They yank me across the beige carpet until it coils beneath me. My heels run across Arek's thighs as we step over him. He reaches out, but his body's agony is too much. There is no more color to his face, his lips. His body is slowly dying.

"Kilon!!!!" I give one last cry.

Just as we reach the door, I see Kilon's massive body erupting from the darkness of the hall and barreling toward the hopeless scene.

I fight, but it's not enough.

They carry me from the Gianda and force me into a waiting vehicle. Navin slips into the car next to me and before I can object, he drugs me with a syringe. I wait for my veins to turn black, but they never do.

"Sleep tight," he whispers.

No. He wants me very much alive. My hands become heavy, followed by my head, and soon the world fades to black.

CHAPTER EIGHTEEN

There are muffled voices.

My throat is scratchy and full, like there is something in it.

Before I even open my eyes, I reach out my hands and they swish within water. My body is freezing while the drugs in my system have made me drowsy and my eyes heavy.

Wait: I am under water.

This alone forces my eyes to open wide and they burn instantly. The surface of the water is nearly five feet above me and bubbles trickle upward from an oxygen tube extending from my mouth. I try to fight my way, but soon realize there are heavy restraints around my wrists and ankles. Luckily, they are only Velcro and I am able to rip them off. I rise, then yank the regulator mouthpiece away as my icy skin touches the cool air.

"We've been waiting," someone says.

It's a chore to pull oxygen through my lungs and I cough repeatedly. Finally, when my spasms calm, I look around. We are in a very large and vintage gymnasium that seems to be abandoned, or at least poorly cared for. However, the equipment in the room is expensive and new. There are computers along the walls, with monitors, and just next to the pool are several medical looking devices that seem to be connected to me by white square electrode patches from my neck to my ankles.

Dr. Karine comes to the edge of the pool deck with a clipboard in his hand. He still wears his thick black-rimmed glasses. "I would suggest you not make any sudden movements."

"What are you doing?" I ask him.

Between my scratchy throat and the sting of my skin, the temperatures have kicked in my body's natural protection, and hypothermia is not far away.

"If your movements get any bigger you will get a shock. So, there is no getting out of the pool . . . at least not until I say."

"Dr. Karine from the Cellar." I do my best at treading water, lightly, trying desperately not to set off the alarm.

He clenches his jaw and looks at me over his wide rims. "How do you know who I am?"

"I make sure I know all of the devil's friends," I say quietly.

"Hey!" The doors burst open and Navin stomps in. It's obvious he heard me. Once he's at the edge of the deck he glares at me while his fists clench in and out. "The devil comes in many forms."

"What am I doing here, Navin?"

Yet he doesn't answer. He walks to Dr. Karine's side and they whisper for quite some time. The water surrounding me is sending bigger and bigger waves as I shake more.

"Hey!" I call out.

"I wouldn't do that," Dr. Karine warns, but it's too late. Something starts to beep. "You're setting it off."

"Why am I in here?"

Finally, they separate, and Navin kneels down on the pool deck directly in front of me. "The cold strips you of your senses. We need the water so painful that you can't think straight. Are you there yet?"

I don't answer, but the truth is yes.

He continues, "Dr. Karine found that water can be a conduit to your unconscious without needing your emotion. The pain crosses your signals."

"I can't stay in here any longer." Everything is starting to feel hot, not cold. The beeping begins again. Only this time, it ends in a jolt. I cry out.

"Ouch," Karine says. "I told you. Gotta be careful."

"I can't." My teeth chatter until it's hard to hear.

Navin stands up and heads over to the doctor, who then hands Navin several papers. "This is everything so far," Dr. Karine mentions.

Navin looks through the papers and nods. He rubs his cheek and looks at me, just as the alarm begins to beep again.

"Please, Navin!" I say, just as another shock plows through my system with painful reckoning. This one sends me underwater. I beg as I finally come up. "Please."

"Are you sure?" Navin asks with a grin.

Again, I am electrocuted, only this time it takes me so long to come back to the surface that Navin is reaching out for me.

"Okay," Navin says. He turns to Karine, "We'll do more tomorrow."

Dr. Karine flips a switch near him. "All right it's off, she can get out."

Stiffly, I take a big stroke but the alarm beeps. This time the shock sears my insides until my eyes bulge. I fight to come above the water, but my body doesn't respond. The surface gets farther and farther away as I sink to the bottom.

My lungs scream in pain, but that last shock was enough to sever my ability to react. Instead, I watch the blue surface and wonder if they'll just let me drown. Finally, Navin dives in. He grabs me under the arms and pulls me up. I sputter and gasp when we reach the open air. "I told you to turn it off!" Navin yells.

"Oops." Dr. Karine lifts an eyebrow as he reaches over and

touches a couple more buttons. "There."

Navin swims me to the side where two of his men are ready to pull me out. They rip me from the water. Navin grabs a warm towel and wraps it around my shoulders.

"I can't move."

"Give it a few minutes," he says as he places small warming packs beneath the towel. Water drips from his hair onto me.

I quickly assess myself since I am nearly hypothermic. But as I do, I can feel that my ability is clouded. *Is Navin in my mind and I just can't feel it?* I search for any tiny Trace of him, but it's not clear. *Is there any rhythm that I don't recognize?*

"Come to your feet," he says with his hand out to help.

I push it away and struggle to stand.

"Remy, I'm not as bad as you believe me to be, I promise."

"The devil's promise? Now doesn't that sound like a disaster. I'm fine."

"You're blue." He grins. "Turn around." He grabs a black eye mask from a nearby table and places it over my eyes, then I feel his hand push my elbow to guide me. After several turns and hallways, I hear the familiar twist of a door lock. Once we're inside, he takes the mask off. This is the room I was in the last time I Traveled to him.

Dr. Karine places several electrodes up my shirt and along my arms. "Don't try to take these off . . . we'll know." He points to the corner of the room where a security camera is in place. Then he turns to Navin, "It's done."

When Dr. Karine leaves, Navin crosses his arms and leans against the wall. I'm still so desperately cold that my mind can't think clearly.

"I've been studying you for years, Remy. Even before you hated me."

"Why?"

He stands tall and walks to me until I hit the wall behind me. "At first? I was intrigued by what you had. Intrigued by your father—the Elite. I just had a feeling about you."

"Feeling?"

"A feeling that you had something I wanted. A feeling that we could be good together. But then, you fell in love with my brother. And I suppose I hated you for that. You also stood so far on the other side of everything I believed in. I'm not sure if that made me love you or hate you more."

"Where does this hate come from?"

"Ephemes killed my mother." His eyes look up at mine and that's when he realizes. "Or maybe you already know that?" He doesn't know what I saw in Arek's unconscious during Tri Planum, so I stay quiet. "Is this from memory? Have you remembered everything?"

"Do you want me to?"

"My mother didn't deserve what she got. Killed by men who claimed she was a witch. Burned at the stake in the name of God. Is that God? She didn't deserve to die like that. Ephemes took it in their own hands and decided they knew . . . but they didn't."

"I understand—"

"But that's just it, I don't think you do. Before you, I was in love with a beautiful woman. But they hunted her and killed her . . . for what? Because Ephemes are desperate to believe they know the answers. It gives them comfort . . . it gives them power, and with those answers they decide who's going to hell. They even feel justified to make that choice. It always amazes me that even though people like you know we were hunted like dogs, you still protect them."

"Your hate has set fire to everything around us."

Navin smiles. "Yeah, well this world needed to burn." He steps so close that I can feel his breath. For some reason I can't step away, and that's when I know . . . he's in my mind. Navin leans in and kisses my lips softly. Just as he's pulling away, I grab his wrist, stick my leg out behind his, and take him to the ground before he knows what is happening. My knee is on his chest when his head hits the ground, and I lean in close, "Don't ever touch me."

He chuckles and places a hand casually behind his head to help his neck with terrifying confidence. I step away slowly, which allows him to climb to his feet and he heads to the door. "Get some rest. We have a lot to do tomorrow. Oh . . . and by the way, we are watching." He points to cameras in the room, then points to my arms. "If you try to take those things off, we will know. I'll see you in the morning."

With a twist of the lock and a slam of the door, he is gone. I rush to the small blanket that lays on the bed and throw it around my shoulders. For hours I try to move and raise my heat. Pushups, squats, running in place, whatever I can do. Eventually the feeling returns to my fingertips, my muscles aren't like molasses, and my teeth stop chattering.

The sheet from the bed hangs onto the floor. With quick hands, I wrap it tightly around the door handle and connect the other end to an empty built-in shelf. Nobody is welcome in here, not tonight.

CHAPTER NINETEEN

I wake up as I'm pulled from the bed and my hip slams against the hard floor. They've somehow managed to cut the sheet; I see it laying in pieces near the door. They cover my eyes with a mask and then push me through the halls. Soon we are back in the big gym with the giant pool and medical equipment. Navin and Dr. Karine are talking in the corner, but Navin comes over when he sees that I've arrived.

"Get in the pool."

"Not on your life."

He points toward the pool. "Get in."

"No," I say coolly.

Navin looks at the men in masks who just brought me to him and nods. Instantly they attack.

I take each one to the ground until they are writhing in pain. There's no longer any need to count the moves that it takes, my body is simply a machine, trained to adapt, switch, and debilitate. More of Navin's people from around the room rush to help, but I take them on. The Void is now with me when I ask it. It is not surprising or unexpected. It is a state that I can exist in if I need to.

So many men and women are piling up, that Navin yells, "Stop!" He picks up a box next to him and presses a button. Instantly my body goes stiff, forcing me to the ground, reminding me of the electrodes that they placed on me last night. Before long, they have me stripped of my clothing and lower me into the icy pool. Navin kneels in front of me.

"Remy, listen, I'm going to win. But you wouldn't be the woman I know and love if you didn't fight me." He stands up, claps his hands together, and yells, "Let's go," to Dr. Karine. Navin pulls his shirt off, leaving only bare skin, and Dr. Karine places several electrodes along his body.

I say through chattering teeth, "You need him to beat me. I see now what Leigh said."

It's obvious this has hit a nerve by the way his cheeks fall. "He did not say that."

"Come on, Navin. You and I both know Leigh."

"Let's go!" Navin says again, but this time more aggressively.

Because of the abrasive cold, I cannot think. It is difficult to find control. My head begins to split with the same headache I used to get when Navin first showed up. I try desperately to help myself by finding any rhythm. *Remy! Just concentrate.*

I can feel him use every bit of my weakness to manipulate my senses.

My eyes roll back into my head, and in only minutes, I am standing in San Francisco just in front of my apartment where this all began. The tap of feet catches my attention and when I turn, Navin and Japha are there, emerging from the shadows, no different than the attacker on that first night. Only they are not human. Japha is no longer an old man with white hair and arthritis—now, his skin is gray, blood drips from his mouth, and his eyes are hollow. He is able to float above the ground and move toward me fast, but my feet are stuck to the ground. I cry out and try to lift my shoes from the cement, one at a time, but they stick like taffy.

Japha reaches for me, but I am suddenly brought out of the Trace and am back in the pool. Navin is kneeling and grinning at me. "Do you understand now? I have the control. So, I can make you see anything that I want you to see. It would all be a lot easier if you just gave me what I want."

I'm shaking violently now from the cold, and my jaw is locked. "What is it that you want?"

"You know what I want. I want you." For the first time, his silence presses against me until the extreme cold suffocates, and all the while his eyes stare straight into mine. A moment passes before either of us speaks and he appears to have become almost . . . human. When he blinks, his eyes return to marble. "If I can't have you, then I will learn everything I need to know about your powers."

"So, you believe I'm the One?"

"I've always believed you were the One."

"If you believe that, then you have to believe that I am here to bring unity and peace to the Ephemes and Velieri."

"Do you know how many times that Prophecy has been translated to fit men's desires—zealots who have decided that they are the only ones to have heard from God? The Manchester Books and the prophecies within them, they were devoured and manipulated for control and power. They don't look anything like their original text. That's the fact. The prophecy says, 'the One will have the ability to destroy when peace cannot be found.'"

My breath is shaking as I pull it heavily into my lungs. I realize suddenly that this is how it will go. No one will ever know the truth; however, most will try to own it.

He continues, "We are tribal, Remy. We survive by destroying the threat before it destroys us."

"You see everyone who doesn't believe the same as you as a threat. You're no different than any other zealot. Why not stand for something rather than against something?"

"I stand for Freedom, Remy."

"No." He looks up with surprise at the stance in my voice. "No, you stand for yourself. Freedom is everyone's right, including Ephemes."

"Maybe so," he shrugs.

"Being fanatical or uncompromising only feeds the same in others, but I suppose you use this idea. You want Ephemes to be less human. You want to hate them. You need to hate them."

"Your lips are turning blue." He grins. "Let's see you fight me off." And with that he turns to Dr. Karine.

My body is weaker than I've felt in months within this icy water. My mind has little power. The shaking in my bones is painful and my muscles clamp around me. Even the smell of this place reminds me of a mortuary.

The stronger the pain in my head becomes, the further I fall prey to Navin. In a blink, I open my eyes and in a series of moments that feel like dreams, I revisit memories. Before long, I realize that they are all memories I once had with Arek. The first time we met, the time he saved me from those men outside Bartholomew Hedlow's home, our wedding, and so many others. My heart races, realizing that Navin's searching, searching for my weakness. At first, he is controlling which ones we see, however deep inside of me, I know that there is one story in my life he is unwelcome to read. He cannot know about Lya and Daye.

With the severe cold, my body is nearly hypothermic, and my mind feels lost. Yet no one else is here to stop him. The memories speed past me just as they've always done with Navin, and suddenly I see the cottage in Spain. My heart races.

What can I do? He can't find out.

A realization comes to me. There are no memories and there is nothing to see deep in my unconscious, if I am not alive. The cottage in Spain draws closer. Arek is slamming his ax into the firewood. There is no time for a decision. Lya and Daye are coming closer, I can feel it.

I blow all of the air from my lungs and submerge myself in the icy pool. I see an outline of Navin coming to the edge of the pool and looking over—it's blurry and moves with the small waves. I hold my breath as the memory of me walking within the flowers in Spain draws closer. Bubbles escape my lips.

Pain starts after just seconds when my lungs are desperate to draw breath. A stabbing ache pierces my chest. My brain is telling me to rise, my body is telling me to end my suffering, but my heart won't let it. I shake my head and scream under water. Convulsions start. More seconds pass and the light above starts to dim. I claw at the cement below me. My body is shutting down.

Don't come up!

My body's decline is blurring my memory.

Stay down!

The darkness starts closing in and my peripheral goes first. Then, strangely, there is peace. The movement of the water above me is like a dance, rather mesmerizing. I can see that Navin is yelling at me from above, but I don't care. Whatever protects my daughters is worth it.

The stiffness is the last of the worst and then it is no different than falling asleep. As darkness comes for me, somewhere outside of myself, as death looms nearby, Navin jumps in the water and grabs me in his arms. He swims to the surface and pulls me above the water, but in a strange way, it's as though my spirit is watching him from the deck.

"Come! Help me!" Navin yells.

Dr. Karine and several others rush to the edge and help pull my limp body from the blue and wet torture device. Navin rushes to do compressions on my lifeless body. I watch from just feet away, and I lift my hand in front of my face. My skin is an olive shade and warm, compared to the blue and freezing woman on the pool deck. Something catches my eye in the corner of the room, so I look up.

There are more people than I expect within this old, junky gymnasium. Each of them looks at me as they pass by, some close and some far, yet most of them smile and within seconds disappear as though they've just walked through an invisible door. Each time they take their last step in a realm that I can see, a bright gold spark fills the air that lasts as long as the green flash at the end of a sunset.

After a minute or two, I am yanked back into the body that now sputters and pukes cold water until it spills out of my mouth and nose. Then I cough until my lungs want to separate from my chest cavity.

Navin sits back on the pool deck and clenches his jaw, but he says nothing. I look at him carefully, then with a scratchy voice I breathe out, "Put me back in and I'll just do it again."

⋁⋀⋁

I'm lying in a four-poster bed with white material draped over the top, and there's a blue light cascading along the walls. The room is decorated with ancient paintings and ornate tapestries. Someone is next to me and I jump in fear as he moves. His shoulders are high, one on top of the other, and his breathing is heavy and coarse. I sit up carefully, trying not to make too much noise, and peer over his shoulder. My heart beats heavily as I follow his profile. It's Navin, sleeping soundly.

Cautiously I slide out of the bed, desperate to keep my feet light as they ascend to the hardwood floor. But just as I step down, a chain clanks to the ground and I discover that it's attached to my ankle. Instantly, Navin grabs a gun from under his pillow and turns to point it directly at me. The barrel is only inches from my nose.

"You're not going anywhere," he says with a raspy voice. "Now lie back down."

I look at him carefully, perhaps to figure out the next move. The chain is long enough that I can step away from the bed until it pulls. Quietly and staring him directly in the eyes, I sit down on the ground, then lean my back up against the wall.

He shrugs. "All right, suit yourself."

To prove a point, he lies back down and closes his eyes. For hours, until the sun comes up, I sit in the darkness until my back is screaming in pain. My throat and chest are still raw from being near death. I nod off for what seems like only moments, until I feel a gentle hand on my shoulder and my body jumps. Why was he touching me so kindly to wake me up?

"Wake up, sunshine." He's squatting low beside me, his hair messy, and if I didn't know better, he'd gotten just a bit of sun. Measures of Arek peek out from his eyes and my stomach twists with anger. The two men couldn't be more different. "We have some things to do today. I'm impressed by, but also curious about, your determination to keep me out now." He points to his head.

"I wouldn't be impressed, I'd be afraid." My eyes slowly bore into his, and even though I never expected it to faze him, I'm disappointed when it doesn't.

He chuckles. "Afraid of what, Remy? I can play your game . . . the question always is, can you play mine?" Within the following minutes, he changes, preps his hair in the mirror, then waits for me to stand.

"What about the chains?" I ask before I stand.

"Oh, that's right. I figure you changed the game and you're now not leaving my side." He comes close to me and as he kneels, he glides his hand down my leg. The cuff around my ankle releases by his fingerprint. "What are you working so hard to keep me from knowing?" When he reaches out to help me to my feet, I refuse to take his hand and push myself up against the wall. My body cracks and aches.

Without any restraints, he leads me to a hall with large mirrors lining one wall and six-foot-tall, ancient paintings of people I don't recognize on another. If I can read the décor, we are somewhere in

Europe. This is nothing like the gymnasium or the school halls that we were in, yet I'm pretty sure they are attached somehow. Just as we pass a window, I see that we are in a very rural area. Some rolling hills, some forests surrounding those rolling hills. No one for miles.

"You're hiding out," I say.

"Wouldn't you, if you were me?"

I don't answer.

He turns and walks so close to me that I am forced against the rock walls. His large hand rests heavily above my shoulder and he leans in so close that I can see the stubble line on his cheek.

I quickly find something to say. "Why would you need to hide, if you are running everything?"

"Not everything. Not yet. But we're almost there."

I chuckle, not because I don't believe him, but because I want him to believe that I don't. "Where are you taking me?"

"You'll see."

We walk through a few more halls, pass a kitchen and an office, but stop before two elegant double doors. There is something perplexing about the look on his face, just before he opens one.

Within this room is a large meeting place with an oval table nearly ten feet long. The chairs are high backed and there's a stodgy aura here. Men and women surround this table, but look up when the door opens and spreads new light across the papers in front of them. Dr. Karine sits at one end, which isn't surprising. However, the blow comes from who sits at the other end.

"Covey?" I say angrily, wondering how many people helped him escape from the Cellar.

Prophet Covey smiles, but says nothing. Three people down, red hair in braids tells me who it is before I can see her face. Prophet Hawking looks up from her conversation with someone I don't recognize and her scowl returns. I recognize several representatives of the Powers, news reporters, the vice president of the United States, and diplomats from the rest of the world.

A churning in my gut begins as my heart drops. It's worse than I could have ever understood.

"I told you I could get her," Navin says confidently.

The last man at the table is turned away, messing with a few folders behind him. When he turns to face me, I recognize him immediately. Isaiah Aldo. The man who is vying for the seat as a Prophet. Yet being this close, there's something more that his presence does to me. It isn't very different from Japha. The same skin crawl, shudder down my spine, anger mixed with fear that I've always felt. While I don't remember what he did, my body does.

I step back, nearly falling into Navin, which makes him laugh. "I told you I have nearly everything."

"Looks like a whole lot of nothing to me," I whisper.

Everyone shuffles in their seats. Isaiah Aldo stands and comes close to me. "Good to see you again."

I'm grateful when the door on the other side of the room opens to take my attention, until I am caught off guard by who is standing there. Tears are dangerously close to revealing my disappointment. Leigh, who hasn't noticed me, comes in and hands papers to Covey.

"Leigh." The name weighs down my tongue. I always wondered, but a small bit of hope had been there, only to die now.

He looks up in panic and growls. "Why did you bring her in here?"

"She needs to know there is no chance. The wheels are set in motion, Remy. Look at this," Navin reaches out and turns a computer to me. A zoom call is happening, and the number on the side of the screen tells me that there are thousands of people on it. "These aren't just civilians. These are leaders . . . around the world. Leaders that want to be free."

"What about Zelner?" I ask of the only Prophet not yet accounted for.

"It doesn't matter. We don't need him."

"What about the money you've made from the Ephemes all this

time. They've made you rich. What happens without them?"

Navin and the others smile. "They've made us rich? No . . . we just waited till we knew where their money was. There is no reason for the Reds anymore. No reason for the Ephemes in any way."

When, finally, a tear falls, Navin stands in front of me and wipes it away, but I yank my head back. "Hey," he says, with suddenly serious eyes. "I will never lose a mother to them again. I will never lose the love of my life to men who want to call the Velieri women witches."

For the first time through this all, I have never felt so hopeless. The world is on fire. The world is done as it is. On the monitors behind everyone, the news channels show the fighting on every corner.

"You used everyone's hate against the world."

"That's right. Hate, Remy. I am killing hate by taking the Ephemes out."

I slowly look at him with horror pulsing the blood through my veins harder and faster than even the night of the attack. "You think that's going to finish hate? Are you kidding me, Navin? The moment the Ephemes are gone it will simply turn to someone else. That is everything you are proving through all of this. Hate doesn't die. Unless everyone can figure out what real love is, hate will always exist."

"Get her out of here. We've got work to do," Covey says as his chin creases.

CHAPTER TWENTY

The night comes slowly while Navin forces me to stay in his room alone. Yet as I sit there, with nothing but silence, my thoughts are never ending. No matter how far gone it feels, I cannot lose hope. The look on Leigh's face told me everything. There was never any chance with him. I now know why Leigh hated me. I stood against the son he secretly backed. Arek's face pops back into my mind and I squeeze my eyes shut, trying to force myself to Travel to him. *Or something! Do something Remy. What can I do?*

I think through my options. Do I know how to reach Tri Planum? We rode through Arek's subconscious and unconscious in the last Tri Planum battle against Alfonzo's men. However, Navin clearly doesn't trust himself or his abilities to fight me alone. He needs Dr. Karine's tactics and machines. A flash of moments pass through my mind: Navin pointed the gun at Ian, just before he killed him. Navin always needed to use my emotion to Trace. He used my fear over a man I used to love. I look up with wonder.

Nearly an hour later, when the darkness has completely surrounded me, the high-tech lock clicks and Navin enters. He lets in just a bit of light, then as he closes the door, he turns on a dim lamp beside him. For the last hour, I have known what I wanted to do. He looks at me for a moment without saying a word.

"We have no chance," I say to him.

"No, you don't."

"You understand that I loved my Ephemeral mother, Ava. More than anything. It was torture to watch her body fall apart. Now I realize why she was so important to me. Lyneva hated me. She's the only mother I knew."

"I know."

"But I watched how they killed Holona. Those men who believed that they were doing God's work."

"Yeah," he says with a glimmer of sincerity.

"I'm sorry," I say carefully. "You had a loving mother and she adored you." His lips part just slightly for a moment as I stand up from where I sit and walk to him slowly. "I know what it's like to lose that."

"You used to love me too," he whispers.

I stand in front of him, "Maybe I did." I grin, then look down at the floor. "I didn't know about your wife."

"Yeah," he says, clearly skeptical of this interaction.

"Can you tell me about her?"

"What are you doing?" he asks.

"Navin, I'm here with nowhere to go. You've locked me up for hours. Maybe tell me why. Give me some reason to fall on your side. What happened to her?"

He is hesitant and his hands draw up to rub his own chest. Finally, he breathes out. "She and my son were walking outside one day. She was pregnant with our second child. Several Ephemes who had something against me decided that they were going to teach me a lesson. So, they raped and murdered her. I came home to find my entire family taken from me."

I stand so close to him that I can feel the heat radiating from his skin. It isn't a lie when the words fall out of my mouth, "I'm sorry."

"They are nothing; they are but a waste of my thoughts."

Ever so slightly, the moment his guard goes down, I manage to peek into his mind. If I'm not careful he'll know. "I see why now." I'm able to break his familiar rhythm and interject mine in his.

Carefully, I dig, deep within his unconscious. It's easy to Trace, but it is one thing to search his subconscious or his unconscious. *What do you have hiding in there, Navin?*

"Do you still see my mother?" Navin asks.

"I do. She asks about you." I choose not to tell him of the sadness that fills her eyes when she speaks of what he's done.

"She does?" His voice turns hopeful.

I feel the first split happen, and instead of living purely in my conscious world where I'm listening to Navin's sad story, I fall into his memories. Again, we are back at the house in the countryside, his mother's cries fill the air, as the Ephemeral men celebrate. I can't find Navin, but when I turn, there is a dark hallway where I can leave the backyard and enter somewhere completely unfamiliar. A young boy is ahead of me and he's panting as he hurries through these halls, afraid of something behind him. I follow him quietly. At the other end of the hallway, we exit into a forest. Yet just as the subconscious can be, the trees have hands and fingers, the shadows move like ghosts in the air unattached to any certain object. The little boy screams and runs away as a bush rips his shirt. Suddenly I see Leigh to my left, but he looks larger and angrier. His face contorts in inhuman ways. "Navin!" Leigh yells, yet his voice sounds like demons.

The boy runs faster so I must hurry. *How do I get to the third level? Why are we here? What is this place for him?*

Meanwhile, in our conscious level in his room, I ask him more of Holona and his wife. There are moments when I'm worried that he's aware of what I'm doing, only to then share a bit more of the women he loved. If I didn't know of his darkest deeds, I would have more compassion for his sad story.

In the second level, I follow the boy away from Leigh and watch him cry as he races through the terrifying trees.

There's got to be a way. There has to be more. Where is it?

I begin to feel that there's a possibility to split. There's a way to get to Navin's unconscious.

Suddenly, Navin, in our conscious, grabs me by the shoulders and shakes me. "What are you doing?" he yells angrily in my face. "You think I wouldn't feel you in there?" His face turns beet red with anger and he grabs my arm. With strong hands, his fingers hurt my skin. He yanks me up and I hit the opposite wall. "You wanna play?"

He drags me through the hall until he reaches a door and yanks it open. Inside this large room, everything appears to be medical in nature. Biochemists in white coats sit at kiosks with gloves on their hands beside walls of pills. This is how he created the injection that nearly killed Briston, and it brings back my concern for Arek and the girls.

It's impossible to know whether they're okay. What I do know is that after Briston nearly died from this, the best labs in the world created its antidote and we kept some within arm's length. I have to believe it worked and they are okay.

Navin throws me inside until I fall to my knees, instantly gathering everyone's attention.

"Dr. Karine!" Navin yells.

Dr. Karine peeks his head out from behind a wall with furrowed brows. "What are you doing? What happened?"

"Do it now." Navin yanks me to my feet, but I rip my arm away with anger. This only makes him seethe more. So, he pushes me through the white coats and into an attached room. This is a strange room. There is a very high-tech chair bolted to the ground. It is unlike anything I've ever seen. Rainbow shaped plastic sits at the wrists, ankles, and neck. Several screens rise from the seat and can be swiveled about the chair, most likely to let someone sit down.

"Go!" Navin growls. He pushes me toward it.

"I'm not getting in there."

"Now."

"No." I turn and stand with strong feet. When he reaches toward me, I grab his wrist and twist until he cries out in pain. He sends his fist across my right cheek, which makes the room blur. In that time, several of his white coats grab me by the arms and I fight as they struggle to get my feet and hands inside the plastic straps. When they finally have it, the straps cinch tightly on their own, including the one at my neck. Isaiah Aldo, Leigh, and Prophet Covey rush into the room as though they've been told what is happening.

"We have no way to know if it will work," Dr. Karine answers.

"I don't care. Do it." Navin makes a hard stance even when Prophet Covey questions him.

"Are we sure about this?"

Dr. Karine swings the screens attached to the seat, all around me. There is one in front, beside, and behind. He's mumbling to himself with worry, which only heightens mine. Then, he places earpieces in each ear that cancel out every noise, but my own breathing. The last and final thing are several electrodes just like every other time.

"What are you doing?" I ask in panic.

Navin's lips move, but I can't make out what he's saying.

"Navin?" I call out. "What are you doing?"

He walks over, pulls the earpiece from my ear, and says, "Stealing every bit from you that I can." Then he returns it.

Dr. Karine stands in front of the monitor and a sound starts, small. This doesn't last long and it gets louder than my ears can handle. I cry out, but can't move my head because my neck is trapped by the piece of plastic. The monitors in front, in back, and beside me turn on. Bright pulses begin. But it's the electrodes and whatever Dr. Karine is working on that I can tell have the greatest hold. I can feel the heat through my body until it seems to be burning me from inside out. Something feels as though it is scraping my brain. Small piercing pain like someone is taking a knife to my insides. Soon my mind starts jumbling. My eyes bulge and pulse.

For several minutes, Navin yells at Dr. Karine even though I can't hear it. At first, I have an instant loss of everything. I don't even remember how they brought me to this room.

I close my eyes when the pain is excruciating and there is no thought or memory left in me. "Stop!" I cry out.

Some men stare from the bigger room that's attached to this one. *Who are they? Why am I in so much pain? Where am I?*

With my eyes squeezed shut, I hear a voice. *Remy, open your eyes.*

When I do, the air seems clearer. Pain continues to be aggressive and unrelenting, however something is shifting. If anything, the pain now sparks the Void. Dr. Karine sees that something has changed, and he raises the level. I cry out for a moment, but only for a moment. Again, the pain is quieted by the brilliance of my senses. Even the sound, the deep drum in my ears, has lessened. Yet what I feel is anger. *No.*

Rage.

It wells up inside of me as Dr. Karine charges harder and the pain digs deeper until I focus my sight. I glare directly at Dr. Karine, Navin, and the others, and somehow, I direct my rage toward them. The room fills with energy so large that the lights shine brighter. They are blinding. The men cover their eyes.

Then, it's like a sonic boom. The room warps and bends in a big bang. Light bulbs shatter, chairs fly back against the wall. Men are knocked back until they hit their heads on the ground. The roof caves in and one last surge of energy peels the paint from the walls.

I look down. The strap on my neck is broken and my hands and ankles are free. The machines are broken and smoky, and the room is nearly dark now from the exploding lights. Navin sits up and rubs his head. This is my chance—I jump to my feet and race to the hall.

Navin yells angrily, but I pay no attention. I made sure to remember the door as he yanked me down the hall. To my right is a door and just beyond this one is another. That is my way out. For the first time in several days, I am outside. That's when I see the large backhouse where the pool was. It wasn't a school; it was an old pool house attached to this Italian Palazzo.

I race through some trees and down several rolling hills, but run into a newer chain-link fence. Only Navin would ruin this beautiful home and land with this. It's fifty feet of chain-link fence with secure electricity at the top.

"No!" I say as I run for several seconds. The gate is locked with multiple impossible locks and when I peer up, I see video cameras. I place my hands on my head as my chest rises and falls. Before long the sirens start and I know I'm trapped. "What do I do?" I cry to myself.

I keep running until suddenly out of nowhere, Leigh is ahead of me with his gun out. "Let me go, Leigh!" I yell.

He puts a hand out to me and I'm confused by the look on his face. "They can't listen from those . . ." He cocks his head at the cameras. "But they are watching so I need you to listen."

"Why should I listen to you?" I cry out with frustration as my eyes continue to roam the fence for a solution.

"Listen to me. We don't have long—they're coming," Leigh says.

"How do I trust you?!"

"Holona once loved me," he says, keeping his gun toward me. "That's how you know. If a woman like that could have loved me, then you must know I used to be a good man. I can help you."

"I don't believe you."

"You have no choice."

I yell with frustration at my predicament.

Leigh speaks, "Do you know why my wife was burned at the stake? Because she told the wrong person that she believed in you— just a baby at the time. The belief in this Prophecy took her from me. That's why she comes to you. But then you died, and it just proved what I thought. You were not the One and she died for nothing."

"Please, Leigh—"

"But, maybe not. After what I just saw . . . I don't know now."
He still seems conflicted. One second he wants to shoot, the next it
is as if Holona has some power here.

Yells and calls from Navin's men are getting closer and I see black
masked guards running through the trees.

"I'm going to come to you, but you will overtake me, use the
gun, and leave through the gate. Beyond this forest, get to the town
and keep going. I can't wait long before I will have to send out who
we have for you." Leigh steps closer.

I feel the tears fall down my face. "Why? Why are you doing this?"

"I love my sons. All of them. Do it now or we will not have
the time."

He gets so close that it takes me a moment to know what to do.
With fast hands I reach out and grab the gun, then take the old man
down just as men exit the woods and give chase.

"Come back," Leigh yells. "Get her!" He pulls another gun from
his pants and I feel the bullets whiz by my head.

I shoot the gate lock and kick it open, careful to not get shocked.
Then I take off like a rocket down the hill and through another stand
of trees.

CHAPTER TWENTY-ONE

I stay far away from the nearest roads, choosing to hide in a dense forest. It's hard to know when I should follow any noises that may lead me to the nearest town. There is one thing to do, find a way to Arek . . . and now Lya and Daye. Yet, here, as the light fades and the temperature drops, getting rescued seems further and further from a possibility. As I pass by a creek, a strange feeling hits me that forces me to stop moving and just concentrate. Someone is near, I can feel their energy.

I slip behind a tree when I hear the heavy breathing of several people. Small whispers fill the air and as I hunker down, I peek around the base of the tree. Several people, moving slowly and deliberately, appear. It is too dark to study them, but I notice that they have bows and arrows, guns, and each one carries a backpack. Their clothes are dirty, but not as though they are homeless, rather more so that they've just been through battle.

"Maybe we should just stop soon for the night?" one of them says—her voice young with an obvious Italian accent.

"No way, we're almost there, Elliot," one of the boys says—he, too, can't be older than his late teens, and he is also Italian.

"I just don't want to get into trouble. What if we get stuck out here or they find us before we reach the Patch?" The fear within her is obvious.

"Elliot, stop!" Suddenly the boy explodes and turns to her as I watch silently from behind the tree. "I'm tired of your crying. That's not going to help any of us."

"Hey, back off," another one of them says, a man who seems just a bit older.

Suddenly a branch under my foot snaps. They instantly pull their weapons as I press myself harder against the bark.

"Who's there?" one of them says and begins walking in my direction.

He's not stopping, and I have only seconds before he turns the corner of the tree to find me. If I say nothing, it will be worse, and deep down, I can feel that they are not Velieri. This doesn't make it safe being outnumbered like I am, but it certainly suggests to me that Tracing will be easier than usual. Just before I step out into the open, I latch on to as many rhythms as possible.

"Who's there?" he says again.

Finally, after I let out a long breath, I step out into the open with my hands up in surrender.

Each of them, four boys and one girl, clearly on defense after whatever they have been through, panics and raises their weapons with intention. "Stop there!" one of them yells. "Who are you?"

"It's okay! Wait, wait, wait!" I hurriedly say. "My name is Remona and I'm alone."

None of them back off, rather they look at each other while still keeping a heavy draw on me. The main guy, who appears to be in his late teens, looks me over with a concerned glare. "What are you doing out here, Remona?"

"I should ask you the same thing." My hands remain non-threatening and I try to keep my eyes light, but the night has nearly enveloped us with darkness.

"We're keeping ourselves safe, that is what we are doing. And new people are not safe." His gun is pointed at me and while I desperately don't want to feel the pain of a gunshot wound again, it helps to know that I wouldn't die from it and he might not know how to kill me.

"That's what I'm doing. I ran away from someone who took me."

"Someone who took you? Why did they take you? What side are you on? Theirs? Are you one of them?"

I swallow hard hoping that they won't see this nervous tick. "One of who?"

He steps closer with irritation. "Don't pretend. I've learned how to kill them, you know . . . the Velieri." He says the name as though he's rarely said it.

"I'm not. I'm not one of them." Immediately I feel that this lie is a mistake.

One of the others behind the main guy shakes his head, "How do we know, man, if she's telling us the truth?"

"Look," I say, and I turn all the way around. I've hidden Leigh's gun in the grass behind the tree. "I have no weapons and I have no idea where I am. But above all of that, I am just looking for a safe place until I can find my husband and daughters."

They are quiet and look at one another.

"I take it it's pretty bad out there?" I keep my voice calm and kind.

Without another second, the young girl, Elliot, begins to cry— her shoulders bouncing with each breath.

The main guy keeps his cool and maintains the height of his weapon. "You could say that."

"What happened to you?" I ask while watching Elliot try to compose herself.

"Our neighbors killed our parents," she says between sobs.

Instantly, my breath catches. "I am so sorry. Look, I promise you that I won't hurt you, in fact, I *can* keep you safe."

The main guy shakes his head. "So, you are one of them? You lied already." He comes at me raging and I back up. Elliot hurries to his side, "Ivan, stop!"

"She lied, Elliot! That's the least of what she'll do," he yells.

"You had your weapons pointed at me! I was scared of what you would do. But I promise that I will not hurt you and I can keep you safe."

Ivan shakes his head and clenches his jaw. Despite his youth, he is taller and looks to take care of his body. He comes so close that I hit a tree behind me and am forced to stay in the direction of his rage. "Our neighbors, who we'd known for ten years, turned on us like that." He snaps his fingers in front of my face. "They killed my parents yelling that the Velieri wanted to be free. My parents didn't know anything about your kind. They didn't deserve to die. You think I'm going to just accept that answer?" His finger clings heavily to the trigger.

"Ivan, let me help you trust me."

"How?"

Carefully I sink into his rhythm, Tracing just deep enough to calm him. He may not even know what I'm doing, as suddenly his face calms and his hand lowers. Just as Arek had done before, I take in a breath hoping to gather every bit of energy I can, and I reach out my hand to him.

"What?" The irritation climbs his vocal cords.

"Just for a second. Please."

There's a long pause where I'm pretty sure he will turn me down, but I dig a little deeper within his psyche just to bring calm to the situation. Finally, he rolls his eyes then takes my hand. Instantly, my body tenses and I feel what Arek must have felt when he passed his energy to John from the gas station. It's not a bad feeling, rather all of the good that I have pulled from inside of me passes from me to him, then returns to me. Just as our blood releases into our body only to return to find oxygen, this feeling leaves me, passes through him, then back again.

After a moment, he looks up at me with different eyes. "How'd you do that?" he asks.

"That doesn't matter and it'll take too long to tell you, but you can trust me. I'm not here to kill anyone and I'm so sorry you lost your parents. If you can get me to a safe place for the night where I can find a phone, I promise to take care of you tonight."

Ivan looks at his siblings. Each of them, one by one, nods their heads.

An hour later, we are in a black forest, being led by just the moon. Elliot has calmed down and she comes to my side. "We're heading to a place called the Patch."

"The Patch?"

"Yeah. It's where all our friends met up. Used to be a club but now it's just a place for us to hide," Elliot explains. She hesitates, then continues. "If you are Velieri, what are we? Human?"

I grin, "No, we're all human, Elliot. That's the thing. In a strange way we're all the same, yet people want to convince themselves that we're not. And any difference is a direct threat to who they are. You are called an Epheme . . . which comes from Ephemeral, unable to live the lifespan Velieri have been given."

"Whoa," she says as she takes it in. Her long dark hair is nearly falling out of an old ponytail, but she doesn't care. Her face has been scratched in several places and there's dirt on her neck and cheeks. "Okay, so you have powers we don't?"

I think for second, then shake my head with a realization. "I don't think so, Elliot. I think we just have the time to experience them."

She nods but just as she does, I get a deep feeling in my chest and I stop walking to look around.

"What is it?" Elliot asks.

"We're close to something."

Ivan speaks up from behind me, "How can you tell? I can't hear anything."

"It's not sound. It's here." I touch my chest lightly with my hand as I lift the other in the air to tell them to be quiet.

One of the brothers, who had gone ahead of us just moments before, calls out quietly, "It's over this hill."

We hurry through some trees and then up a steep hill where we then carefully look over the edge. On the other side, there is an old town. Ancient buildings built close together with the surrounding rural area made of thick foliage, extend for several blocks. I can see smoke, but I'm not sure whether this comes from the homes, or if there has been chaos here as well.

"What have they told you about here?" I ask them carefully. "Has this town seen trouble?" They all nod and my heart sinks. By their reaction, I realize Navin's plan has gone further than I even understand. "So how do you know that you'll be safe here?"

Ivan shakes his head. "We don't. But our parents, before they died, made sure we had a place to go and they said if we can get in quietly, it will be okay."

"Okay. Where do you go?"

Ivan pulls out a scrap of paper from his pocket, then uses a light from his watch. "Here is the entrance to the town, and this is where they wait for us." He points at the northwest corner.

"Who is waiting for you?" I say, worried. It would not be a good idea to surround myself with Ephemes at the moment.

"Those who have fought them off." Ivan looks at me with pride and even though I smile back, inside there is nothing but fear for these siblings. They don't know what or who they are dealing with.

"Come on," Ivan says to the others, but I stop him with a hand on his arm.

"Wait. Go that way." I point to the back of the town. "It may take you longer, but it's okay . . . this is the right way."

"What about you?" he asks.

"I don't think there's a place for me with a group of Ephemes. It's too dangerous."

"No," Elliot says quickly. "No, we'll make it okay. You can come."

"No, Elliot. I really don't think it will be. But honestly, if you can do one thing, help me find a phone?"

Ivan nods. "I'll bring one to you."

"Thank you."

Together the siblings head down the steep hill, struggling to keep from sliding down. All I can do is wait, so I roll over and take a moment to rest, staring at the sky full of stars. Two falling stars pass within a few minutes, mesmerizing me and keeping my mind off Navin. It's quite possible this forest is crawling with his men searching for me. Yet, you would think, I would have a feeling.

Nearly an hour passes, and I begin to wonder whether I should wait any longer. There is too much opportunity for Navin to draw closer, the longer that I wait. Just as I sit up in order to continue the journey, someone runs up the steep hill toward me. I can only see the outline of a small figure. Then as they get closer, I hear the breathing and realize it is Elliot. Jumping to my feet, I meet her halfway down.

"You okay?" I ask as we come together. But as I walk closer, trauma on her face is revealed. She has a phone in her hand that I take, but my attention is on her. "Elliot? What's happened?"

"It wasn't what we thought!" she cries. "They're killing them! They're killing them!"

"Where?" I ask. "Can you take me?"

"Come!" she cries and rushes down the hill. Suddenly she falls and I grab her arm to help her up. Once we get down the hill, we race toward the northwest entrance. "Come!" she yells again.

But as we reach the gate that leads within, I slide on my heels to a stop. I can hear the fighting inside. Yells, cracks, pops, grunts, and growls come from somewhere just inside.

"Elliot, listen to me. Go back up that hill and wait."

"No!"

"Elliot, please. And here . . ." I quickly type in Arek's phone number and hand it to her. "Call my husband and tell him where we are. His name is Arek. Can you do that?"

After a few moments of sobbing, she realizes that she will be of no help to me and, in fact, might make things more dangerous. With that, she turns away and runs back. After breathing out my fear, I carefully enter the back entrance and hunker down in the shadows. Just ahead under the dim streetlights, I see Ivan hiding behind the rear tire of a parked car.

"Ivan!" I whisper. He looks at me with fear in his eyes. "Where are they?" I ask.

He points over his head and behind him at the group of houses squished together on a small plot of land. Then a long line of men moves down the street ahead of us. Before I can warn Ivan, they come upon him and instantly attack. Like a bat out of hell, I race to help Ivan. In the time it takes for me to get there, I dig deep, hoping to find that these Velieri are untrained. It feels like most of them are . . . but one.

"Hey!" I yell.

They see me running directly toward them and several of them laugh. I am a woman. They are men. It is obvious that these are their thoughts. When the first one takes a swing at me, I miss his fist by sliding on my knees beneath him. It takes me all but seconds to wound him enough that he is on the ground. Six of the seven men run toward me, while the seventh holds back, and instantly I know—he is the trained one. The first man, I take out his knees; the second, I use to hide from the third only to take them both out at the same time when they aren't ready. In just a few minutes, I have brought each one of them to the ground in pain. The seventh man looks at me with heavy eyes. Blood is already striped down his cheeks.

We stand off, just staring at each other wondering when the other will attack. I can't wait too long, or the other men will begin to recoup. He suddenly sprints at me and as he does, I take that moment to delve deep within his mind. It is obvious he has trained to protect himself and this stops me for a moment, but only for a moment. I realize within those seconds how strong I have become and how deep I can go, despite their strength.

Even though it takes him only seconds to reach me, as I Trace within his mind, it feels much longer. This man's fears lay so shallow within him, you would think this would be the first they would rid him of in his training. Instead, I grab them and manipulate what I can. He doesn't notice at first as we fight. Three moves and he falls, only to jump back up. It is then that he stops and looks around. His eyes grow wide, and he strangely slaps his face. I'm in his mind and he's confused at what he sees.

"Let me," I tell him. With a flick of my wrist, I swipe the air as though moving books on a bookshelf.

In his mind, I have sent wood through the air and it stacks up around him until he cannot move. It looks just like a coffin, only standing upright. He panics as he pounds it with his fists and claws at the enclosed space. Strangely though, in our true conscious, there is no wood. He is fighting the air. Had this been Alfonzo's men, or any of the Protectors, those trained beyond just the common Tracing, it would have been much harder. But this man cannot see that he is free and capable to move in any way that he wants. All the other men, who are still writhing in pain, look at him strangely.

"Let me help you," I tell him. With just a slight change of his mind, the coffin pulls away one plank at a time, but I then surround him with the moist and cold stone of a cave. I circle my finger in the air and the cave wraps tighter about him until his chest is pressed by the rock. In reality, he is free.

"Ivan!" I yell, as I let the man suffer in his claustrophobia. "Where are your brothers?"

He points to the house behind us, and I run over to them. I know that the farther away I am from this lightly trained man, he will be able to see reality, but I have no choice. The homes are full of smoke. Bullet holes line the walls. A few people lie on the ground, lifeless. After I check their pulses and realize they are gone, I move on. I pick up a gun near one of them and check that it's loaded, then continue with the gun raised. Soon, I hear fighting in a different room toward the back, and I rush in. Several men are fighting and Ivan's brothers are doing their best against the attackers. Their faces are swollen and bruised, and blood is dripping down their Ephemeral faces. If this had been any of the trained Velieri, they would already be dead, but instead, they are able to fight back despite their bodies breaking down faster.

"Hey!" I yell. This catches everyone's attention. Instantly I let shots ring out, hitting each of them in their chests. "Come on!" I yell to the wounded brothers. Just as they pass, one of the men hurls himself at me, taking me to the ground with his heavy body. In seconds I swing my legs around and catch his waist with my thighs, locking my feet so that he can't get far. His blood is seeping onto my clothing from where I shot him. He rears back to release a punch, but I keep him off balance by pulling him toward me. As he falls, I yank his shirt high on his back and wrap it around his neck. I push away with my legs and squeeze tightly with my fists until he falls asleep, and I roll his heavy body onto the floor beside me. Already the other men are starting to get their bearings and climb to their hands and knees, so I quickly escape. Before long we are back on the street and running through the throng of people, under the dim streetlamps.

"Come on!" I yell and call Ivan and his brothers to follow me out of the gate we came through. Unfortunately, they don't follow—rather they look at one another, even with the yelling that we hear from down the street. "Come on! We don't have a lot of time!"

"No!" Ivan says urgently. "We have to save them."

"Who?" I ask as I keep my eye on a group running down the road about a quarter mile from us.

"Come with us!" he says.

"We have to get you out of here," I beg.

"No." His resolve is clear. "I cannot leave them."

There is only a split-second decision to make, so I swiftly run toward them and pull their arms toward the nearest building. "Keep in the shadows!" I warn them.

Once we stand, hidden by a nearby building, we stop for only a second. "Where is our sister?"

"She's hiding on the hill. She's safe." With command, I take control, knowing what they are up against. "Take me now."

"Over here." Ivan and the brothers run from one overhang to the next, taking advantage of the dark. Before long, Ivan checks this way and that, then he opens a rectangular ground floor window and snakes his way inside. Each of us follows and I barely disappear, just as several men pass.

We now stand in a basement with storage beside every wall. Ivan rushes away so we follow. In the very back, through several hallways, we come upon large moving crates stacked on top of each other. Ivan and his brothers quickly pull the crates aside, revealing a door. He opens it with a key, we rush in, and he quickly locks it behind us. It isn't until I turn around that my eyes grow wide and a strangled breath escapes my mouth.

It is a large room with no ventilation, and looking back at me are upwards of fifty people. Scared eyes stare back at me. Men, women, and children, holding tightly to one another. Most are bloodied and dirty.

"You see," Ivan says.

"Yes," I whisper.

One of the men jumps up. "What are you doing, bringing her here?"

Ivan places his hands on the man's shoulders. "No, no listen, she helped us. She's okay."

Suddenly the stomp of feet overhead fills the room. Every eye stares at the ceiling. "Shhh," Ivan says quietly.

I move to Ivan and his brothers and turn away from the people in the room. "What do you expect to do, Ivan? These people are here because the world has gone crazy, how do we save them from that?"

Ivan shakes his head. "I don't know, but we will. If you are one of them, you can save us."

My heart drops. He clearly doesn't know what he's dealing with. "I don't know about that."

"But . . . you—" he pleads, but I interrupt him.

If only he knew my story—I'm new, I'm a baby. Yet, I think about what just happened with Navin. I don't know how to do that again. I don't know how it happened the first time. In just a whisper, I say, "Okay listen, just give me a second to think."

If they go out as they are, they're dead. I can't teach them what to do . . . that'll take too long.

Finally, I look back at Ivan. "How long have they been here? How long can you keep them hidden?"

Ivan shrugs. "Don't know."

"Okay, listen. I'm going to go find your sister. I need the phone I gave her. Can you keep them quiet?"

"You're going to leave? How do we know you'll come back?"

"Ivan," I look at him closely, "does your gut tell you that you can trust me?"

"I don't trust my gut anymore." The look on his face is hesitant and uncomfortable. His world makes no sense to him anymore. I understand completely. "Please, Remona, come back."

"I will. I promise."

With that, I leave them and close the door. Then, I pull the heavy crates back to their original position. In just minutes, the brisk night air hits my skin, and the smell of gun powder fills my nose. I press myself against the walls using the overhang shadows, so that when people run by no one can see me. There is so much yelling, and distant screams send chills through my body. *How do we fix this? It all feels too much.*

Several men block the gate from which I need to leave. For a moment I stand against the siding of a small home just watching them, wondering how I'll sneak past. I close my eyes, quickly finding the Void. My body turns light, and I feel my arms tingle. Beyond the Void, I listen. Their rhythms are chaotic until I find each unique cadence. *Can I do five at once? Tracing is easy compared to Tri Planum, but for five men?* I start with one of them, riding his rhythm easily, then two men, and so on. As I do, each of them begins to show signs that what I'm doing might be working. I can see the look of confusion in a couple of their faces, while the others are oblivious to the way I control their every moment. Soon I find that I have all five in my grasp.

"Good job, Remy," I whisper.

Each man robotically turns away from where I hide in the shadows, which means that they are all facing different directions. One of them, as if in slow motion, tries to slap his face with a heavy hand, obviously feeling that something is off, but unable to know what. It's risky to step out into the light, but I do. Since they are turned away, none of them can see me. Carefully, watching every direction, I walk toward the gate, which ultimately means, toward the men. As I come closer, I keep the rhythm tight. Once I get close enough, the men make micro turns with their feet, keeping their eyes pointed away. It might look ridiculous to anyone watching that these men somehow turn just enough again and again, their second-hand-clock-like-movement, in order to miss me walking directly through them.

This is way easier than fighting.

I reach the gate and turn around—every one of the men is still facing away. Finally, I run knowing that once I'm a certain distance, they will recover and wonder what the heck just happened. I let the smile stretch across my face.

"Elliot?" I call in a heavy whisper once I reach the top of the hill. I'm just a bit out of breath, but not like most would be. "Elliot?" I call again.

Finally, her small voice catches my attention, and she steps out from a grouping of trees. "Did you find my brothers?"

"I did."

"Did you help them?"

I hesitate. "I'm going to try. There's a lot of you in the Patch and I can't do it myself. Where's the phone?" Her trembling hand pulls it from her pocket. "Did you call him . . . the man I told you to call?"

"Yes."

"And?"

"And he told me that it would be a couple of hours before they can get to us."

"Did he sound okay?"

"Strong, he sounded strong."

Relief fills me. "How long ago was that?"

"I don't know, an hour?"

I quickly dial and soon Arek picks up. "Elliot, what's happened?"

"Arek," I am so grateful to hear his deep voice. "It's me."

"Remy." He sighs into the great abyss of thought. "Thank god. We're coming to get you. Maybe an hour."

"How are you so close?"

"I told you . . . I always know where you are."

My heart flips. Somehow this has been true. "You're all right?"

"Yeah." He whispers as though he's around a group of people. "Luckily Briston was the guinea pig for this and Hugh knew exactly what to do."

It had been a while since I thought about Hugh. "Dr. Hugh, is he okay?"

Arek continues, "He's fine. When it all started, he was with a celebrity client who has plenty of security. Lya and Daye are okay too. How are you?"

I shake my head as I look over at the scared girl next to me. "I have a problem. I got away from Navin . . . I don't have the time to tell you how. But now, I've found more trouble."

"You do that well," he notes.

"I promised a young group of Ephemes . . . they lost their parents to the uprising. I promised them that I would help them, but it turns out that there's a large group of people here . . . Ephemes . . . trapped in this town. They're hiding well, but it won't last forever. About fifty of them."

"Fifty Ephemes . . . Remy, we don't have time to help fifty Ephemes."

"Well, I can tell you now that I don't have an option. So, I try to do this alone or I wait until you can do this with me."

"Remy." There's always a reserved patience in him for everything that I do. It's been long enough now that I realize Arek loves me, but loving me has more than enough challenges.

"Arek, listen . . . they're stuck in a room underground and if they get caught, they will be slaughtered just like every other Epheme in this town has already been. Some of them are wounded . . . badly."

He sighs. "Okay. Can you hold off until we get there?"

"I'll try. But hurry."

Elliot and I wait for longer than an hour. Her body is restless, but the shadow beneath her eyes tells of her fatigue. As we sit against a large tree listening to two owls hooting and swooping through the night to catch mice, I recognize the breath of someone who has just lived trauma. Trauma that will cloud her deepest places and eventually hide within her unconscious waiting for that very moment that it will defy her, confuse her, and trick her into believing false experiences and a false self.

She falls asleep on my shoulder, and when I place my hand on hers, suddenly I see through her eyes her parents dying as they tried to save her, and my eyes brim with tears. I let go of her hand when my abilities become too much to bear.

Every few minutes screams and yells echo through the night sky and I hope that they don't come from the Patch. I find myself pacing after a while. Finally, deep in my gut, I know that Arek is nearby. A whistle bounces off the trees—Kilon's whistle that I know so well. When I see Arek, I run to him. He wraps his arms around me, turning every moment beyond this one less important. I feel the instant relief washing over me. When he looks me in the eyes and runs his hand down my arm, he shakes his head. "How did you do it? How'd you get away from him?"

I shake my head, "I don't exactly know . . . it's a story I need to tell you. But not now."

Kilon, Sassi, Lya, Geo, and Daye have all come. Even Peter arrives behind them and I'm grateful for his youthful spirit for Elliot. He is only a couple of years older. Geo holds a metal box in his hands, and he quickly sets it down on a rock. Daye grabs me for a hug.

"You're okay," I say to her as her veins once again look a normal color beneath her skin.

"We are. But the world is not," Daye says with heavy but wise eyes and I wonder . . . *Do mine look like that?*

Elliot comes closer. "Everyone, this is Elliot. Her brothers are in there with the others, doing their best to stay safe."

Arek nods at the young girl. "We're here to help."

"Thank you," she whispers.

Geo lifts a drone from the box and in just seconds I can hear the whir of its motor as it bounces up in the air. "Remy, help us figure out where they are." He points to the box, inside of which is a computer, and soon, as the drone flies over the town, we can see everything that is happening.

Sassi shakes her head, "Look at that." The drone passes over piles of rubbish and bodies that are strewn about the town. Several Velieri run about, some as predators and others celebrating.

"They're looking for leftovers," I tell them.

"This is how it is everywhere," Sassi warns. "Unfortunately, we can't save everyone."

"Not yet anyway," I say quietly. Everyone looks at me with no surprise. "Okay, follow this row of houses. Through here," I point at the screen as the drone flies through. "If you go through this store . . ."

Geo sends the drone into the building, hoping that it doesn't catch the eye of anyone around. So far, this small town is too distracted with destruction to pay attention to it. "There! Behind those crates . . ."

The drone shows us that the crates are still set and hiding the entrance to the Patch. Geo looks up at Arek, "What are you thinking?"

Arek takes in a deep breath, but no one strategizes like him. Finally, after several moments, he nods. "Peter, you stay here with Elliot. Keep her safe." Arek turns to me. "What distance are we from the entrance to the Patch?"

I think for a moment, "An eighth of a mile?"

"Okay. Kilon, you go around from the left and continue to circle the building in the shadows. I'll go from the right. Geo, Daye, and Lya, you will get in and help one group. Sassi and Remy, you help the other. When you are out, Kilon and I will each take a group and hopefully get them out safe."

We all look at one another, not ready to walk away from these Ephemes, but not ready to face what is next.

CHAPTER TWENTY-TWO

As we come to the gate, I notice the same men are there. They are quietly talking, their guns hanging from their shoulders. I lean over to Arek and quickly tell him what I did before and he smiles. He doesn't have to say it for me to know. His Remy is back no matter the memories that have not returned.

"Can you do it again?" he asks.

I chuckle. "Of course, I can do it again."

As we walk through, I dig deep, riding their wave. Each time I do this, I realize why Tracing, although powerful, is also dangerous. It feels like at any moment, within the darkness and pain of people that we are inevitably connecting to while digging deep, you will fall in and find it difficult to get out. *I hope that's not a thing . . .*

Arek runs his hand down my arm, "It's not," he answers my unsaid question, which makes me shake my head.

The guards' eyes are turned away and their bodies move in a rotational clicking of sorts, never able to see us. Geo, Kilon, Sassi, and the others hurry through, but take a moment to recognize the simplicity.

"Huh," Kilon quips. As we begin to run, hoping not to get caught on the open road, Kilon shakes his head with a slight grin. "Let's not think about how many times we could have used that."

Keeping in the dark spaces, we press ourselves against the buildings. If one person finds out that we are here, they will make sure everyone knows, so that can't happen. Arek points in the opposite direction once we reach the outside of the store where the Patch is. Kilon nods and heads away, while Arek takes the other side and the rest of us enter the store. But immediately, as soon as I've stepped foot inside, someone heavy and sweaty runs into me, nearly knocking me to the ground. In seconds this man I don't recognize has his gun pointed in my direction and takes a shot. The bullet enters through my lung and exits out my back. Instantly it is hard for me to breathe.

Before he can take another shot, Sassi throws herself on him, wrapping her legs around him with such force that they spin in the air and fall to the ground. Sassi lands directly over him and quickly bends his wrist until the gun falls to the floor. Lya kicks it away and points her own toward him.

"Don't say a word. Don't call for anyone or I'll take a shot where it hurts the most." Lya is shockingly intimidating to the point that my eyes widen.

Arek and Kilon hear the commotion and come inside. I'm still sucking my breath through a straw as I bend over, coughing blood.

"Is it out?" Arek asks as he runs to my side.

"Yes. I think so," I wheeze.

Kilon stands over this man, then rips some material from his own shirt and stuffs it in his mouth. "You're lucky, son, that there's already been too much death here. Keep your mouth shut." The man nods in obvious panic.

Kilon ties his arms and legs, then he places duct tape over his mouth. There is a closet nearby. Kilon notices it, rips the shelves off the wall, and pushes the man inside. "Here, take a rest."

Finally, Kilon and Arek leave again to circle the building while we make our way to the basement. We head down the stairs and through a deep cement room with storage on every wall, then we move the crates and I knock on the door. "Ivan," I say quietly.

After a moment, we hear the lock turn and soon all of us stare at the scared people inside. We are no longer the minority here. In this town at this moment, the Ephemes are the minority. One click away from Navin's end goal—ultimate genocide. Ivan smiles, his young eyes full of hope that wasn't there before. "You came back."

"I told you I would. We're ready to get you out of here. . . Okay," I say aloud to the group. "We're going to split you in two groups. One will go with Geo, Lya, and Daye here. And the rest will come with me and Sassi." I turn to Geo . . . "You go first."

He nods. "Okay. Everybody make as little sound as possible. Follow the shadows of the buildings and if you see anyone press yourself against them. We're taking the back gate."

I help several of the people who have been wounded get to their feet. Soon half of the group exits the room, trying to keep the children as quiet as they can. We wait just a couple of minutes until they have enough time to leave with either Arek or Kilon. Then we gather the last of the group and rush through the storage and up the stairs, to wait at the door until we see Kilon coming to us from the back of the building. Sassi and I usher them out the door into the open where there is no longer the safety of walls.

One of the elderly is very slow, so Kilon takes her on his back and her white hair falls over his shoulder, as she holds on for dear life. Finally, we make it to the end of the building where we need to cross a road to get to the gate. Sassi looks at me carefully when we see that the other group has already escaped. There are no more men standing guard and for some reason this worries me.

"Give me a second," I say to the group. I hurry forward, checking from one direction to the next, feeling uncomfortable with the quiet. The air is tense. Many have died here, and I can feel them in the air. We are not alone. "Come on." I finally wave the others through. They run. Several make it to the other side and Kilon hurries the older lady on his back across the road.

Suddenly, a shot rings out. A woman running across the road cries out and falls forward with a powerful plunge. She's been shot in the back.

"No!!!!!!!" I yell.

I run to her, her Ephemeral body already convulsing with pain. It takes only seconds before she dies in my arms, just as another bullet whizzes by.

"Hurry!" Sassi yells at the others. Our eyes meet.

"Where is it?!" My voice is broken and angry.

"Somewhere up there!" Sassi yells back as she helps a little girl who has just tripped. Another one of the group is shot, then another. This time I see the orange glow when the bullet releases from the chamber. Several of the Ephemes crash to the ground. The sniper is up in the church bell tower just fifty yards away.

"Get them out of here!!!!!" I scream at Sassi and Kilon.

Kilon recognizes my thoughts and yells, "No!!!"

"Go!!!" I yell back.

I run as fast as I can, feeling the excruciating blow every time someone falls just after a shot. My breathing is still shortened and wheezing from the healing wound to my lung. As fast as my feet can carry me, still several more shots are fired and several more men and women fall to the ground. Sassi is trying her best to get those who are still alive across the street.

I reach the church and throw the door open. It is small and ancient. The rustic floorboards bend and scream with every step that I take. Just behind the pulpit are the stairs to the bell tower. Upon hearing another shot, I fly up the stairs in the intense black. I stumble several times just from sheer fatigue, but the anger that burns within me makes it easy to dig in. At the top of the stairs, I kick the door open and rush inside. The sniper is covered in black, but it surprises me when Navin's mask with the red Xs on the eyes and lips hangs from his back pocket. Suddenly, I realize that these snipers aren't just Velieri from the town—Navin has sent his men out. The fight ahead of me is bigger than I expect. At first, he does nothing and neither do I. At least this gives them time to get the Ephemes out of this place. Suddenly he whips his gun toward me, but I pull mine faster than he can and shoot the gun out of his hands by placing the bullet through his palm. He cries out. Then he leaps toward me, but I'm ready. A front kick to his chest as he lands sends him back and he slides along the floor.

My head begins to pulse in the same familiar way, like an alarm to my system telling me that this is no ordinary Velieri and I must be careful. I cast my net deeper within his psyche and I can tell when I've turned into more than just Remy in his eyes: the monster staring back at him, just as I play with the shallow parts of his fear. He tries harder and I feel the compression on my body as he tries to negate what I'm doing to him. In an unexpected move, he turns to the window, letting out one more shot and one of the women who has almost made it to the gate goes limp in Kilon's arms.

"No!" I yell.

I use the high adrenaline to take him down, so I sweep his feet out and send him to the ground. Then I end it with one shot.

Breathing heavily, I pull myself off him. When I peer outside, there are seven Ephemes lying on the road. They missed freedom by mere feet. I'm angry beyond tears. I wonder to myself: *Is this it?*

Is there an end to this?

"There is." I hear the whisper and turn around. It's only there for a second—a shadowy, human-like figure, looking like Beckah, but disappearing too fast to tell. Even when it's gone, it leaves evidence with a shade of purple lingering for just a few seconds. "Beckah?" But no one responds.

Before long, I reach the gate. Sassi, Kilon, and I take all those who are left up the hill and we rejoin the others. Elliot cries as she reunites with Ivan and her other brothers while Peter smiles as he watches on.

"How do we get them out of here?" I whisper to Arek.

"The Gianda here is willing to put them up for the time being. There are some shuttles waiting at the bottom of this forest. We just have to get them there." Arek looks at me then reaches out and runs his fingers down my cheek. I'm surprised when it stings, and blood covers his skin. "The belltower, huh?" he asks as he raises an eyebrow.

"There was no one else," I respond.

"I'm beginning to believe there's never anyone else." He wipes his fingers along his shirt, then kisses my temple.

"Now you're gettin' it . . . it only took six hundred years."

CHAPTER TWENTY-THREE

Later that night, we gather at the Gianda after having brought the Ephemes there for safety. All of us, including Briston, Diem, and Gal on the computer, meet in the conference room. I don't let them get very far before I tell them what I know.

"Navin is here in a villa that I've never seen before. It's old and has several buildings around it," I explain.

"Is it like the one we found before? Are there more Ephemes there?" Gal asks as she scratches her arm.

"No. Not that I saw. It seemed to be just me, but I didn't get to look everywhere. There's something more though." I look at Arek with care. "Leigh was there with them."

"What?" Sassi asks.

"Navin has Hawking, Prophet Covey, and . . . Leigh."

Briston is the first to show his anger. His voice, which is normally a growl, is even deeper now. "Leigh? Leigh is there with them and knew he'd taken you?"

"Yes . . . he was well aware."

Everyone looks at one another.

"Isaiah Aldo was also there."

"Remy?" Sassi asks carefully. "What did they do? Why did they need you?"

"He doesn't need me. Not anymore. Don't you see, he still hopes that he can use me, but at this point he's done enough damage to the world that he doesn't need me. He wants what I have . . . not me."

"I can't imagine Navin being great at Tri Planum . . ." Kilon growls.

"I don't know that he is. But Dr. Karine is helping him with everything. Tri Planum and so much more. Look what they've done to this world already . . . there's no stopping him now. But there's more . . ." I hesitate before saying anything.

Everyone is looking at me with concern.

Arek cocks his head to the side and touches my arm. "You said something about how you got out."

"Yeah. Something happened that I don't understand."

Geo comes closer and stands next to Daye. Their chemistry is palpable, and I can't help but let my glance linger. Does she feel the same way that I do when Arek touches me? I certainly hope so. Geo clears his throat before he speaks. "What happened, Remy?"

"They attached me to a machine. It's obvious that Karine is doing anything he can to control this. It nearly took me . . . it's hard to explain . . . they wanted to know more so they were using this to search, and I felt it getting closer to finding things we don't want them to know." I sneak a glance at Arek. "I tried to battle it. I tried to keep everything protected. But I felt things coming . . . I was fighting so aggressively, doing everything that you have taught me all along, but no matter what I did, it just kept getting closer to the surface."

Lya steps forward with panic. "Please tell me my father didn't waste all of these years hiding us, just to have you give away everything?"

"Lya!" Arek warns her.

"Your father?" Sassi furrows her brow and uncrosses her arms. "Who's your father?"

"It's just like you to ruin everything . . ." Lya spits the words at me.

Sassi races toward her and her long and muscular frame towers over Lya as her eyes stare with rage. "You'd better watch what you say." It isn't long until Kilon is standing behind Sassi as backup for his wife.

"Back off, Sassi." Lya clenches her jaw and steps toward her until they are nose to nose. My heart skips, never having seen Sassi like this. Everyone is confused.

"What's going on?" Briston calls from the screen.

"Tell her, Remy," Lya mumbles.

"Lya!" Arek yells.

Lya turns to him with arms flailing. "She's going to ruin it again! All the work you did. All the years you kept it from him and yet you just keep believing in her. I bet you he knows. I bet you she couldn't hide it from him."

"Knows what?" Sassi looks at Arek. "Arek? What is she talking about?"

"Just tell them!" Lya yells.

Silence drops over the room. Kilon and Sassi are staring at Arek and me with such confusion. Briston finally speaks up. "Tell them. It's time."

Arek clears his throat and breathes in. "Lya and Daye . . . they are ours. Our daughters. Remy's and mine."

I've never seen Sassi's beautiful eyes so wide. At first it is confusion, but turns to displacement. "What are you saying?"

Kilon starts looking at the girls and turns his head from side to side.

"No," Sassi rubs her head and shakes it. "What are you saying?"

Kilon interrupts, "Sassi," his voice is surprisingly calm and clear, "look at them."

Sassi turns to him and he points to Lya and Daye. The rest of the room does the same. Sassi takes a moment and stares. But the longer she does, the more questions seem to enter her mind. "What? How?

What . . . I . . ."

Arek steps toward her. "I'm sorry. I couldn't tell you. I couldn't."

"You didn't trust us?" Sassi asks with pain in her voice.

"It wasn't that. I didn't trust everyone around us. The more who knew, the more problems."

Kilon's face is starting to change. I'm surprised when a smile comes across his face. "How? When?"

"Remy was pregnant, a couple of years before she died," Arek explains. "She had them in Spain and we did everything we could to make sure that nobody knew. Not even you."

Peter chuckles, "Whoa. No way."

Gal and Diem are hollering from the monitors. "I knew it! This is it, the Prophecy happened. It's here! Aye!!!"

But Sassi is the last to come around. I walk to her with my hands out and grab hers. "Those months that Arek and I gave you off. Then, we would disappear here and there before I died."

"How did I not know?" Sassi is mad at herself. I can see it. The look in her eyes is near fear that she didn't know.

Arek walks to her and takes her face in his hands. "I made sure that you didn't know. Blame me. I had no other choice but to make sure that no one knew and they couldn't use you to get to them."

"I can't believe it."

"Well believe it," Lya responds. "All that, Sassi, and in one moment, she gives it all away to Navin after all these years."

"I didn't." This time it is my voice that is abrupt and strong. I stand up in front of my daughter feeling the same emotion well up within me and look at her with serious eyes. "Just when it got close, I saved it. I hid it." I turn to Geo, "Something happened from the anger and fear . . . It created an explosion."

Geo looks at me suspiciously. "What do you mean?"

"I mean, everything inside me and my desperation to keep Lya and Daye safe manifested until I screamed. All the lights flashed; the machine exploded . . ." I'm trying to gauge the way people are watching me and I can see the confusion on all their faces. "Whatever came out of me was so massive, it made a ripple through the room and they flew back."

"Who flew back?" Arek asks.

"The men."

"How many of them?" Kilon asks with a furrowed brow.

I hesitate. "All of them."

"Without touching anyone?" Sassi asks even though it is obvious that she has not recovered from the new turn of events.

"Yes. The day that you all came to the school when this all started . . . I watched Arek push Navin back without touching him." I look around unsure how to understand what happened.

"Yeah," Arek admits. "But that was one man. Not a roomful."

Lya changes the subject. "So did you tell him about us!?"

"No!" I yell back. The room falls silent. "Our secret is still safe. You are still safe." I walk to her with intimidating steps.

Lya doesn't back down.

Arek changes the focus. "Let's all take a moment. Sassi, Kilon . . . and everyone else. We're sorry we couldn't tell you. It's the hardest thing I've ever done."

Kilon walks to Arek and places a hand on his shoulder. "It's real." He nods his head and begins to smile. "It's real. The Prophecy is real."

Kilon walks to Daye, the softer of the two, and places a hand on her face. "How did I not see it."

Daye smiles and touches his hand.

Sassi turns to me with an almost smile. "Twins."

I nod.

She breathes out as if this is her way of acceptance.

I look at Lya for a moment, wondering what I have done to her. Then I turn to Arek. "What are we going to do? He's here in Italy and I know where."

"Guaranteed that as soon as you escaped, he left," Geo says. "Navin's not going to stay around. Not a chance."

"Don't we at least find out ourselves? Arek? Do you really want to be this close and not try?" I ask.

An hour later we travel down the road toward the villa where I was last with Navin. None of us have slept, yet none of us can feel the fatigue due to the adrenaline pulsing through our veins.

The black sky is turning a dusty purple in preparation of the new day. We are dressed in dark colors with weapons ready and night goggles hanging from the loops on our belts in case we need them.

We stop a mile away then walk. When the villa finally comes into view, everything is eerily quiet. It's silent enough to be a cemetery. My heart is thumping against my chest as we reach the chain-link fence that I escaped through.

"Watch for cameras," Arek whispers as he uses pliers to cut the metal fence. Soon there's a big enough hole for us all to climb through. I point out my exit route and when we get near, we find the door open. Inside, things are strewn about, and it is obvious that Navin left quickly. Still, we search with caution.

"This is not a good idea, mate," Kilon says in the strangely quiet hall that I ran through so quickly before. "We're playing on his grounds, on his turf. I don't trust it."

"He's not here," I say quietly. "I can't feel him. Can you?"

Everyone, one by one, shakes their heads.

We pass by the doors to the swimming pool, and when we look in, there is nothing left of Dr. Karine's equipment. "He used this . . ." I mention to the others. "He called the cold a conduit . . . no different than using my emotion."

"Going old school, are we?" Sassi says sarcastically. "They've been doing that since the turn of the century and even longer."

Arek kneels and touches the water. He shakes his fingers off. "Yeah, but it's smart . . . people have forgotten to prepare for those older methods."

Geo looks at me, "It's one of the first things we taught you. Do you remember? At Sassi and Kilon's cabin, I Traced you in the cold forest. Hypothermia causes confusion and hallucinations; those are easy to use against someone. How'd you get out of it?"

"I wouldn't come back up."

Kilon turns to me with a grin. "Back up?"

"Yeah, from the bottom of the pool. You can't read a dead body."

Kilon high-fives me. I look at Lya, hoping that she'll understand the great lengths I went to, to keep her safe. There is a glimmer of recognition in her eyes.

"Can you hear that?" Peter asks.

We all remain quiet. A deep pounding comes from somewhere.

"What is that?" Sassi asks.

Geo follows the sound. He ends up at a far wall and places his hand on it. "Feel this."

Kilon and Arek rush over.

"Someone is on the other side." He presses his ear against it. "There are voices. People are yelling."

Everyone instantly knows. It is obvious that we are all thinking the same thing: *What has Navin left us now?*

Geo runs to the nearest door leading outside.

"Check the door before you open it!" Arek yells. Geo is smart and carefully checks every inch before he kicks it open. Soon we are all outside and just behind the gym is a built-on structure with no windows. When we look closer, there is a square cutout no bigger than a matchbox with a lock and swinging door.

"What is it?" Sassi asks as Geo cautiously gets closer.

After a moment, Geo's worried voice carries across the breeze, "Arek."

Arek joins Geo. With careful precision, after making sure it is safe, he turns the lock and opens the small matchbox-size cutout.

Terrified voices cry out. "Help!"

"Who's there?"

"Please get us out of here!"

Fingers reach through the hole and Arek touches them to let

them know he's there. "We're here," he says to them.

At that moment, Peter comes from the gym. "Look what I found." In his hands is a laptop computer.

"Where did you get that?" Kilon asks.

"Navin left it for us, I have a feeling."

Arek opens the computer. Instantly a video begins without us touching anything. Navin is there.

"You can't save everyone, Brother. It's time to stop trying. There are hundreds of these all over. You'll never know where and how many. Sorry about that. It's important to know, I'm doing this for all of us, for our freedom."

At the end of the video, we hear the clank and unoiled squeal of moving parts within the walls of this added structure. Suddenly everyone within the room is screaming and crying. Multiple fingers come through the cutout.

"What's happening?" Arek yells.

"Water!" One of the ladies cries. "It's filling with water!"

"Look around!" Arek yells at us. Kilon runs as fast as he can around the entire building, hoping to find something to save these people. The rest of us glide our hands all over the walls. Sassi runs out after checking the gymnasium and yells, "The pool is draining!"

Arek runs into the gymnasium and searches the pool. He dives into the ice-cold water and finds the hole. For a moment he stays down there, trying to find any solution. When he comes up, he yells, "Find anything to plug this. Give me anything!"

Many of us run around throwing him this and that, but there seems to be nothing big enough to stop the flow of water. For a moment he can slow it down, but we soon realize that Navin has planned for it all and another hole begins to drain. When he realizes it's of no use, Arek jumps out into the cold air, his clothes pressed heavily to his puckered skin. We run out to find that the water is high and even though this small hole is letting water pour out, it is not enough.

Arek and Kilon find ground tools, such as hammers, axes. They begin to swing away. The walls are made of cement a foot thick. It doesn't matter how strong they are or how hard they hit; it does not make a dent.

For what feels like an eternity, we try everything we can. Water pours from the square cutout, but it isn't enough. It's an awful sound. The screaming, the cries, the torture. Until it all comes to a stop.

The water has risen all the way to the top. We continue to work, well beyond the amount of time it would take to save whoever is in there.

Unexpectedly, Arek yells at the top of his lungs and punches the cement wall until his knuckles are bleeding. Several minutes later, after we've all stared in silence while wondering whether there was a solution that we just couldn't find, Geo shakes his head. "This has to end."

CHAPTER TWENTY-FOUR

"I can't fight like this anymore . . . in constant defense," Arek tells everyone in the car as we drive to the airport.

No one says anything as we pass towns that feel gravely apocalyptic. Sassi's eyes are full of anguish, however I know her, and the resolve will follow. "We need to be the best. We need Gyre. And I don't mean just enough . . . we need to be spotless. And Remy . . ."

"Yeah?" I say from beside Peter in the backseat.

"There are two things we need to do. One, we need to find Navin and the only way is to learn to control your Traveling. And second, we all know the only person who can help us with Navin's unconscious is Lyneva."

All of us look up at the same time with surprise.

"We all know she's been with him since she was a child. Hopefully she'll know something about him if he's trusted her enough to tell her," Sassi continues.

"But how do we get her to tell us anything?" Peter asks.

"Navin's turned his back on her. She's been in the Cellar all this time . . . I'm not sure she won't freely tell us." She turns to Kilon, who has been peering out the window instead of paying attention to her. "And you."

"Me?"

"Yeah, you. You are going to go there."

"Where?" Kilon dramatically balks.

"You know where!" Sassi raises her eyebrows and cocks her head. "You are going to dig deep."

Kilon takes in a big breath. "Yeah okay."

"Diem?" Arek turns all our attention to him on speaker.

"Aye?"

"How many of us can we pull together?"

"As many as you want."

"Okay call them . . . we head back to Switzerland and change our tactics. It's time to play offensively."

"Aye, sir," Diem says with a pound of his chest.

CHAPTER TWENTY-FIVE

In my mind, I continue to replay the drowning. The horror and pain those Ephemes must have felt is difficult to imagine, so I find myself sinking further into the abyss of hopelessness. Arek notices my heavy eyes, "What's going on in that head of yours?"

"Watching the way people treat others on this earth is not easy. Not even during my Ephemeral life, when I knew nothing of this battling underworld. Our guarded nature was created to protect us from danger. However, we've misused and misunderstood our primal instincts for so long, conjuring up reasons to hate so that creating tribes is justified. There's comfort in saying you're wrong and I'm right. Lines are specifically drawn to declare your side righteous. What is a sacred belief to one, might be pain to another, but the world doesn't want to work that hard to understand this. We draw lines to enforce our beliefs and criminalize those that suggest the slightest difference—all in the name of convincing our own selves that we are okay because we have the best answers."

Arek nods. "Unity, I'm beginning to believe, is as fictional as fairytales." He hesitates then continues. "I know my brother; he won't stop until they're all dead. Ephemes represent our chains. But we all know it is the most powerful and elite within the political world of the Velieri that sold their souls to force us into hiding."

"We hide in the name of acceptance but cannot reconcile what that damages within us."

Above the clouds on the plane back to Switzerland Arek calls everyone he can, bidding them to join us. I watch him as he rubs his head and neck, desperate to find an end to all of this.

"Is this a good idea?" Briston asks Arek. "We'll be like sitting ducks—all together."

"Well, being separate hasn't worked so far," Arek admits. "When people feel alone, they start looking for comfort from anywhere. Ephemes will begin to join forces and there's more of them than there are of us. The Ephemes in power will begin to use anything they can against us, nuclear . . . chemical . . . whatever they can because they will assume that we are no different than Navin."

Briston nods, "I'm here for it, Arek. Whatever we need to do."

Hours later, we pull the large SUVs into the driveway of Arek's home, and . . . I guess, my home . . . in Switzerland. "We bought seven hundred and fifty acres . . . hoping to live a quiet life," Arek says as he meets me behind the car to grab our things.

"Seven hundred and fifty acres? That's a lot." I reach in and wrap my hand around the strap of my bag.

"I suppose it is, but we were ready to be secluded." He brushes his shoulder against mine.

"And we've lived nothing but the opposite." I turn back around, letting my eyes roam the perfectly sliced horizon on one side and the rise and fall of the mountains on the other, with a beautiful valley in between—where our home sits.

A small dusting of snow has already touched the ground even though the fall just branded the air with dry leaves and the sweet smell of pine.

"It's enough land to have everyone come to us. We establish

ourselves here," Arek says as we take the stamped walk up to the house. "I've been preparing a long time, years and years, with the best technology you can find. All seven hundred and fifty acres are droned every hour. There's a thin line of electrical wire around the entire border that will tell us when anyone comes onto the property, and the drones can reach any acre within the border in less than one minute and fourteen seconds. I know this property like the back of my hand."

When we enter the home, not everything has been fixed since the last time Navin came after us here. The wall that was shot through is now just drywall and mortar in some places, but for the most part, when I walk through the door, there is an instant barrage of memories. Now this place feels like my own. I wander through the rooms realizing that most of the choices of décor were mine. He didn't touch anything or change anything. As I pass Masey she looks at me carefully, casting her potent territorial glare.

"I changed the pictures in the main bedroom," she says as she passes me in the hall. "Hope you don't mind."

"Hey Masey," I say as I set my things down. "I get it. You want your hands on everything, but get it through your head . . . I'm alive, I'm here, and I have him." I wink at her slyly, then pick my bags up to take them to our room. With one last look, I catch her frustration.

It's not until I'm closer to our room that I see Arek looking at me mischievously. "What?" I ask him.

"You couldn't help yourself?" he grins.

"Should I?"

He slowly lowers his head close to mine with a large smile. "I've got things to do and prep, so you get some sleep and I'll come in soon."

"Okay."

Later, just past midnight, Arek finally walks into our room and I look up from my pillow when the door softly closes.

"It's just me." He begins to undress and breathes out a heavy sigh. "It will take us time to get everyone here."

"Where will we train with Gyre?"

"There's an old monastery on this land. I've modernized it some, but there are also underground tunnels from long ago that you and I resurrected where we store heavy artillery. We've used it in the past. That's where we'll go. It's armed, it's protected, and it has everything we need including space."

"We stored heavy artillery here? We must have known this would someday come."

He nods. "When Japha and Navin joined forces . . . even when we didn't know Lyneva was involved, the writing was on the wall. Someday, if they continued to grow and especially with their conspiracies, it was only a matter of time until it got out of hand. You and Sassi intuitively understood more than Kilon and I did."

Without looking at me he sighs and sits on the bench in front of the window even though there is just darkness and the moon outside. His head falls into his hands. His hair is growing back from being shaved months ago after nearly losing his life. I climb out of bed, my cold feet touching the creaky wooden floor, and I carefully wrap my arms around his neck.

"It'll be okay," I whisper in his ear.

"Eventually . . . I believe that. Just what happens before it is?"

When I look out the window, the moon is as large as I've ever seen it, and the stars are in a constant swirl about the sky. A thought comes to me.

"We need to bring Ephemes here," I finally say.

"What?" he asks with surprise.

"Not yet, but we do. As many Ephemes as we can. Then we send them out to train others."

Arek shakes his head and chuckles. "Leave it to you . . ."

"What?" I turn to look at him.

"The queen of hope, the queen of dreams."

He takes my hand and stands up. He brings his face so close to mine that I smile. "My Queen." Lifting me into his arms, he kisses me, warming my lips until they swell, and a deep pulse begins behind my cheeks. Slowly he walks to the bed, never letting my skin cool, and when we are there, he lies me down and crawls on top of me.

"Arek," I whisper.

He shakes his head. "No more talking."

ᏙᏙᏙ

When I wake up, just outside our window where Switzerland displays its greatest beauty, the backdrop of the tall peaks, and the turning of the old summer's grass to yellow, I can't help but notice a lynx. Wandering alone across the meadow, stopping for just a short moment as though something has passed her in the grass, the lynx is the most beautiful color. I sit up though, understanding what this means. Every time I have seen a lynx it is just before the storm.

The leaves from the few trees surrounding this house are beginning to accumulate on the glass roof and a bit of misty rain is turning them into unique shapes. Arek is still sleeping, so I quietly make my way through the room, throw on a sweater, and head down the hallway. I find Sassi in the kitchen, waiting for her coffee to brew. The moment she sees me, she smiles and raises her long, lean arm, inviting me to come to her side.

"What is ahead of us?" I ask after a few minutes of waiting.

"Let's not think about it. It's too early. Coffee first, think after."

Several large sounds come from the front of the house, so Sassi and I look at each other curiously. "Are you expecting someone?"

I laugh, "A lot of someones."

We head toward the front door and out onto the driveway.

A long caravan of trucks, SUVs, and cars are making their way toward us. Both Sassi and I smile at each other when we see Briston at the helm with a handsome smile on his face. He parks his extra-large black truck and jumps out, pulling me into his arms for a hug. "This," he says with gratitude. "The first installment of soldiers are here."

A horse whinnies from the trailer attached to my dad's truck and I quickly walk to the window in order to pet her nose. "Who's this?"

"That's Nan. She's mine."

I smell her sweet muzzle and run my fingers along the velvety skin. Just beside her is another one. "Why horses?"

"We brought many in order to get to the Monastery. Besides, I couldn't imagine something happening to them while I'm here." Briston runs his rough hands down her mane and she turns to him, clearly knowing her owner.

"What a beauty," I whisper.

Mak comes around the corner just in time. "Yeah she is." His eyes are suggestive as he looks at me.

"Mr. Mak. You've come to learn Tri Planum," I say in a spooky voice.

"I've come to do whatever we need to get our lives back."

Aita slips by his side, her bright red lipstick making her thin lips and frown more severe. "Hello."

"Good to see you, Aita," I say carefully. The horse nudges me just in time and I turn my attention back to the sweet animal.

Briston leans against me, "Gyre will be here tonight and we'll go together."

"Hopefully it will be different than last time."

CHAPTER TWENTY-SIX

Briston, Arek, Sassi, Geo, and I jump on horses with lights attached to their harnesses to guide the way.

"Where's Kilon?" I ask.

"Look behind you." Sassi rolls her eyes.

When I turn, I see Kilon walking out of the garage leading a dirt bike.

"There's enough horses for you, Kilon," Briston mentions.

"Oh, Kilon doesn't ride anymore." Sassi's tone is filled with a playful annoyance.

Kilon stops and looks at his wife with aggravation. "If you'd had the experiences I have had on those dangerous animals . . . you'd be doing the same. You all just do your thing and I'll do mine."

"And it has nothing to do with the rider at all." Sassi looks at me with a grin.

"Baby, you can make fun of me all you want . . ." He kicks his leg over the dirt bike and sits down. The size of his body makes the bike look like a child's. "But I will always know where I'm going on this thing."

"And so will everyone else." By her words, this is clearly not the first time they have had this argument.

He revs the engine and takes off along the valley.

Even though my Ephemeral life was lived in the city with little to no animal interaction of any kind, I can feel the comfort and ease return to me. Much of the trek to the Monastery is steep, but after a thirty-minute ride, we arrive. A small light extends out the window of a lower floor telling us that Gyre has already arrived with escorts and my stomach flips with nerves. There's no telling what we are here to do.

Arek helps me from the horse, and in the darkness, he stares at me for a moment. "It'll be okay."

"I know."

His thumb runs up and down my cheek until I give a faint smile.

There are eight rough-cut stone archways before you reach the doors leading into the main hall. While it is dark, there is just enough light telling us exactly where Gyre is. We follow the dark halls, passing the decrepit remains of a dormitory, cloister, refectory, and possibly an old library. But before we reach Gyre, I feel my body change. I slow my pace and recognize the expansion and retraction within me. Geo notices that I've slowed down. "Remy?"

"It's happening," I tell them, just as my hand involuntarily squeezes into a fist. My knees begin to buckle, when the seizure begins and my body falls.

CHAPTER TWENTY-SEVEN

Navin is sleeping and I'm lying on my side facing him in his bed. I try desperately not to gasp or make any sound, but it doesn't matter. He grabs my wrist with his eyes still closed. "You're back." His voice is raspy from waking. "You don't know how you're doing this, do you?" His eyes open and he squeezes my arm even harder.

"Let go," I growl.

Suddenly he jerks my arm toward him and rolls over on top of me. "Why do you think you always come to me?" His face is just inches from mine. "Because we're connected . . . Did you know that?"

"Don't mistake your obsession for connection."

"No, don't you remember?" He smiles so eerily, so menacingly that the panic sets in. *What don't I remember?* "We planted something a long time ago."

"What are you talking about?" His body is hot as he rubs his nose up and down my cheek.

"Do you know why you Travel to me?" His finger swirls along my cheek, past my ear, and into my hair as his eyes try to stare gravely into mine. Keeping my eyes focused on the ceiling where the fan slowly turns, his breathing increases with irritation. He pulls my hair until I'm forced to look him in the eyes. "Look at me. You loved me."

I chuckle, "Navin, you're delusional."

"Am I? Think deeply. Those memories are there. You were with us . . . you lived beside me, ate beside me, and touched me as if Arek didn't exist."

"That's not true."

"It is true." He drops his forehead to my cheekbone and breathes heavily. I can feel him trying to Trace immediately, but I can't fight it. My body writhes uncomfortably as though trying to get out of this—get out of whatever spell he's using. "Did you know," he whispers, "that when you Travel, you can't fight the Trace. You're weaker here. We knew that would be the only way. Take you from what you know . . . let your body in the other dimension convulse and cry out in pain, easily letting me slide in. That was our chance . . . to plant within you, within your spirit that when you Travel, it will be to me. I am the gravity that pulls you and there's nothing you can do about it."

I cry out suddenly as I fall into the deeper Trace he has been trying so desperately to make happen. My hand refuses to stay where I desperately want it to remain, and instead raises to his face. My fingers softly glide down his rough skin and he smiles. A tear runs down my temple as the war rages within me. *Why?! Why after all this time is he able to control me?*

He slowly lowers his lips onto mine and no matter the fight within me, I cannot stop.

Somewhere in my chest, a warmth begins, and my mind returns to a memory. Isaiah Aldo tortured me for weeks, no different than in the Cellar. Tactics that would not be permissible in war, were used on me. Navin would come to my aid each night, pulling me from the chains and carrying me away. He tended to my wounds with a warm cloth, and he would feed me and give me water. Every day this continued. Isaiah tortured me and Navin saved me. While I was weak, there would be plenty of time to break in where he needed to. I try to peek about the room where I've landed in this Travel. His wall is still covered in maps and information, there are pictures that I've seen before hanging on his wall, a talisman sits on his nightstand, and his gun rests just beside it.

My body begins that familiar push and pull, the expansion of my molecules, and I know I won't be here long. Just as Navin is about to reach for my lips again, I blink and wake in the dark halls of the Monastery. This time it takes a moment to recover, having stayed longer than before. My body is fatigued beyond measure. Arek has my head in his hands and he runs his thumbs along my cheeks. "Remy," he whispers.

Sassi squeezes my hand. "Are you okay?"

Unexpectedly, tears fall from my eyes. Navin had been able to get in for the first time in a long time. The memories of their torture for all those months have returned. They are caught in my breath, they are caught in my lungs, strangling me until I can't breathe. I sit up and cough, hoping to free myself. *What do I do with the memories?* They're haunting, they're dangerous, connecting me to Navin— enough to experience him as an anchor pulling me to him in my weakest moments. "He's making me do it."

"Do what?" Arek asks.

"Travel. This isn't a gift. This is their doing. They knew how it would weaken me. That's why I only see Navin. I don't Travel to any- one but him. He wants it that way; he made it that way."

Everyone looks toward Geo with questions, but in Geo's eyes, I can read that he doesn't know either. "This is why we need Gyre."

After a few moments they help me to my feet and we continue through the dark halls toward Gyre.

We enter what used to be the church. It is lit by candles and the shadows play along the ancient stone walls. Though the ceiling is not perfectly intact, it is obvious that this place—these stones—were once beautiful. There are no longer any objects, chairs, pews . . . rather there are only four walls and a blanket that Gyre sits upon in the corner. Gyre does not look male or female, alive or dead, and does not sound human. I am afraid of Gyre's shriek, just as I was before. The small being has wandered through my thoughts and instantly the whisper within my head begins—no matter the training that I have been given.

"You are stronger, but are you ready?" the voice says.

"Ready for what?" I expect the others to look at me, but soon realize that Gyre is not just speaking with me. The others are just as transfixed as I am—possibly in their own conversations.

"To be everything you ARE."

"I am ready to defeat him."

The small voice continues within my mind. "Impossible. Not without understanding. Not without a greater knowledge of all that YOU define."

"And what is that?"

"You cannot know all. Power does not exist within our immovable lines, but outside them. Try to know or understand everything and you will fail. We follow what is alive—alive by spirit—alive by the evolution of our souls and we do not need to have solidified answers to be ushered into the presence of our ultimate selves."

Gyre has been on this earth a long time: walked the bloody fields after battle, eulogized many dead, helped others in their quest for alchemy. There is no doubt that this being knows more than most and these words defy every ego on this earth. Without knowing the answers, we are afraid. We use words, concepts, beliefs, and rules as a weapon to demonize one another.

"All sit." I hear the words, then open my eyes. Gyre, in the corner, waves a pointy finger telling the old woman what is to happen. None of us can hear what is said, but we wait for instruction.

The old woman waves her arm at us. "Come sit."

We sit in front of Gyre on the stone floor. Gyre sets incense between us, then takes a drag of a long pipe. Carefully the old woman walks behind each of us and pushes our eyelids closed.

"Breathe deep," she says, in translation of Gyre's inaudible ghostly words. "Tri Planum," she says, "is not just to fight. It is to find. What lays there? What hides there?"

As I suck in a deep breath, trying to be free for whatever is to be learned, my body feels as though it is falling. When my feet touch ground, I open my eyes. Just ahead of me are the others, looking around at the strange surroundings where we suddenly find ourselves. Everyone stands in the forest I have seen so many times before. The fog drifts through the trees. Several yards away, there is someone walking toward us. When they come closer, they smile, and all of us are surprised. It is Gyre—no longer feeble, no longer shackled by a failing body.

"It is time to look," they say, their bald head covered in strange tattoos, their voice suddenly strong. It is the voice I hear when Gyre is speaking within my mind.

"You look refreshed," Sassi says sweetly.

"It is only within the earthly body that I am destitute," Gyre responds. "Let us go. Let us look."

They take us through the forest that feels so strangely familiar. The same forest where I stood with Geo when he first taught me about Tracing. The same forest where Holona and I have met again and again. Gyre nods and looks at me. "Yes." This time their voice is in my head and not out loud. "Yes, there is something that happened here. Something that draws you back again and again."

"Does anyone recognize this forest? Why do I always come back here?" I say as my feet snap branches and needles. Water drops from our skin due to the thick fog and I pull my jacket tighter about my body. Sassi says something to Arek so quietly that I cannot hear. They walk several trees away. Suddenly Arek stops, looks around, looks at me, and it is obvious that something has just occurred to him.

"What?" I ask.

"They cannot tell you." Gyre's whisper floats through my mind.

Suddenly I hear crying in the distance, and it makes me walk a bit faster. I don't even recognize when the rest of the group—Arek, Sassi, Kilon, Geo, and Briston—all back off, letting me walk ahead. Several birds fly away as I make my way to the top of a hill. Just as I pass over the edge, I stop and take in what's in front of me. Gyre also stops at my side. I see a small home that does not look to belong in this forest; smoke from the chimney is billowing, but it is the feeling within my soul that speaks louder than all other senses. I want nothing to do with this place and before I even recognize it, my feet have taken steps backward. Until Gyre places a spiny hand on my arm, stopping me mid-stride. "It is the only way," Gyre's healthy voice whispers.

"I can't." Suddenly I realize that all the times Geo and the others have trained me, Tracing deep within my mind, have begun in a forest or involved hands grabbing for me from beneath the floorboards in a dark home. That same feeling—the nightmarish shadows, the windowless places—the fear returns as if the walls are thick with danger. The aura surrounds this home well beyond the borders.

"It is the only way," Gyre says.

Suddenly the trauma, whatever happened within this home, scratches at my skin from the inside trying to be let out. "I can't," I say again. This time my voice cracks with terror.

I look back at the others as they watch from the bottom of the hill on the other side. *Do they know what happened here?*

"There's only one way to know," Gyre says as if answering my unsaid question. Gyre takes my hand and gently pulls me forward, but I plant my feet heavily into the earth and look back at Arek. There is fear in his eyes and for a moment we simply look at each other. He nods his head as if to say, *It's okay.*

The crying from the home grows louder and I begin to recognize the tone of my own voice. It is me crying. However, I've never heard this before—never heard the brokenness and the heartache that warps everything in its path. No bird, no squirrel, no piece of grass, no speck of dust will keep its integrity in the path of this pain. The cry turns to screams and pain—physical, as well as emotional. My heart pounds my chest and my throat is dry as I slowly follow Gyre down the hill to the front door and closer to the tortured sound. My hands shake as I reach out to open the front door. Still, I don't remember. I don't know what has happened here except . . . my body remembers. It is ravaged with pain until every part is shaking and tingling with numbness.

My shaking fingers twist the knob and I enter once the door is open. The same place where the fingers reached through the floorboards when Geo was trying to teach me how to battle the Trace are in front of me. I have returned again and again, never realizing that this place was deep within my unconscious. Suddenly a cry fills the home from somewhere in the back, making me jump out of my skin. Slowly and methodically, I travel through the rooms looking for me. The old me. Whatever me this is who can sound so broken, so shattered.

Gyre stays several steps behind but does not leave me alone. The sound of water draws me to the kitchen. Navin stands at a basin washing a knife. From the hand pump, water runs red as he pushes the handle again and again. Somewhere in the house, I cry out, and Navin squeezes his eyes shut, then turns to look down the hall.

That's where I go, following his gaze, knowing that at the end I'll maybe understand what has happened. I recognize these dark halls where Geo tried to help me understand, trying to help me fight the Trace. The darkness surrounds me and seeps within my skin like a deadly poison. I reach the last room at the end of the hall and step inside. Isaiah Aldo, Japha, and Covey are there. Doctor Karine stands over me as I lie in a pool of blood on the bed. I'm writhing in pain, as Dr. Karine holds something small in his arms. My breath catches when I realize it is a baby.

"No!" I let out a soft cry as my soul suddenly allows the memory back in. "This is not real . . . this didn't happen," I cry.

Gyre touches my arm. "Be honest with yourself. It is the only way to break free."

After a few moments, Dr. Karine shakes his head and covers the baby with a bloodied cloth. He walks toward me, then passes without knowing that I am there, heading straight to the kitchen where Navin waits. Navin looks up as he enters, but the doctor shakes his head. "No, I could not get the labor to stop. It's not working. This is the third. I've done everything I know to do."

Navin wipes his brow with a hand and growls. "I don't believe that. You can figure it out."

"I can't. Everyone is looking for her. They got close last time, Navin. If they find us with her, we'll be put to death." Dr. Karine's eyes are tired and just slightly afraid of Navin.

"You'll get it," Navin demands. Then as if realizing what Karine is holding, he hesitantly walks toward him and lifts the rags for a second. This seems to make him sick, and he quickly pulls away, going back to the water basin.

Tears fall from my eyes as the wave of memory overtakes me. It is on the edge of return, but not quite there. So much of me wishes that I could remain in the dark and refuse to know anything else. *Stay down. Stay silenced. Stay in the catacombs of my soul.*

Dr. Karine leaves the kitchen and heads toward the back. He walks through a door into the back yard. Several yards behind the home is a hole already dug in the ground and a shovel sticking out from the hard dirt. Carefully he lays the tiny body in the grave and begins to cover it up. After he's done, he walks away, wiping the sweat from his face with his shirt. Instead of following him, I notice the dirt piles beside this one. There are two more and I drop to my knees in front of them. The memories return, breaking the fragile glass barrier I built to keep them inside. Bubbling out from the greatest wound, the rawest place, my cries rise with no barriers. They consume every part of my physical being until my body shakes uncontrollably. Navin tried again and again to be a part of the Prophecy. He stole from me, hoping it would lead to our power together. Instead, he was disappointed by the death of each child.

My body convulses as the tears fall down my nose and into the dirt below where the babies lie.

"Remy!" I hear Arek's panic as he finds us in the backyard. Only moments later, he drops to his knees and lifts my broken body into his arms.

"They all died." There is no fixing, no healing, no magic wand that will now make me forget.

"I'm sorry," he says repeatedly. His strong body absorbs as much as it can, but there is nothing that will easily repair the damage.

Gyre watches without words.

More screaming erupts from the home, and I pull myself away from Arek. He watches me carefully, but the louder the cries become, the more it draws me back. I climb to my feet and run back inside, but it isn't the same.

It has returned to the hell with no windows, only darkness, and the floors break beneath my steps. Creatures manifest from the shadows of every corner and with each turn, I scream and run away from their distorted hands as they reach for me.

"Don't retreat." I hear Gyre in my mind. "You know what happened here. Don't let the nightmare continue. Call it out. Break it down. Burn it. Be free. Your deepest layers are mixing with each other . . . which is dangerous. The second level is your nightmare, and the third is hidden truths. Don't let them become one. It's too hard to know how to fix one versus the other."

The headless beast steps out from the shadows, not human and not animal. The beast is covered in holes all over its skin that pulse with each breath. Teeth emerge from its cheeks and its eyes are just slits in the pale effervescent skin. It hesitates for just a moment, then charges me.

Gyre is suddenly at my side. "Don't move."

The beast has a screech that pierces my ears, and its claws take chunks out of the flooring from the sheer power of its run.

"Don't move. Stop it in its tracks."

The panic sets in. "How?!"

"You know how." Gyre is practically touching my shoulder with their chin as their voice encourages my stance.

"I don't!"

The beast's screech forces me to cover my ears. It is only seconds from hitting me and its body is three times my size.

"Stop it! Find the voice and go deeper. Beneath the Void, beneath all of it, you will find your power!"

But just as I begin to see the air as crystalline, the beast crashes into me, sending me flying across the house. Pain explodes through my body and my bones feel crushed as I hit the wall, causing a body-size indentation. When I slam into the ground, everything stops. The air changes, the sounds of the house disappear, and I'm left sputtering on the ground. I taste blood in my mouth, and I can't catch my breath. I feel hands on me. When I open my eyes, I'm back in the room with the ancient Gyre and I'm lying on my side on the hard floor in the Monastery with my body writhing in pain. Arek and Sassi kneel over me, but the pain is so severe that I roll to my knees, press my head into my hands, and moan. Even though it just feels like my body is broken, when my mind clears, the feeling in my chest reminds me that nothing is worse than the ache of my soul. At this moment, I'm convinced I will not come back from what I have just learned. I groan with the intensity. Tears fall down my nose and come to rest on my tense hands. Arek's hand lands on my back and I feel the instant soothing of his caress. He drops his mouth to my ear. "Breathe. I got you." I moan as my ribs scream. So, he repeats, "I got you."

The old woman comes to our side. "Gyre says we are done today. Take her home. She will need to sleep. Give her this." I do not see what she passes to Arek, but it doesn't matter. I am so grateful for the release and all I want is to crawl into a hole and pretend that none of this ever happened.

CHAPTER TWENTY-EIGHT

I sit alone in the early morning, watching the horses graze from the patio that faces the meadow, backdropped by white-capped mountains. The air is crisp and jacket-worthy, but I didn't want to take the time, so I now sit here shaking. It almost feels good . . . needed, maybe? With a cautious finger, I check my swollen lip from my nasty fall at the end of my time with Gyre. It is nearly healed with just a small scab, but my attention is on it, nonetheless.

"Does it hurt?" Sassi asks.

I turn to find her tall frame covered in the long puff jacket that I wish I had. She also holds a mug with steaming hot coffee that I wish I had. To my delight, she pulls a mug from behind her back and hands it to me. "I figured you might need this."

"You're a life saver, thank you."

With that, she steps down beside me and sits until her hip is touching mine. "I told Arek that I would go today."

I look at her carefully. "What do you mean?"

"I mean, it's my turn tonight with Gyre. We give you a break."

I shake my head while breathing out and cast my eyes back out to the Alps. "Be careful what you ask for."

"Yeah, I figured that's what you would say." She takes my hand in hers, interlacing her fingers with mine. "We never knew, Remy." For the first time, it is as if Sassi can't look at me. "We never knew the lengths to which Navin went . . . they covered your memories so that you couldn't tell us. I'm so sorry, Remy."

I'm surprised to see the tears in her eyes. "Sassi," I whisper.

"No." She stops me. "Kilon and I swore to keep you safe, but we didn't."

"It's not your fault. It's Navin's." Sassi gives me a sideways glance. I say with a grin, "Lots of other people can take blame . . . but not you. Not you."

"It's impossible. I will always feel the guilt because I love you so much," Sassi confides.

"Love me so much that you listen to what I say. We cannot blame ourselves for things that happen outside our control."

Once again, the lynx travels across the white meadow, until she stops, looks up at us, and sniffs the air. "I saw her yesterday," I whisper, hoping she does not run away.

"She's beautiful," Sassi says as she takes a sip of her hot coffee.

The animal sees us and seems to be intrigued by our presence. She takes a few steps toward us even, and when she comes to a stop her head nods. "Did you see that?" I ask Sassi.

Sassi scrunches her forehead together, "I did."

After a minute or so, this beautiful creature slowly turns and runs away—her fur blowing in the wind until you can see her pale skin beneath.

A strong scent of coffee tickles my nose, begging me to take a sip.

"What do we do until Gyre is ready?"

Sassi rubs her perfectly round shaved head. "It's time to train. We need to see what Lya and Daye can do. I mean, after all, for the fact that you are their mom and Arek is their dad, I can only imagine how good they might be."

I turn to her, "Sassi, look at you here apologizing, when I'm the one who should be. We owe you an apology for not telling you sooner about Lya and Daye."

"No." Sassi looks down at her feet as she kicks some dirt around. "No, Kilon and I talked about it. If it had been us, we would have done the same. There is nothing a parent wouldn't do for their child."

Finally, we look at each other, then I place my arm over her shoulders.

Sassi clears her throat to speak, "First, today we go to a special place. A hot springs sits about an hour hike from here. I feel we're supposed to go there this morning."

"You feel that?" I ask as I look at her strong profile.

She gives one deep nod. "I was told."

"By whom?"

She chuckles. "By the divine Power that brought you back to us. Her voice can be loud when I'm listening." Sassi's nose wrinkles as she thinks. "Actually, her voice is loud whether I'm listening or not . . . and we're supposed to go to the hot springs."

An hour later a large group of us begin the trek to this sacred place. Each of us have a pack with a mat, towel, change of clothes, water, and a snack. Several times along the walk my legs burn and my breath increases when the incline steepens to an almost impossible degree. Daye touches my arm gently at one point. When I look at her, I'm shocked by her eyes. They look just like mine. I've noticed Geo watching her for days now. Their quiet conversations in the corner at meals, how he touches her lower back as he walks her to her bedroom at night, and the sweet but shy way they say good morning. At this moment he stands just a few feet away from her as she catches my attention. "You've got a friend." Her slender finger points to my right and just between the trees, I recognize the brown spotted fur of the lynx.

The cat seems to stop when we do and follow quietly out of arm's length as we climb. How Daye knew that it was following me, I'm not sure that I'll ever understand.

Here and there, through the hour, I keep an eye out, wondering if the lynx will follow the entire way, and she does. The weather grows worse the higher we climb, but this only lends a hand to the beauty of this hot spring once we reach it. We are high enough that the clouds part until we see the swirling galaxies. Steam rises from the blue water. It is not small; in fact, it is the size of a pool. The only difference is that it is surrounded by snow-covered ground, with only the trees providing the forest green.

There's an aura here that ignites my skin and warms my chest. Instantly I recognize what Sassi was saying. This spring is different, eerily so. Almost as if the volcanic activity that leads to its heat is less about nature's phenomenon but something grander than that . . . something that encompasses nature, man, space, and everything in between.

"Find your place," Sassi says as she sets her things down. Quietly we all obey and in just minutes we lie on our mats. I've learned enough now to recognize that our quiet spaces are our infinite spaces. I lie in my void, recognizing its perfect circumference around me. I feel the heat from the water on my left and small flakes of snow fall on my exposed skin. After several minutes of silence, my skin starts to rise. It begins with my fingertips and spreads till it touches my entire body.

"Remy," the rich voice whispers. I'm so deep within the Void, that it takes me a moment to recognize it. "Remy," the breathy voice echoes in my head. I open my eyes. The sky is a bluish purple, so pristine and clear that it feels as though I can see even beyond the galaxies. Stars burn and flash within my sight and the grandness of it all takes my breath away. They are the same colors that I saw in New Orleans on the wooden bridge. The air feels thick—not heavy or troublesome—rather thick with energy, alive and vibrant. I sit up and recognize that it isn't just the sky that has turned these colors, but the air around us. Everyone is still there, lying on their mats, their eyes closed. And once again, what is before me is beyond what I can understand. The thick lifeforce that I can feel all the way through to my bones, brings me to my feet when once again, my eyes detect ghostlike movement. I squint my eyes to see better. The best way that it can be described is a busy sidewalk in New York if there were only spirits left on this earth.

"They're always around." I turn to find Holona, once again. "We don't know while we're alive."

"What don't we know, Holona?" I ask her quietly, hoping to not disturb whatever this is that rustles through the air, never needing to obey the laws of this realm.

"We don't know anything beyond ourselves." She turns to me with a weighty grin. "I wish I had known or been able to see what you are seeing. They're fighting for us. They see more than we do. And yet most of us feel so alone all the time."

"The world makes us feel alone. People make us feel that way." I've recognized this for years, and this quite possibly might be the first time I've said it out loud. Everything that still weighs heavily on my soul from my old life to this one flashes in my mind and my shoulders rise. She sees this and gently lays a hand near my neck.

"No, Remy, the world would be free if we recognized more of the light than wading in the dark."

"Holona, you and I both know that what is light to one, is dark to another. We're tossed around, abused, until the world doesn't carry anything that we once thought it could. If we could find the light, I guarantee that we'd follow it till the ends of the earth, but I'm starting to believe it's nearly gone."

She nods, takes a moment, then continues, "They didn't believe me. They didn't want to."

I look at her carefully. "Who? Who do you mean?"

"The men who gathered around as I was tied to the stake. If they believed me, then it would ruin the dogma they'd carried for years, the dogma they'd been taught as children. But I understand . . . if I could prove that I wasn't a witch and that things weren't what they'd convinced themselves to be . . . if they were wrong about just one thing, this would mean that they'd have to second guess everything. They were willing to sacrifice my life in order to protect their rules. They didn't recognize that rules and limitations are a hinderance to God, not the path to him."

"Holona, how does this end? Do you know?"

I'm afraid when she turns to me and her eyes are drowning. Her cheeks rise until the small delicate wrinkles crease at her temples. "No . . . but what I can tell you is this: it is coming. When the last bit of light leaves the earth and there is nothing left but darkness, that is when there will be nothing left to lose and people will claw and beg for an end. Darkness cannot live without light."

She softly walks over to Lya and Daye and stands over them. "She has you and her father in her. And won't back down even in the gravest of situations."

"Who?"

She answers as though she doesn't hear me. "She won't be able to finish what she starts."

"What do you mean, Holona? Who? Lya? Daye?"

I hear a breaking branch behind me and swiftly turn. There, the lynx waits. However, something is different, and I find myself lost in memory. I walk in a field with a lynx—steady and slow. Then another memory and another. Suddenly my heart rips open with all the passion for this animal that I would have if it were mine and connected to me beyond what words can say. When peering back over my shoulder, I see that Holona has gone. The sky is back to darkness and the steam rises over the water as snowflakes fall.

Again, I hear the crunch of snow and when I look back, the lynx has drawn closer. A vision of my hand running down her speckled fur as she sleeps beside me makes me want to close the distance. Her name was once Vi and pronounced just like the letter. There's no way this could be the same animal, but still, she crawls low to get closer.

I'm startled when a hand touches my arm. Arek is standing next to me and staring at the lynx just as I am.

"Could it be her? Vi?" I ask.

Arek has grown accustomed to me remembering things and no longer looks surprised. He shakes his head. "I don't know. But powerful things have surrounded you all your life. Vi was just one . . . they were drawn to you . . . connected to you . . . always. Many of them."

I kneel down and reach out my hand. The lynx backs away at first, but the longer I keep quiet, she slinks toward me making the softest sounds. "Vi?" I whisper. Now everyone is up and watching from a distance. The cat is hesitant, backing away and eyeing me closely. "It's okay, Vi," I say again. Finally, she sniffs my fingers and then presses her cheek against them. Before long, her purr makes me smile and rumbles beneath my touch. Within moments she rolls at my feet, gently kneading her claws in and out of my shin. "Hi." I look up at everyone with a smile. "You're mine now," I whisper to the lynx that crawls on my knee to investigate my face.

"Okay everyone," Sassi says. "I brought you here because of this place. It's been known to share with people. To give them insight, visions, possibly the future. Each of us will go in one at a time. You will submerge yourself all the way and listen for what is told. This could help us in training for Tri Planum."

Peter chuckles. "What if we can't swim?"

Kilon passes by Peter and pushes him easily into the steamy liquid. "You're first, big mouth."

Peter's arms and legs flail as he falls awkwardly, making a big splash in the hot spring as Kilon chuckles. He comes up instantly laughing, but Sassi kneels before him from the side. "Go under and count to ten. What you see, if you see anything . . . it's for you and no one else. You got that?"

Peter grins. "Yeah, I got it."

He sucks in a big breath and submerges until the top of his head is covered. It's growing colder so I wrap my jacket tighter as we all watch on—wondering what this place could possibly tell us. Vi has trotted a few feet away but doesn't go very far, keeping her eyes on me. Peter emerges from the water, wipes his face with his long fingers that have yet to grow their meatiness of age, and then he turns to us with raised eyebrows. "Whoa, that was intense," he says. "I don't know what to do with that information."

"You will." Sassi smiles. "Okay, Kilon, since you felt the urge to push him in, it's your turn now."

Kilon pulls off his jacket and then long sleeve shirt revealing his massive build and I notice as Sassi appreciates him. Finally, he crawls into the water making funny faces along the way. Then, each of us takes a turn. Arek practically dives in, staying under water for longer than twenty seconds. No one says anything about what they see, however you can tell by their faces that some experienced very little and some found it very intense. When it comes to my turn, I step to the edge of the water. There's a rock just under the surface, providing me a natural stair. The water is hot against my skin, feeling good in the middle of the snow-covered mountains. But it's more than that . . . I feel what Sassi says about the special hot spring before I plunge fully. My mind starts to wander, pulled in every direction almost as though the water is playing games to find out about me. With one last look at Arek, I submerge. At first, the warmth of the water feels as thick as melted butter, but the longer I resist coming up, the more it turns from my outer senses to the greater sense within me. At first, I wonder if it will be like visions or the way memories come to me, but instead, it's a feeling like someone is watching me. When I open my eyes under water, it is beautifully clear, and the blue is near turquoise. That's when I hear a voice—one so deep and powerful that I'm sure I've never heard it before. It says, "She will die for all."

"Who?" I think to myself. But in the water just ahead, Lya and Daye are there. I wonder suddenly if I've stayed too long, and they are now letting multiple people in at a time. They are submerged in the water, their hair floating around their faces, bubbles covering their skin and coming from their noses.

Again, the voice breathes out. "It will happen for the greater good."

My eyebrows furrow as I stare at my daughters for a moment longer. Then with a quick push off the earth floor, I pop out of the water. That's when I see Lya and Daye standing on the edge, and now I know. My knees are weak from the thought. *Who? Who will die? Please no.*

Arek wraps a towel around me, covering me from the instant freeze. With his hands on my shoulders, he looks at me carefully, "Are you okay?"

"I don't know," is all that I will say, abiding by Sassi's rules.

Lya emerges from the water in a few minutes, her face solemn, but that's not new. It isn't until Daye comes out from the water crying and screaming that we all panic. "Daye!" Geo yells from the side as he reaches out to help her. She grabs his hands, her face contorting as she cries, and he pulls her out of the water and into his arms. She fills the air with her sobs.

"What happened?" Lya asks.

Sassi clears her throat. "She can't tell you."

"The hell she can't! Why not?" Lya's hair is still wet, and she shivers.

"Because I told you. What you learned is for you, not us. It is not safe for you to know what she does." Sassi comes to Daye's side as Geo holds her closely and kneels. "Daye, what you saw is not definite. It is what can be, not what is."

Daye's cries calm, but it is obvious that whatever she saw down there was more than she expected.

CHAPTER TWENTY-NINE

Hours later, we have all gathered in a great hall off the ruins. Briston, Peter, Diem, and Gal are laying out weapons for us all. Arek, Geo, and Sassi are talking quietly in the corner—more than likely discussing how to teach everyone all at once. Mak, Kenichi, Aita, and Masey are the latest to arrive. Quietly, I sit in the corner of the grand hall, as the lynx sleeps at my side, and I take a moment. Perhaps I'm hiding after what I saw in the hot springs. Perhaps I don't want to face Navin after knowing what he put me through so long ago. It's all jumbled together in my mind. Lya has been concerned for Daye since her time in the mountains, and I watch as she places an arm around her sister.

I want to go to them, to treat them as my daughters, but I don't know how. Instead, I watch them, carefully protecting myself from what I can only assume will be the greatest rejection of my life. Daye has shown her love for me, but Lya still can't accept that I am here and that somehow, I stand in her way.

Finally, Arek calls us all over and we stand on several black mats pulled together for training. "This afternoon is about the fight. No mind wars. Not right now. This is about weapons and our skill. We must be prepared for anything. And we never know what Navin will use against us."

Lya crosses her arms. "Have we figured out Adam and the rest of the Fidelis from San Francisco?"

"Yes," Arek nods. "They are on their way here. Today is extremely important, because tomorrow we have invited as many as we can." Arek looks at me, knowing what we haven't told the others about tomorrow. I can see that he is hesitant, but in my gut I know that it is the right decision. Gather as many people here as possible, teach them what we can, and then be ready to conquer Navin and his followers.

We stand in two lines, facing one opponent. I am with Mak first. Arek is with Kilon. Sassi stands across from Briston, and so on. We will fight our first opponent, then take a step to our left and fight the next until there is no one left. The clock is set to five minutes. Weapons are lined up on the floor of one side of the grand room. SWAT gear rests on tables on the other side of the room. We have a choice to go after the safety gear first or the weapons. As the countdown begins, Mak grins as he bends into fighting position. Aita stands near the door, choosing not to fight. Her red lipstick is all that I can see out of the corner of my eye.

Masey stands on the side with her medical bag in hand.

Three. Two. One. Neither Mak nor I let the other close the distance. We are immersed in hand-to-hand battle in seconds. He does well, better than the last time we fought, but it doesn't last long. I find it hard to stay out of his mind and at one point he shakes his head while I strike again and again.

"Stay out," he tells me with a raised eyebrow.

"Sorry," I say, just as I swipe his ankles, knocking him to the ground and stealing his breath. He tries to scramble to his feet, but I straddle his back, wrapping my arms around his neck, and within seconds I catch him in a bow and arrow choke. This looks exactly how it sounds—he is the bow and I am the arrow. I have wrapped his shirt around his neck with one hand, placed my bent leg against his middle back, and taken his pants with my other hand. I press my shin against his spine, while pulling his neck and leg in the opposite direction until he chokes and taps. He coughs and tries to catch his breath, until the bell sounds and it is time to move on to the next opponent. I put my hand out to help him to his feet and as I do, he shakes his head. "Let's just put you in a room alone with Navin. He won't know what hit him."

He doesn't realize the weight of what he just said and that I have been in many rooms with Navin. Yet Navin doesn't play fair. He uses multiple people and tactics, technology and science. "It hasn't worked so far," I simply state.

"It will," Mak says as he moves to the next spot.

Geo is next and we are a fair fight. Geo's gift is intuition, our spirits, and understanding the connection from this world to the next, but he holds his own in a fight. The five minutes ends without either one of us hitting the ground. His nose is bleeding and my skin is bruised, but that is all. We shake hands and move again.

I fight my father until both of us are blue in the face. He took me down once, and I took him down once.

Sassi had mentioned that we were to watch Lya and Daye in battle. Daye adapts well, but she does not have the drive that Lya does. I notice Lya, her breath is gone and her hair is wild, but it is the determined expression on her face, no matter the opponent, that lets me know she will not stop until she wins.

I find myself going lighter against Daye, but I figure the others will train her just fine. It is when I reach Lya that something shifts in me and in the air. Her eyes are hard and cold toward me even before the bell rings. While I know I am her mother, the look on her face forces something in me to forget nurture, and the competition begins. The bell is loud and instantly she attacks, but I use it to my advantage, and she falls on her back in less than a minute. I say nothing, but neither does she. She doesn't have to because her face tells me everything—she is raging. Hand to hand battle, we are away from the line of people in seconds, slapping, striking, kicking. Angry grunts escape her mouth as she tries harder and harder. It isn't until this moment that I realize how truly good I have become. She is unable to pass or hurt me, which only riles her spirit more. She wants me on the ground. Within the first three minutes, I have taken her down three times and she refuses to let me help her up. With everything she has, she tries to connect, but cannot. I twist around, sending a high kick at her chin and she doesn't see it until she's on the ground. My mother's heart instantly feels bad, but the truth is this . . . she's been training longer than I have in this life. Arek has taught them to protect themselves since they were children, but still she is allowing her rage to get the best of her. Again, she clambers to her feet. We've traveled so far that she can grab a knife and swipe it toward my chest. The tip of the blade slices my shirt and skin at the same time, and I feel the sting. She does not back down and comes at me again and again. The bell rings and everyone stops, shakes hands, and moves spaces. But soon they realize that Lya is not done with me. She comes at me harder and faster, aggressively trying to take me to the ground. Repeatedly I take her feet out from under her, but I cannot stop until she stops.

"Lya!" Arek yells from a distance.

At this point, she sees red and does not hear her father's urging. Finally, I take advantage of the reach of her arm. I grab her flailing wrist, pull it directly to me, and take out her feet. This time I do not let her stand and swiftly straddle her with my legs, then press her wrists to the ground. "Stop!" My voice is commanding and seems to break her out of the madness.

Arek is at our side quickly. "Lya, what are you doing?"

Tears come to her eyes when she realizes everyone is watching. "Get off of me!" she shouts.

When she drops her weapon, I let go of her wrists and step

back. Arek places himself between us, but it doesn't matter when Lya rushes away.

At first Arek stares in her direction, but soon decides better than to go after her. "She needs a minute. Let's give her one," he says as he checks my chest. A long cut just below my clavicle has poured blood down my shirt. He breathes out and shakes his head. "I don't know why," is all that he says.

Kenichi calls us back because we have one more fight before we've fought everyone. Only now, one is left without an opponent, so Kenichi bows out of the fight. Arek is my last and after what just happened, I am tired.

When we stand across from each other, I look him in the eye. He winks just before the bell rings. In only seconds we are deep in battle. It takes him a minute and a half to take me to the ground, but I find that a win. We begin again, and this time I decide to do something just a bit different. Just as he's about to take me down again, I roll with his kick, wrapping my legs around his—he rolls with me. We grapple until the bell rings and, just as it does, we are left on our backs, gasping for breath, our legs still intertwined.

"You're amazing," he whispers to me. A second passes before he finally lets the truth leave his lips as he stares at the ceiling, "I should never have let him touch you. I can't ever let him touch you again." He says this almost as though he is convincing himself.

I reach my hand out and lay it on his chest while keeping my eyes upward as my breath still hasn't calmed. "He won't."

His green eyes are bright behind his flushed skin as he finally rolls over to his hands and knees to stand. He reaches out and helps me to my feet.

"I'm going to go find her," I whisper as we stand together.

"I'll come with you. I know where she is."

CHAPTER THIRTY

I'm surprised when Arek leads us back to our house. I follow him through the hallways, and he opens the door to an empty room. Two French doors that lead to the patio are standing wide open, which is allowing snow to waft in. I place a hand on his arm and when he looks down on me, I connect with his perfect eyes. "Let me."

I walk to the doors and step into the frigid air. My clothes are still sweaty, so the wind pierces my skin. There's a hammock attached between the railing and the house, where Lya lies, her skin wet where she's wiped away the tears.

"Hey." I keep my voice quiet and pleasing.

"Hey." Is all that she says back.

After a few more minutes, when my body and voice shake from the cold, I suck in a large breath and am ready to dig. "I know you have something against me. If I knew what it was, maybe I could fix it."

"You can fix the thirty plus years that you were gone?"

"No, I don't think I can." Lya looks out over the Alps, and I can tell that her guard is down. "Lya, I'm sorry. I'm sorry that I missed your life. I want you to know that I wish everything could have happened differently. I wish I could have been a mother to you."

"Well, you weren't. But it doesn't matter, because we did fine without you."

"I can see that."

After a few moments of silence while the questions still loom within the air, finally, I hear one that I can understand. "Why?" she asks. "Why were you the way that you were? Why, when you knew we were coming into this world, couldn't you just let it be. But you had to dig into everything. Remona Landolin, the hero? Was that what you were trying to do? Ephemes died at the Red Summit . . . so what? It wasn't the first time, and it certainly wasn't going to be the last. You had to personally bring everyone down? Did you ever back away from anything? You knew we were there. You knew we needed you."

The truth was, even with all my memory returning, this was a question that I had asked myself many times. Willow and Remy had mixed, never quite allowing me to return to the driven Remy that I used to be. "I don't know. I can tell that if I was who I am today, I never would have done what I did. Or at least, I don't think I would. My mother had turned on me. A woman who I knew hated me for most of my life . . . the person who should have loved me the most. Maybe that was what drove me to do what I did?"

"Or maybe part of you just felt too important or special to care what would happen to us if you weren't around?"

Her words hurt, but the truth was that I didn't know if that was the answer. It could be. Maybe I did feel above consequence?

"I don't know," I whisper. When I look out to the meadow, the lynx is lying beside the nearest tree, looking up at me. "Or maybe," I turn back to Lya, "maybe you're just like me and you can't stand that."

Lya's eyes shoot directly to mine and she takes an uncomfortable breath.

I continue, "Part of me thinks that you would do the same. And you're trying to convince yourself that the pain you felt from not having me there was my fault, and you would never cause anyone that pain—but maybe that's not the truth. You seek justice more than anyone I know. You want good to win just as I did, and yet sometimes, don't you hate that your mouth gets in the way? Your ego gets in the way, and it pisses you off. You can blame me for every-thing, that's okay, but you only blame me because you're afraid that if you don't, you might have to accept that you're just like me."

"I'm nothing like you," she says pointedly.

Arek suddenly emerges from the room. "I disagree. It's one of the things I love the most about you. After your mother died, I would look at you and be grateful that within every molecule of your perfectly made self—even if you were driving me crazy—was the greatest gift: a woman who knows truth, who will fight for the underdog, and demand justice. But most importantly, she would never dim her light to appease those who disagreed with it. Remy fought to have you. She fought to make sure you would live without the stigma that she did. She made me swear to protect you and to give you the life of freedom that she never had. It's because of her that I knew what to do."

There are tears in her eyes and my heart sinks. It's difficult to know what her emotion means or whether she'll understand my sacrifice. Fear envelops me when I think about the hot springs and the sacrifice I was told one of my daughters might make. If anyone would give her life for the greater cause, it would be Lya.

Suddenly Arek's phone rings and he walks away to take it, leav-ing the two of us silent. After a moment, I hear her restrained voice, but I don't look at her out of fear of what she might say.

"Look, I'm sorry. I've never really thought about it like that. I guess I never knew all that you went through to get me here."

"Lya," my chest rises and falls. "I . . . I'm sorry that I wasn't there for you. I don't remember everything . . . not yet . . . but you know what happened the moment that I saw you? I instantly remembered the love that I had for you. There was never going to be anything greater in my life than you and your sister."

I'm not sure that Lya believes it, but it doesn't matter. It's said. I leave her alone on the porch and walk back inside. Arek is coming back, and I can tell by the look on his face that there is news.

"What?" I ask.

"They've found more people. The Ephemes that were missing . . . a group that I sent out have found more of the camps and more of the dead. Navin's planted them everywhere." He breathes out, then cracks his neck uncomfortably.

"What can we do?" I reach out and touch his rough jaw.

"All we can do is make sure we are at our best, then we go fight."

"You are the strategist."

He cocks his head to the side as if this is too much pressure on his shoulders. "I suppose I am. I just don't see what to do yet."

"You will."

CHAPTER THIRTY-ONE

Once again, we sit before Gyre within the dark room. We have been asked to be still and be led, but after the last time, my body is tense. It helps to know that tonight it will be Sassi's memories. In fact, Gyre insisted that we do more than one, and since Kilon and Sassi are married, it's their turn. I'm fairly certain that when Kilon heard that, if Gyre wasn't the greatest in the world, Kilon might have tried to put Gyre to sleep and run.

Instead, we now sit quietly, waiting for what is next. Waiting to find the deepest parts of Sassi and Kilon. The transition is seamless as I feel the rise in my chest and then in a flash, I see Gyre—healthy and able, once again—walking toward us through a dark hallway. Behind Gyre's head is a clocktower and the moon is sitting to the left of it. It takes a moment to figure out our surroundings, but it's easy to recognize when Sassi and Kilon do. I hear her cascading breath blending with an ache so deep that the earth can feel it.

Sassi and Kilon stare at each other. It's obvious that they believe they've made a mistake.

I know the feeling. To confront what drives us means unbearable pain. *If we return to these moments, it feels like death, but Gyre says it is our path to life. The irony.*

I'm still uncertain that the return to what Navin did has provided me any such release.

"It will," I hear Gyre. "Deep in our souls what we have hidden causes decay, and yet it is only the living that this happens to."

A tear slides down Sassi's cheek. "We're back." Pain adds a depth to her voice that her rich soul can't cover.

"Babe," Kilon whispers, "I can't do this."

Sassi places her hands on his chest. "Kilon," her tone is loving but stern. "Yes, you can. It's not fair to her . . . it's not fair to us, to keep her trapped."

Gyre comes close. "Just because we are here . . . changes nothing. She dies again and again in your unconscious without you ever recognizing it. It shadows every choice you make and everything you do."

Kilon loses himself for a moment as Sassi runs her hand down his back. He bends over to breathe.

While I watch Sassi and Kilon try to defeat their resistance, Arek comes close to me. "Listen, Remy, I don't know how much you remember . . . you're a part of this night more than you know. Just be prepared for whatever we see. I don't know how it rests within them, but Sassi and Kilon's memory might mix what was real and what wasn't."

"Mom!" we hear from a near courtyard that we cannot see.

"Oh my god," Sassi breathes out, then she passes Gyre and runs to the courtyard. A beautiful woman with a long statuesque build, who looks to be a perfect mixture of Kilon and Sassi, is racing through the garden. I know her. I've seen her before as Sassi and I walked through the bayou.

Nayo is out of breath from panic. Soon, the Sassi and Kilon from long ago come from a nearby doorway. The Sassi beside me is holding her heart as she watches the scene.

"Nayo?" Sassi calls out with concern.

"Mom!"

"What's wrong?"

"They're taking her!" Nayo yells. "They're taking her!!!" she screams again.

The real Sassi beside me places her hand to her mouth with tears in her eyes. Then we watch as Nayo runs out of the courtyard, followed by Sassi and Kilon. Rather than follow them, we are pulled by her memory, again falling through the air like Alice in Wonderland, and we land in a chaos of screaming and yelling. How to explain the travel through this moment is much like the beginning; when Navin first tried to steal all my memory and I was in a time warp. My body plunges forward in time and existence, with stars enveloping me and memories passing faster than light. *What is happening?* At first, I can't tell. We are in a dark house that looks to exist in the 1600s or 1700s. Sassi and Kilon begin to run through the halls toward the yelling, so I follow without thought or question. Gyre, younger and preserved, stands within a doorway of this dark home, but says nothing as we pass.

Finally, we reach the main room. The yelling is now understood. Arek is not there, but Sassi, Kilon, and Nayo—as they were on this day in the 1600s—point their swords toward Isaiah Aldo, Japha, and seven other men. Five of them surround the Remy of that time. It looks as though I have been drugged and am nearly unconscious in the arms of one of the men. As I watch myself in second hand, memories zip through so briskly and prickly that I grow exceedingly uncomfortable watching.

"Oh my god," I whisper to myself. "I know this night." Arek nods, his eyes uncomfortable behind flushed cheeks.

"Isaiah! Let her go," Kilon growls. His chest and arms are tense as he holds his weapon. Nayo and Sassi are beside him, until Nayo quietly backs up, trying to be inconspicuous. With soft feet she backs out of the room and only once she's out of eyesight of Aldo's men, then and only then, she runs back through the hallway from which we just came. We follow her as she leads us through a back door and around the corner of the old homestead.

"No, no, no," I hear from Sassi as we watch Nayo within Sassi and Kilon's unconscious. I've had that feeling before, like even though you know what happens, and you've pictured it repeatedly, you are hoping and praying that the outcome changes.

We race around the homestead behind Nayo, until the door bursts open ahead of us. Isaiah and his men come running out. We watch as the Sassi and Kilon from that night have not backed down and give chase until they're outside with them. Muskets and single shot guns explode from each side, but take time to reload. Kilon and Sassi are so strong and so effective that they pass right through several of the men with ease. Yet, as the memory seeps back into my soul, along with the heavy chest and the tense muscles, I turn my eyes to Nayo. She runs straight to Isaiah Aldo. They fight with knives, slicing the air this way and that. She catches him across his neck, but not deep enough to stop him. He yells and jumps back. The man is now angrier than before. Two of his men carry my drugged body away as the fighting continues.

Nayo grows angrier and works harder against Isaiah—she grunts and yells with rage. Aldo is nearly losing the fight. In a slick move, she manages to get him off balance and he falls to the ground. She swiftly steps on his neck.

"Let her go! Tell them to let her go," Nayo warns him. Aldo chokes as she presses her foot harder. "You have one more chance, Isaiah. Let. Her. Go."

It seems that Isaiah is just about to relent, but then something changes on Nayo's face. It's difficult to understand what just happened. Sassi yells from the depths of her soul—a cry only exclaimed by mothers. *"Naaaaayyyooooooo!"*

One of Isaiah's men has thrown a dagger. It lands directly in Nayo's chest. She falls to the ground in panic and pain. "Ahhh!!!" she screams as she finds it hard to crawl backward.

"Nayo!" Kilon yells as he battles two men.

Sassi doesn't have time to run to her before another one of the men attacks Sassi, knocking her to the ground. Isaiah makes his way onto his feet and stands over her. She tries to kick him away, but the pain is too much, and the dagger has paralyzed her left side. Isaiah drops to his knees, one at a time, and pulls a knife from his belt. He grabs her hair and yanks her head back. She fights as much as she can, but her body is no longer obeying any of her commands.

"Nayo!!!!" I hear from somewhere in the distance.

Remy, as I was that night, has woken and I pull against my captors. Isaiah does not take much time or care and he runs the knife along her neck.

"*Nooooooo!!!!!!!!!*" Sassi cries. There is no sound like that of a mother losing a child. Those screams cover the earth with poison. Nayo coughs with wide eyes, and then Isaiah finishes her with a knife behind her ear.

The man who had me that night places a cloth over my nose and mouth, and I watch as I fall under its spell once again. Kilon's deep voice fills the air in an enraged yell. Then he flies toward the men. Isaiah sees that he's woken a mother and father's pain as they strike and attack, trying to reach him. Everyone in their path is falling. Isaiah runs toward the men who have thrown me in a carriage and he jumps inside. Kilon can get close enough just to touch it for a second, but the carriage races away.

Sassi already has her daughter in her arms. She rocks back and forth, letting strangled sobs out, and when Kilon reaches her side he drops beside her, taking his wife and daughter in his arms. It is all too clear now why Kilon raced after Isaiah in the courthouse.

I've not realized that I've been holding my breath.

"How does this help us?" Sassi begs from beside Gyre. "Watching this again. I can't!"

Gyre turns to her and lays a hand on her arm. "Open your eyes." She looks up as tears fall down her cheeks. "I did not create this for you to relive. We rode your unconscious . . . It was already there."

Sassi looks at Kilon. "I thought I'd done well."

Kilon nods with tears in his eyes.

Gyre speaks up again, "Her memory will never leave you and that is okay. But it is the decay of your spirit, the lies we tell ourselves, or the humanity it steals from us that is the problem. We do not wish your daughter to go away, she is just fine. It is you that we wish to help live infinitely better. With this here you can be easily manipulated."

"What do we do?"

Gyre raises a hand, and I can feel the pressure in my chest as my body rises. Then we fall again, riding the darkness full of stars as time passes too fast to comprehend. I land on my feet with knees fully bent but hear yelling before I straighten myself. Arek lands beside me and we look at each other with concerned eyes since we are alone.

"Kilon!" Arek yells. Together we run through a jungle, missing large branches by ducking and weaving. There is a fog of particles in the air floating past my face that is too light and thin to wipe away.

"What is this?" I call to Arek.

"Don't know," he answers, as he cuts a branch out of his way.

We follow Kilon's yelling until Arek slides to a stop, leaving him teeter-tottering over the edge of a large cliff that falls nearly two hundred feet below us. Kilon stands at the edge of this cliff yelling, "Sassi!" This directs our eyes below. Sassi is stuck on a small ledge on the side of the cliff that is so small her toes hang over the edge.

"Sassi!" Kilon yells again.

Sassi is struggling and turns to him with fear in her eyes. Gyre appears from the rainforest, but says nothing. When Kilon sees him, he's angry. "What are you doing?"

Gyre shakes his head, only making Kilon angrier.

"What are you doing? Get us out of here. I'm done!" He tenses all his muscles and lets out a large uncontrolled raging growl. "No more!"

"Kilon!" Sassi calls to him. "Stop it! Look at me. We don't have to be here. Change it! Let's change it!"

I step forward when I remember this place. The air becomes so thick with these white floating specks that I lift my hand in front of my eyes to look closer. They land and stick in my eyelashes, until I blink to get them to fall. Kilon begins to try and crawl down to Sassi, but Sassi yells at him to stop.

"This can't hold us both! You know what you have to do, baby," Sassi calls out.

"This is . . ." He growls and paces on the edge. "I can't . . . no . . . nah . . . this is just . . ."

Just below her feet, the cliff starts to crumble. I watch as the pebbles hit the mountain all the way down until I can no longer see them. Sassi screams. "Kilon!"

Suddenly the wind picks up and the air is now so full of these gray specks that we can barely see one another. Sassi is also surrounded by these floating pieces.

"Do you remember?" Gyre says, walking closer to Kilon.

Kilon's tear-filled eyes watch the thick air. It finally sinks in. "We left her ashes here."

Gyre nods.

Kilon raises his hand in the air and catches a handful of dust.

"Losing one," Gyre says calmly, "does not mean the other must also be lost."

Kilon looks at him carefully, then back to Sassi. "Babe, I got you."

Sassi nods. "I know you do." Once again more of the ledge crumbles away until her fingernails claw at the wall behind her but to no avail.

Kilon is doing everything he can to calm himself; pacing, breathing, and, ultimately, he is lost.

"You can either be sidetracked by what you have lost, or preserve what you have," Gyre says again. "Only you, Kilon, can accept the particles falling on your skin, your hair, your clothes . . . Nayo is everywhere, in all moments." Kilon looks around, studying the mountain he stands upon. More of the ground breaks away and Sassi screams. "I got you!" Kilon yells. All of us know the danger of dying within these levels and what it can possibly mean in our conscious. Kilon closes his eyes and when he opens them, there's a fraying rope beside him. Swiftly he begins to send it down. "Grab this!" Kilon yells.

It reaches her, but her hands are clinging so desperately that it's difficult for her to let go. Without much thought Kilon tries to use several vines protruding from the mountain in order to climb down to her, but one of the vines breaks and he nearly falls himself.

"Kilon!" Arek yells and rushes over, but Gyre places a hand up, telling Arek to stop. "Sassi grab the rope!" Kilon yells. She groans and growls as her footing falls away until just her toes are left holding on. Just as the last of it falls, all of us let out a cry and I close my eyes. When I open them again, Sassi has grabbed the rope. Kilon is grunting as his body slides on the ground toward the edge of the cliff and he clasps the fraying cord. "Ahhh!" He yells.

"Hold it!" Arek yells. "I'll help!"

"No." Gyre warns.

"No!" Kilon responds between growls. *"Ahhh!"* He cries out from the pain in his muscles. Through clenched teeth he speaks to Gyre, "If this is our memory . . . I can change it! If this is our subconscious, it never happened!"

Gyre nods.

"Mevu ti longyv nalu! Mevu ti longyv nalu!" Under his breath, he chants this again and again as he pulls the rope. It means *"I release its hold over me."* He closes his eyes and before long his muscles don't have to work so hard. One foot at a time he slides back until Sassi gets higher and higher. Finally, she reaches over the edge with bloody fingers. Kilon pulls her up and over until they drop on the hard dirt together as the particles continue to fly through the air. After a few moments, I feel my chest rise, then the ground falls out from under

me. We land in Sassi and Kilon's cabin. For the first time, I smile. Kilon is bending over Sassi, who sits on a rocker next to the fire. This cabin is old, and they wear clothing from long ago, but there is no covering up Sassi's belly. She is pregnant and glows from deep within. Suddenly it isn't so hard to breathe. The way they look at each other, young and happy. Excited about what the future holds. The weight of this world no longer resides on their faces in this memory.

Then we return to now—this moment, kneeling in front of Gyre, the old ambiguous being. The smell of earth and dust fills my nose. And there is a chill to the stone room. Sassi and Kilon look as though they've been through war and I understand. I was there just yesterday.

Gyre points a finger toward them while speaking in their high-pitched, hoarse voice. "The pain haunts until we are blind."

"Are we fixed?" Kilon asks.

Gyre's eyes close. "Fixed is not as essential as being awake."

Kilon rolls his eyes, but Sassi elbows him. She wipes the tears from her face, then quietly and gracefully she leaves without a word. It isn't until Arek and I make the trek back that we hear her cry from somewhere we cannot see.

CHAPTER THIRTY-TWO

In my dream, I take a step, but fall through the ground and keep falling. Darkness surrounds me as my hair flies up and around my face. My stomach hovers in the air, tickling every inch of my insides. There is nothing to stop me from crashing into whatever is below me. I blink and instantly I wake up on a bed. My face is pressed in the sheets and the room is dark.

"Remy." I hear his voice and turn to see Arek lying beside me. He reaches out a hand and runs the back of his fingers down my cheek. He kisses me and as he does, I run my hand down his hair and feel the way his skin warms mine. After a while, it changes and his skin grows cold. When my eyes open, it is Navin kissing me, the weight of his body is holding me down. I yank myself away, but he holds on and smiles. Every time I push away, he keeps me close until I try to yell, and nothing will come out.

"I don't think so." His voice is raspy and evil. It reminds me of those first moments when I saw Navin and his stone-like eyes in San Francisco. I didn't know then what would become of this. I didn't understand who he was to me.

I slap him hard and yell again, but this time my voice is met with a calmer one. "Remy."

My heart jolts awake and I'm grateful to realize that it was all a dream. I hadn't Traveled, and I wasn't experiencing anything but a nightmare.

"It's okay," Arek says as he pulls me closer. The glass ceiling is dusted with snow and the air is crisp. Arek's skin warms me immediately as I sink deep within his arms.

"Did I know what happened to me?" I whisper. "Did you know what Navin did?"

He takes a moment before speaking and I'm convinced we both need the moment before he answers. "We knew something had happened . . . your body knew . . . but you didn't know what. I didn't know . . ." he doesn't finish.

"Our babies lived," is all that I can think to say.

I look up into his eyes as he looks into mine. He drops his forehead to press it against mine. "They did, but you didn't."

With this admission, I am reminded that no matter the pain that I have gone through, Arek lived his own. I run my hand up his jaw and cup his head in my hands. I lift my lips to his forehead and kiss him. "Navin has taken so much from us."

"But he couldn't have the one thing he wanted . . . you and your babies. I got those." He grins.

"I love you, Arek." A small tear escapes the corner of my eye.

He sees it and rolls over until his face is over mine. "Don't cry, baby. This is going to end . . . I promise you."

CHAPTER THIRTY-THREE

My jacket is thick as I hike the trail. I'm not supposed to be alone, but I just need a minute. One moment by myself in order to take stock of what is ahead. My cheeks and nose are especially cold as each step I take brings me higher and the view expands beyond what my eyes are capable of seeing. I am convinced as the land sweeps and the small snowflakes begin to flurry that there is nothing more beautiful than this space in the world. I can only imagine what horrors are happening out there. Although we must, it takes every bit of our strength to turn on the news: killings on every street corner, explosions in busy buildings. Now it isn't just the Velieri hiding, it's everyone. With my last step as I just reach the clearing, I breathe in the pine and the clean air.

The prisoners are still chained, the camps are still there. What lies ahead seems too much. We need to save them, find Navin, figure out how to bring him to justice, and then do our best to recover what the world used to be. So many are dying.

Unexpectedly, I hear a clearing of the throat behind me. When I turn around, Beck is there. "Beck! When did you get here?"

"I told you I'd join you all. Everyone was still asleep and I saw you sneak out of the house. It's been a long time since I've been here in Switzerland," he says as he looks out over the beautiful scape. "I found some things for you."

"For me?"

He shakes his head, "No, for all of you . . . for all of us." With steady hands, he sets a backpack on the ground and pulls his phone. "Here." He comes closer to let me see. "Here, I have found years of Navin's computer system history. It's phenomenal. This man has been using the internet since it began. That's how long he's been working under the radar to do what he's done. But Remy, I found something important. Look at this." He swipes left and a new screen pops up. It is a map and there are dots covering several places. "Here are his camps. For every dot, you should find the prisoners."

"Beck, this is huge! How did you do that?"

His grin says enough, but instead he shrugs, "I told you. I'm the best. I guarantee that Navin thought of me when he told his Black Hats to be safe. But I have my ways. His men are good, I can tell you that, but I'm better."

"Do we know where Navin is? Where he spends most of his time?"

Beck gets smug. "Look what I've done . . ." Again, he moves to a different screen. "It's been one week since you saw me. I broke into all security cameras around each of these places. It took me a minute, but I soon found Navin going in and out of this camp. But a day later, he was at this camp. He stayed there two days, then a day later he was at another camp. The man doesn't want to sit still, and with Arek after him, I don't blame him. Not at all."

"That's why it's hard to find him."

"Well, and the question is this . . . once you do find him, are you ready? He has an army, do you?"

Our eyes meet. I step toward the edge of the mountain to take a second to think, and look out over the gorgeous view. "Not yet. But

Beck," I turn to him, "we will. I need you to find someone for me. In fact, several people. Will you do that?"

"Of course, but just one more thing. Those prisoners who are still alive . . . well, I found a computer system for several of these camps, and something is to happen in a few days."

"What do you mean? Do you know what?"

"There is a timer. These camps are all part of one trigger."

"What does that mean?"

"It means, he plans on killing them all. Just as he and Japha did at the Red Summit. Just like the atrocities they've committed over centuries."

"Can you stop the trigger?"

"Yes, but first, he will be prepared, and all his Black Hats will know. You never rely on the computer system alone. They will have a backup plan, just in case Navin assumed you might hire me."

"You're that confident?"

"Yes, I am. You have several things to look at here, Remy. Navin has years of planning under his belt . . . he has Black Hats, Doctor Karine, and many of our most decorated Prophets and Powers. The only way to win is to stop running and attack him directly. With me, we can do it. We just have to be ready."

CHAPTER THIRTY-FOUR

Within two days, more people have started to arrive. Adam and Commander Wakefield drive in with a convoy. The reunion is blissful between us all, but especially between Adam and Lya. Watching Lya drop her guard for this frumpy but kind man is something to appreciate.

Sometime later, while I am training with Kilon outside, sweaty and worked, the sound of more vehicles coming down the private road lifts my eyes. My mouth raises into a grin as familiar faces smile back at me—one specifically that I hoped to see again.

Jay, the Ephemeral doctor who saved me just months before with his fancy cars, hangs his hand out the window in a wave. Our eyes meet and it is like lost friends. "Jay!" I holler as he comes to a stop. His wife, Patti, sits in the front seat, while behind them a procession of cars wraps along the road for miles.

Kilon walks up behind me and obviously remembers him. "How'd he find us?"

"I asked Beck for a little favor . . . it's time we bring in a little flavor to our group."

"And Ephemes are going to give us that?"

"You'd better believe these will."

I run up to the car once it stops and as Jay steps out, we embrace each other as old friends. "Beck found you! I knew he could."

"He did. He called me yesterday morning. So, I rounded up the Panel Beaters and here we are."

"All of you!" I say in a fit of laughter.

"Yeah, well, when all the madness started, I seemed to be the only one with the proper information. We lost a few of us but let me tell ya . . . old men with their cars are the most dangerous of them all. There's nearly five hundred of us."

"Five hundred?!"

"Not the cars. Just forty cars, but five hundred men. It's tough to break some of these guys away from their cars, but some of them are wealthy. One of 'em was able to get us a carrier, assuming you might need our transportation after everything that just happened."

Kilon shakes Jay's hand and just about that time, Arek, Briston, Peter, and Sassi emerge from the house. Pontiacs, Camaros, Barracudas, Mustangs, Firebirds, El Caminos, GTOs, Chevelles . . . the list could go on . . . are lined up with their engines rumbling.

After Arek says hello, Jay asks, "I'm sure we'll need to hide them for now. Is there a plan for that?"

Arek turns to Peter. "All right, Peter, I need these cars parked within the crater."

"The one a few miles from here?" Peter asks.

"Yeah, that's the one."

Peter's face brightens up. Arek is trusting his brother for this job. It is obvious in his eyes that he is grateful. Just the day before, his girlfriend and her family came into town. So now he is moving up in the ranks and in love.

Immediately Peter runs to a few of the first cars, giving them instructions, yet Jay lifts his radio up to Peter. "Have at it. They'll do whatever you tell them to."

Peter smiles as he takes the radio, then provides details. He soon leads the motorcade of cars toward a safer destination.

Jay stays with us, "I knew meeting you would someday come in handy."

I grin. "I can't guarantee that's true, Jay. But it's good to see you."

Patti, his wife, comes to his side. "Welcome, Patti. Let me show you around." I give them a tour through the house, then once we wander outside, their eyes widen as they notice the miles of large tents across the land. Rows of people are lined up and training under Atum's watchful eye.

Jay shakes his head and looks at me. "You've been busy."

"We have." There is something in Jay and Patti's faces that tell me it was not an easy choice to come here. "Have you been okay?"

It takes nothing more than my concern before Patti begins to cry, and she excuses herself. Instantly Sassi offers her some tea and they disappear within the house.

"I've never seen anything like it," Jay begins. "Our neighborhood alone, a quiet and friendly place, turned into something I didn't recognize, overnight. We were sleeping—everyone knows we're doctors and we work from home. Wounded were being delivered to us every few minutes. Friends, family, strangers were all the same . . . attacked in the middle of the night by something nobody understands. I started to gather those I knew would want to know . . . people I knew could handle the truth. We met in our large auditorium where we keep our cars and work on them. I told them how I met you and what you said to me. Then, when you had Beck contact us— I asked everyone what they wanted to do. And you know what they said?"

"What'd they say?"

"They said . . . no one should have to hide who they are. No one. And they wished to fight to make sure that happens. Before we knew it, we were on the carrier boat heading to Switzerland."

I rest a hand on his shoulder. "Well, you rescued me, Jay. The least we can do is keep you safe . . . for now."

"They killed my niece and her husband. It's now my fight."

"I'm so sorry." After a moment of hesitation, I touch his shoulder. "Welcome to training."

As the nearly five hundred Panel Beaters make their way back onto the property, a strange thing happens. Our large group of Velieri, who have been drilling all afternoon, stop and turn to the new men and women.

The Ephemes walk slowly as they see our groups with weapons and glistening skin in the cold air. Everyone is tense. The Ephemes and Velieri working together?

To most of Jay's group, we are a brand-new idea that most likely hasn't sunk in yet. They are hesitant. Especially when the Velieri do nothing to alleviate their concerns; rather, they eye one another like two sides of a battlefield. But this is just a meadow, and we are all victims here.

"Listen to me!" Jay bellows from between the two dueling sides. He climbs onto a nearby rock wall so that he can be seen by them all. He first addresses his own people, "I know that many of us saw things and experienced loss beyond what we could ever have imagined. The last few days have been intense for us all. But it's those things that brought us here. Those things made us decide it couldn't just be us against them." He turns to the Velieri, "We know who you are . . . and we don't care. We see your power, we see what you can do that we can't, and we don't care."

Arek steps up beside him and sets a hand on his shoulder. "You are all welcome here. And it's important that we work together. It's the only way. We have one common enemy . . . The GENOS. They stand for neither the Velieri or Ephemes. We welcome you here and in fact thank you for being willing to come. Some of us have gathered sleeping bags, blankets, pillows, food, and many more things from the surrounding areas. There is a place for everyone here."

For just a moment longer the two sides wait carefully, wondering who will be the first to break the barrier. Finally, a woman on the Epheme side and a woman on the Velieri side step toward each other with their hands out. Instantly the line breaks. The two groups weave together, in and out, shaking hands, hugging strangers, and dropping pretense. Jay and I share a smile.

For three days, people arrive. Beck can connect with groups from all over the world. Hok and the Brazilian Fidelis, the New Zealand Fidelis, and every other Fidelis with tents on their backs hike onto the property.

Arek turns to Briston with concern as we meet within the kitchen of the main house. "I need you to pull in every favor you can," Arek pleads with my father. "We need equipment. Helicopters, drones, weapons, a constant air guard so that we aren't just sitting ducks."

Briston smiles a mischievous smile. "Already done."

"What?" Sassi asks.

"As our group started to build, I contacted Colonel Mitt. He's ready to fight this and he agreed emphatically to give us anything we need. We are now within a no-fly zone and the colonel and Beck are working together to broaden that."

Arek shakes his head. "I should have known you'd already have it covered."

There are newcomers every day. As people gather, Arek has naturally become the leader. He flourishes in this, and I watch him from afar as he manages to build soldiers from both Ephemes and Velieri. While I grab water when I'm out of breath from training, I look across the meadow as two helicopters hover slowly over for protection, and all I can see for a mile are rows of people training. Each section of new and old soldiers are being led by the best. Lya, Daye, Sassi, Kilon, Arek, Mak, Diem, Gal, and even Peter have their own army that they stand before. For the first time since the uprising began, I wonder about hope. *Do I feel it? Today I do, but will I tomorrow? If I find that Navin has ten thousand to our two, will I still feel the same?*

Suddenly I hear my name from the porch above me. Beck leans

over, his eyes showing a clear concern, and with his forefinger he calls me up to him. Beck refuses to join the crowds. He stays locked in our office and I bring him coffee throughout the day. In moments, I'm standing over him as he sits in front of his computer.

"What's going on?"

"You know that timer I told you about?"

"Yeah."

Beck swivels his chair and turns to me with a big sigh. The look in his eyes already tells me that I don't want to know what he has to say. "What?"

"I've found a connection to the Cellar's security system."

I furrow my eyebrows and think for a moment before I speak. "What does that mean?"

"When that timer goes off, it will shut down the security system within the walls of the Cellars. No more locks . . . nothing. What happens when you give the devil the key?"

"How long do we have?"

"Not long enough."

CHAPTER THIRTY-FIVE

Everywhere I go, Vi, the lynx is always just a few steps away. While she never gets too close when anyone else is near, when I am alone, she lies by my side. Sometimes even close enough that I can rest my hand on her back.

The days are long. While some have been chosen to watch the news to inform us of the chaos happening outside these property lines, others have been chosen to train. "Don't think about anything else. Your mind and body have to be at their best," Arek tells everyone.

Time and again I check on Beck, his eyes red from staring at the screens, his hair a mess. But the further he gets, the prouder he becomes. "He's got nothing on me," Beck said last night.

Meanwhile, every dusk Gyre continues to take us within.

Again and again, I revisit the house where Navin, Japha, and Isaiah kept me; where they continued to torture me, forcing me to bury babies. Sassi and Kilon cannot seem to release Nayo, and Arek continues to battle those white stone walls where the water sweeps him away. Geo finds himself revisiting those moments of Beckah's death repeatedly. Daye often leads Geo away with a hand on his back after he's struggled to make it through a session.

The truth? You never feel adequate or capable enough. How do we counteract all these years of Navin's preparations? The killing, the hatred, the lies.

Now, we have a timer . . . a countdown that continues to squeeze tighter around us until we are suffocating.

One night as Arek and I watch the stars through our glass ceiling, an idea comes to him. He rolls over and runs his hand down my cheek. "We're afraid and in constant defense. Remember in Tri Planum . . . once we were the aggressors, everything changed."

"Okay. What do we do?"

"We make things happen on our terms."

"How do we do that?"

"We do what Sassi says. We talk to the person who knows him best. The one who has nothing to lose and everything to gain from helping us. The one who feels abandoned by my brother."

"Who?"

"Lyneva."

I sit up in the bed within the dark room.

He continues, "He raised her. She knows everything about him."

"What if she won't tell us anything?"

Arek takes a moment to run his fingertips up and down my leg, and my skin lights up. "She will."

"We don't know who to trust within the Cellar."

Arek grins. "I'll send Gal and Diem to get her. She's here in the Switzerland Cellar . . . and they can have her here tomorrow."

ᴠᴧᴠ

By midday, a large, guarded van pulls into the drive. We meet it with apprehension, especially Briston. His hands have been sweaty all morning and I wrap my arm around him. Elizabeth has chosen to stay inside. When the van door swings open, Lyneva is sitting on the middle row, her hair messy, her eyes red and tired. I've seen this before. She's haunted. Withering away from who she was with Navin. Her wrists and ankles are clasped with chains and she's wearing a gray jumpsuit that I recognize. Having gone through it myself, it is difficult not to feel sorry for her.

The guards help her weary body step out, then they walk her inside. Arek, Briston, Geo, Kenichi, Mak, Beck, and I follow. "Let her sit," Briston says to the guards. She shuffles to the couch, and I can see that her eyes have fallen on the painting that I first noticed. The one Arek gave me for our anniversary when my first memory of my mother came back to me. Repeatedly I remind myself that she isn't Velieri anymore, rather still Epheme.

She looks small and broken. It's difficult to not forget how she begged Navin to kill me. Or how much she hated me and the Prophecy over my life. My hesitant voice wavers, "How are you?"

She looks up without an ounce of aggression. "Fine."

If we get her on our side, she might tell us what we need to know. "Can I get you something to drink? Tea?" I ask.

Her voice is childlike and reserved . . . fearful almost. "Tea would be nice. Thank you."

They speak with the guards while I rumble about in the kitchen, telling them that we will be okay with her alone. Once they leave, I hand her the hot tea in a mug and for the first time I recognize gratefulness in her.

"Are you okay in there?" I ask as we all sit down around her.

"I'm fine, thank you."

Briston begins. "Lyneva, we need your help and I'm willing to offer you something to get it."

"I don't know where Navin is. He hasn't come to get me . . . like he said he would." It's hard to notice whether her eyes are near tears, or if it is just the weight of the Unyielded within them.

"How many of these camps did he create?" Briston throws a

couple of pictures on the table in front of her as she sips her tea.

"You found the camps?" she whispers as she studies the pictures.

Beck speaks up, "Not all of them, mate. I've found twelve. All within Bryers."

She nods.

"How many more are there?" Beck asks.

"I don't know." No one believes her and she can sense this. "I'm telling you; I don't know."

"Tell us what you do know," Briston requests kindly.

She breathes out and shuts her eyes for a moment. "There were fourteen when I was last with him. But the more people he took, the more he needed, so there could be more."

Everyone looks around carefully. Mak speaks to Beck first, "There are nineteen Bryers around the world. I guess we can just assume that he will eventually take them all."

Lyneva speaks up, "Once the uprising started, there was no need to take more prisoners. Those prisoners are only there for one reason."

I sit farther on the edge of the chair, "What reason is that, Lyneva?"

She takes three long sips and looks out the window before she responds. Then finally, as though she's figured out there is no escape, she turns back. "He knew you would never let them die without a fight. He wanted to draw you in."

"Me?"

"Yes. He's expecting you to find them and try to save them."

"And if we don't?" Arek asks.

"Then they die and everyone in the Cellars go free. And that means he has ruthless killers that hate you. They all hate you." For the first time I see a change in her eyes from victim to momentary anger.

"Lyneva . . . do you hate me?"

There is a long silence. "I did. But not anymore. I suppose I wanted what you had . . . power, love . . . and yet here I am. Without any of that."

"Do you remember your life as my mother?"

"No. Not much."

Strangely, in my chest, I feel that she is lying. For the first time I understand what Arek has been saying about Ephemes never able to lie to Velieri. It's true—the prickly sensation in my chest has told me. When I look up at Arek, I can see that he feels the same.

Geo takes front and center with his arms crossed. "Lyneva, what do you know about his weaknesses? What has he told you?"

"His weaknesses?"

Geo steps even closer. "Yeah. We need something to use against him and we know you have it."

"I don't know."

"Do you want to go back to the Cellar?"

Lyneva's eyes change, and her chest rises and falls with fear. "No."

"Then I'd suggest you help us. I need to know what this man fears. What has he gone through that we can use."

"Oh . . . I get it. You're talking about Tri Planum."

"You know about it?"

"That's why Dr. Karine is there. He's trying to teach him how to do it. But it wasn't working. Navin's been unable to do it without help. He uses tricks . . . ways to force your brain and body to ummmm . . . to fail you. Extreme cold, flashes of light, pain, and so much more. It allows Navin to be able to do Tri Planum by weakening his opponent. But he couldn't do it without all of that," Lyneva explains.

"Lyneva," Briston continues. "We need to know how to get in."

"His mother's death was huge for him. But we all know his biggest weakness." She looks down, but after a moment looks up at me.

The rest of the group understands and takes a glance toward me.

"Do you know about my Traveling?" I ask.

"I overheard them talking about it once. They planted something in your memory . . . when you were a little girl. Do you remember when I would take you to see Japha?"

"I do."

Geo shakes his head. "We need more than that. What did they use against her?"

"I don't remember."

"That's not true," Geo growls.

"I don't remember."

Geo rushes toward her, pointing his finger in her face. "Every time you lie, we know. Try it again, I dare you!"

"I don't remember!" she cries.

Briston comes in with his calm nature. "Do you want your freedom?"

"You know I do."

"Then you tell us what you know. We will know if you are lying."

She sees the serious looks on each of our faces. "There was some way that he hypnotized you as a child. Just think of your memories with Japha. Something is there that doesn't belong. Could be symbolic, but it could be physical. He's haunted you, hasn't he? You've dreamed of him all your life . . . even as an Epheme."

"Yes. I've seen him all my life, even after death."

I can picture his white hair and arthritic fingers.

"Gyre," Geo says to me. "We'll ask Gyre to retrieve it."

I won't admit that I've had enough of Gyre.

"Listen to me. I do not work for Navin anymore. I do not give him my loyalty. I want this to end just as much as you . . . please. Please, free me from the Cellar," Lyneva begs as tears come to her eyes. "If you want to get him: Holona and you. That is all. While I don't believe Navin can truly ever love anyone but himself . . . the closest he came are you two. That is the truth."

"What about his wife?" I ask.

Lyneva stares at me. "Her love still would not replace the importance of his love for you. You had power. You had gifts."

"Thank you, Lyneva. If we need anything else, we will ask,"

Briston says kindly.

The guards walk back in and suddenly panic fills her body. "One night out of the Cellar? You can keep me chained. Whatever needs to happen . . . just please . . . give me one night. Let me stay."

"No, absolutely not," Mak and Arek agree, surprisingly. Although I can tell that Briston and Kenichi are swayed.

"Please. Remy, you understand . . . I know you do."

Her pleading pulls at my heart.

"Remy, please. One night away from there."

"Okay. One night, but the guards will stay with you. You are to stay in the room and that is all. Tomorrow morning you will go back, but I will speak with the Powers to give you leniency," I tell her.

The men look at me with wide eyes, but I ignore it.

"Are the Powers still in place with the uprising?" she asks.

"Most of them were able to get into hiding in time, but we lost a few," Briston tells her.

"I can't believe his plan worked," she whispers.

Geo looks her over with suspicion. "What do you know about the plan?"

She looks up in fear. "Only what he told me. He has the best of the best hackers."

Beck pipes up, "Whoa, whoa, whoa, easy now. The 'best' is over-zealous, don't you think?"

"Well, I don't see that anyone was able to stop him," Lyneva says to Beck.

Beck glares at her before he says, "That's because they didn't call me."

Lyneva nods, "Well then, good luck."

The night falls quickly and only after we have checked on all our leaders do we feel comfortable enough to sleep. Nights have become shorter and shorter as Arek is constantly working with Beck to find Navin. This night I fall asleep without Arek and at nearly dawn I wake to find he's still not there. It's quiet through the house, but something doesn't feel right. I sit up as the sun is starting to rise.

My skin tells me that someone is nearby. My hair rises on the back of my neck.

"Who's there?"

Someone jumps out from the shadows and wraps a wire around my neck, pulling it tight in seconds before I can even get my fingers in. Instantly my windpipe is squeezed, and the darkness starts to overtake me. I can't breathe and I throw myself back. They hold on until my skin starts to rip beneath the wire. The only sound I can hear is that of the wheezing through my larynx. My eyes pulse beneath the pressure of my trapped air. It is impossible to even cry out for help or fight.

Just as my arms are losing the ability to flail and my sight is disintegrating, I hear the door open and Arek yells from across the room. Finally, I fall to the floor and the wire loosens. I gasp for breath and for a moment lie on the ground desperate to recover. When I look over my shoulder, Arek is crawling toward me, but there is no one else there.

"Who was it?" My voice is still strangled.

"Lyneva." He kneels over me and wrestles the last bit of the wire from my neck. "Are you okay?"

"Lyneva?" I sit up swiftly. "Where is she?" I look down and see that he's bleeding beneath his shirt. "What happened?"

"She got away. But she won't get far."

Together we jump to our feet and run out. Sassi, Kilon, and Beck have already heard the commotion and come to help.

"Where'd she go?" I ask.

"She's out there, running!" Kilon catches a glimpse of her and gives chase. We all follow, sprinting outside in the melting snow without jackets. I grab my boots and throw them on to trek through the ice.

Across the meadow, then up the mountain and through the trees we follow. Her head start gives her time, but Kilon is fast and catching up quickly. We weave through the pines, getting hit by wet branches so hard that it stings, until I hear Kilon yell. "Stop!"

Finally, I reach the very top after Kilon and Arek. They're frozen. Just ahead, Lyneva is backing away. The edge of the mountain is not far behind her, which is why it makes my heart lurch when she takes steps backward.

"Stop, Lyneva," Kilon says gently. "We're going to try and help you."

Lyneva shakes her head as tears fall. "No one can help me. They've attached to me . . . they're haunting me. That place has stolen so much."

Beck and I are the only ones who know what she's saying. Both of us step toward her but must stop when she threatens to jump off the cliff if we make any more movement.

"There's a way . . . I did it," I tell her. "We'll get you out of there."

"It won't help." Her fearful eyes look over the ledge, then when she turns back to me, something has changed. "Do you want to know something? I've always hated you. When you were a little girl, and everyone told you that you were special . . . I hated you then. He never loved me . . . but when I found out he loved you . . . it made me hate you even more. It doesn't matter what you do . . . he's got everything planned and there's no way you're going to fix it." She breathes out as if to enjoy the scenery and the fresh air one more time.

"Lyneva?" The small voice stretches through the cold air from behind me as though it is slower than the speed of sound.

Lyneva looks up with wide eyes. A hand touches my shoulder and soon Elizabeth steps in front of me. The sisters stare at each other and, for a long moment, there is silence. Finally, Elizabeth's sweet voice begins.

"Lyneva, please don't do this."

A large tear leaves a trail down Lyneva's cheek. "I have to."

"No, you don't. I'm your sister and I'm telling you that you don't have to." Elizabeth's elegant hands are out toward her. "You're different now. I can feel that."

"No. I'm not." Lyneva grins out of surrender. "Elizabeth, you were always kind. No matter what. Even after all that I did to you."

"Because you're my sister."

"I've never been a sister. Sisters don't do what I've done."

"Please Lyneva . . . it's okay. We'll find a way. Briston's going to find a way to help you."

"Elizabeth?" Lyneva says after she takes a breath.

"Yes?"

"I'm sorry." Without another word, Lyneva turns to the edge of the mountain, raises her arms out to the side, and steps off until there is nothing left but falling.

"No!" Elizabeth cries and runs to the cliff's edge. Briston chases after her and takes her in his arms. I stare out into the emptiness, the place with no foundation, the air that does not and will not hold us. It is a different kind of void than the one that helps me see clearly. From this void, there is no turning back. I drop to my knees and think of the words she just said to me. Memories flood my mind of all the times in my life that I knew I was her burden. I was the stain on her life—the irritation that just wouldn't go away so that she could figure out her own worth.

After a few minutes of silence, Elizabeth comes to me. The sadness colors her face and her eyes look at me with such love that I want to look away. She places her hands on my cheeks. "You've always belonged to me. You were mine and I have loved you every second of your life. You may not have come from my body, but you have always been my heart."

I fall into her arms—the woman who cared for me when I had been stuck in a corner for too long. Then together, arm in arm, we walk back down the mountain. It isn't long until we find one of the guards, beaten. The other is nowhere to be found.

Diem shakes his head and Masey wipes the blood from the guard's forehead as he sits up against the wall. "We can't trust anyone."

Masey looks up at Diem, then her eyes turn to me.

CHAPTER THIRTY-SIX

As we do every night, a group of us kneels before Gyre, hoping that somehow we can be rid of what hides within. None of us look forward to these moments. They're hard—aggressively so—and within my soul I fear what might be found. We are silent on our way to the ruins as the night stars sparkle. It is the strong, crisp wind that has given us this view, and while my face is freezing, my eyes are grateful. Everyone is silent.

Sassi's rich voice rises over the wind. "I have to remind myself again and again, it is better to have it revealed within Gyre's presence than Navin's or Covey's."

Many of us nod.

The androgynous and wise Gyre sits in the corner, eyes closed, breathing so slowly that when I try and match it, it is impossible. "Tonight we do not play in the truth of our unconscious, rather we will face our subconscious." Gyre's lips do not move, yet I hear this in my head perfectly. None of us say anything, but we do look at each other with concern and fatigue all rolled into one. "It is our subconscious that turns our true fears and pain into nightmares. It sifts through our existence, tossing and turning the truth, becoming stories of such grand delusion we become confused with reality versus fiction."

I think of the first time Geo taught me, that night at Sassi and Kilon's cabin before we went to the Bryer looking for Ian. They couldn't go to the deep unconscious since I lived within the unbridled ugliness of the stories of my subconscious. I remember vividly being unable to see Arek, and the white scaly monster in the field that chased me till I fell. This seems so long ago.

"We need whatever you have," Arek admits to Gyre. "Give us all you can."

Gyre nods. Soon I can feel the split happen from my conscious place in the room. My body shakes and my skin perks. Within moments, I land—as if dropped from the sky—onto dry dirt that sends puffs up around my shoes. Instantly the heat of the sun scorches my skin and I look up from my crouched position. A more modern version of the Colosseum in Rome, where the gladiators faced their own deaths, surrounds me. More medieval than not, there are many large metal doors around this Colosseum. The stands are empty and at first, I wonder if I am alone. However, when I turn, Sassi is kneeling across the circular arena—the puffs of dirt billowing from beneath her feet as if she just landed. Then I see Kilon, Arek, Geo, Daye, Diem, Gal, Lya, and lastly Briston. Each of us stands in front of our own door, waiting for whatever is next. Sassi notices me first, then follows my gaze to the others. Around each of our left ankles is a heavy and rusty ball and chain. I try to take a step, but the ball is so heavy that I cannot move it but a couple of feet before I am tired.

A screech blasts, in fact several screeches that make a dissonant chord until many of us cover our ears. The corroded doors are opening. My heart pounds, wondering what will be behind mine. Gyre knows everything within my unconscious mind. Anything that is there, I am working against the oldest and wisest Velieri who exists today and there will be no fight if I am not careful.

As my door slowly opens, I search the grounds, hoping to find anything that will be of help. But there seems to be nothing . . . just dirt. Squinting my eyes doesn't help to see what's behind my door, and yet there's a shadow that appears to be pacing from side to side within the dark hypogeum of this Colosseum. This being is not small, that I know. Inch by inch the door struggles to open. Suddenly I hear a scream from beside me and when I turn, Lya is flying through the air with a dark creature, as if it has just barreled toward her and thrown them both across the dirt. I take a step toward her in panic but the ball and chain stop me. "Lya!" I yell.

"No!" Sassi wails. When I turn to her, I suck in my breath and place a hand on my chest. Nayo is there. But it is not Nayo, rather something of nightmares. Her beauty is no longer available to our eyes, as a creature from a different place has taken over. Kilon's door has yet to open and he struggles to get to Sassi. When he can't, he yells, "That is *not* her, Sassi. Get it together, love! It is not her!"

When I see Arek, he points to my door and mouths, "Don't watch us . . . watch yourself!"

Finally, my door opens just enough for whatever is inside to attempt its escape. Its limb reaches out—colorless and scaley—not human nor animal, and its body cannot break free quite yet. This only makes it angrier and more possessed. Clickety-clack, the eroded door takes an inch at a time. Finally, the door opens the last inch, which allows the monster's freedom. Instead of running directly toward me, it climbs the walls of the Colosseum. I've met this beast before. The memory of the lake surrounded by the field of high grass, when its terrifying dull but shiny rounded back peeked over the weeds as it crawled toward me. Today is no different. This beast is shiny and scaly like a sea creature, but it moves like a spider. *What is this? It must be something to me, otherwise why would it continually show itself?*

Somebody screams behind me. I cast a short glance toward the others and see terror on Sassi's face as she watches a grotesque version of Nayo come at her; she backs away. Kilon is not far from Sassi, but he has covered his ears with his palms. The door in front of him has opened, revealing a darkness within, and I notice that his feet are sliding across the dirt as if being pushed toward the black underground of the Colosseum.

"Arek!" I yell as he is surrounded by ten very large and very angry men. Their bodies are covered in deep scars, and they have every painful and torturous weapon attached to their bodies by leather. All at once, they dive for Arek.

I search for my daughters, hoping they are somewhere near, but my monster is eyeing me now. Even though we all understand it is Gyre that is feasting on our weaknesses, the pulse of danger is thick and heavy within my neck and chest.

"This is not real. This is not real," I continue to tell myself. The monster that has wedged itself between my fears and reality now turns to me as its mouth opens wide, showing several rows of sharp, daggered teeth. Yet it has no eyes, only porous black circles in their place, almost as if it is part fly. Everything is pounding within me. There's nothing more important than grounding myself, and quickly. How fast I forget how to control my mind. I am in the nightmare, which means my fears are driving my imagination. *What do I do?* Suddenly the white and shiny beast leaps off the building and chases after me. It slithers and claws at the same time—unnaturally fast. If I don't run, it will devour me in seconds. Then I remember Geo's words the first time I met this animal: "You can't outrun it! If it's not real, there's no way for it to hurt you!" So I stop. My heart is pounding until my knees shake. I can hear its heavy panting and underlying growl as it races to me. When I turn, sweat is pouring down my face and chest. Out of the corner of my eye, I see Daye tied to a column as the building shakes and begins to crumble. Geo is doing everything he can to release her as he chants, "It's not real, Daye!"

The white scaly beast knocks me down and instantly bites my arm and I feel the pain. I scream in agony and use my other arm to hit it. The mind is a brilliant thing, and it doesn't matter that this beast is not actually real—my mind is convincing my body that its teeth have sunk into my skin and is ripping my flesh from the bone. I hear a voice calmly whisper, "It is you."

I open my eyes and listen to the whimpers escaping my throat. "This monster is mine," I whisper as tears roll down my face and the teeth crash down harder, forcing me to cry out again. When the pain settles for just a moment, I gather my thoughts again. If this is dwelling within me, then I have accepted it. "If that is true then I have power over you," I whimper. This doesn't work. The pain is so intense that there is no convincing my mind that this is not happening. Just behind the monster on top of me, I can see that Lya is crouched and bleeding, her eyes filled with tears as she awaits the dark figure that crashed against her and has been haunting her every move as she tries to hide. Daye is thrashing to get free of the chains that have wrapped her tightly to the collapsing building as Geo grabs her face to convince her of what she must do. Each of us is losing. Not one of us is ready to fight Navin, if we can't defeat our own unconscious. Blowing my breath out to calm myself, I close my eyes. Clearing my mind of the chaos, of the pain, is my only option. I go back to the basics, what I learned from the very beginning, and I take my rhythm back. The monster releases, only to clamp down again on my leg. But this time I don't feel it. I open my eyes to see if it's still there and it is. It shakes its head like a dog with its toy, but my leg feels nothing. I watch as the sky above fades from light blue to dark blue, filled with massive amounts of stars. The Colosseum is not dark but everything has been filtered with gray. Then the air turns crystalline, as it has many times before, and I enter the Void. Everything still plays out around me, but now my body shifts into a state of reserves. I watch as Daye is crushed by more building and I yell, "Daye!"

As if I will it into existence, I notice a sword just feet away from us. With a hefty punch to its ear, I knock the beast loose from my body and crawl as fast as I can, bleeding on the dirt until it's red. I reach the sword as the beast grabs my back with its claws. Without pause, I twist around and send the sword through the beast's gut, then rip it out to the side. I stand above the staggering monster and raise the sword over my head and give one last stab to its chest.

I turn and race toward the others as fast as I can with the heavy ball and chain. Everyone is overwhelmed. Sassi has fallen and cannot fight Nayo. Whatever Kilon has seen within the darkness has him nearly crawling on the ground toward Sassi. When Arek defeats one man, another immediately takes his place. Then, as if in slow motion, I watch as Daye finally gets her arms free from the column, but the moment she hurries away Navin steps from the dark corner she passes. With one step toward her, he wraps one arm around her shoulder and the other around her jaw. In seconds I hear the crack as her eyes roll in the back of her head.

"Daye!!!!!" I yell as I begin to run.

But then it happens, just as it had before. As Navin pulls a knife to press it deep behind Daye's ear, the sonic boom warps and bends the stone arena. Walls crumble as the energy from within me breaks out through every pore of my body. Lightning lights up the sky, rain begins to fall, and everyone flies back as if blasted. Every man fighting Arek hits the stone with such force that I can hear their bones crack. My body drops to my knees, out of breath, and without any more energy.

All has gone silent.

Until finally, I hear the rustling of hesitant footsteps and small voices.

When I look up, we are back in the chambers with Gyre. Everyone is looking at me with wide eyes and concern. "What?" I say.

But only then do I notice something terrifying. Something unexpected and impossible. I still sit in front of Gyre, only now . . .

I am floating three feet above the ground.

Gyre stands, with pressed hands in prayer position. There is no smile, but Gyre's head drops into a nod as my body slowly descends.

VVV

Within the living room of our home, while Sassi and Peter gather drinks for everyone, Gal turns on some music and I find myself mesmerized by the rows of tents in the meadow. The scene I look upon is nearly silent, within the canopy of low fog with patches of clear sky, revealing a heavy moon. When we head to Gyre after a long day of training, everyone else who has traveled from afar are ready to drop their tired heads on their pillows. The security team makes their rotations through the sleeping community. One of the military helicopters passes by to my right and for a moment looks to be directly in the middle of the moon.

Before long Arek comes to stand beside me. "What are you thinking over here, alone?" he says with his drink in one hand as he hands me mine.

"I'm thinking . . . what's it like to be out there? Those who know nothing about what is happening, yet their world has turned to chaos. Don't you think about what's happening outside of this property?"

Arek nods, then leans his tired shoulder on the glass. His warm skin instantly fogs the chilled window. "Yeah. I do. But we have to worry about what's in our reach. Your father has many teams out there helping, and Prophet Jenner has built core groups to gather those who need help, whether Velieri or Epheme. So, I guess, I just know what I need to do and that's my focus."

Over the sound of everyone chatting and laughing, someone calls my name and finally grabs my attention.

I turn to find everyone looking my way. "What was that, Remy?" Peter asks.

"What?"

"How'd you do what you did . . . in that Colosseum?" Peter asks again.

"I don't really know."

"That's what you were talking about when you escaped from

Navin." Sassi sips her tea as she sits on the couch.

"Yeah."

Even Beck has heard the music and comes from his sequestered hole to grab a rum and Coke. Geo, who is never far from Daye now, crosses his arms and steps toward me. "What did you feel when it happened?"

"Scared . . . angry . . . like we'd never get out of there, honestly."

Geo looks at Kenichi. "A sense of defeat."

"I suppose so."

"Kenichi?" Geo asks.

"I've never heard of this before," Kenichi admits.

The song "At Last" comes on the radio and Kilon stands up. He's been eyeing me since I was standing at the window. "Let's not worry about it." He heads toward me with his hand out. "It's too late and we've done too much today already. It's time to dance."

I smile and take his hand. He pulls me in as a father would a daughter and then we dance to Etta James. Many of the others join, and the rest sit around drinking to calm their nerves.

After so much, during a time of madness, we find a moment to come together and just exist. Not as though we have a battle ahead, but as though we've already won the war.

CHAPTER THIRTY-SEVEN

I've managed to secretly make my way to the dilapidated church. It is the middle of the night, and when I walk in, Gyre has just woken. "I was waiting," I hear that voice say within my mind even though their physical mouth never moves.

Carefully, while the old lady sleeps, I sit before Gyre just as I always have.

"What is the One supposed to be able to do? I mean in the Manchester Books, why is the One so powerful? And what if I can't do it?"

Feebly, this ancient being struggles to move, yet still comes to me on hands and knees. In this close proximity, I'm awestruck by the powerful energy I feel within my body. It forces me to close my eyes and breathe. I feel a bony hand take mine.

"Is the One able to exist without the other levels? Should I be able to rid myself of the unconscious and subconscious? Is that what I'm trying to do?"

"We need the levels; they can be the holder of great joy . . . just not the demons within them. However, the One will know when all comes together how to weave in and out without the knowledge of others . . . They will know how to force more levels so that the wrong person cannot control within."

"It can't be me, Gyre. I don't know how to do anything that you speak of."

"You will. If you learn that there is more beyond the three levels of our psyche, you have the power to exist in all levels at once . . . but one thing more . . . you have the power to go beyond Tri Planum."

"Impossible," I whisper to myself.

"Not impossible. Only if you decide it to be so. When everyone fights within these parts of ourselves and the enemy seems to be guiding all that you are saying . . . The One will be able to surpass all of it. You will drive the nightmare and shadows of our fears . . . and you will conjure up the dead and demons of their past."

"How?!" I cry out.

"I've told you . . . you will go beyond the three. . . even if only to your enemy."

The bony hand pulls from mine, so I open my eyes. Gyre's gray eyes stare into mine until I feel as though my insides are being pulled from my skin. "What are you doing?"

"You will be able to control more than the mind . . . you will control the physical."

"It's all too much. I've seen power in myself . . . yes . . . but not enough. No more than the others."

"Close your eyes and do as I tell you." I obey the command. "Drop into the Void . . . the one that has become second nature . . ." Before long the air becomes clear, and my body is light. "Now open your eyes and see me."

When I do, I shriek and back away in panic. Gyre has turned into an evil version of the bony old being, with eyes sunk back into their skull and skin melting away. I can't bear to look. Suddenly I hit something behind me. When I turn around, I see Gyre again . . . only this time Gyre's face is young and normal. Still androgenous, but thoroughly alive and healthy. "Look over here," Gyre's voice calls to me, and that's when I see the old Gyre of today. All three in one room.

"What is this?"

"The ability to collapse the three levels into our conscious reality. This is the ability of the One."

"But you can do it. Then you're the One. Not me."

"No. I have not collapsed Tri Planum . . . this is just what it would look like. I am not capable. No one is. In this, you can direct him. Lead him, steal from him—he will give you anything to get away from that feeling."

"But the One . . ."

"That's right. You will know . . . somehow."

Something comes over me . . . fear, anger, disbelief . . . and I shake my head. "You're telling me I should be able to do something you can't?" This comes out in a near whisper. My heart thumps against my ribs until my body pulses. "I'm sorry, I have to go." I jump to my feet and head out of the ruins.

"Running from me is not the same as running from who you are." I hear Gyre speak to me as I step out into the night's chilly air. I look up at the stars, close my eyes, and breathe in. Within the hour, I hike to the edge of the cliff with just one light in my hand. The moon is bright enough that I can see the drop ahead.

"Remy?"

"How did you know I was here?" I whisper.

Instead of answering, Arek comes to stand beside me.

"Do you think she had peace when she jumped? Lyneva? Do you think it had just become too much?" I ask.

Arek doesn't say anything at first, but I can tell he is staring at my profile. Finally, he speaks, "There were many times I thought about ending it all after you died."

"Why didn't you?"

"Somehow, I had to hold on to the hope that there was more. We'd already seen a miracle. How could I not believe that more could happen?"

"I am so far from being a miracle. I just ran away from Gyre after they showed me something I can't do . . ."

Arek gently sets a hand on my neck and smiles. "It's always the things we think we can't do that become the foundation of who we are."

\\\\\\

"I've found him." Beck's voice seems to have deepened from the endless nights. His eyes are red from constantly staring at computer screens. I carry a full mug to him and lay it gingerly on the folded paper towel with dried brown coffee spots. Just beside Beck's computer is a muted television that is skipping through news channels every few minutes as though on a timer. I find myself watching in horror at the atrocities happening around the world.

"Don't pay attention to that," Beck warns me.

"It's hard to look away."

"We can do nothing to help without the proper training, or without a plan." Arek had reminded everyone this the day before. "We cannot strike until we're ready."

When Beck doesn't take a sip of his coffee, I realize how serious he is. "Navin?" I ask.

He nods, wipes his tired eyes, then turns his screen to me. "Yes. Look here." His thick finger points to a red line. The red line has red dots along it as it crosses the mountains and valleys on the map. "He has a pattern. Every two days he travels. Smartly so . . . never stopping for too long. Last night I had an idea. Don't ask me what made me think of this . . . but I started to investigate bank accounts. Covey, Hawking, Zelner. Who is truly running the show here? Within Covey's account there were large sums of money transferred that stopped the moment he went into the Cellar. Then a week after he managed to weasel his way out of there, the transfers started again. Every four weeks two million dollars are deposited into his account. It comes from a business called . . ." he looks at me with a smile before he continues, "GENOS*79."

I take a seat in the chair beside him. "GENOS . . . I get, but what about the seventy-nine?"

"I'm not one hundred percent sure, but the Red Summit happened in 1979. That's not the interesting part. I knew, of course, that this was Navin, but I went into the data bank and searched for the name of the person or persons who created this business license. And there it was."

"What?"

"Navin Rykor, Simon Covey, and Rita Hawking."

"What about Zelner?"

"Nope, he's clean so far. Money was also being transferred to Hawking from this business. There's a list of people who were getting money deposited. And you'd be interested to know that it's not just from Velieri, rather, the richest and loftiest of the Ephemes as well. Current and past presidents, megachurch leaders were of the highest paid, and any big business within that realm. And lastly, most surprising of all, there was money being transferred to the Reds. Our confidants and protectors were not actually on our side, but Navin's."

"You're kidding. They were willing to let their own people die in order to fund themselves."

"Yep."

"I can't say I'm totally surprised."

"I hacked into GENOS*79 as best I could and found that they own two jets. I identified their itineraries and quickly found that A4057-1118—this jet—without surprise . . . is following the same pattern that Navin takes. Moving every two days and never quite sticking with a pattern long enough to allow people to follow. However, I'm brilliant."

I smile.

"There is a way, because they have to be a part of the highway in the sky, to know when they're moving."

My heart starts beating fast. "Beck, tell me now or I'm going to jump out of my skin."

He picks up his phone and turns it to me. There is a map with the same red line, but one thing more that I see is a black square sitting just above one of the red dots. "That is where this plane is. The tracking shows that their next stop is here." He points to the map, to a distant Bryer near Bangkok.

"Wait Beck, you know where he will be before he goes there?"

Beck nods with a sideways grin. Instantly I wrap my arms around his neck as we both laugh.

$$\text{\textbf{VVV}}$$

As the sun falls, Beck and I search for Arek or Briston. We pass by rows and rows of men and women with weapons, getting better and better. Every morning we train their minds, and every afternoon we train their bodies. People stand at attention when they see me.

I can hear loud voices from within the warehouse beside the ruins. When we hurry inside, I look across the large room full of Ephemes. Every one of Jay's men and women have their phones out. They are watching the same colors and shapes pass by the screen that I did, when I didn't know how to fight Tracing.

"Jay, would you come up?" Arek calls Jay to the front. The war veteran obeys, placing his phone in his pocket. "Go ahead and put your phones down," Arek says to the others. "We are taking a chance with you all. There will always be more of you than there are of us. No matter how many years we stay in hiding, this won't change. But you have to understand, our only defense to your numbers is our skill over yours. Yet, here I am." His eyes look the crowd over with concern. "I am about to teach you a defense against one of our skills. While this will not be enough to keep you safe from the Elite, it will help you with those who have not been trained. I am putting my trust and faith in you . . . Ephemes," he places a hand on Jay's shoulder to show his kindness regardless of his heavy words. "I am going against everything I've been taught and I'm teaching you how to make it harder for us." He looks around and lets the silence fall on the crowd. "But here's what I know . . . we are at war. We haven't the time to battle one another. You need us, and we need you. Can we trust you?"

Jay turns to his large group of Panel Beaters and raises his arms in question to encourage the crowd to respond. One of the men stands to his feet: "You have my word."

"And mine," another one says. Then another and another.

"Let's take it back," Arek finally interjects. "Let's take back our freedom . . . together."

"Yeah!" several of the Ephemes call out.

With that, Arek turns to Jay. "It is your job to not let me in, Jay. For five days you have been taught how to not let me in, so show me."

"A'right," Jay answers.

The two men stand directly across from each other and Arek crosses his arms in front of his chest. He closes his eyes while Jay stares intently at Arek. "Keep me out, Jay," Arek whispers.

Jay squeezes his eyes closed, showing how truly difficult this task is. Again and again, Arek stops only to remind the man of how to keep Velieri out. But each time, Jay is quickly Traced. Geo finally emerges from the corner of the room, whispers something in Jay's ear, and steps back. Finally, Jay sticks his hand in his pocket and closes his eyes. Several minutes pass until Arek opens his eyes. A smile forms on both of their faces. "Good," Arek says. "What did you do?"

Jay says loudly, "I kept my attention by telling myself the same thing again and again."

"What was that?" Arek asks.

"What Geo told me. He said, 'Tap your fingers on your leg and with every tap say the same thing.'"

"So, what did you say?" Geo asks.

Jay sheepishly grins. "The alphabet."

There's chatter amongst the crowd until Geo addresses them. "It doesn't matter what you say, it's the attention that you allow your mind to give to them. If they get in, they ride your confusion. They break your rhythm by capitalizing on your attention. That's how they do it. So, you guard yourself next to Velieri, until Velieri can't find a way in."

Suddenly we hear screams from outside. Each of us have our weapons in our hands within seconds. Kilon runs to the door, "I'll check it out."

In just a moment he returns with a strange look in his eyes. "We're in trouble."

Arek swiftly turns to the group of Ephemes in the room. "Stay in here. Jay, lock the doors behind us and don't come out until you hear one of our voices."

"For sure," Jay nods and hurries behind us to make sure he barricades everyone in.

We run out and find a large group of people gathered within one of the rows of tents. Kilon, Arek, Geo, Beck, and I run to it. Hok hurries to us. "Someone's here."

Arek shakes his head in confusion, "What do you mean?"

Hok points to one of the tents, "Look inside."

All of us bend to enter the tent, and my breath catches the moment I step inside. "Oh no," I whisper. Blood spatter covers the material walls and has pooled on the ground next to the body of one of the Fidelis.

"He was from the Gianda in Brazil," Hok says.

"Do we have any idea what happened?" Geo asks.

However, just then, someone from the group yells from outside. "There's more!"

Arek races outside. After several minutes of searching, we find nearly ten who have been slain. As we stand within the last tent, Geo, Arek, Briston, Sassi, Kilon, Gal, Diem, Hok, and I are all there. "Someone is here. If we don't find them now, there will be more."

Suddenly yelling and screaming begins again. We race out to find someone standing in the meadow with their arms pointed behind them. "There's someone dead in the field!" the woman screams.

Finally, Arek turns to Peter, who has just run up with Lily. "Peter, get every one of the Ephemes into the house or the warehouses."

"Okay!" Peter starts yelling at those standing around and immediately the meadow is abuzz with movement and panic.

Briston checks his gun, "Is it a group?"

Arek shakes his head. "I don't think so. I think it's just one."

"How could they get away with this when surrounded by so many of us?" Gal's hair is wild and free as though she's just woken from a nap.

"That's what I'm afraid of. Gal and Diem, you go that way. We'll follow the trail from the body we find in the meadow."

"Aye!" Diem hollers as he's already weaving in and out of the tents with Gal.

Then, we race toward the body in the meadow. We find one, then another, and another. Arek's eyes move from the body in the grass, rising inch by inch, as though something occurs to him. I follow his gaze and quickly realize what he's thinking. Just ahead are the ruins. The place where Gyre has trained us each night. The place where Gyre sleeps.

"Gyre!" Arek yells at the top of his lungs.

"No!" Sassi lets out a cry as we all run at full speed toward the ruins.

At the door to the ruins, the guard has been slaughtered. We enter with our weapons at the ready, and the air is thick with something vile. There is a maze of halls ahead—too many for us to stay together. As the others find their own path to follow, the pounding beneath my skin calls me toward the darkest hall. Someone's wicked presence climbs my skin and attaches to me, giving my body what almost feels like pain. The discomfort repels and draws me in at the same time.

As I take steps through the ancient rubble with nearly no light to guide me, I raise the flashlight from my phone. It provides me with a spotlight, leaving everything else in utter black. Part of me fears what's ahead, while the other part of me is eagerly anticipating. I hear the small rustle of something ahead—like that of a scurrying mouse. Unexpectedly, I hear Gyre's voice, "Be careful."

"Gyre?" I ask the darkness. I hear the voice again, like the breeze flowing through a forest, "Be careful," Gyre whispers.

"Gyre?" My hands are shaking, causing the light to bounce ahead of me. Finally, I reach the dead end and it opens into a larger room of debris. Carefully, my light travels the walls. Something moves away from my light. "Be careful," Gyre says again.

"Hey!" I yell. Just then, my light hits the man's eyes and as it does, he lunges toward me. I cry out when his knife plunges into my chest and we fall to the ground. Instantly, I can feel that he's punctured my lung and I struggle to breathe. My phone flies to the other side of the room, spraying light on the falling ceiling. He is strong and trained to attack my mind first. The only thing that saves me is how good I've become. As we grapple, I keep him from stabbing me again, while our minds fight to take control. He has nothing against me. I am stronger and as the fight continues, I can hear his breathing getting heavier, yet my wheezing tells me I have a collapsed lung.

He manages to get away for a moment, and he scrambles to use his phone. When it lights up, I gasp at who it is.

"Meryl! How did you get in here!?" I haven't seen him since the Cellar.

He points his gun at me as he places his phone to his ear. "Do it now!"

Not long after, my body feels the push and pull again. *Not right now!*

I'm incapacitated when I Travel. My eyes start to roll back and Meryl grins as he steps closer. He grabs my hair while my body fights to stay aware. Convulsions happen before the darkness comes and the pain within the strong aching twitch of my muscles gathers so much strength that I cry out. He stabs me again. Then, I fall into the abyss.

CHAPTER THIRTY-EIGHT

I wake with a start while Navin kneels over me. He was prepared. So, when my sense comes back, the pain from the knife he's already plunged below my ribs makes me convulse. We are in one of his camps and rows of prisoners watch on. Their eyes are terrified as they watch us in the grass.

"Do you see?" Navin yells to all of them. "This is the woman many Velieri call the One. If she's so great—if she is amazing—then why is she so weak here and now? Why has she not found a way to save the world?" Navin looks down at me with a juxtaposition of love and hate. He comes closer to my lips, while twisting the knife and making me scream. "You cannot save them, Remy. I will not have my life's work ruined by you, no matter how much I love you. Do you understand?"

When he leans so close that I can feel his breath on my cheek, it opens a chance for me. I wrap my arms around his head, yank it down to my chest, and despite the knife sticking out from my abdomen, my legs climb until they can constrict around his neck. With the prisoners watching on, Navin coughs as my thighs choke the breath from his body. I twist him over until he's lying on his back in the grass, and I'm now looking over him. This happens so quickly that his guards aren't ready and it takes them a moment to race toward us. His face turns the deepest red—almost purple—and he's frantically clawing at my legs. "Listen to me, Navin. Time is up. We've got you."

His guards finally reach me, and they start to pull me away from him, but I'm too strong. This only lifts his head off the ground. When my body starts to Travel back, my thighs loosen. One of the guards hits the knife in my side and this finally forces Navin's freedom. He falls back to the ground, sucking in the air as they rip at me from all sides. "Time is up!" I cry out, just as the world turns black.

CHAPTER THIRTY-NINE

I cry out as I return to the ruins. My body is wrecked. A desperate wheeze scrapes through my throat. Arek and the others are around me. My brain is still convinced that Navin's knife is in my side, only this time I realize it is Meryl who has given me my true wounds. With a collapsed lung, it's like breathing through a straw. I struggle to sit up and panic as I look around, "Where's Meryl?"

"He's dead," Arek says with a straight brow. I look down at his bloody hand as he kneels beside me. With care, I rest my hand on his. His eyes turn to mine and for a moment, we simply stare. I've never seen his eyes like this. This man fights for integrity no matter the cost, but today it has been a high price to pay. His strong green eyes, although bright in color, have lost a bit of life. "He nearly killed you . . ."

"How did nobody see Meryl?" I ask.

"We don't know," Briston responds.

"So does this mean that Navin knows where we are?" I ask.

"That, or he will soon. Your Traveling . . . it is a liability for you now. One second more and you would have been gone." There is fear in Briston's eyes.

"Navin knew what he was doing." I rest my hand on Arek's face. He looks up with interest, so I nod. "There's something in me. Whether by memory—be it my unconscious mind, or my physical body. It draws me to him, and I believe they're studying it . . . learning how to use it. It was like he was ready for me to be there. He was prepared and had a knife in me before my mind was aware. Will Gyre know? Can they find it . . . whatever they planted? This isn't a gift . . . it's strategy. Japha is written all over this."

"Arek, Remy, Briston, you have to come," Sassi calls from the nearby darkness. Leaving Meryl, we head toward the orange glow where Gyre takes us beyond ourselves. There's an energy in the air— not good and not bad—that forces my skin to ignite. I raise my hand in front of my face and see that the energy alone has caused me to shake. Once we get close to the room in the ruins, my breath catches in my chest. Something has happened. Something terrible. The air— despite the usual orange glow—is not clear. Opposite of the Void. Its haze is supernatural and attaches to my skin as heavily as moisture.

There is no denying the tragedy on Sassi's face as we draw near. We enter with hesitation. Gyre hangs from a wire attached to the ceiling. Any exposed skin is covered in blood so thick that it has dripped off Gyre's toes and onto the floor. "There's a wound behind the ear as well," Sassi says as tears fall from her eyes. The old woman lies on the ground next to the wall, also slain.

It is Geo's response that surprises me the most. Geo falls to his knees and tenderly touches Gyre's feet with trembling hands. He speaks a strange language while closing his eyes. Between Beckah and Gyre, Geo has lost his family. I watch as Daye slowly comes to his side and touches his shoulder. He turns his cheek and presses it against her hand until she kneels beside him. When she does, she wraps her arms around his head, and he buries himself within her comfort.

"What do we do now?" The words tumble out of me before I can

question them. "How do we do this without Gyre?"
But no one says a word.

CHAPTER FORTY

Before sunset, we stand with shovels in our hands and lumps of dirt where we've buried those we lost. While I find my soul heavily burdened over the events of the day, my eyes look around at the sheer numbers that this group has grown to. Together we take a moment of silence. I look up into the falling sun, without care about the fact that it sears my eyes. A storm is moving in from the north, but it won't hit us until late. Beck and I have yet to tell the others of what he found. As he stands beside me, he nudges my shoulder. When I look at him, he cocks his head to the side, telling me to follow. We move through the crowd and continue to walk alone along a creek that runs through the meadow.

"Listen," Beck says. "You can't win this if he has control over you. Just as I've found a way to track his path, your Traveling is more powerful. I wish I knew the psyche as well as computers, but I don't. No matter what, sending you to Navin will never be good for us until we can figure out his hold on you."

"I know."

"Have mine ears deceived me?" he says facetiously as he pulls his ear forward with his fingertips. "Did you just say you agree?"

"I did." I smile.

"You are definitely not the same as you once were."

"All I can hope is that this is a good thing."

"It is. Who you used to be waited for no one despite how stupid rushing into anything may be."

"I have an idea."

"What's that?"

"While Geo is helping me find whatever Navin has within me, I need you to figure out how to get me viral. Can you do that? Can you mess with the algorithms?"

Beck chuckles. "What do you think, love?"

"I think you should be insulted by my question."

Beck leans in and kisses my cheek. Then he begins to walk away, but before he does, he turns back and points at me. "Don't forget what I said when we first met."

"What's that?"

"You let me kill him."

✖✖✖

"We have to do this. Now. Whatever it takes. Whatever happens to me. It's a waste of our time if we can't figure out how he's controlling my Traveling," I tell Geo as he washes his hands in the kitchen sink after digging the graves. He turns the water off and I hand him a towel, but he says nothing. His eyes are still red and swollen while his thumb and fingers grip the porcelain until I'm sure that he's going to break it.

"We need Gyre." Even as he whispers, his voice cracks with sadness. "I can't do this without Gyre." Finally, he turns to me and leans his hip on the countertop. I reach out and take his hand.

"You can do this."

He shakes his head while staring at the black tile beneath our feet.

304

"Geo, you can do this. Gyre taught you everything. The reason you were chosen is because, out of all people, you wouldn't need Gyre's guidance forever. I came so close to dying today because of Traveling. If we're going to do this . . . if we're truly going to end this, I can't be afraid of the moment when whatever Japha and Navin planted will be used at just the right time. But Geo, I'm afraid. Meryl would have killed me."

"There's a reason that Gyre takes us into our unconscious and I don't."

"But you've done it before. With all of us in Spain when we were trying to figure out Tri Planum."

"It's not the same, Remy."

"Why? Why isn't it the same?"

He stretches his neck side to side and breathes out. "We're taking you back to your original childhood, before you can even remember. There are limitations to a child's brain. If I resurrect these moments with Japha and Navin, searching within the most delicate parts of your mind, there is a chance that whatever they did . . . if I mess with it . . . it could ruin so much. You could change. Children are fragile, but their ability to stamp down these memories, to cover themselves in story is resilient. What if I reveal something that can't be reversed? Gyre would know how to do it . . . but I don't trust myself."

Suddenly something occurs to me, and I sit on the counter next to him. "It's because of Daye, isn't it?"

"What? No."

"Geo, she lost her mother once and it changed her life. You don't want to be the reason she'll lose her mother again."

Geo squeezes my hand, then looks up at me. "It's dangerous territory. Japha was one of the most powerful of his time."

"You can do it. I believe in you." He looks away. The pain of losing Gyre overwhelms him and he closes his eyes. I come closer. "Geo, you can do it." A few more seconds pass. "Geo, you can do this."

"Geo." We turn to find Peter standing in the doorway. It is

apparent that he has heard our conversation, when he continues, "Geo, I saw Gyre and I saw Meryl."

"What? When?" I ask.

"When I had my turn at the hot springs. I didn't know what to do with what I saw until now. I knew Gyre was going to die. Do you think Meryl stood any chance against Gyre? The springs took me there, to the ruins. Gyre spoke to me while hanging as though it was nothing. The words were clear, 'If I stay, he won't learn. Geo will be greater than I.' Then Gyre said nothing more and I came out of the water."

"You saw Meryl kill Gyre. So, you knew it would happen?" Geo asks.

"No. I didn't. But I wish I did. Maybe I would have been able to stop it," Peter says and looks down.

I interject quickly, "But you just said the truth, Peter— it was Gyre's choice to die. Meryl couldn't have taken Gyre's life, unless Gyre wanted it." I turn to Geo. "You see, you have what it takes to help me."

Finally, Geo pulls me into his arms—not for my comfort, but for his own. His voice is but a whisper. "Okay."

"When everyone goes to sleep tonight. Just you, me, and Arek. The less energy the better. Right?"

When Geo pulls away, it's as if he's thinking. Then finally he nods. "For this . . . yeah."

Hours later, when the masses have settled into their tents after the horrifying day, Geo meets me in my room. The windows are tinted to keep others from looking in, yet we can easily see outside. Vi, the lynx, is curled up in a ball just under the overhang. At times she looks up because of a sound, but she'll quickly settle back into her place. We wait while Arek finishes talking with Beck, and soon he walks through the door, surprised to see Geo there.

"What's going on?" Arek asks. Before we respond, Arek can feel the tension and knows without an answer. "It's dangerous."

"I told her," Geo says.

"What happened today was dangerous and we can't let that happen again," I plead with him. "How close did you come to watching me die again? I had no ability to fight Meryl off. None." I pull on the end of my sleeves until my white sweater covers my fingertips.

Arek doesn't argue, however it's clear that what he had to do today will affect him for a long time. "Everything that happened to you as a child . . . don't you realize, it's those things that made you fall into Lyneva's trap in the first place. It is what caused your execution. Why? Because someone a long time ago messed with your innocence. It scrambled a part of you and we have the chance to make it worse. Even Gyre knew to leave that part of your memory alone."

"Let's go," I say to Geo.

Arek breathes out with frustration. "Remy!"

"He's controlling me, Arek. Doesn't it bother you that he still has some way of controlling your wife?"

Arek raises his voice at me, the anger coloring his cheeks. "Of course, it does. But one thing at a time! I almost lost you today." The words trail off, heavily burdened with guilt. Just about the time I wonder if he won't continue, he does. "We have thousands of people trusting that we are going to help them get through this! Remy, there is no time to fix you if it goes bad. Everyone needs you as you are. Your daughters need you!"

My chest gets tight, and I hurry toward him. "You're right, my daughters need me. They need me to show them what it truly means to live, Arek! No fear. Never under the control of someone else! If anyone can do it, Geo can. I believe in him. I believe in me!" With that, I walk out of the room, grab my bag, and leave the house. Geo follows as Arek drops his head.

Nearly an hour later, Geo and I reach the hot springs. Vi has followed, keeping just enough distance between her and Geo. Vi's tail sways back and forth when I look her way.

Just ahead, a consistent wave of steam rises from the water as I drop my bag beside the spring. I reach down and glide my fingertips along the top of the glassy surface. This place is magic, and I feel it to my bones.

"Sometimes . . ." Geo says as he takes his shirt off, then his pants, ". . . this place helps. It counters what we do in the past, since it's known to provide you with a clue to the future. Gyre took me to one in Japan quite often. Let the water be the conduit for truth." Geo steps into the pool, so I take my clothes off as well and lower myself down. Just then, we hear the quake of branches and Arek emerges from the trees. Vi gets close enough to sniff him as if to say, *Are you safe?*

Without a word, Arek undresses. Beneath the stars and the shadows of the large moon, I am mesmerized by his every move. He can step into the water with his long legs and touch the bottom while his perfectly sculpted chest still sits above the surface.

Geo clears his throat. "Remy, you're going to slip beneath the water and hold your breath. While you do that, this place will want to tell you of your future, but you're going to request the past. Then, we will all be there in your past. Arek and I will most likely look the same, but you, you will be a child. If we can get to where we need to go, you will even think like a child. This will be problematic, but necessary. Do you understand?"

"Yes."

"And . . . it's important that you listen to me. Having the trust and innocence of a child is dangerous when trying to reveal your earliest traumas. Keep your eyes on Arek and me if things go awry. Got it? Don't look at the problem, look at us. The only people within your memory will be us three. What that means is this . . . nothing can scramble your perception and memory but . . . You."

"Me?"

"Yes. You."

"What if I start to Travel?"

"I'm hoping I can prevent that. Do what you can to keep Navin out of your mind if you do Travel. Don't let him know where we are. I have a feeling he's been trying," Geo explains.

Arek chuckles. "Yeah, trying is all my brother was ever able to do."

"Yeah," Geo agrees, "but this time he has Dr. Karine."

"Give me a second," Arek says to Geo. The water looks as if it's glowing under the stars. A long nearly neon cloud sits in the middle of the speckled sky. It has a glow of purple and pink.

Arek swims toward me, takes my head in his hands and kisses me. We look at each other for a moment as the beads of water roll down our faces, then he backs away, giving Geo the signal to begin.

"Let the water soothe your skin and feel yourself floating," Geo tells me. "Let the Void come as you fall into your past."

I close my eyes as the air hits my warm skin and soon I feel the Void. I am in perfect harmony with the earth and for a moment, I just let the peace sink in. Just as Navin and Japha did so long ago when they struggled to steal my memory, I am suddenly standing in the stars and memories pass by me so swiftly that it pulls my skin with them. I know Geo doesn't want me here for very long—my memories as a child are sacred and layered—but my mind as a child doesn't recognize what is real. I can feel my mind turning from the consistent and heavy thoughts of an adult to the energetic and woundless simplicity of a child.

I can feel us dive younger and younger. We're getting closer. It's obvious within my spirit.

"Close your eyes." I hear Geo's words, but I don't see him.

When I do, a brisk spring cold hits my cheeks with the smell of recent rain. Drops of rain make patterns along my skin so I open my eyes. Lyneva is beside me, only this time she towers over me. I look up at the woman with thin lips and an angry expression. "Come on!" She rips at my arm, frustrated by the precipitation, and it's so aggressive that my feet stumble, which only irritates her more. "God, you're so . . ." She doesn't finish the insult. It doesn't matter though since I don't need to hear the words to know the way she feels about me. It is my love for her that forces me to overcompensate and lift my feet high as we walk inside the castle.

It warms just a bit within the stone walls and before long one of the servants meets us. "Here." Lyneva hands me off to him. I see Navin down the hallway to my right and Lyneva hurries toward him while the servant takes me to the left. When I look back for just a moment, I notice the grin on Navin's face as he watches me walk away.

"Sit in here," the servant says as he reaches for a door handle that I've seen before. I furrow my brows when a feeling rushes over me. It's telling me to run. Fast. Hard. *Whatever you do, run.* The voice is unexpected. Instead, I take the moment to look around. My mind goes in and out of thinking like a child, then for just brief moments, I remember why I'm here. I've seen this door before—within Tri Planum. When the servant opens it, he pushes me in then closes it just as I run back toward it. The room is dark, only lit by a fireplace. Just as before the overwhelming sense of dread forces my heart to race. A mirror is in the corner of the room across from where I am standing and my young eyes, no more than four or five years old, stares back at me. My dress is dirty at the bottom from the mud and rain and my long hair is twisted into braids. The smell of smoke is seeping into my dress and eyes. The panic grows to an unimaginable level, and I grab the handle of the door. It's locked from the other side and doesn't budge.

Nothing good happened in this room.

Again, for just a split second, I think about that moment within Tri Planum as I entered this room with the heavy and ornate furniture. Only this doesn't last long before I'm living this moment. Now. It's happening. There's a door on the other side and somehow, I know I'm supposed to wait. I'm waiting for the man with white hair to enter. I can't begin to count the number of times my mother has brought me here. Tears come to my eyes. I do not wish to see him. Ever again. His arthritic fingers and his colorless eyes.

My body shakes. I push my back against the wall, terrified for what's next. When the handle across the room begins to shake, my tears come faster. Soon, I see his arthritic fingers reach around the thick wood. Slowly he enters the room. There's no greater discomfort, no bigger moment to wish for my father to be here, to save me.

Japha sees me against the wall and his eyes pinch even tighter around the edges. He locks the door, then places the key in his pocket. "Come here, Remona." His crackling voice hurts my ears.

I can't help myself before the "no" slips out.

Before I have any control, I feel him digging around in my head and suddenly, no matter how much I fight it, my body is being pushed to him. I am no match for his strength or his manipulations. My four-year-old body is now hyperventilating as I am driven closer and closer. The bottoms of my shoes make scratches along the floor. Finally, when I am close enough, he reaches out his hand and touches my hair. It makes my skin crawl.

"You don't even understand, do you? You are no one. They say you are the One but it's not true. You're just a silly, stupid little girl who gets into trouble and deserves the punishments your mother gives you. Do you understand?"

I nod even though my body is still under his control.

"Now, show me. Show me what you can do."

With fear in my eyes, I shake my head.

Rage explodes within him. "Fine. Again! We'll have to do this the hard way! You know what's wonderful?" he says as he leans toward me, bringing his lips close to me. "You're just a weak, stupid child . . . what is real, Remy? What is happening in this room? Look at me!"

I refuse to look at him. I've closed my eyes because I'm scared. Terror hurts my temples and my shoulders, while his evil raises the skin and hairs on my neck.

"Look at me!"

Unexpectedly, I feel as if I'm flying. This forces my eyes to open. I scream. Somehow, I'm hovering just inches below the ceiling and above his head. My body is horizontal and facing down. "Help!" my tiny voice screams.

Japha flicks a finger, and it shoots my hovering body across the room until I painfully hit the wall. I cry out. "Is this real, Remona?" He laughs a sadistic laugh. "You have no power, no abilities, and you'll never know."

Deep within my mind, something is happening. His conscious words, the echo that bounces within these walls, is just a cover-up for something going on within my mind. Even as a child, I am aware of this. An eerie chant is so quiet, so in the recesses, that I'm unable to know what it's saying. *What is he doing? Why is this happening? Where's my dad? Somebody help me.*

"Look at me!" I open my eyes. Japha flicks his hand once more, but this time I split into two of me. Two Remys now hover next to the ceiling. She's quite far from me at the beginning and at first it almost helps me. Another girl. Another me within the room. It's scarier to be alone. Japha shakes his head, then with his arms crossed in front of him, he circles a finger, and the other Remy turns her head. Her eyes suddenly open and they're white. She raises her top lip and growls like an animal when she sees me. I scream even louder. Japha claps his hands together and the other Remy and I crash into each other. Immediately she tries to claw at me, and I cry out. "Daddy!" I holler. "Momma!!!!"

"Your mother has no desire to help you."

I manage to maneuver my feet against the ceiling and move myself away from the animal version of me. Japha flicks his hand and once again I split. A third girl hangs just below the ceiling. Her eyes are red, and her face is beyond pale. Both Remys crawl toward me, their voices more like screeches and moans.

"Daddy!" My voice is that of a terrified child. My body shakes in terror. "Help!"

As the other Remys reach and yank me around, I manage to hold on with my fingertips to the molding and press myself into a corner. They cover me like a pack of wolves as I cry.

"Remy." A familiar voice returns. I open my eyes and try to peer around the wild but young Remys. Geo and Arek are there. Just as Geo said, they are the same, while I am but four or five. "Remy," Geo says again.

"Help me please," my tiny voice quakes with fear.

"Remy, do you remember why you're here?"

"My mother brought me," I answer.

"Yes, she did . . . long ago. But that's not why we're here. No, listen, if you can tap into the Remy that's older. We need you to listen for what Japha's doing."

"Is this real?" I cry as I fight off the other girls; their eyes are painful to look at.

"This did happen to you. He was able to manipulate your young mind to believe he could do this. He's attached himself to your fears and subconscious young mind. But this is what I think, Remy. I think he did this to you again and again to use your emotions, to use your fear to plant something. Something that would draw you back to Navin again and again when you Travel. If we know what he did, we might be able to reverse it."

"I can't!"

Several seconds pass as Japha plays a bit more. He cannot hear or see Geo or Arek even though it seems that they are only feet from him.

"Remy," Arek says, and he walks over to stand under me as a child. "Remy, let me help you." He reaches out his hand to me and I try to grab it. When I do, he pulls me down to the carpeted floor and wraps his arms around me like a father would to his daughter. "Look up."

When I do, I recognize that the other Remys haven't noticed I'm not there. They are clawing and scraping at the ceiling instead. "What is he chanting, Remy? Listen for a moment."

I cover my eyes with my small hands in order to listen. At first,

I don't hear anything, until finally I feel the foreign being within me. It's traveling through every nerve ending and firing in my brain. *"Tre kilou neu fumen caretsiva sui."* I finally hear. Repeatedly, he says it. When I say it, *"Tre kilou neu fumen caretsiva sui,"* Arek's chest vibrates when he asks me to say it again. So, I do.

Only then, Japha comes to stand over us, but I soon realize Arek is no longer there and I'm alone with Japha. Even the duplicates of me are gone. Japha kneels in front of me, but I just lie there, nearly catatonic. This wasn't the first time he'd done this, and it wouldn't be the last. His clammy hand runs down my arm and even though I want to rip it away, I can't move. Soon his hand lands on mine and he touches something that is in my hand. I didn't even know it was there.

"Remy," Geo says quickly, "what is that? What's in your hand?"

As difficult as it may be, I try desperately to lift my hand so that I can see the hard thing in my palm. When I do, a gray wooden coin sits in my hand. *Wait, I remember. I've seen this many times.*

"Just as before," Japha says, "read what it says."

I shake my head at first, but this only angers him. He reaches out and squeezes my cheeks until they hurt. "Read it!"

"Tre kilou neu fumen caretsiva sui." I read the words, yet I do not know what they mean.

Japha continues, "In the Manchester Books, they speak of the One. I've always heard since I was a child, this One would have gifts that none of us could ever understand. But you know what I think, I think there is no One." He sits down beside me as I curl into the rug. "You have done greatly. I'll see you again soon."

His voice disappears and I feel my chest trying to take deep breaths, but I can't. I suck in water and choke. When my eyes open, they sting. I'm underwater, staring ahead at the rock wall of the earth. Then, I'm being yanked up until my head emerges into the open air. My eyes roll back into my head.

"Remy!" Arek's voice yells.

I can hear it, but I can tell I'm not breathing. My body is hot. I'm pulled from the water by both arms and lain across the cold ground. "She's not breathing!" I hear Arek yelling. "Remy!" His hands wrap around my face, but I can't see him. "Remy, come on, baby."

Geo squeezes my hand until it hurts. "Remy."

Finally, something releases in my chest and I'm throwing up water. After some time, when my throat is scratched from retching, there's another sound. I recognize my cries. I'm crying as the water leaves my lungs. Soaking wet, Arek pulls me into him. My head lays against his chest as he runs his hands down my wet hair. "I'm sorry, Remy. I'm sorry."

Geo gets up and watches us for a moment, then he turns to place his hands on his head as he looks at the stars. *"Tre kilou neu fumen caretsiva sui."* In a whisper he translates, "Within me, I capture your spirit."

"What does it mean?" My throat is angry and swollen.

"It's an old scripture used in the Manchester Books," Geo explains. "He used it . . . basically turned it into a spell. Connecting your spirit to his."

"Not to Navin?"

"To both of them."

"So what do we do?"

"You'll have to take it back."

"How?"

"Return to that room. If you take out Japha, you take your power. That talisman is somewhere. It has to be within your memory . . . within that room."

The quiet is interrupted by a grave voice yelling. Even Vi jumps to her feet and cowers a bit behind a nearby tree. As the yells draw closer, I recognize that it's Lya. Something isn't right. Arek helps me to my feet, we grab our clothes and then we run . . . meeting her just as she rounds some trees. My body is starting to absorb the freezing temperatures outside.

"She's gone!!!! He has her! He has her!" The fear and pain in Lya's voice is palpable and sends chills down my arms.

"Lya!" I cry out. "What's wrong?"

Geo reaches her first and takes her by the arms. "What are you saying? Who, Lya? Who?"

"Daye!" she yells back. "Daye is gone!" Blood is dripping from Lya's mouth and her eye is black. Others are now reaching the hot springs after running and are now out of breath.

"What happened to you?" Arek asks Lya as he places his hands on her face.

"I tried to stop them. But there were too many. Black masks with red Xs. We were at the Ruins and I swear she let them in."

"Who let them in?" Arek asks in confusion.

Hok races up the mountain and, just in time, he answers, "Masey. We now know who let Meryl in."

"They came in and took Daye. I couldn't stop them!" Lya cries as Adam reaches for her.

"Where is Masey!?" Geo asks.

"We can't find her!" Hok yells. "We think she left with them."

"So, he knows we're here."

CHAPTER FORTY-ONE

We've gathered at the house. Beck clears his throat and interrupts the chaos from the doorway. The group turns toward him. "Listen, time is running out. If we had the option of ignoring the Bryers, we would take it. But we all know the Bryers give us the key to the larger picture. The Cellars." Beck's eyes are red from exhaustion as he looks at me directly. "You and I may be the only ones to understand the evil there. If they are free, Navin has all but won."

What happened there is imprinted on my brain. The Unyielded no longer see truth in any capacity, which is humanity's true danger. "So, what is more important—the Cellars or the Bryers?" I ask with a heavy voice.

"We have no choice. The Bryers have the answers to stop the system. Navin's hackers set up a scheme that they believe is impossible for us to break. However, they didn't realize my skill. Arek," Beck calls out, to which Arek looks up. "No one has strategy like you. We need the Bryers, but we also need to focus on the Cellars. My guess is they've planted someone in the Cellars as a fall back. At least I would."

"A fall back?" Peter asks.

"Someone who can still release the Cellars if something goes wrong at the Bryers," Beck explains.

"Not to mention," Sassi begins, "if we let all those people die . . . the Ephemes will never forgive us. They will see the deaths of all their people and choose to believe that every Velieri is responsible. More reason for war."

Arek nods, while he rubs his eyes. "It's just the facts. We need to bloody take him down now. If we try and wait until everything is perfect, until we have the perfect upper hand, it will never be. We have only days till every prisoner is killed within the Bryers and until the unthinkable happens at the Cellars. Plain and simple. And don't doubt it: Navin will use Daye in any way that he sees fit."

After so much time and so much energy spent over the last years, to never knowing what Navin was up to, the room is silent. Aita is holding on to Mak's arm as he rubs his chin with contemplation, the color seems to have drained from my father's face, and it is Arek I watch, knowing that his mind is reeling.

After several moments, Arek clears his throat. "I know my brother. He did this because he wants us to come to him." He turns to me, "He wants you to come to him. I know there's still something in him that believes he can turn you. He'll never stop trying and it's even more dangerous with Dr. Karine." Arek grabs a marker from Beck's desk and walks to a white board in the corner. He draws visuals of every Bryer and every Cellar. "We need people at all of these places at once."

"What do you mean?" Sassi asks.

"It means we split up. Gal takes a group to one Bryer. Diem to another. Mak, Peter, and as many leaders as we can trust. We separate. Remy and I face him, if something happens, it's only us. At least this way, people will live on for the fight. Beck, can you help everyone get into the Bryers?"

"Wait!" Kilon growls. "You've got to be kidding. We separate? That's your answer, mate?"

"It's the only answer. We have no other choice." Arek knows this is not what anyone wants to hear.

"That's not a choice, it's suicide." Kilon flexes his arms out of aggravation.

"I agree with Kilon!" Sassi's tone is deep and stern.

"No!" Kilon turns away from Arek for the first time. "This is wrong. It's too dangerous. I separate from my wife, for what? One last ditch effort to take out a man who has been preparing for years?"

"Which is why we have to do what he's not prepared for," Arek answers quietly.

Mak steps forward with Aita directly at his side. "I agree with Arek." A wave of surprise passes from one of us to the next, until it gets back to Mak, forcing him to shake his head. "I know. But he's right. We have to come to Navin with everything we can."

Finally, Peter comes forward. He looks at his brother. "There's enough of us to cover the Bryers. Now is not the time to be without Sassi and Kilon."

Kilon messes the top of Peter's head. "This kid . . . see, he's right."

Briston nods. "Those of us who have been around, who have been through the Cellar, we go there." Briston turns to Kenichi. "Kenichi and I will gather our elders, those we can trust, and we'll take the Cellars. Beck, we can handle it inside. If you show us where to go and what to do, we'll do it."

Finally, Arek seems to let down his guard as he walks to Kilon and places his hands on his shoulders. "I hear you. You and Sassi will be with us."

Kilon finally lets out the breath he has been holding.

"Beck, did you figure out what I asked?" I interject.

"I did. It's ready. In fact, I called some reinforcements," Beck says. He walks through the living room, exits into the hall, then returns just a few minutes later. Following him is Andrew Vincent.

His confidence fills the room as he walks to me.

"You joined us."

"I was always yours, my lady." He takes my hand and kisses it, then he addresses the rest of the group. "Beck called me and I'm glad he did. Listen, Remy and I are going to get through to anyone who will listen. We'll reach for the world."

Peter laughs, "The world, huh?" Andrew gives him a stern look, which changes Peter's response immediately. "Wait a minute, what do you mean?"

"I figured out a way to fix the algorithm and address as many people as we can," Beck explains.

Peter clears his throat. "Wait, you figured out how to send somebody viral?" He then tries to downplay how cool he thinks this is. "Yeah, okay. That's a solid trick."

Beck continues, "She and Andrew will put out a video. Over the years, Andrew is the only one both the Velieri and Ephemes have completely trusted. They know his face. They know his name."

Arek steps forward. "We go live and let everyone know that they can help and hope that the world does the right thing. We send crowds of Velieri to stand outside every Cellar. We encourage teams to fight. They'll reach the Cellars, they'll reach the Bryers, and they'll battle those on the streets. Anything that helps. Beck can walk each team leader through shutting down the timer. Beck, can you explain?"

"Navin's rigged it so that each timer has its own code. I need every code given to me in sequence. The Bryers' codes must be inputted in a specific order. But that's not all; once that is done, we need Navin's fingerprints and eyes to access the main timer. Once we do that, I can hack past his system and shut it down."

Peter nearly chokes on his drink. "Oh is that all?"

Briston rubs his neck. "Are we sure about this?"

Everyone stays silent. We can hear the rain that has started to fall.

"I'm not sure about anything anymore . . . but we have nothing to lose. Navin must be stopped," Arek says quietly, as though he has surrendered.

"And if we fail?" Kilon asks.

Arek nods. "That's why we send Kenichi and Briston to the Cellars. If the prisoners at the Bryers die and our team leaders have failed, the most important thing is to make the inmates stay where they are. Beck, is there a default should that happen?"

"Yes. The Cellars were built with not just one override to their system ever being hacked . . . but two. Only the person who designed the system for the Cellars knows about there being a second override," Beck says confidently.

"Who designed the system?" Peter asks curiously.

Beck looks down, cracks his neck, and then looks back up. "My grandfather. I'm trusting that Navin didn't know about this."

"Do we know for sure?" Sassi asks.

"No." Beck chuckles with irritation. "We don't know anything for sure. But what I trust is that I can read the system better than anyone."

"So, what's the first step?" Mak asks.

Arek explains, "The video. We send that out. Get the streets back on our side as much as we can. Once we do that, we divide. Send people to the Cellars, to the Bryers, while Sassi, Kilon, Remy, and I find Navin himself."

"What I know . . ." Andrew Vincent begins. "What I've seen, is that people are dying in far bigger masses than those who sit in those camps. The streets are dangerous. Everyone has lost someone at this point and I'm not sure we'll ever be able to come back. Navin is our most important target. Our chances of returning to normalcy at this point are small, but our chances of returning to normalcy with Navin are zero."

"Aye, okay," Diem nods. "Then what do we do?"

Beck pulls from his pocket an earpiece. "Each of us will have one of these. These connect us all. You'll follow my instructions for every turn. And if I know what I think I know, I can turn the timer off."

VVV

Hours later, Andrew and I stand in front of a tripod with a camera secured on top. "Wait a minute," Andrew says with a raised eyebrow. He walks to the corner and pulls over a nearby stool, then crawls on top. "You know what my father always said?" he asks me as he stands. "He said the little man stands for himself, but a large man stands for justice."

I smile. "I like that, Andrew."

"You always did." He chuckles. "I kinda like this . . . I can say things that I've already told you and get the credit for a new gem."

"You two ready?" Beck asks from his place behind the computer.

Andrew suddenly shakes his head and climbs down. "Just one thing first. Can I connect to this TV, Beck?"

"Sure."

Andrew pulls out his phone and connects his screen to the TV. "Tell everyone to come in for just a moment."

Soon, everyone gathers within the small office in the main house. Briston and Elizabeth, Adam and Lya, Arek, Diem and Gal, Kilon and Sassi, Mak and Aita, Kenichi, and Peter all make space within. I look around for Geo, but he isn't there.

"I need you all to watch this. Especially you . . ." he says to me, then he turns it on. A silent video shows the devastation. There are clips from all over the world where fighting has decimated much of the cities. At the end of the video, a man runs up to the cameraman. He is clearly in India, and he's covered in the powdery rubble from head to toe. "Whoever this is, we will fight! This silent, invisible killer . . . where are you? Who are these people . . . who is fighting? We don't even know. Yet we lose our lives every minute. Show me where to go and I'll fight." Andrew pauses the screen and turns to everyone.

"Listen," he says, "I know what the Prophets want—they want us to say nothing. But it's time to tell everyone the truth. Give them answers about who it is they're fighting. Give them direction. We need them . . . we need everyone. There are far more people out there not involved with Navin than involved with him. We just have to convince them of that."

Aita steps forward, "They have said we will all be in trouble . . . if we say—"

"The truth?" Andrew asks her. "I don't know about anyone else, but the truth is the only thing that I'm actually willing to lose my freedom over."

Peter stands and shows us his phone screen. "This is my school." All we can see is a building on fire and people running about in chaos. "When you put weapons in the hands of people who can't think for themselves . . ."

"Exactly," Andrew nods as he runs his hand through his short hair. "Listen, it's time to forget all that was . . . and extend our hand to the future that will be if we take it back. I'm ready to take it back . . . Are you?"

"I am," I say loud enough to turn the heads of the others. Arek reaches down and takes my hand.

"Do you understand what this means?" Arek asks me. "Everyone will know who you are. That will never end."

"Ephemes won't understand why I'm even speaking to them. Is it important that it is me?"

Gal flips her long hair so there's a large wave above her forehead of coppery color. "It don't matter whether they understand . . . we do. What they need is a face to connect what's good. That is you."

My heart is nearly going to beat out of my chest when the room goes silent. After a few moments, Beck says my name and brings me back. "You ready?"

"Ready as I'll ever be."

Finally, Beck turns on the camera, sits in front of his computer, presses a few buttons, and then with his finger, he points at Andrew. Andrew clears his throat, then begins to speak. "Many of you know me. You have watched me for years on your television and trusted me to give you the truth. If you can see this, if you can hear, stay with me for just a moment. As you all know we are under attack. Many of you have asked me why. Many have wondered who is at the middle of all of this. I do not have time to go through history with you, but what you need to know is this . . . I am Velieri. Centuries ago, my kind was hunted for one simple reason . . . longevity and nothing more. We were killed for how long we could live, then forced into hiding, and for years . . . for years we have been afraid to say who we are. But listen to me . . . nothing has changed. We are all human. We can fix this. Beside me is Remona Landolin . . . a woman," he connects eyes with me, then continues, "who has fought for change. She was convicted because she chose to stand against hate. The hate that's killing us. I ask that you listen to her, listen to me."

I begin to speak, my words starting slow, but then picking up as a strange feeling encompasses me. My body ignites with electricity and my fear falls away. "There are many of us who know that what's happening is wrong. More than a week ago, a man known as Navin Rykor, who is the leader of a group called the GENOS, called for all his people to attack and leave those who are not like us for dead. We are not in a fight between Velieri and Epheme; we don't need to be. We are all human, all of us. The GENOS wish to kill all who are not like us and, in turn, are doing the very thing that forced every Velieri into hiding so long ago. What is your heart telling you? To all the Velieri out there . . . don't run, don't hide. We fight against tyranny. We know what it is to be hunted . . . don't let it happen again. We fight for the person next to us; we fight for everyone even when they are different than us. All those who are listening, all those who don't know which side to choose . . . let's take our humanity back. Let's take a risk within our souls . . . I know you can feel it right now as I speak. This is a call to action. This is to tell you that you can make a difference. Start now, enter the streets, and take them back." My eyes become watercolor. "Stand up for the marginalized. You never know when it will be you. Decide now to fight for *all*."

Beck writes a number on a white board behind him. At first, I don't understand what it is, until he crosses that one out and writes another. Suddenly the realization sparks and my eyes widen. The first number was 10,000; the second 575,000; until the numbers of zeros keep building: 603,487,953. I look up at him with shock. He nods but turns his finger in a circle telling me to continue. So, I do.

"On your screen right now," I say as Beck changes the video, "you see a map of the world. On it, we have marked in red every territory, every region, where men, women, and children are being killed by these so-called GENOS. All Velieri know their nearest Cellar. Protect yourself as best you can by Tracing heavily and stand outside its walls with us. We ask that every one of you, ready to take action, ready to defeat those who are dividing and conquering in the most inhumane ways, get to these places as fast as you can. It is our choice to stop oppression. It is our choice to bring the world together. Listen to me: save those who can't save themselves. We will be making this map available on the website that is flashing at the bottom of the screen. Join me, join us. Don't let those who choose hate win. We won't disappear. We won't go quietly."

Beck nods his head when our live ends. Even though we are done, he turns back to the white board and writes 939,075,837. When he turns back around, he has a look on his face like *I told you so.*

"How'd you do it?" Peter asks.

"I told you I could, so I did. You went viral. Navin for sure saw that."

"What if it does nothing?" I whisper.

Andrew shakes his head and smiles as he shows me his phone. "Look." He scrolls up, addressing the comments on our live. "They're there." He turns to Kilon, "Turn on the news." We shift through the channels and our video is being replayed repeatedly. Every station and every journalist. Some are speaking to people on the street. A woman runs up to a journalist in Cincinnati and yells at the camera, "Remona Landolin! We are here!!!!!!!!! Let's take it back! Every Epheme in the Cincinnati area can find me! I'll keep you safe. And every Velieri who believes in the right of every life to be free, come help! Josephine Calle—" She then shares how they can find her, gives a war cry at the top of her lungs, pounds her chest three times to tell of her loyalty to me, and races down the road with a large group of more than forty or fifty people. They are not the only ones. There are more; every channel brings a courageous new cast in a terrifying play.

"What now?" Sassi asks.

"We meet Navin where he'll never expect it." Arek takes the knife he's been nervously opening and closing and stabs the desk beside him. Beck jumps back with surprise.

"Where's Geo?" I finally ask.

Peter finally speaks up. "He went after her." We look at him with surprise. "After Daye . . . I saw him leave."

"And you didn't say anything?" Briston asks.

Peter thinks for a minute. "No."

"Why?" Arek asks.

"He already lost one love . . . I don't want him to lose another." Peter shrugs his shoulders and crosses his arms in front of his chest. "I wish him the best."

CHAPTER FORTY-TWO

One of our daughters is gone—the one with the smile that lights the room. Now, as I look around the crowd we've assembled upon this beautiful property, as each group prepares for the battle ahead, it's difficult to imagine that inevitably we will lose some . . . and for what purpose? While the purpose feels necessary, it does not change the question. Nearly every grouping of people in human history has been pillaged and plundered in the name of land, religion, or race. And here we are again, never able to recognize that ultimately, we do not have to conquer or control one another in order to own our own beliefs.

I slip into the Void, the place where I can exist without fear. There is a heightened beat to my heart that hasn't left since I found that Daye was gone.

"He won't answer his phone," Sassi whispers as she comes near.

"Who?" I ask.

"Geo." She looks at me carefully. "You're in the Void." She says this as more of a question than a statement. Yet when I don't answer, she takes my hand. "I can feel it," she whispers.

She's right. When her fingers lace with mine, I suddenly remember a quote from the Manchester Books that says, "You may stand alone and exist in Power, but stand with two and create it." A force sends lightning through my skin, weaving in and out between us.

"We're going to end this," I whisper.

A tear falls down her cheek as she nods, but she refuses to look anywhere but the Swiss Alps ahead. "You're damn right we are."

"What if this is the last time we're together?"

Sassi turns to me with stern eyes. "You know just as well as I do, there is never a Last Time that we will be together. There is waiting to see someone again, but eventually the waiting ends."

I nod.

Minutes later, I am standing beside my father. "In record time we have divvied up our groups into enough teams to go to each Bryer and Cellar. We've done a lot, Remona."

"We sure have."

Every leader gathers in a circle as the rest of the people prepare. Suddenly multiple helicopters come over the mountain tops, followed by military planes. Briston smiles. "Ryan Jasper. They'll be guiding us from the air. Each leader heading to a Bryer will connect with one of Ryan's pilots. Kenichi and I have gathered more of our elders within the Cellars." My father turns to me, "Thire wanted me to tell you hello." I smile when I think of the guard who saved me from Meryl and Davi in the Cellar.

Hok stands to attention. "Every Fidelis from every Gianda around the world, they are fighting with us."

Jay, who has since become an Epheme leader far beyond what I could expect, talks to his group. They look scared but determined.

Next to Sassi and I, Peter can't help himself and he smiles so large that Kilon nudges his shoulder, "What's going on in that head of yours?"

"Nothing . . . I just thought we were all gonna die, you know. But now I'm like . . . maybe not."

Kilon shakes his head.

Arek interjects as the helicopters land. "Not all of us will be traveling the same distance, so we will wait twenty-four hours before completing the plan. Because of Briston's connection with the military—or at least what is left of the military—they are providing military aircraft to get people where they need to go. But that leaves us to deal with Navin and his men. Beck, do we know how many they have?"

"Navin moves around with a posse of about forty. But there are many more within each Bryer."

"I've reached out to Alfonzo, but he hasn't returned my call to help," Arek explains.

"And he won't. He's just as connected to Navin as we ever knew, I bet," Peter growls.

"We don't know that. There's a lot going on and not everybody is going to take this cause. This is ours. Navin is ours." Arek cracks his neck. "Expect the best. They'll have abilities because of Dr. Karine and all that he can provide. We have to be careful."

"How do we know who Navin's men are?" Peter asks.

Beck speaks up, "I found emails that gave his men instructions. Every one of Navin's men will either be wearing the mask, or must have it on them somewhere. Even they need to know who the others are. The only people we won't know are the civilians he has called to action, but they'll be easy to Trace."

Peter stretches his arms overhead confidently, "Good enough for me."

There is urgency to say goodbye to the others. Arek notices the concern on my face and comes to my side. "We need to leave now. We need to find her." The edges of my jaw hurt from my clenching. He reaches out and rubs them softly.

"It doesn't help her for us to act on impulse. It's what he wants. We'll bring her home, I promise."

Mak slowly comes to me. He looks at Arek with kind eyes. "May

I have a moment with her?"

Arek nods and steps away, releasing my hand at the very last second.

"So, you're leading one of your own groups?" I ask Mak.

"Yeah. Which means I can't protect you."

"As if you could anyway. It might mean that I can't protect you though."

We smile at each other, and he reaches out to take my hand, then he turns serious and steps closer. "Remy don't try and take on the world alone. Please. Be safe."

Somewhere within my spirit, I have a strange feeling that saving the world might cost us more than we've bargained for. "I promise."

Quietly he hugs me even when Aita comes near. Immediately after, I turn to her and despite her discomfort, I wrap my arms around her. Her body stays rigid and cold, until the very last second, but as I pull away, she does her best to smile.

"Come back safe," I whisper to them.

"We will," Mak says with a nod.

A few moments later, just before we are about to leave, Peter, suddenly looking like an adult, walks up to Arek with a serious brow. "I'll make you proud, brother."

Arek grabs his head with both hands. "I know you will. But listen, you've already made me the proudest man. You're honorable, strong, and committed. Take that with you and come back to us safe and sound. We may not share the same mom, but you are more brother to me than any of my others." Arek places his forehead against Peter's, until Lily appears through the crowd with tears in her eyes. Peter is leaving her to take on his own team, and it's obvious that she is terrified. Arek releases Peter and pushes him toward the woman he loves. Peter takes her in his arms and then kisses her.

Across the way, Adam and Lya are leaving each other. He is leading a team, but she is insistent about coming with us to find Daye. Commander Wakefield also has a team. The Reds have easily mixed with the Velieri and together the army has grown beyond what we could have ever imagined. It's quite the picture; the beautiful landscape soaking up the tears and goodbyes.

Even the group we saved from Italy came to our aid. Elliot and Ivan, who lost their parents to the Velieri, have joined us with those capable from the Patch. They arrived last night. How they trust us and stand by our side, I might never understand.

Sassi, Kilon, Lya, and Beck will come with Arek and me. Briston, my handsome father, connects eyes with me. He grins but it is not without worry. He has prepared his own group for the Cellar. As I slip into his arms and feel his heavy breath, there is no greater connection to my father than at this moment. "Listen to me, don't be the hero. Be smart. Do you understand?" Briston whispers in my ear.

"Why is everyone saying this to me?"

"You're more Remy now than you've been in a long time. And I know you when you have something to save."

"You wanna know the truth?" I say quietly to the man who raised me. "There is no more Willow . . . not anymore. And he'd better not touch a hair on her head."

"I love you," Briston whispers. "I'll see you on the other side."

"Love you, Dad."

He hugs me one last time, then leaves to kiss Elizabeth.

I climb the rock wall that helps me stand above the crowd. With a megaphone, I clear my throat. A strong confidence brews within my belly.

"Well, we don't know what's ahead, but you all have worked tirelessly and that's not in vain. There is no choice but to put it all out there at this point. If we sit back, evil wins. Everyone has a right to be happy, to be free. Everyone has a right at life. The GENOS want to take life away . . . that's why you're here. When things get hard, just remember why it is that we're here." I notice Vi, my lynx, has come the closest to the crowd that I've ever seen. She sits near the wall, looking up at me with her pointy ears. "I heard once that a lynx carries a reminder of quiet observance. To remember that there's more to life than what we can see and hear. When you're in the fight, when you're in the depths . . . just remember that there is more happening than what you can witness. Trust in that. Someone once told me that we never will understand who and what is petitioning for us . . . and I believe that. And when all this is over, we'll come together and celebrate our win."

Briston calls the cavalry in, and soon each of us separate, climb into our own military plane, and whisper one last goodbye to the land we've considered home for the last few weeks. Standing in the back of the plane, I stare at Vi, and she stares back. Suddenly and unexpectedly, she walks to me, slowly and methodically. I get lost in the intelligence of her eyes. When I reach out to touch her, she doesn't flinch, rather my hand glides along her fur with ease. It's nearly impossible to explain, but something travels between us, spirit to spirit. Vi's tongue travels up my arm as she licks me for the first time. I look at Vi from where I've landed and, within her eyes, I can see that she's calling me back after all is said and done. I nod and with that, she walks down the ramp and eventually travels across the meadow. After a few moments, she sits down stoically in the meadow, facing my direction.

CHAPTER FORTY-THREE

"He's staying in the penthouse of the Chateau Barbury on Fifth Avenue," Beck says with his computer open and on his lap as we are strapped in the plane.

"New York?" I don't know why I'm surprised.

"The hub, the center of hustle . . . they have everything within reach," Beck explains.

The rest of the group seems to need no explanation. Sassi shakes her head and closes her eyes. "Prophet Hawking's home."

"Yep." Beck sips his drink.

"Take a look at this." Beck turns a computer toward us and instantly we see New York, but it's no longer the same. Fighting on every street corner, military everywhere, cars on fire. "Fifth Avenue."

"It doesn't matter," Kilon growls. "Nothing's going to stop us now. We go in whether there's thousands or twenty."

"Look at this though." Beck zooms in with a satellite. There are guards with masks and red Xs on their eyes and mouth standing at every window, entrance, and exit.

We stay quiet as we let that sink in with the knowledge that we have military planes full of our team and men who studied under Alfonzo Geretzima to be Umbramanes with Arek. "They are the best. They can enter anything, anywhere, and never reveal themselves. I'll lead them, and they will surround you," Arek explains to our group.

"We cannot kill Navin at first," Beck explains. "We need him. Besides, I want to kill him." The smirk on Beck's face makes everyone grin.

After ten hours of flying, we land nearly a half mile away. "Based on his patterns, he should be there another two days," Beck says as we enter a meeting place in the basement of a Velieri hotel. A man wearing a very masculine and tailored suit waits for us with his hands behind his back.

"We've been waiting for you," he says.

"McGregor?" Arek asks.

"Yes, that is correct."

"Thank you for housing us while we wait," Arek says as he throws his bag of weapons over his shoulder. "Every team is waiting for the twenty-four-hour mark. Then we'll check in with each other and if everyone's in their place, we'll go."

It's been a while since we have seen anything that isn't torn to shreds, but this hotel is pristine. McGregor speaks as we climb stairs into the main portion of the hotel. "Prophet Jenner made sure this place was protected. Tanks sit on each side with her men watching every entrance and exit. Here are keys." He hands out white cards to each of us.

Arek looks at everyone, "Take a room, get rest, get ready." Then, with a strong hand he takes mine and together we enter an elevator that takes us to the top floor. We enter quietly and he throws his bag of weapons on the desk while I walk to the window. Smoke billows from many parts of the city. Unexpectedly, tears come to my eyes as I wrap my arms around myself.

I don't even notice that Arek is speaking to me until he wraps his arms around me.

"I need you to listen, Remy." He presses his lips onto the back of my neck. "Remember something for me. This connection that you have with Navin, this ability he has to call you to him . . . whether it's gone, or if it happens again, just remember that you aren't that little girl anymore. If you keep him out of your mind, you keep safe."

"Yeah," I whisper.

Finally, I turn around and fall into his arms. "How will this end?"

For the first time Arek says nothing as his strong fingers softly stroke my hair. After a moment, he lifts my chin, then drops his lips onto mine. I can taste my salty tears within our kiss. "It's you and me, Remy. That never ends . . . no matter what happens. This . . . you and me . . . forever."

CHAPTER FORTY-FOUR

We all gather in Beck's room, where several monitors have been set up. At first, we wait in silence. Finally, after several minutes, the leaders begin to check in.

"Beck? Are you there?" We hear Mak's voice.

Beck, who has been leaning back with his hands on his head, jumps up and grabs his microphone. "Mak, we're here, mate. Turn your camera on."

Beck presses a couple of buttons, then points toward the video square that will be Mak's. It's the first camera to go live and suddenly we can see a long fence, just like the one we found before.

"We're here." He speaks in a hushed tone. "I've circled the camp several times and it seems that the computer system is within this building." Mak points his chest toward a makeshift brown building where several guards are positioned while he stays covered by foliage.

"Be careful, Mak," I say quietly as I watch on helplessly.

"You know I will," Mak answers. "Do we wait?"

Just then, we hear another voice coming through.

"Beck, I'm checking in." Hok's voice comes through loud and

clear. Soon, his camera displays a view of a long bridge leading to another Camp.

"Good to hear from you, Hok. Mak and Hok, yes, we wait," Beck says quickly. "Just sit tight."

Hok hunkers down with the rest of his team. "We've also found the computers. It's the same as Mak, they aren't where I thought they would be."

Lya is watching intently, waiting to hear Adam or see him on the video.

Ryan Jasper is the next to connect, then Jay, and Gal. But there is no Adam. Not for some time.

"Where is he?" Beck rubs his head. "We have to have all of the codes at the same time, or this doesn't work."

Lya pulls out her phone, but after a few minutes shakes her head. "It's not showing me where he is."

Each camp looks similar, although it can be night or day depending on the time zone. I detect tension in their voices. The last two leaders for the Bryers check in, everyone except for Adam.

"Where is he!" Lya cries out.

Soon, those at the Cellars come through. Briston checks in, then Kenichi, several of the Powers that I have noticed over the years are also there, and Thire. It surprises me when one of the faces that pops up on the screen is Zelner. As if Briston reads my thoughts, he addresses everyone over their mics, "Zelner is with us. I've been working with him for a while and everyone can trust him." Those at the Cellars are not outside them like the others. They are elders who have slipped within the forgotten doors and known the codes to slip into the basements unseen. Each one looks eerily familiar. The mildewed walls, the darkness, and sounds of the tortured. I can smell the filth as I watch them hustle through the Prisons.

Beck addresses them, "Briston, Kenichi, those at the Cellars, you will wait for those at the Bryers. Keep hidden and wait for us."

Still Adam has not come through. "Where is he?!" Lya's intensity is growing with every passing minute.

"We have to trust that he'll be here," Beck says as he wipes his sweaty forehead.

Somewhere in the back of my mind I picture Geo and Daye—how he would slide his hand down Daye's arm, then lace his fingers comfortably between hers. And Daye would lean into him. Across the desk from Beck, Arek is standing with his arms crossed.

"We'll get her back," he mouths. "You and me."

I nod.

Beck has managed to get sixteen leaders on two screens. We can see the unique scenery from Japan to Switzerland, to New Zealand, to Africa and beyond. Each group is covered within the foliage or adjacent building, or whatever they have been able to find for cover. Gal is the closest to us in New York, deep in the Catskill Mountains. Diem is back in New Orleans. This was Briston's idea, to keep the couple closer to us than most. Jay has made his way back to South Africa, and Ryan Jasper is somewhere in Asia. My father is in the Cellar that I know best, Switzerland.

"Okay everyone, listen." Arek begins to speak to the leaders. "Stand back until we can get to Navin—hopefully by then Adam will have made it. I will tell you when we have breached the perimeters. Let the Umbramanes within your group do what they do best. They will get in and find us our codes. It's a half mile from here to the Chateau on Fifth Avenue. We have no idea what kind of protection Navin has on the climb to the forty-second floor. It could take us some time."

Gal jumps in, "What if Adam doesn't get here?"

There's a bit of silence until Beck clears his throat. "Then we forget the prisoners at the Bryers and I turn my focus on the Cellars. I'll access the secondary system to override and hope I can do it in time." Beck sighs, then continues, "We have to have these codes in order. Does everyone know their order?"

"Aye," Diem says first and the others follow.

"Then sound off." Arek looks at Beck who has the list in front of him. One by one the groups sound off, starting at one and ending at sixteen, which is Adam's place. Lya is now pacing back and forth. Beck ignores her as best he can. "We need the codes in that order. Once we have them, within just moments of entering them, we must have Navin in order for this to work. Once we get him, we release the prisoners and keep the doors to the Cellar locked. From there . . . we take care of Navin and everything else. Do you got me?"

"Yeah," one says, while another says, "Aye."

"Be ready to get those people out of there. Get your plan together to get them as far away from there as possible."

Gal speaks up from the mountains, "Listen all, I've already studied the area. Our system isn't where I expected it. It's in the guards' quarters. Which means I somehow have ta encourage 'em out of there."

"Aye," Diem says, "I have to do the same." The husband and wife work together even when miles apart. "We're stacking firewood just at the fence line." He turns his camera toward the fence to show many of his people helping out while keeping within the shadows and dark. "As soon as you say go, we'll light it, which will draw them out. Then the Umbramanes get in."

Arek nods. "It's a good idea. Do whatever it takes."

Hok jumps in, "Diem, we'll do the same." He commands the others he's with to search for firewood. "Give us time and we'll be ready to go."

Peter's voice breaks through sounding heavy and older than I remember, even though it has only been a day since I've seen him. "Have any of you heard them in there?"

"Who," I ask him.

"The prisoners. They're screaming and crying."

"Focus, Peter," Arek comes close to his brother's square on the computer. "You hear me?"

"I do."

Briston's voice comes through, "Do you see this?" Everyone turns their eyes to what he sees. "At my Cellar, there are thousands of them." His chest camera is staring outside. People have gathered. Just like the day Leigh drove me there. The Velieri have gathered. However, these are not screaming and yelling for my death, they are concentrating. Serious faces, Tracing everything they can.

"It's the same here," Kenichi says.

Arek looks at his watch, "Once we start our timers, our goal is two hours and fifteen minutes. Are you ready?"

The leaders agree together. Finally, Arek notices that all have spoken and he leans into the camera. "I'm setting my timer. Two hours and fifteen minutes. That's all we have. Be safe, all."

The beep of his timer fills the room and instantly we grab our weapons. "Come on, Adam," Arek whispers.

CHAPTER FORTY-FIVE

We stay hidden within the alleys of New York City. It does not look like the tourist attraction that it always has been. There are people on every corner, but it isn't obvious who they belong to—exactly as Navin wanted it. Valentino, Bergdorf and Goodman, among so many famous buildings, stand like fortresses over the brokenness.

Beck continues to check his phone while his computer is tucked into his backpack. Everyone is covered from head to toe with weapons. Meanwhile, on an open tarmac one mile away, several military aircrafts wait for the very moment that we need them to retrieve us.

In the dark I hear Sassi cry out in surprise, so we race to her. She's standing at the edge of the sidewalk beside a building teetering over a gaping hole that has been blown open, revealing the city's darkest underground. Kilon reaches out and pulls her back from falling.

Twelve Shadow Ghosts, whom I've never met before, surround us on all sides. Arek knows every one of them, and just that morning I saw them studying the map of the Chateau Barbury. At times I've noticed the stealthy way they move—nothing like ordinary humans.

I have my eyes on one Umbramanes, his mustache dark and his eyes hooded, only to look again in seconds and it's as if he's vanished. If I didn't know better, I would believe they're ghosts, just as their name implies.

"It's strange that just months ago, Alfonzo's ghosts were coming after us," I mention quietly.

"They were following what they were told by their Prophets, and you were a criminal," he responds.

One of the men overhears our conversation and steps forward. "Excuse me, Miss Rykor. My name is Kelly and I was there with Uri, when you used Tri Planum against us. I want to apologize. We were doing what we were told was best."

"Nice to meet you, Kelly." I shake his hand.

"But Remy, I just wanted to tell you . . . all of us . . ." He points at the surrounding men. "We no longer serve those against you. You have our loyalty."

"I appreciate it, Kelly." The cold night air chills my throat as I take in a nervous breath.

"Of course." He walks away.

Beck calls everyone over and we huddle within the darkness of a nearby alley. "Listen, this is where we must be careful. Once we cross this street, Navin may have his men perched about in protection." He shows his map. "We are here. Arek?"

Arek nods. "We'll enter in twos. Anyone who is not part of the Umbramanes must travel with a ghost. They will keep you hidden."

Sassi pairs with one, while Kilon pairs with another, and so on.

Arek and the other Umbramanes speak to one another through earpieces as we hide against the building across the street. My eyes bounce from the entrance to the top floors. "Navin is up there. I can feel him." Suddenly the familiar feeling, right before I Travel, fills my body. "Arek . . ." I gasp and he turns to me with concern, "it's happening."

"Can you do anything to stop it?"

Before I can answer and just as he reaches out to me, everything goes black. I wake up on a hard floor of black and white tile. The room is massive. There's an echo with every move that I make. Beautiful murals cover the walls, and the ceilings are lined with gold trim. Large windows wrap around with views of what I know is now a disheveled city, but within the black sky, all the lights of a cityscape create the façade that life is as it once was. For a moment I close my eyes. If only this could be true. I pretend that all is as it should be, and New York is hustling below. Tingling runs across my skin, telling me Navin is nearby.

Across the indoor pool are several large metal ice baths and medical equipment that doesn't belong within this luxury penthouse. I carefully walk around the pool, gliding my hand along the wall, then enter a wide hallway that is painted the color of heavily creamed coffee, trimmed with picture frame wall molding. It is dimly lit with a night light. I stay silent and up against the wall in case someone appears. As I round a corner, I stop and pull back when I see a man guarding a door. He's sitting in a chair and listening to a podcast on his phone. That's when I know . . . something or someone important is in that room.

What should I do?

There's a closet just to my left. I hurry over to it and twist the handle to get in. It screeches just a bit, which makes my heart twist. I carefully sneak a peek at the guard, but his podcast has covered up the sound. Finally, once I'm inside there is safety in the dark closet.

Just at my feet is a metal door stop. I pick it up, lean halfway out of the closet and heave it over the railing. Then, hurriedly shrink back inside and close the door. In seconds a small crash fills the echoey halls, immediately concerning the guard. He leaves his post and rushes down the steps.

That's my cue. Instantly I race to the bedroom door, already feeling my body begin to tingle as though I'm preparing to return. Opening the door, I see Navin at his desk, and while he pours over his papers and computer, he fidgets with something between his fingers.

I got you. I know exactly where you are.

Finally, I feel myself fall back into the universe and wake up exhausted.

"You okay?" Arek asks.

"He's up there . . . waiting for us."

Before we enter the building, the Ghosts gather to go over the details. They look at the map of this building, its entrances, its exits, how we can get to the top floor, and the quickest way down. I can feel the confidence of the Umbramanes.

"There are three elevators, but only one can take us to his penthouse. The freight elevators don't begin until the fourth floor. We need to somehow skip floors one through four," Arek explains. On our ride over here, something interesting I learned is that the Umbramanes were the inventors of roof topping, or what others call urban climbing.

"I'll go in the actual front door and make my way up with Kelly." Kilon volunteers to take the most dangerous route. Then I realize, Kilon will do anything he can to stay away from heights and the only other way we can get in is to scale this high rise for at least the first four floors.

"You'll be the only ones inside for the first few floors," Arek warns him.

"You don't trust me?" Kilon grins as he checks his weapons one more time beside Kelly.

Arek lays a hand on his shoulder. "With my life."

"All right then." Kilon puffs up his chest and shakes out his arms.

"Besides, Kelly will protect you," Arek grins.

"Just put everybody to sleep," I tell him as we part ways.

"Be careful kid," he says to me with a wink.

"Of course. It's me." He raises an eyebrow, telling me that he knows just what that means.

We split up—each person with an Umbramanes. Arek fires something that appears to be a gun, but it is thick and round at the base. Instead of releasing bullets, it sends a wire high into the air, which pierces the wall and attaches its claws to prevent it from coming back out. Then he shoots a second for me. Fifteen yards away, I watch Sassi and her Ghost do the same.

"Are you ready?" he asks.

"Do I have a choice?"

"No."

Arek wraps the wire around my waist, clipping it into place. We are dressed to blend in, covering our faces with black masks and our hands with gloves. We begin to climb one foot at a time. It's obvious that Arek would be much faster if it wasn't for me. My fingertips hurt after very little time, but once they turn numb it is better than the first few pulls. Arek stays below me.

"You're doing great, Remy. Just a bit more." His voice doesn't even sound like he's working hard. I can see out of the corner of my eye that Sassi is about at the same height as me. With each grab I lift a bit higher. We're coming upon a window and trellis, where I notice a blinking red light.

"Arek," I say quietly. He looks up and I point toward the light.

He brings his finger to his lips, telling me to stay quiet, then he climbs past me and ends up beneath the trellis near the security system. He notices some wire and pulls a knife from his pocket. With one hand he opens the switch blade, then cuts the wires easily. The red light instantly disappears, so I nod at him. I reach up and prepare my next grip, sinking my shoe into the faintest crack of mortar. Unexpectedly, a guard rushes out onto the balcony with his gun toward me. He can't see Arek.

"Stop!" he yells. In my peripheral vision, the Umbramanes swiftly grabs Sassi and covers her with his own body. They disappear as they blend into the building.

"Come this way," Navin's soldier above me growls.

"I can't," I say quietly enough that I wonder if he can hear me.

"Slowly make your way to me."

I notice Arek sweating as he climbs silently beneath the balcony. You would believe there is glue on his hands when his arms reach out, appearing to extend beyond normal human capacity. The guard is completely unaware because Arek's every move is completely controlled.

I climb closer, when he threatens to shoot. He takes hold of the wire around my waist to pull me toward him.

"What are you doing?" the soldier asks, pressing his gun under my chin. When I look over his shoulder, Arek is already there. Navin's guard has no idea. "Answer me," he demands.

Arek reaches out and twists the man's neck. He drops to the floor and his gun slides several feet away.

"You're dangerous," I whisper.

"No more than you, my love."

Before long, we reach the fourth floor and release ourselves from the wires.

"Let me go in first," Arek requests.

He presses the earpiece in his ear and speaks to his fellow Umbramanes. "In three."

Somehow, he breaks the lock on the sliding door silently and swiftly, then he enters the room covertly.

He leads me in the darkness through hallways and upstairs.

"Yeah," Arek says to someone speaking to him in his earpiece. We are pressed against the wall. "Just outside the main door. Coming now." Arek reaches out his gloved hand and turns the knob on the door. As he opens it, I see Sassi's beautiful eyes over his shoulder as we enter the room. One by one, Kilon, Lya, and the rest of the Umbramanes find us.

Once we begin our climb, making our way to Prophet Hawking's Chateau, we run into guards that are strategically placed. Arek, Kelly, and the other Ghosts speak to each other with hand gestures and take the men out in seconds. Even when they must fight, they do so ever so quietly and quickly. No one has a chance against them. They have memorized the details of each room in seconds—camera locations, number of guards, and whether there are exits.

We finally reach the only elevator to the penthouse. It is rigged with cameras and multiple locks. Beck pulls out his computer and begins tapping away.

"Give me a second."

"We don't have one."

Arek places large black tape over the lens.

To open the elevator doors, Beck bypasses the system. Once he does, we all cram inside and make the last climb to the thirty-eighth story. There are forty-two stories in all, the Chateau occupying the last four.

Finally, a bell rings and the doors open, but all of us stay hidden within the elevator. Arek steps in front of me and wraps around me like a shield. We hear the click-clack of shoes on the tile of the foyer, then a man presses the button repeatedly and looks inside wondering what has happened. He sees us, but before he can call for help, he is pulled inside. We leave him handcuffed and out cold within the elevator as the doors close.

The foyer is grand and beautiful. One of the Umbramanes quickly climbs the wall like a spider, keeping above the cameras' sight, and disables them.

It's the middle of the night and just like when I Traveled here, there is only dim light from tiny night lights along each hallway and in each room. This penthouse is beyond what most can afford. Chandeliers, grand piano, commercial grade kitchen, and a massive dining room among so many other things. It is obvious that Navin has been living the high life.

Beck whispers, "Security is off. Be cautious of individual monitoring. He'll have cameras everywhere. If it's not a part of the main system, it won't be shut off."

"Ten-four," Arek says.

We slip through the foyer, past the grand room, through halls, checking the rooms to make sure we have not missed anyone. Navin's obsession is obvious. There are cameras everywhere, computers and desks where his GENOS have hacked into systems, and security so thick that Arek and the Ghosts must be at their best. "You follow us," Arek tells us. We do our best to stay out of their way. They clear rooms in seconds while talking to one another in code.

I feel uncomfortable. Why was this so easy?

Beck shakes his head, "It's not easy . . . we're just that good."

"Get out of my head, Beck," I whisper.

Arek turns to me with serious eyes and whispers, "Guard better."

He's right. I've let the task distract me.

One by one, room by room, several floors of endless perfectly decorated house draw us closer to the room where I know Navin sleeps. Then I see his room at the end of a hall.

"This is it. He's in that one." I point toward it.

Everyone draws near.

After a moment, we enter.

But it isn't what I saw.

"What is . . ." but I don't finish my sentence. The dark bedroom is empty, but for two chairs in front of the desk where I saw Navin. Prophet Mannon is in one. His head lies unnaturally to the side as though he's asleep or dead. He's gagged and blindfolded with ropes wrapped around his chest securing him to the chair. My panic rises when my eyes turn to the chair just beside him. In it sits Prophet Jenner. Blood streams down her face, and she is also blindfolded and gagged. We keep the light off, but draw near. This terrifies Prophet Jenner.

"It's okay. It's us," I whisper and touch her hand.

Sassi hurriedly pulls the gag from both of their mouths and uncovers their eyes. Mannon wakes with a start, but his mouth is so dry he can barely speak. "Navin . . ." he licks his lips, "he's next door."

"Are you okay?" I ask.

Prophet Jenner's tears stream down her face. "Daye," she whispers.

"You know where she is?" My throat tightens as I wait for her response.

"No. But she's here. And Geo . . . I don't know where they are. He let us see them and then took them away."

I turn to Arek. "I thought this was where I saw him."

Prophet Jenner interrupts, "He's not far. . . Next door, I believe."

Once we have the prophets free, we slip out of the room and back into the hallway. We open the next door quietly. Navin shoots up in bed to see nearly twenty of us pointing our weapons toward him. Arek places his finger to his lips, warning Navin to be quiet.

"Get up," Arek says quietly.

Navin smiles. "Welcome."

"Get up," Arek commands.

His eyes catch sight of me and he stands. A sadistic smile has spread across his face that makes my stomach churn.

Navin notices Beck. "Ahhh, Beck. I should have known. How'd they convince you?"

Beck steps toward Navin angrily. "They told me if I helped them, then I'd get to kill you."

"Fair trade," Navin agrees. He sniffs the air. "Has anybody told you, you still reek of the Cellar."

Beck attacks with an obvious intention to kill him, but Arek stops him swiftly. "Back off, Beck!"

Beck has trouble pulling away, but finally he relents. Sweat pours down his face and his cheeks are flushed. I've noticed that Beck's anger lifts his large shoulders to his ears.

"Put your hands behind your back and turn around," Arek commands Navin.

However, Navin's reaction concerns me. He raises an eyebrow and cocks his head to the side. "Look, you don't want to do this, brother."

Arek's chest rises and falls as the veins down his biceps grow with tension. "Don't call me brother, and you're right; I don't want to do this. I want to kill you, right here, right now for what you've done to me . . . to my wife. But I need you to know something. It was never you. She was never going to choose you, nor was she ever yours. That Prophecy that you believed so deeply—the one that you assumed was yours to steal . . ." Arek steps up to his brother, who is only an inch shorter than he is, then he reaches his hand out and forces Navin's head in Lya's direction—who now stands next to me. Arek leans close till he's speaking in a whisper. "The Prophecy is already realized. I know you see it. You see what you always wished for yourself. She's mine."

"What are you saying?" Navin chuckles uncomfortably.

"You never knew. My wife . . . my child. Now, where is my daughter?"

"Apparently she's right there." Navin is confused, until you can see the change in his eyes.

Lya steps toward him. "Where's my sister?"

No matter how many years Navin has mastered never showing weakness, for the first time within his eyes is the antithesis of calculated. It starts slowly then builds until his eyes grow wide and his mouth opens just enough. He looks at me, then to Lya repeatedly as Arek continues. "There is no greater betrayer to your own self than jealousy over what someone else has. Tell me where Daye is."

Navin rubs his neck with a heavy hand. "I have no reason to tell you anything."

"How much time do we have?" Arek asks Beck.

Beck checks his watch. "Nine minutes."

"Give us the code," Arek commands. Navin looks at him with a clenched jaw and a grin. With a kick to his heel and a twist of his wrist, Arek knocks Navin to the ground so hard that his head makes a sickening crack, and he grabs it in pain. "Give us the code."

Beck has already prepared his computer with a clear vision of every leader's body camera as they wait patiently in the shadows for us to begin. His raspy voice is quiet as he speaks with them. "Is everyone ready?" Everyone responds with an out of breath *yes*. "Adam, are you there?"

A small crackle can be heard. Beck leans in closer, "Adam?" He runs his finger along the volume and the crackle gets louder. This time, there's a voice, but it's difficult to hear. "Adam?" Nearly a minute passes, leaving just a few minutes left. The crackle happens again.

"He's having trouble with his system," Beck says. "Adam, mate, I need you to check your pack. I gave you an extra in case this one didn't work. You're breaking up. Change it over, mate. Change it over." The timer is counting down. Navin is growing more confident.

After another stressful minute, Adam's voice comes in loud and clear. For the first time I watch Lya smile.

"Call in one by one!" Beck commands.

They sound off.

Peter is first, "Seven-five-zero-two-seven-three-eight-four -three-four-two-three."

Followed by another, then another, and another. I keep my eyes on Navin, who can see what is happening as clear as day. Beck enters each code into the system until Navin is the only one left. Arek presses his gun to his brother's head. "Give it to Beck."

Navin spends much of his time staring at me, until finally he turns to Beck. Through tight lips, he says, "Seven-nine-eight-eight -three-two-three-zero-zero-one-one-eight."

The keys make a tapping sound as Beck enters the last code. Finally, Beck and Arek force Navin to look into the screen for facial recognition and place his finger prints on the scanner. Instantly, something happens on the screen as Beck replaces the computer on the desk. "It's done," Beck says as he rubs his head and smiles. "It's done," he says again with relief.

Arek rushes to the monitor to look at the video. Kilon takes over guarding Navin. "Mak," Arek says cautiously, "try to open the gate."

From the left-hand corner, we see the gate getting closer as Mak walks toward it. With tense hands, Mak twists the fence lock and pulls. The screeching sound of metal fills the air as he pulls the gate apart. "It worked!" Mak yells. "It worked!"

Leader after leader opens the camps' doors and I can hear the hesitant excitement from their teams. "Listen everyone," Arek begins with an intense voice. "Listen, the hard part starts now. We still have to get around the guards . . . and get everyone out. Be careful, be guarded. You can do it."

We watch as they attack. Navin's guards explode from the camps' buildings and the fighting begins. We are helpless in New York as they wage their own wars to free the prisoners. Lya watches Adam's camera. I keep my eyes on Mak's. Arek can't help himself as he watches Peter run ahead of his team.

Navin says nothing. He watches on with not a word and I can't help but steal glances. One by one the prisoners see that their captors are being defeated. At first many of them are scared, but the leaders call out. "It's okay! We're here to help!"

Peter enters one of the buildings and immediately is attacked by several of Navin's men. It's hard to watch. Arek's knuckles have turned white as they hold on to the table. Guttural wheezes and cracks from punches can be heard. Weapons of all kinds fill our ears. Finally, Peter defeats his attackers, which allows us to take a breath. Just ahead of him, he stares at a room full of malnourished and poorly cared for people. They hide behind one another. "We're here to help you. If you stay with each other and stay behind us, we'll get you to safety," Peter says, softening their fear.

Even though many of these prisoners are fatigued, injured, and starving, the spark returns to their eyes. Suddenly our teams within the Bryers are no longer small—many of the captured join the fight. We smile at each other.

"It's done," I whisper.

Beck hurries to Navin and pulls his knife. "So now we kill him."

"Wait!" I yell. "Where is she?" Navin seems to be unphased by what has just happened. "Where is she, Navin?"

When he says nothing, I lose all my senses. I rush toward him and with a powerful fist, I punch his face until he spits blood.

"Where is she?!" I scream at him.

"Wait!" Beck's voice tells us a story we don't want to hear. Every one of us turns back to him. "It didn't work. I knew it. It didn't work." He's staring intently and his fingers pound frantically on his computer keys. "Briston? Kenichi? All of you who are at the Cellars, what do you see?"

"Where's my father?" Beck points to the screen that is his and he turns up Briston's volume higher than everyone else. We can hear him breathing heavy as he hurries through several halls.

"Briston?"

"Let me check one of the doors!" I'm grateful to hear my father's voice, but as we watch his footage, our bodies are tense when we hear an alarm blaring suddenly.

"What's happening, Beck?" I cry out.

"I knew he wouldn't make it easy," Beck whispers.

I'm about to ask again, but before I can, Briston reaches out his hand to an armed door. It opens with ease. "Beck, what do we do?"

As we listen to the sounds of fighting at the Bryers and our people having success, it is overshadowed by the weight of my father standing in a prison of the most dangerous criminals with doors that are no longer secure. His breathing has grown heavier, and I can't help but let panic slip in. "Beck, what do we do?"

Kenichi is now calling out from his Cellar. "They are becoming aware . . . look!" Kenichi stands with several guards in a room full of monitors of every floor and every cell. A couple of the criminals, wearing their gray suits with black numbers, slip out of their cells and rush to the nearest doors.

"Beck!" Thire yells. "It's happening here! We have to do

something. We only have moments."

Arek looks at Beck and covers his microphone. "What do we do, Beck?"

"The only thing I can do," he looks at me with an apology in his eyes. "I can lock everyone in. I can't lock the individual cells, but I can lock everyone in."

"Can they get out first?" I ask quickly.

"There's no time. I have to do it now."

Arek breathes out, then without another moment gives a definitive nod. "Do it." Arek leans into the microphone. "Those who are at the Cellar, listen to me. We have no other choice but to secure the main doors. No one will be able to get out. This is our only chance."

We suddenly hear Mak, out of breath and running with several freed prisoners beside him, "No! What are you doing?"

"What I have to, Mak," Beck says.

Briston, Kenichi, Thire, and several of the Powers, men and woman at the highest degree of skill, finally all agree. One by one they admit it is the only way.

"It's happening . . ." Beck punches a few codes, while Mak yells, "No!" once again.

We watch the screen as blinking lights for the lock on every exterior door soon turn red. In one fell swoop our most powerful and elite men and women, our oldest and wisest on our side, are now trapped. Briston's camera catches sight of criminal after criminal realizing they are free and taking to the halls like madmen.

"Hold tight. We'll come get you," Arek says as the veins in his forehead pop out.

We turn to Navin. It's obvious by the look in his eyes that we fell right into the trap. "You're alone, your most powerful alone with the most dangerous of all Velieri, and I still have her . . . your daughter. I guess you have no choice, but to do as I ask." Navin stands up, wipes the blood from his face, and steps toward his brother. "I'll take you to her."

Navin leads us through the halls toward the pool. We enter and immediately see that Dr. Karine is across the pool, standing next to Masey and a large army of men in black masks with red Xs. We raise our weapons fast, as do they. Many of us yell, "Put your weapons down," but not one of us will ever take that chance.

"Where is she?" Lya yells at Navin. She walks directly to him and places her gun against his head, behind his ear.

"You can do that . . . but it doesn't help anyone," Navin says quietly.

Rage deafens Lya and she pushes the weapon harder against him. I can see her finger pulling the trigger.

"Lya!" I yell. "Don't."

Tears begin to stream down her face. "Where is she?" Lya's hand shakes with anger. "Where?!"

Navin calmly clears his throat. "Over there."

My eyes study the room until I remember the ice baths against the wall. That's when I see the long blonde hair hanging from over the edge of one. I run toward her and as I get closer, I see Daye in one and Geo beside her in the other. Lya passes me and nearly jumps in the ice bath as she tries to pull her out. Daye's face is nearly blue.

"I wouldn't do that!" Dr. Karine says.

"Lya!" I cry out.

Navin's voice rumbles from deep within his chest. "Dr. Karine, tell them what they need to know."

The doctor walks to the edge of the opposite end of the pool. He rubs his hands together. "If you move them, they will die."

"Why?" I turn to him.

"What do you know of Tri Planum, Miss Landolin?"

I glare in his direction. "It's Mrs. Rykor. I know Tri Planum . . . everything about it."

"Well then you would know that if they are defeated in their subconscious, or unconscious, then they could possibly never be anything but comatose in their conscious." Dr. Karine cocks his head to the side, chiding me with his brilliance.

Navin stares directly at me, so I turn to Arek. We look at each other for some time, until finally Arek closes his eyes. "What do you want?" Arek asks his brother.

"I want freedom and I want everyone who stands in the way of that gone. Briston, Kenichi, you. And I want . . . you." This time there is no smile or grin on his face, just truth as he looks at me.

Arek turns to face his brother. "No more games."

"Life is a game, brother. I will work to get what I want. You either choose to fight me in all levels, or everything stays the same. There's no way to release your daughter without going in yourself," Navin finally says. He lifts his thumb and forefinger making an inch measurement between them. "I'm this close to having everything."

Arek takes a few more steps toward his brother. "I will fight you and I will win."

"All of you in Tri Planum . . . against me. Sounds fair enough. But no Shadow Ghosts."

I shake my head. "You have Dr. Karine."

Navin looks over at Dr. Karine and nods. More GENOS with black masks, burst onto the pool deck from every one of the five doors until we are desperately outnumbered. "Many of the GENOS were Ghosts too. They left Alfonzo to join me." His Umbramanes outnumber ours by far. Slowly, as if to make an entrance, Leigh appears from one doorway and Covey from another. My heart drops. Arek glares at his father.

Dr. Karine presses a button, which closes the doors to the pool.

"I should have known." The disappointment in Arek's voice is loud and clear. Leigh looks at him carefully.

"The Prophets are done," Leigh explains. "There is nothing but sides to take . . . as much as I'd hoped it wouldn't come to this."

"It never needed to come to this, Dad. He's killing Kenichi and Briston and you are just allowing it," Arek says quietly through a clenched jaw.

"It's not what I want. But if it is the only way . . ." Leigh admits.

"You can't be serious!" Arek exclaims. "We could have been so much more than this. So much more. The Rykors have always led. Led with purpose . . . led with integrity. When did that stop? When did you cash in?"

"I didn't cash in. I claimed stake in freedom," Leigh answers.

"This isn't freedom. This is a massacre. This is the easy way out. Hate is always easy," Arek growls. "You could have stopped this before it began."

"And what good would that have done. The world is already a mess." Leigh pulls the hammer back on his gun. Then suddenly he raises it toward me and shoots. I feel the pain in my stomach instantly and, before I know it, my hands are covered in blood.

The GENOS start shooting. I race toward the ice baths where Lya stays with her sister. Before I can stop it, Lya gets hit several times with bullets. "Lya!" I scream as I feel hot pain in my back and fall to my knees.

My body is paralyzed, and I drop to the black and white tile floor.

∿∿∿

When my eyes flutter open, it is without understanding of where I am or how much time has passed. The mural on the ceiling revives my memory and I sit up as if I'm on springs. Only then do I feel the constraints on my wrists and hear the clink of chains. My tired eyes peer closely at the chain and leather strapping me to the ground.

"You're awake." Navin takes several steps toward me, then kneels. Any other moment in life, to have any other man look at me with these eyes would be something to desire, but the memories are still locked away within my chest. He reaches out and drags his knuckle down my cheek. I look away. "Everything I've tried to create . . . it's happening. I wanted to kill Ephemes for the freedom of others, and look . . ." He points to a monitor in the corner where chaotic footage of the world at war plays. "I've wanted to fight my brother my entire life and here he is." He points toward the tub where they are lowering Arek's lifeless body. My face flushes with fear. "But none of that means anything unless you . . . you exist with me. That, I have to admit, I haven't figured out yet. But you're predictable. I take something of yours and you come find it. And here you are."

"I will never choose you."

"Maybe not . . . not with the way you are right now. But I've planted something in here before," he touches my forehead with his fingertip. "I remember telling Dr. Karine and Japha that it would never work. Until it did. I can do it again."

"Traveling." I look into his eyes and know I'm right.

"Yes. We had to wait for that one. You were just a kid when we made sure to do it. But it finally happened. When it came out that you were the One and it seemed everyone wanted a piece of you . . . that's when it started to work. Your fear was the catalyst to your Travel. I never would have thought."

I look around and notice that Kilon, Sassi, Lya, Daye, Geo, and Beck are all motionless and lying within the cold water. Unfortunately, I see that the rest of the Umbramanes have overtaken ours. Kelly is dead. It's in the corner of the room that I see two very familiar and scared faces looking at me. Prophet Jenner and Prophet Mannon are once again tied to chairs and unable to help.

"What are you doing with them?" I ask.

"Getting everything I want." He stands up and takes out his phone. Soon he starts a video and is instantly connected to the rest of the world. "I told everyone that I would take those out who stand in the way. The Prophets . . . they are the old way. It's time to usher in the new." With that, he pulls a gun from his pocket and points and shoots. Mannon cries out in pain.

"Noooo!" I yell.

Navin turns the camera toward me. "And the One? This is the One they have followed all these years. Spent years protecting. And for what? Here we are. There's nothing she can do."

He twists his body around again and points the gun at Prophet Jenner. "Navin, don't!" I yell. "There's no reason to kill her."

"I guess I should keep her . . . in case you need a little push?" He nods, then turns to Mannon and the bullet makes my ears ring. Only this time, Mannon no longer moves. He is no longer in pain. Blood drips from behind his ear. The deepest and most guttural cry escapes Prophet Jenner.

Navin walks to me and whispers, his lips next to my ear. "Try and save them all, Remy. I think you'll realize soon that this Prophecy . . . this idea that some Higher Power chose us . . ." His laugh is dangerous since he does so without care. He kills with the strangest conviction—believing that he is doing what needs to be done. *How do we fight this?* "It is all a lie. A dangerous lie that kept us hidden in the name of money and power."

"The same things you've sold your soul for." My eyelashes are wet and heavy as I stare directly into his eyes.

"Put her in," Navin tells the others. His men pick me up and begin lowering me in the water. It's so cold that the pain is instant. It's impossible to tell whether it is fire or ice . . . I suppose it doesn't matter to my nerves. What matters is that it rapidly takes my mind to a weakened state just like before. All I can think about is the pain, the intensity, the desperation to get out of the freezing water.

Dr. Karine comes over and places electrodes all over my skin. Then Navin sits on the edge of the bath, "I'll see you soon."

As soon as Dr. Karine returns to his computer, he presses a few buttons and that's when the buzzing from the electrodes starts. It's not just that. Navin has closed his eyes and is already digging. His Trace is no different than the first time I met him on the streets in San Francisco, only now he must work harder, even in my compromised state. I cannot tell if Leigh is joining in this fight as he stands in the corner. Isaiah Aldo stands near. The severe cold pulls my strength from my mind in order to reinforce my body's defenses.

"Good night, Remy," Navin whispers.

CHAPTER FORTY-SIX

My actual self, the body that exists within Prophet Hawking's New York penthouse, is captive to the freezing water that nearly paralyzes my muscles. With this, and the help of Dr. Karine, Navin has better control than I've ever experienced since being trained. Our injuries don't help—the water is red from my blood. The multiple shots I took have slowed my blood, which has slowed my healing. Navin feasts off this in order to take us to the next level.

The shift begins and soon my mind splits in two realities.

Within the second reality, I wake on the ground outside. It is nighttime and I am facing the stars while my fingers touch soft grass. To my right is a fireplace and chimney and nothing else. It stands alone with a stack of wood burning orange with squares of black where it will soon turn to ash. Someone else's fingers softly lace with those on my left hand and when I turn my head, I smile at Arek lying beside me. He rolls over and kisses me as he has done so many times. My palm presses against his warm skin as I close my eyes. I hear the wings of an owl . . . or maybe a bat nearby, which grabs my attention.

When a hard finger pushes my face back to be kissed, I gasp at the sight of Navin—not Arek. I panic and crawl away.

"Remy, come back," he says.

When he gets up to come after me, I flee. His feet make padding noises through the mud, telling me that he is not far behind. Just ahead there is a fence that seems to cover miles of land. Luckily, I catch sight of a metal handle and I rush to it. The latch gives me trouble under the pale light, but finally I am able to throw it open.

I shriek and brace myself, as I nearly fall down a set of stairs. The door of the fence has turned into an interior door of a home. This is how I know we are in our place of dreams. It is not reality and the more I believe it to be so, the more lost I will become. I struggle to catch myself before I fall down, but Navin reaches me. He rips the door from my hands and because of this I plunge down the stairs. Every bounce on each step, I feel. Once I land, I moan. Soon, Navin grabs my hand and yanks me to my feet.

Within the ice bath in my conscious existence, I keep my eyes closed so that Navin and Dr. Karine don't know I am awake, but even there, it is as though my body feels everything that is happening in my subconscious.

Back in my subconscious state, I raise my knee to my chest and with one large kick, my foot connects with Navin's knee. I hear the pop and feel the actual crack. He cries out as this sends him to the ground. This gives me time to race away.

"Remy!" he yells angrily.

Within this old home, lit only by the spotted blue light of the moon through the windows, I grow increasingly scared as potted plants come alive and shadows have eyes. I run and run until something occurs to me. I am going nowhere. The hall is extending longer and longer, never allowing me to reach the other side. I don't know whether to stop or continue.

Soon, I feel another split within my mind. This isn't good. I know what this means. It means he has me on a revolving reality enough to dive deeper and press further. He has been able to fulfill Tri Planum.

The third level appears in a flash. I'm now on the streets of a city, but at the base of each high-rise are moats like those around a castle. The sky is a combination of black and red with fast-moving dark clouds. I run through the streets alone, wondering where everyone is. It can't be just me. Navin, Dr. Karine, and the others have us all.

Strangely, I notice a high-rise building like the ones in New York, but it has moving parts. Square objects travel along the outside of the building. As I get closer, it becomes clearer. There are chairs—large wooden ones like the old-fashioned electric chairs that would execute criminals and I recognize that there are people in them. They are appended to the exterior of the building like a train track dug into the ground. The chairs can move sideways, then up, then across, and back down. The chain within the track makes heavy clunking noises. There are three chairs traveling at different stages of the building and a large crowd has gathered outside to watch like zombies. They do not help or appear concerned, rather they seem to have no care for the people who sit strapped by leather and iron within them.

I get close enough to take a better look. Each person in the three chairs is wearing an iron mask not much different than a scold's bridle used throughout the centuries to silence women who were thought to be rude. Only these masks look to be extremely heavy and secured with train-size bolts next to their temples and jaws. They cannot make a sound or move anything but their eyes. The closer I come, the more I recognize their scared eyes, even when I can't see their full faces.

"Daye!" I yell and come so close to the moat that I nearly fall in. Her terrified eyes drop quickly to mine, then the next chair passes. It is Geo. And the third chair is Kilon. His eyes seem to be shut, but I can see his hair splaying from beneath the metal.

What do I do? I say to myself as I look around. That's when I notice that the track enters the building next door. I follow carefully, keeping within the shadows of the building. Every few minutes, I check in with my conscious self to make sure that I can still move and have not been completely taken over.

Navin is trying to control every thought, every sight within these three levels and I feel it. Why doesn't he just kill them? The thought enters my mind again and again. There must be something he needs with the others in order to get what he wants, but what is it?

Even with Dr. Karine, Navin's abilities are elementary at best. Clunky and unnatural, he tries to move through my mind with precision, but I know where he is at all times. I can track his sound, his rhythm whether he likes it or not. When my fingers and toes wiggle in the ice bath, this tells me he hasn't been able to go deep enough yet.

In this last level, the greatest task is to cross over the water surrounding the buildings. Precious time passes as I try to figure out what to do.

The entire time, I do my best to keep my thoughts protected. How do I battle him alone? Our conscious should be our best . . . and yet I lay within the strangle hold of freezing temperatures and whatever confines the electrodes have placed on me. I'm not sure what they've done to the others. *Where is Arek? Is he also in his own hell? Is he within the levels that I am?*

I check in with my conscious state again. My body has started to shake violently. As carefully as I can, I peek through slitted eyes. Navin is in a chair not too far away, his eyes closed as he works hard to dig within me and get what he wants. Dr. Karine is at his computer, paying more attention to our vitals than to my body. Leigh is nowhere to be found and Isaiah sits beside Navin. It's obvious their plan is to work together.

With slow and meticulous fingers, I pull one of the wires of the electrode attached to my thigh. It's more difficult than I expect, then finally it pops off with a small splashing sound. I hold my breath and glance with small eyes toward Navin and Isaiah. They are too busy and don't notice.

So, I pull another one, then another. With each one gone, I feel the difference. That's enough for now. I don't want them to notice that I'm awake, so I leave the other electrodes alone.

Within my subconscious, I am still running through the hall that never ends. *But what if I stop running?* So, I slow down and teeter to a stop within the hall of this mysterious, dark mansion. I wait for a moment and nothing happens. *Maybe I'm right?*

But then, the shadows reach for me. They are now palpable and drawing close and the sound that comes from them is beyond frightening. The ground begins to shake, and the walls start closing in. Faster and faster the walls become a prison around me until I can't breathe. Stopping wasn't the answer. So, with nowhere else to go, I run. Chasing the end of the hallway like an animal chasing its tail. The end will not get closer, and it feels hopeless.

Within the third level, is it my unconscious? Is it Navin's? Are these memories or something drawn up and devised by Navin? My feeling is that this is his design. Our unconscious does not normally appear so nightmarish, so fictional—that is usually our subconscious. Our unconscious is usually our deepest and most hidden memories.

Within the high-rises of this third level, I follow the track to where these chairs enter and exit. But the moat stands between me and the large doorway where these chairs disappear. I look down in the murky water just as something large and scaly swims by.

What can I do? Just then, I see a wire of lights overhead. The zombie-like crowd is still not paying any attention to me, rather they watch Daye, Kilon, and Geo move across the building, their bodies jolted with each turn of direction.

I climb a nearby truck and reach up to grab the row of lights. With a heavy yank, I test out its security. It feels strong enough. Carefully I hang from it, letting my toes slowly release. Then one hand in front of the other, I make my way across. At the door, I finally let go and rush inside. It's an industrial building and completely empty except for five of these wooden chairs. Four people sit confined within them. I race to their side and see Arek within the first one. I'd know his green eyes anywhere.

"Arek!" I reach out and grab the metal mask, but it is screwed into the chair with large bolts. He can't say a thing to me. His hands are bolted down, his feet, his body . . . everything. Lya, Sassi, and Beck are next to him.

"What do I do?!" I cry out as I yank until my fingers bleed, but it's useless.

Suddenly the track comes to life and pulls Arek's chair onto it. The chain clicks like when you climb a roller coaster.

"What do I do?!" I climb onto Arek's chair, tugging everything as best as I can. "I can't." My chin quivers, and my body shakes with energy and fatigue at the same time. Arek's eyes stare directly into mine as the tears fall down my cheeks. "I'm sorry, baby. I'm sorry."

His chair travels through the empty warehouse toward the door that will let him through. Sassi, Lya, and Beck are not moving yet. When I can't follow Arek, I run outside. If I can figure out what Navin's doing with them, maybe I can stop it. Again, I use the lights to climb my way back across. Once my feet land on solid ground, I study the surroundings. I watch as the chairs move along the face of the building. What is he going to do to the building? My eyes cover every inch of it, but I can't find anything but the track.

"Close your eyes and listen, Remy." Holona's voice comes from deep within.

So, I do. I'm distracted by the clink of the track chain and that's the only thing I can think about. Until something different hits my ears. There's a whirring sound from somewhere behind me. With careful movements, I turn, and that's when I see Navin. He's staring at me from the building across the street. When we lock eyes, he points his finger toward Arek, Daye, Geo, and Kilon. The whirring sound gets louder. Navin lifts a box in his hand and presses a button. When he does, shots from his building fire directly across the street.

"No!" I scream. The earth shakes as the bullets penetrate multiple parts of the building, narrowly missing Geo. "Stop!" That's when I understand. He has them here because of me.

CHAPTER FORTY-SEVEN

It is difficult to move my muscles since they are frozen. I reach a level of cold that I've never experienced before. Even for my brain to tell my body to move, there is a disconnect that makes it that much more difficult. Keeping my eyes closed, I try not to grimace as I reach for the last few wires. My body is desperate. It fights the urge to jump out of the water. But I also realize that within my subconscious and unconscious, I am losing the battle.

Next to me, the others seem to be doing nothing. Not a sound comes from their direction and that's how I know that I'm alone. Somehow, I have to battle Navin without him knowing. It's not just Navin that I work against, but Isaiah Aldo, Leigh, and Dr. Karine. I work and work to wrap my finger around the wire, then pull until the last two electrodes pop off. Whatever connection that Navin believes he has with me that allows his power over me, is gone.

Within the subconscious, I stay as invested as I can, never wanting to lag behind Navin's Tracing. Only now, without the electrodes, I feel a difference. My brain is clearer. The words Arek said to me long ago come back as I push to remain ahead of this game: *"We cannot continue to be defensive; we have to take our power back."*

Within all three levels, conscious, subconscious, and unconscious, I stop for a moment. *Think Remy. You can do this. What needs to be done? I need to save them. How? Why am I here? Why doesn't Navin just kill us? What does he want?*

Suddenly it occurs to me. Where is Navin? If he's expecting to shift something . . . if he's expecting to change something within me, where is he within these places?

It's just a distraction. Where is he? Instead of running, I need to change the narrative. I need to find him.

In our unconscious, I look up at him as he presses the button again. A barrage of bullets sends parts of the building flying, only this time Daye is hit by a bullet.

"Daye!" I yell.

What do I do? I can't do this alone. Please! I can't do this alone.

"Remy", I hear the soft voice behind me. When I turn around, I've never felt such relief in my life. Holona is there. Her long dark hair hangs heavily around her face and her green eyes.

"Help me," I say out loud as I feel myself crumbling. "What do I do? How do I save them?" She comes closer and looks up at her son, Navin. I feel her sadness within my chest. "Holona, what do I do? He's going to kill them. He's tearing the world apart."

"He thinks he's doing the right thing," Holona admits. She turns to me calmly, although I've never felt more pressure in all my life. "Remy, he's using the fact that he's still everything you hate. It's locked and stored. He's using the fact that you've shackled him to yourself."

I look at her, then raise my eyes to Navin.

She continues, "Find him."

"He's right there." I point toward the tower, but he's no longer there.

"You still believe that it's his choice of where you are. It's not his choice. It's yours." Holona explains. "You are the One. So, I suppose

369

the question is, what does that mean? What can you do that they—even together—cannot?"

My eyes widen and my heart skips a beat. "A back door? One he cannot see," I realize.

"Make him believe you're exactly where he wants you." She nods as I close my eyes.

From my conscious, within the New York penthouse, I begin to dive. At first it seems complicated. There's too much to take care of . . . too many people against me. For several moments I wait—listening for the old reliable rhythms within each spirit. I hear four unique cadences and, while my eyes are closed, the rest of my senses are heightened. I'm not even sure how, but I grab all four and ride these rhythms within them. Dr. Karine is the weakest, especially without his electrodes. Navin is next . . . but I notice something different. The air changes against my skin. It turns cold, and blasts of wind hit my cheeks. I can't keep my eyes closed any longer and when I open them, once again, I am standing in darkness with thousands upon thousands of sparkling stars surrounding me.

Navin is using Isaiah Aldo to lead him. I can hear it. Navin doesn't trust himself enough to go alone . . . to fight me alone. I disrupt their cadences as secretly as I know how. I don't want them to feel where I am, rather they need to believe that I'm still running through the hall in my subconscious and standing outside the high-rise in my unconscious. It surprises me that once I figure this out, it is easy to accomplish.

Meanwhile, because I've made them believe I'm still where they want me . . . I can find my own path. I can figure out why I'm so tied to Navin that we can't seem to defeat him. Once I establish control, it's time to search. *Where is Navin really?*

I wander through memories. Moments when I hated Navin. Moments when he stole from my life. They pass quickly, except for one. Soon I drop into the memory.

Holona is there as I stand on the hilltop overlooking the house on the hill. The house where Isaiah Aldo and Navin took me. "What do I do?"

"Burn it," Holona says.

My surprise shows. "But I'm in there." I can hear my cry from within.

This is when she turns to me sternly. "No, you aren't. That's where you have it wrong. A part of you has lived there since it happened and yet you don't need to. Do you hear me? You're not in there. You haven't been for a long time. Burn it."

One moment, I am on the hilltop, and the next I am beside the house with fire in the palm of my hand. It does not burn my skin or make a mark, and I'm not sure how it got there, nor do I care. I peer within the window just as I hear my screams from inside. I am there, my body convulsing in pain, while Navin watches.

"I . . ." I begin but cannot finish.

"You are no longer there, Remona. Burn it," Holona repeats.

Finally, I kneel beside the house. I drop my hand to the ground and let the flames lick the dry grass beneath. Soon they catch and a small fire begins but gathers strength faster than I expect. Holona blows on the fire and it's as though she's thrown kerosene. The fire shoots across the house, bubbling the paint and blackening every edge. It's unexpected when my chest grows tight, and my throat feels the painful lump. It was just a moment ago that I hadn't remembered any of this, but now I can't help but picture those years of torment. As the entire cabin goes up in flames it takes everything within me to know that this is not actually happening, rather it is but a stain on my memory that I have not released.

Finally, we climb the hill once again and by the time we are at the top, the heat from the house has made my body glisten. I turn around just in time to see the last bit of fire cover the rest.

Then, an unexpected weight is lifted from my body.

"I can breathe," I whisper. Without it, it is hard to believe I ever lived with it.

Holona smiles, "I know." She looks me over carefully. "There's more."

"I don't have time for more . . . we have to get everyone out."

"The weight of your fear keeps you from letting this go. And letting this go is the only way to defeat him. Trust me."

"Okay," I whisper.

I close my eyes for just a moment, then when I open them, I have dropped into the hallway that I know so well. It is the dark gloom of my memories that makes the air thick and my feet like stone. The room where Japha, Navin, and my mother took most of my childhood awaits me. I walk to the door in order to enter, my chest tight as if in a vice. One turn of the handle stands in my way, and I hesitate.

"Go," Holona says.

I twist the knob and step inside. The last time I was here, he made my mind split in three. Japha always had that ability to make me feel crazy. Only now, I know why I'm here. There's something in this room that has forever tied me to Navin. Something here forces me to Travel to him. To give up secrets that I don't want to give.

The crackle of the fire seems to set pace with time, sometimes slow, sometimes fast, sometimes unexpected. Long ago Geo explained that memories, when tampered with, will be different than what really happened. So, I look around trying to remember those moments in this room when I was just a child.

"It was so long ago," the words tumble out.

"But just a moment ago, really."

"I can picture Japha opening the door while I sit on the couch afraid of what's to come. As he walks in, I can see that he's repeating something over again and again," I tell her as I make a circle about the room.

"What does he say?"

"*Tre kilou neu fumen caretsiva sui.*" Only now I know the translation because of Geo. "Within me, I capture your spirit." I turn to

Holona. "Geo told me this at the hot springs. He told me to return to this room. If I take out Japha, I take my power. I have to find the talisman."

It's not as if Holona knows the answers, rather she's learning just as I am. Suddenly, the handle in the room begins to shake and twist. I press myself against the wall near the door. That's when it occurs to me that I don't have a weapon.

Holona glares at me like a mother would. "Remy, it's your choice. Give yourself a weapon."

I close my eyes and when I open them, I lift my hands in the air. Within my right and my left are two Glocks. When I catch Holona's expression, it makes me smile. She raises an eyebrow, impressed at my skill.

"Okay. I get it," I whisper more to myself than to her.

The door shakes on its hinges as a key turns the lock. I step to the opposite side of the door and press my body against the wall. Finally, the door opens and Japha steps inside. I take a shot and my bullet hits him in the back. He flies forward and quickly turns to me with his hand up. The energy that stands between us makes it hard for me to come closer. This man is beyond dangerous. Over the years, his power has grown and never been challenged by anyone else.

"*Tre kilou neu fumen caretsiva sui,*" I whisper again and again. He's afraid of my words. So, I say them louder. Then louder. Unexpectedly, he jumps to his feet and lunges toward me. My body flies back. His arthritic physique is nothing to be afraid of, but we all know the internal power someone can have over you. He wants to affect my mind so that my body becomes useless. I can tell he's getting in because the room starts to move slowly. It's so slow that every time his hand moves it has a lingering effect like the tail behind a falling star. That's when I notice his other hand. Within his palm between his crooked and disjointed fingers, he rubs a wooden coin just like the one Navin had. My heart begins to race.

"*Tre kilou neu fumen caretsiva sui,*" I say the words, yet they come out slowly. My mind starts to fade, which allows this old man's body to stop my weapons from turning toward him.

"Remy!" Holona yells.

The room becomes dark, and he begins to mess with my mind even more. I can feel that he's trying to pull me in two, then possibly three. His eyes are nearly translucent. This is not someone who understands right and wrong. He does not understand humanity or bleeding for someone else. He does things to me because he wants what I have and sees my life as a profit margin.

"Japha is dead! This isn't real!" Holona yells.

Suddenly everything stops. I look toward Holona, who stands nearby, and see it in her eyes. She's right. In fact, this is *my* memory. Japha has evident power over me, even now. Something starts in my toes and rises, gliding all the way through my body like a shot of light. I was just a child, but I'm not anymore. I'm strong now, capable of more than this. I control this memory.

Anger erupts from deep down. My cheeks flush with rage. I can feel it building beyond what I've ever known, and then it explodes. But not just in this room. It erupts outside the high-rises with the red and black sky. It erupts within the long hallway that has no end.

Within the room with Japha, I twist my hand. He crashes against the ceiling, and the talisman falls to the floor. Instantly, I grab it from the ground and place it in my pocket. He falls to the floor then reaches out in order to fight back and I feel the familiar crash of his evil against me. Only this time my energy and his clash so violently that the walls wave as if soft; my energy wins and he flies back. When he hits the fireplace, his body explodes into a thousand pieces.

After a few moments, when my awareness returns to me in my conscious state, I am no longer in the freezing water in the New York penthouse. Within the pool room, I stand in a warped bathtub, its metal melted to the tile floor beneath my feet. The water that was once ice is now an inch high and boiling around me. The room looks to have been through an explosion as Dr. Karine lies lifeless against the back wall, pieces of his computer thrown this way and that. Debris has covered the top of the pool. Navin is rubbing his head beside Prophet Jenner, whose straps have broken. Isaiah is trying to get up but is too dazed.

"Remy," Arek's gravelly voice says from beside me.

I turn to Arek. Only I realize I am now looking down on him. He has reached out to me. Once again, my body hovers over the deck floor and my feet no longer touch the ground.

CHAPTER FORTY-EIGHT

Tri Planum is not over. Although I defeated Japha from my memories, Navin still has us controlled within the other levels. Arek, Geo, Beck, and Sassi are the only ones who have come back to life within our conscious state. There's an energy coming from my anger that has lifted me in the air once again. My body feels weightless. It tingles from the inside to the outside. My cheeks and my neck are on fire—somehow, I know it is connected to the thrill of defeating Japha.

"Remy?" Arek's voice calls my attention down to him and before I know it my feet have touched the tile. "You are the One."

"It doesn't seem to matter, Arek. What has this done for anyone?" I say as he places his palms on my fiery cheeks.

"Arek!" Geo says with a nervous tone.

I peer over Arek's shoulder and that's when I see Lya, Daye, and Kilon. They have been thrown about in my outburst, but now lie unresponsive within the inch high water.

Geo has Daye in his arms as Sassi kneels over Kilon. Arek, Beck, and I rush to Lya and pull her wet and comatose body up.

"They won't come out of this until we can free them." Sassi grabs her weapon and points it toward the end of the pool where Navin had been. But he's gone. So is Prophet Jenner.

Leigh and his men are just now coming to.

Geo turns to us quickly before everyone across the room gets their wits about them. "Let's get them safe. I'll stay with them while you go after Navin," Geo suggests.

Soon, we move Kilon, Lya, and Daye through the doors and down some steps. We find a room in the back of the house, one that can be locked and barricaded with furniture. Geo prepares his weapons, as we do ours.

"You'll be okay?" I ask him.

"Of course. I'll be with you in the other levels. Just tell me what you need."

With one last look, Sassi, Arek, Beck, and I leave them behind a wall full of furniture. We race through the penthouse searching for Navin. Several of his men are waiting for us as we enter the hall. Instantly, a barrage of bullets hits the walls, destroying Prophet Hawking's home. Navin has kept his best men for himself. Trained fighters respond to every strike and kick instinctually. We fly in and out of rooms. Under my breath I pray that Navin hasn't gotten away again.

Arek finally stops and looks at us. "This ends now."

We all look at him with a nod. "This ends now," each one of us says.

While we race through the penthouse in search of Navin, taking on his men until our bodies hurt, I find that the hall within my subconscious has stopped growing. I can now reach the end. My awareness has changed. I can feel the danger before it happens. The shadows that once were reaching out for me, now run beside me as though they belong to me. I reach for a door at the end of the hall and instead of hoping that something safe is behind it, I choose what is there.

When I open the door, I step out onto a mountain—the edge of the cliff that sat within Arek's subconscious the first time we went through Tri Planum. Only this time, instead of being forced to climb before the bottom dropped out from beneath us—and Alfonzo's men repelling to catch us—there is a dark sky with a bright yellow strip of sunset over miles and miles of mountain peaks. And standing on the edge, looking away from me, is Arek. He turns around in his pure strength and perfection, so much that it makes my breath stick.

"You found me," he says.

"I did."

From above us I hear a catcall, and when we look up the mountain, Geo is standing there. He directs us to come up with a twist of his hand, so we begin to climb toward him.

"Navin has no help now," Geo says as we reach him. "Sassi and I have found the others."

"Who?" I ask.

"Lya, Daye, and Kilon."

He leads us up the rest of the mountain until we are surrounded by brilliantly large redwoods. Sticks made to look like symbols we don't understand hang from large branches above our heads, which tells us that we are getting close.

"I think he was trying to tell us something," Geo says. Arek and I aren't sure what he means until we enter a clearing and see Sassi and Beck standing in front of three piles of wood. I've seen the same setup before. Each pile of wood is about six feet high with a sturdy and tall log standing in the middle. I'm in disbelief about what I see ahead.

"You think he's trying to tell you something?" Geo asks Arek.

Lya, Daye, and Kilon are strapped to the middle of their own pile of wood. Their heads are tied to the standing logs by rope within their mouths and although I can see in their eyes that they know what's happening, because they are trapped within their unconscious, they cannot move here either. They are aware but incapable of much else.

"It's the same way Holona died," I look at Arek.

Sassi turns to Geo, "Does this mean we are still in Arek's subconscious?"

But instead of letting Geo answer, for the first time in what feels like forever, I know the truth and answer before he does. "No. We're in Navin's. He hated that his mother died because of them and he hates that we're preventing him from exterminating those who did it."

Arek walks to the edge of the pile. "I know you can hear me. We've got to start with your unconscious first. You remember that? We have to free you there first before the others or we risk your mind. You understand?"

Even though they can't respond, their eyes look at us and I can tell that they know. A tear runs down Daye's cheek. Geo steps to the pile where she is held and climbs carefully. He reaches out from halfway up to touch her hand. "We're going to get you out of here."

"We guard them here for now while we work on their unconscious," Arek says.

Within the unconscious, I am still staring at the building where the chairs clink around the outside of the building. Only now two of the chairs have broken leather straps, which forces me to look around. *Where are they?*

Lya, Daye, and Kilon are still trapped by the metal masks and straps, but Geo and Arek are no longer. My eyes search the strange dystopian city. Finally, I see them. Coming from the large warehouse, they climb the lights and land on the street near me.

"Where is Navin?" Geo asks.

I turn my head to the high-rise where he stood a short time ago, but he isn't there. Instinctively I know he never wished to face us by himself. "He's hiding."

"The irony," Arek whispers. Then something occurs to Arek. "I know where we can catch him."

"Can you take us there?" Sassi asks.

"Of course, I can."

I close my eyes just for a moment as I feel the change. It starts within but then the air turns hot. A small wind that's humid hits my face. Instantly sun scorches my shoulders and when I open my eyes, I'm looking at a place that I remember just slightly. "Wait. I know this place."

Arek nods. "Yeah. He lost her here."

We stand outside a courtyard in a city center. "When are we?" I ask.

"Sixteenth century France. It's where Navin lost everything," Arek says with heavy eyes.

"So, he's hiding here?" I ask.

"It doesn't matter where he thinks he's hiding. This is his unconscious. We navigate this . . . he can't keep Lya, Daye, and Kilon in those masks. It's him that is keeping them controlled by their minds . . . we switch the scene . . . switch the narrative. Come on."

Arek hurries through the courtyard, where people pass by with goods and baskets. Past the courtyard is a garden and just beyond this a small home. Ahead I see a woman. She's beautiful with kind eyes and short dark hair. She holds the hand of a child, and is pregnant with another. I see a large breath lift Arek's chest, and I can tell that he doesn't want to be here.

As the woman and her child walk along a path just outside this home, I hear the gallop of several horses. Three men on these large animals hurry toward her. She's about to let them pass, but they stop to engage her.

"Here he comes," Arek says and turns behind us.

Navin is sprinting across the field toward these men and this woman.

Instead of letting him pass, Arek stands in his way. Navin slides to a stop, staring directly at his brother.

"What are you doing?" Navin asks through gritted teeth.

"Taking control," Arek tells him.

CHAPTER FORTY-NINE

Within our conscious, we race through the penthouse fighting every one of Navin's men until we've scoured every room. "He's not here!" Sassi breathlessly yells as she runs to us.

Together we make our way down the building, from elevator to stairs, hitting every floor and taking out anyone in our way.

Back in our unconscious, Arek stands in Navin's way.

Suddenly it comes back to me. "I remember this," I say quietly as I look from Arek to Navin, then back again. "Your wife. Ephemes killed her."

His eyes cloud over with sadness, but it's more than that. The rage within him is about to burst as he keeps his eyes on the men and his wife.

The men jump down from their horses and start circling Navin's wife and child.

"It's still there Navin. It's feeding off you," Arek mentions. As if to mimic the men circling Navin's wife, he begins to circle his brother. It's at this moment that it occurs to me . . . just like Kilon's ability to send people to sleep, or Geo's ability to connect the energy from every realm, or Sassi's and my ability to mix with those who walk in spirit, Arek's ability becomes clear. Within his strategy, he can pull people to their suffering within themselves. He can control Tri Planum in ways that others can't.

Arek continues, "Let my daughters and Kilon go."

Navin's jaw clenches and his chin quivers as he turns to Arek. "This is just a memory." Spit sprays in the air, but he tries to hold his pain close.

Arek continues to circle his brother. "But does it feel like it? Can you watch what happened to them again and again?"

The men surrounding Navin's wife and child begin to taunt her by pulling at her dress—she yells at them to leave her alone. "Run!" she yells at her child.

Navin's body is so tense, it seems that if you knocked him over he'd break into a million pieces. For the first time, my anger turns to sympathy.

"Navin," I say quietly. "You've continued this long enough. Let Lya, Daye, and Kilon go."

"And if I don't?" His teeth stay connected in the vain attempt to cover that he must want to run to them.

"You no longer have Dr. Karine," Arek tells him. "This doesn't have to end. I can force this to happen . . . again and again and again . . . until—"

"Until what?!" Navin interrupts. "Until I grovel, until I beg? . . . because I'm telling you brother, it . . ." he takes a hard step to Arek, "won't . . ." he takes another, "happen." They are now face to face.

None of this seems right. Within war, there are casualties; within beliefs, there are contradictions; within pain, there is the ability to hurt others, so where do right and wrong live? Two brothers, staring at each other, their anger pulsing from their veins to puffed up chests.

Within our conscious, the world in which we all exist in body and mind, we have fought our way through the building, checking every corner for Navin. His men continue to attack, but we've prepared long and hard . . . and with each of them, they last but minutes. I am able to take down men double my size in just a few moves, sneaking in fatal blows when they least expect it.

We reach the lobby and look around, sweaty and bloodied. It's quiet. We keep our weapons high and search carefully. I hear the loud crash of something falling over behind the watchman's desk. Carefully Sassi and I walk around it and find a young man without a mask and without a weapon crouched in the corner. He sees us and throws his hands in the air. "Don't shoot, don't shoot! I'm not one of them."

"Get up," Sassi orders him.

He awkwardly stands to his feet trying to keep his hands up at the same time. "Where's Navin?" I ask him.

"Who?"

I can feel that he's lying so I raise my gun again and point it directly at him. "There's no time. You either tell me where he is, or I take you with us to find him."

"Okay, okay! He ran across the street. There are weapons in a bunker."

"Where?"

"In a bunker . . ."

"What building!" I yell at him.

"The Ivory House. It's a small restaurant at the bottom of the Paige building. Beneath the restaurant is a basement and Navin's there."

"How many men went with him?" Sassi asks.

"A few," he answers.

"You're getting on my nerves, kid," Sassi yells. This is one of the first times I've experienced Sassi's panic and it's unsettling. "How many?!"

"Less than ten!" he cries out.

We tie him up quickly and shove him in one of the rooms.

"Hey," Beck says. We turn to see that he's been checking the internet from his computer and phone. "You're not going to believe this."

"What?" We hurry to his side within the quiet lobby.

"See those . . ." he points to the cameras hanging from the ceiling in the corner of the lobby. "Every room in this entire building has one. I was able to download the video from upstairs . . . what Navin did to us and," he looks at me with apologetic eyes. "and what you did to get us out of there."

"Why? Why did you do that?" I am wracked with fear suddenly. My entire life I have been forced to run because I was different. People cast me out because of the Prophecy long ago, or they praised me with what felt like false hope—expectations that I couldn't live up to.

"Because it's time." Beck stares straight into my eyes. "We don't have time to play around anymore . . . we don't have time for your reservations about who you are. People need a hero. They want a hero. They want someone who can do what they can't and experience what they never have."

I place my armed hands over my head and turn away. "Beck."

"Look! Velieri have now seen it. Andrew shared it. And Ephemes," he comes to me with his phone in his hand, trying to get me to look. "Ephemes have a choice. They either see the miracle that you are, or they continue to believe there is no purpose and no one to save them. It's their choice . . . but either way, everyone deserves a choice. Now look." We watch as he scrolls. The video is on news stations and social media sights. Again and again, it begins with us trapped, until whatever is inside of me erupts and decimates everything in its path. My body lifts in the air as the power ripples through the room.

Andrew Vincent, from wherever he is, has already made a video. "Andrew," I whisper, impressed by his ability to keep up his status as everyone's favorite journalist.

"It's why he's the best," Sassi agrees.

Andrew's deep voice has always soothed his listeners, and at this moment, I feel the same. "Whatever you do, watch this video. I am here to tell you . . . do not look away, do not run. I told you that she is the *One*." The video plays, then he begins again: "People are being murdered, our cities destroyed, all because of one man. I'm calling all those who are willing to take the chance to fight. Get out there. Velieri or Epheme . . . we are all human. All capable of taking this fight. Fight with us! Fight with her!"

"I can never go back," I whisper.

"We were never going to be able to," Arek says as he comes close. "Nothing was ever going to be the same anyway. Let's end this now."

I nod. "It ends now."

CHAPTER FIFTY

W e are about to step out onto the streets of New York. We've seen the smoke from the windows and smelled the destruction, so we prepare our weapons before unlocking the sliding door. My Glock is full, and I hold Kilon's favorite gun, a Sig Sauer 1911, in my right hand. Sassi's eyes watch me prep it, so I lay a hand on her shoulder. "We'll get him out, Sassi. He's going to be okay."

"I know," she nods, yet I'm not sure she believes me.

"Are you ready?" Arek asks.

"Yes. Let's do this!" Sassi says with full power deep in her lungs.

"Maybe." Beck admits.

Arek gives him the side eye, then reaches down and twists the key that's already there to unlock the glass doors. When we step close, they open with a swish, revealing the pandemonium. Under the streetlamps, it is no longer a ghost town. People are running this way and that. There is fighting all around us. Fires everywhere. Like a SWAT team in heavy gear, we push through the debris, following the instructions we were given by the man who saw Navin. We see the

Paige building just across the street and the doors to the restaurant below, but immediately wonder how we are going to get there with the madness surrounding us. Cars whiz by and I'm forced to jump out of the way.

Meanwhile, within our subconscious, we still wait at the base of the firewood. Lya, Daye, and Kilon remain unchanged, hanging lifelessly like ragdolls, trapped by their unconscious.

"Where is Navin here?" I ask. "Don't you find it strange that he shows himself in the third level but not this one?"

"Something's going to happen," Sassi says as she sets her hand on her chest. "I can feel it."

She's right. I listen carefully. I feel rhythms that are not ours. We keep watch, this way and that.

"They are just sitting ducks without their unconscious free," Geo says as he tries to get to the top of the mound where Daye is strapped. "Yet we cannot risk freeing them without it."

Out of the corner of my eye I see something pass from one tree to the next.

"Did you see that?" I whisper.

"What?" Beck asks.

"Something's out there." The sun is falling, which makes it difficult to see.

"Where?" Arek asks as he steps a bit closer to the forest. Suddenly an arrow whizzes by him, forcing him to duck, and in just seconds, the wood pile beneath Daye and Geo lights up. The fire spreads fast around the base.

"Where'd it come from?!" Sassi yells.

"From there!" I point toward a small grouping of trees and race toward it. Another arrow flies past. Then another.

Before we can stop it, the fire rips across and up, nearly reaching their feet. "What do we do?!" Sassi screams as she tries to climb to Kilon, but the flames are too big. Kilon, Daye, and Lya are unaware.

"The only way is to defeat the unconscious," Arek says. He raises his gun to the trees and lets bullets fly. It doesn't matter that he can't see who it is. His jaw clenches with such force and I can see the rage in his eyes. "Come out," he whispers.

Meanwhile, deep within the unconscious, we still stand in the field, keeping Navin from saving his wife or his child. "Let my daughters go," Arek growls at his brother once again.

The men aggressively push Navin's wife to the ground and raise their weapons toward her. "No!" Navin yells as he watches on.

Arek sweeps Navin's feet out from under him. Faster than our eyes can see, Arek holds a knife to Navin's ear. "You have seconds to release them or I swear to god you will watch her die again and again."

The man attacking Navin's wife takes her by the collar of her dress and begins dragging her toward the house. I am desperate to cover my ears from her screams.

"It would be one thing, brother, if it was just me. But it's not." Navin knows something.

I instantly look around the field.

It takes me a moment to see them, but then I do—Prophet Covey, Isaiah Aldo, Prophet Hawking, and Dr. Karine. Then my heart drops when Leigh comes to stand beside them. "How did we not feel them?" I wonder out loud.

"I don't know," Sassi says honestly.

I notice a change in the air, and the drag of my mind . . . then, within the second it takes to blink, we are back in the dystopian city where moats surround the buildings and the sky is an even brighter red than before. The orange stripe of sunset has thinned.

Lya and Daye are still there, trapped beneath the thick welded metal. Their fear is obvious within their wide eyes behind the masks. Even though Aldo, Covey, Hawking, and Leigh have managed to bring us back to their designed third level, Arek still has a hold on Navin, only now Navin lies on the ravaged street. Suddenly, the whirring sound starts again, and I look at Navin.

"Who's doing that?" I yell at him. Arek presses the knife harder to his head.

"What?" Arek asks me.

I turn toward the building across the street where Navin once stood from the upper floor and bombed its counter building. There, looking down at me, is Isaiah Aldo holding the button in his hand. He grins as he presses it. Instantly an explosion rings out. Just ahead of Daye's chair, as it moves across the building, is a large hole where the bricks have been blown away.

"Stop!" I yell.

Navin says nothing, but a grin spreads across his face. Isaiah engages the weapon again and again and again. The ground shakes as the brick building flies apart brick by brick. "Arek!" I yell, as I run toward the moat. Prophet Covey, Hawking, and Leigh are there with Aldo, to keep the mind battle under control. They don't say much, just concentrate with hard eyes and clenched jaws.

I yell at the top of my lungs at Leigh. "Do you know who they are, Leigh? Huh?! Do you care?"

Despite the fact that his face has been emotionless this entire time, I can see a flicker of confusion by what I'm saying. "Look at them! Look into their eyes. Your granddaughters are up there! Or do you care?" Leigh steps forward, so I continue, hoping that this gets through to him. "That's right. We hid them from you for years! But here they are. Your flesh and blood . . . their very existence means that you are a part of the Prophecy just as much as I am."

Leigh's eyes widen and he peers closer.

"You're a fool, Leigh. He's going to kill your grandchildren. Holona's grandchildren!"

CHAPTER FIFTY-ONE

In our conscious, we reach the double yellow lines in the middle of the street with our weapons drawn. Suddenly we see Navin and his men waiting for us under the overhang of the Paige building. Their guns are pointed directly at us, and they're shielded behind large black shields.

"Oh my god," Sassi says.

Arek shakes his head and turns to us. "Find cover fast!" Before we can even move, the guns begin to riddle us with bullets. Sassi and I land behind a nearby car that has been flipped on its side. Pain rips through my side and I cry out. Sassi, too, is hit.

"Sassi, are you okay?"

"I'm fine, I'm fine." She winces as she pulls herself to sit against the car.

"Sassi, listen to me. I thought of something. Can you distract Navin?"

"Which level?" she asks through gritted teeth.

"The unconscious. If you control the unconscious, you control his conscious right? Do your best to keep the attention off me."

"Okay," she says while her body is shaking with pain.

Against a nearby building, Arek and Beck are aggressively shooting at Navin's men. It's hard to know whether we will come out of this. It seems to be out of our control. Everything is out of our control.

CHAPTER FIFTY-TWO

Within our unconscious, an unexpected car zips down the road of the mangled city. Behind the steering wheel is Sassi. That's when I realize this is my chance: while Arek has Navin, and all eyes are on Sassi. All I can do is try.

If I hurry, it'll only feel like seconds that I'm gone. I need the back door that Holona helped me find. Soon, I stand in the Void, the stars swirling about me in an unexpected pattern.

"Holona!" I call out. For a moment, the silence remains, and I know that I can't wait too long. "Holona!"

"I'm here." Her deep voice is behind me, and I turn around.

"I know what I need to do. Take me to a memory of Navin when he was a child."

She says nothing for a moment and lets the request sink in. Finally, she nods. "Okay."

"But it can't be yours. Listen, I know you exist in a place that has power beyond anything I can do here. You must find Navin's memory. Not yours. I know he's your son, but we risk everything if we can't do this."

She nods. "This is not my son. Not the one I raised." She reaches out her hand and when I touch it, we dive deep into a memory bank. Passing this one and that, until we come to a halt near several little boys—not one older than ten—running around the courtyard of a castle I've seen before. That's when I recognize this place. Arek took me here once. This is the castle of Arek's grandfather, who was leader of the Protectors until he died and Leigh took over.

Holona and I are watching carefully as these boys of the Renaissance run around happy and playing—a rather different childhood than mine. "Which one is he?" I ask Holona.

She points to the one that I already believed to be him. "The leader," she says.

This doesn't surprise me. Navin, with his sharp eyes and pale skin. I shake my head. "I need him alone."

The shift happens almost instantaneously, as though whatever place Holona exists has more ability than I could ever fathom. Suddenly, I am in a room, still during the fourteenth century, with a fire glowing in the fireplace. Only this time a boy stands in the corner, quietly humming, his face pressed against the stone walls. I remember this well, as my mother always punished me this way.

"Navin," I say quietly.

It is unsettling when his eyes turn to me. It is Navin . . . although at the same time, it isn't. His eyes aren't as cold, his jaw not so tight.

"Who are you?" he asks.

"No one of consequence. I'd like to give you something." With nimble fingers, I pull the talisman from my pocket and show it to him.

"What is the manner of dress you have on?" he asks inquisitively.

"This is what we wear, where I come from."

"Where are you from?"

"Far from here." I grin and kneel, still holding out the talisman. "I don't have much time, but I'd love if you could help me by taking this. It's for you. I made it for you."

"What is it?"

"It's valuable. So, if you keep it with you, you'll have good luck. I need you to take it and read it to me."

Carefully he makes his way toward me. When he gets close enough, he reaches out and takes the talisman from my palm. He studies it for a time.

"Do you like it?" I ask.

"Very much."

"Can you read what is on it?"

"Fumen kilou neu tre caretsiva sui." He rolls the talisman back and forth, looking at the mysterious symbols along it. He reads aloud, "Within you, you capture my spirit."

"Very good." I pull out mine from my pocket and show him. "This one's mine."

"What does yours say?" he asks.

On it, it says the words that are just slightly different than his, *Tre kilou neu fumen caretsiva sui.* "It says, within me, I capture your spirit."

Young Navin studies the perfectly carved wooden piece, then looks up at me perplexed.

"Read it again for me?" I fear this won't work, but this is my only chance. "Please?"

This time Navin grins. *"Fumen kilou neu tre caretsiva sui,"* he says again.

"And again."

Again, he repeats it, as I do mine. Something happens this time that didn't the time before. My skin crawls and my heart lurches. Even Holona looks around. It's as if a weight has fallen from my body.

"Did you feel that?" I ask her.

She nods, then looks back at me. "It's done."

"Is there a way to be sure?"

"We can only try."

I lean over the child, cup his hand with the talisman in mine, and smile. "You'll forget all about this," I say Tracing his innocent mind, just as they did to me.

The young Navin returns to the corner of the room, places his face against the wall, and I can hear his faint whisper as he repeats the words: *"Fumen kilou neu tre caretsiva sui,"* again and again.

Holona nods as I turn around. "You can't use this in Tri Planum. This hold over him . . . it won't work in there. He needs to have someone to Travel to. You have to free yourself and the others from Tri Planum and then you can use this."

"I just hope it works."

"Me too." She looks at me carefully, then gives me a weak smile. "Hurry back," she says. "Listen, Remy, when all seems lost . . . just remember one thing."

"What?"

"Just remember, there's always something greater petitioning for you. You're not alone. And when it gets hard, it's important for you to remember that."

"Okay."

"Now hurry! They need you."

CHAPTER FIFTY-THREE

Just a short time ago, this dive into Tri Planum was nearly as foreign as the sound of Velieri when I was first attacked. Yet now, I jump through these tunnels faster and better than I could ever have expected. At this point, Arek's rhythm is the most familiar to me and if I wait silently long enough, I can close my eyes and pick through the many to find his. That's how I get back to them so fast.

I slide back into the unconscious that Navin created to keep control, and it's obvious that it has been only seconds, since Sassi is still trapped in the car that she crashed into the building. Suddenly I see Navin running to where Isaiah, Leigh, and Covey are hiding.

My eyes swing about desperately, searching for Arek. "Where is he?!" I yell.

Beck and Geo both point toward the street where Arek had been holding Navin down. Instead of the brothers, there is now a hole in the street and smoke billowing from it.

"Arek!!!!" I scream.

I race over to the billowing smoke. There's nothing there as I cough and feel the burning effects in my eyes. "Remy!" I hear from behind me. When I turn, I see just his arms and his head peeking out over the side of the moat. It takes me just a second to reach him and pull the rest of his body up. When he finally peers at me, I see it in his eyes. There's no more being careful. Rather, we simply need to attack.

"You can do this," Arek says. He places his hand on my face. "I'm with you."

Beck and Geo help Sassi out of the car while the horn blares. With a few yanks of twisted metal, she slithers out with only a few bruises. I help Arek to his feet and then together we race across the torn road and into the high-rise where the rest of the men remain.

Taking the stairs, we fly up two to three at a time. Again and again, we hear the bombing. "When he hits them, they're gone!" Sassi yells.

"He won't!" Anger has erupted within me, and I fly past Sassi. She stops for a moment, surprised that I have taken the lead. We finally reach the door that will lead us to Navin as the entire building shakes. We kick our way in and without another word Navin, Isaiah, Covey, and Leigh are on guard. The only way I can describe the fight that happens next is beyond anything that can happen within the real world. Only in our minds can we catch bullets, evade strikes, and our moves—and our enemies'—are faster and more precise than anything in the conscious world.

My cheeks flush and the light within my eyes dims, then brightens, then dims again as if we're under a strobe light. I can feel the energy of the room turning into a lightning ball, one that Willow used to teach her kids about in school. Starting like an electric pulse within my fingertips, then moving through my arms and into my chest, is a heat so warm and a shock so bright that I pay little attention to my ability to win this fight. Isaiah has chosen me as he always has before, like I was the reason for his insanity. He wanted to break me, he needed to. Perhaps he just wanted Navin's attention, or Japha's power . . . but no matter what it is, he faces me right now. And this lightning, this thrust of power within me, envelops me so quick that I give him no room. Not a second to move. Not an inch of space.

Within our conscious, Sassi and I continue to hide behind what we can in order to get closer. Our guns are hot within our palms as we shoot what we can and help each other from the others that attack us. Arek and Beck also make their way closer.

Within our subconscious, the nightmare has begun. The fire still climbs, licking at the heels of Daye, Lya, and Kilon. Our daughters remain comatose, but Kilon has managed to open his eyes. He can't speak, but we can see the tears in his eyes from pain. Creatures of all kinds have emerged from the surrounding forest, forcing us to battle them all at once. I've never fought for anything so hard in my life, but the lives of my daughters. They didn't know me as a mother, nor did I know myself as one, but here we are, desperate to create anew what was stolen from us.

But it is within my unconscious that the truth has come. Isaiah is desperate to take me down, to murder me once and for all, but my abilities are out-maneuvering him in every way. And suddenly I understand what Gyre was talking about. A fourth level. No one has ever done more than three. Whatever the Velieri founders believed the *One* would hold the power to—feels within reach.

"Go," Arek commands me as he fights Navin. Navin grabs Arek's neck, but Arek climbs the wall with his feet and flips over Navin's head—something completely impossible in the physical world.

I close my eyes, listening to Isaiah's moves. Then when I open them again, the room is still there, but there's a fourth layer over it. My body is keeping pace with Isaiah, yet somewhere I've connected to a deeper place than just our unconscious. I return to the place Navin took me so long ago when he tried to steal my memories and convince me that I was his. Stars cover everyone and everything in this room like a translucent screen.

"You will still see me. I am there in your sight," I whisper to Isaiah. I step away from him, and he continues to fight the air. I watch him for a moment as he wails and tackles nothing. Somehow, this screen of stars, the place I called the Void, where all things become perfectly clear, has meshed within the unconscious. As if I can copy and paste myself. Isaiah doesn't see that I'm not there anymore.

I walk to the other side of the room and reach out to touch Navin. With one fingertip against his shoulder, he flies against the wall and hits so forcefully that the brick wall turns to dust. I push him again, only this time he flies out of the high-rise building and into the air, and I follow. It is my choice whether he falls several stories to the ground or whether he stays in midair. I decide to play and let him hover clumsily several hundred feet in the air.

The dark star-studded curtain that I now travel through holds us above the apocalyptic city. Navin panics, never having experienced floating with nothing protecting him from a fall. I walk around him, feeling the power pulse through my veins. I touch his hand while closing my eyes and remember what Gyre said. *You can direct him. Lead him, steal from him, he will give you anything to get away from that feeling.*

I open my eyes and Navin is in an absolute panic as he sees himself behind me, still fighting Arek within the third level.

"What are you doing?" he cries out.

"Leading you."

I cock my head to the side, telling him to look at the building where Kilon, Daye, and Lya have been bound. "Warehouse," I say. Suddenly, Navin and I are in the warehouse and I am strapping him to a chair. The heavy iron mask wraps around his face, while the turn of the motor twists the train track-size screws in place. He yells as the metal closes in on him, and I cannot hear the end of what he calls out. "Remy, you don't have . . ." but the clank and the squeal cover up his words.

"Let them go. And you know how. Unconscious level first."

I back away and the chair is taken by the chain and motor out of the warehouse. Soon it is climbing the building, where Daye, Lya, and Kilon still remain. "If you don't let them go . . ."

I look back to the building across the street and in a blink, I am there, holding the button to the cannon. I press it, and the large explosion happens just at Navin's feet. He feels the pain from the shrapnel that hits his shins and blasts his legs. Even though he can't cry out through the metal mask, his eyes show the scream.

"Let them go, now. I'll make this unbearable. The only way to get out of there is to take us out of this place." Somehow because of this overlaying fourth level, I am able to speak to him, just as Gyre spoke to us. While I stand in the building far away, he can hear my voice in his head.

Suddenly, all of us are within the subconscious. The fires are out of control, and I recognize the feeling that we are no longer battling in Tri Planum. There is no longer an apocalyptic city, and no longer the high-rise and chairs. The three piles of wood have turned black, gray, and orange, and the flames lick at their skin.

I look around as the others fight monsters and evil of all kinds, but Navin is nowhere to be found. Closing my eyes, I take a moment to listen and feel where he is. It doesn't take long to know his fear. For the first time since this all began, I can feel that he no longer believes in his power but recognizes mine. I rush toward the forest, leaving the others. Within the fog and lowering sun, I see Navin hiding behind one of the trees. When he sees me, he turns his gun in my direction and shoots. Before I understand what has happened, his eyes have grown wide as I hold my hand out in front of me. When I turn my palm over, the bullets are dust within it and fly away with the wind.

Once again, my face has turned grotesque. I overtake him almost immediately. I drag him through the trees as if he is a rag doll. Upon reaching the fires, there is one set up for him. The creature I have become in his eyes can drag him up the wooden stake with ease. Then, I start the fire. It engulfs him in flames faster than the other fires. He has no power anymore. "The only way to get out of here is to take us out." My whisper speaks in his ear, even though my lips don't move, and his cries of pain are loud and piercing.

Suddenly we are back on the streets of New York with no sub-conscious or unconscious to fight. Just here. Just now.

"We're out!" I yell.

"Remy!" Sassi says as she points toward the penthouse from where we came. There, with their weapons and armor ready, are Lya, Daye, and Kilon. Sassi smiles and so do I. Arek, across the way, shows his relief.

I have beat Tri Planum. The fourth level is mine. And now, there is no coming in and out of the Void . . . it is always. I live here.

CHAPTER FIFTY-FOUR

Lya, Daye, Geo, and Kilon race toward us, ducking and avoiding gunfire as best they can. Navin's army has formed a barrier across the street behind many tanks and ravaged buildings, and it has become large and takes shots at every moving target. Isaiah, Covey, Navin, Leigh, and even Hawking are nowhere to be seen.

Lya comes to my side, and we hide behind the nearest car.

"What do we do?" Daye asks.

"Why don't we dive into our own Tri Planum?" Lya asks.

"No. We have to keep ourselves out of it . . ." I don't explain, but they can see that I have my reasons.

Suddenly, a loud noise comes from the other end of the street. Several large tanks push their way through the heavy debris, kicking aside torched cars.

"Who is that?" Sassi asks.

We keep our eyes on the tanks coming closer while also trying to fight the GENOS. They get uncomfortably close.

"What do we do?" Daye cries out.

Soon the rumbling slows down and the tank gun turns toward

the GENOS. A barrage of bullets fly, taking many of them out. After a few minutes, when the gun slows down, we hear the screech of the hatch. For the first time in months, a familiar and kind—but dirty—face smiles back at us.

"Caynan!" I yell.

"I couldn't let you have all the fun! Look!" He points the opposite direction of the street and on the other side is a man I don't recognize. With the GENOS still recouping who they have lost, Arek and Beck return to our side. Arek's eyes fall on the man walking our way. A large army of men and women follow behind him.

As the sun begins to rise, Arek takes several steps toward this man with his hand out. He is older, dark skinned, with a mole on his cheek just under his eye. There is nothing extremely terrifying about this man, however, I can tell that he means business.

"Alfonzo," Arek says as they shake hands.

My eyes widen. I study him and then his group. The Umbramanes. I have now been chased after by these ghosts, worked with some of them, and now . . . here they are—the best trackers in the world. Navin comes to my mind, and I smile at Sassi when I see the pleasure on her face.

"The end is near," Sassi whispers with a grin.

Kilon runs his hand along her neck, "That's for sure."

"Arek." Alfonzo's thick Spanish accent bounces in the air beautifully.

"I didn't know which side you were on," Arek admits.

Alfonzo looks around Arek's shoulder and his eyes fall on me. "Neither did I, til I saw what Andrew shared." He walks toward me with his hand out, so I shake it. "It's a shame I didn't believe in you before. But here we are. Our forgiveness will be in our actions."

"Thank you," I say quietly.

"Where is he?" Alfonzo asks.

"Not just he," Arek explains. "They. Navin, Covey, Hawking, and Isaiah."

"Isaiah." Alfonzo Geretzima says with a sly grin. "He believes he's the best. Is he the best?" He turns to the Umbramanes when he asks the question.

"Hell no," one of the men in the front says, with his arms crossed in front of him.

Suddenly we hear a rough, gravelly voice that puts us all on edge, and every one of us twists around with our guns pointed toward him. Leigh, bloody and broken, walks up with his hands in the air.

"Stop!" Sassi yells. "Don't move a step closer, Leigh!"

Arek moves toward his father with so much anger, it's difficult to know whether I should hold him back or let him go. "What are you doing?" Arek yells.

Leigh reaches for his gun and the rest of us start yelling. "Wait!" he cries out. His old and wrinkled hand pulls the gun from his waist band, then he throws it toward us. It slides across the pavement until it lands at Kilon's feet.

"What are you doing?" Arek asks, his voice calming slightly.

"I didn't know," his eyes turn to me, "what they did to you. I didn't know about your daughters. And I thought I was choosing freedom." His sorrowful eyes turn to Arek with such pain it's hard to look away. "I'm sorry, son. I'm sorry I didn't see what you were telling me." Tears come to Leigh's eyes and my heart drops. This is a man I have never seen. The hard shell crumbling right before our eyes. "My intention," he lifts his dirty hands in the air and twists them about, "was never money or power . . . I just truly wanted to be free." He walks to Arek and rests a hand on his cheek, "I see you now. You believed in something that I just couldn't. I didn't want it to end like this . . . and I'm sorry." The father and son stare at each other with tears pooling at the bottoms of their eyes. Arek's chin quivers. "Navin is at the Old City Hall Station. They have more weapons there."

He turns to Lya and Daye, "You're beautiful."

"Will you come with us?" Lya asks her grandfather.

"No, I will show you where your enemy is." The look in Leigh's eyes after he says this is one that will haunt me until the day I die. He turns to me one more time. "My wife? You still speak with her?"

I nod but say nothing.

"If you see her before I do, tell her that I love her."

"I will."

The haunting within his eyes turns into determination. Unexpectedly he runs out into the open streets with no cover, but pulls a second gun from the back of his waistband. When he reaches the intersection, he turns and looks up, pointing his gun directly at one of the GENOS in the fourth floor window and shoots. Then he turns and takes out two more GENOS, until they finally understand that he's no longer on their side. His eyes connect with mine, just as the GENOS begin to shoot. His body convulses in pain as blood sprays in the air. In only seconds he is riddled with bullets.

"No!!!" Arek yells angrily. Arek reaches for his rifle, lays it over the edge of the tank, and singlehandedly takes out many of Navin's men to save his father. Kilon joins in, trying to get the rapid fire to stop so that Leigh can make it out alive. My eyes fall on a man standing behind a nearby post, his sights lined up on Leigh.

"Leigh!" I scream.

Arek takes a shot at this man, but it's too late. The bullet hits Leigh just behind his ear and his body goes rigid. Immediately, he falls to the ground.

All of us, including Caynan, Beck, and the Umbramanes, take out nearly every GENOS within this block and Arek races toward Leigh. He sets his hand along the older man's shoulder and closes his eyes. Just then a barrage of explosions sends us into cover. Arek wraps his arm around me as we press ourselves tightly to the metal of a car.

Beck is shaking his head as he's staring at his screen. "What?!" Arek asks just as bullets whiz by my head and I can feel his arm and body instinctively press us harder.

"Look," Beck says, shaking his head as he turns a computer to us. An aerial view of the city shows GENOS—thousands of them—filling the streets and closing us in. Their black masks with red Xs along their eyes and mouths are undeniable. Tanks are trudging through the chaos, but there are too many of them for us. Even with the Umbramanes and Caynan and his vigilantes, we are but a fraction of the amount of people coming our way.

"What do we do?" I whisper.

For a moment Arek says nothing, his brain on overload. "The only thing we can do . . . fight."

"We can't defeat all of them."

"Maybe not. But we can try."

Suddenly, a plane flies overhead, unleashing a massive attack on us with artillery. Arek wraps his body around mine as the road around us flies in the air like raindrops on a lake. The sound is agonizing, and my fingers wrap his shirt in my palm as I keep my head glued to his shoulder. People around us are getting hit from every which way. Sassi and Kilon are under an overhang nearby and I can hear their cries of pain and fear. The plane passes again and again, never letting up. By the look on everyone's faces, there is no getting out of this.

CHAPTER FIFTY-FIVE

I have no idea how much Arek's strong body has taken from this air raid as he covers me completely. Beck cries out with anguish when he's hit. Caynan races the streets while avoiding what he can and tries desperately to get back to the tank.

"Do you hear that?" I ask suddenly when a small growl comes to my ears. Arek looks up at the sky as blood drips down his temple. Together we see several tiny dots on the horizon. "What is that?" I ask.

"Yes!!!!" Beck screams to the sky. "Military planes! They have to be ours!"

"Make sure they know we're down here!" Arek yells at Beck. Arek pulls his phone, but it's been demolished by stray debris from the buildings. In just seconds, Beck jumps to his feet as he talks on the phone.

"They know!" Beck yells with laughter as he waves his arms in the air. "It's Gal and Diem!"

As they fly overhead, all of us cry out in joy. "Yessss!!!!!" Kilon bellows.

There is no better relief than this. Someone has come to our aid just in the nick of time. "Gal and Diem!!!" we all cry out.

They streak across the sky directly in our enemy's path and engage in a dog fight. It doesn't take long before smoke and fire engulf the enemy aircraft just before it crashes.

"Let's go!" Arek commands and we race along the streets. Soon, the multiple planes that have come to our rescue fly low, sending the masses of GENOS fleeing, which gives us an opening through the streets. "Come on!"

Heading straight toward the Old City Hall Station, we fight those who challenge us, but it is the military aircraft that leads our way. Finally, we descend into the subway.

"I figured it out," I whisper to Arek as we pass the Brooklyn Bridge City Hall stop. The subway has not been saved from the war happening in the streets, and there's fire, smoke, and debris everywhere. We pass bodies—GENOS, Ephemes, and Velieri alike. We have all been victims of this uprising. Beyond the ravaged underground, it is a ghost town. Eerily I have never experienced such quiet within an echo chamber like the subway.

"Spread out," Arek commands. We no longer take the subway cars since they lay broken and unusable. The systems within each city are now shutting down. We keep close to the tiled walls with our weapons ready as we move deeper beneath the city. "Stay low."

Geo and Daye stay beside each other as we pass the arches covered with mosaic tile of the old-fashioned subway. We hear the recorded voice and bell, but it is anything but typical. Arek peers back at me and again I wonder, will I ever experience his eyes without the weight of the world? Soon, we realize, there are GENOS on the other side of the stalled subway cars. We peer at them by climbing the stairs and looking through the windows.

Arek and the Umbramanes move in first. I've never experienced something so quiet, so perfect.

We can see men ahead who have not noticed we are there as they unload piles of boxes of ammo within closets along the tunnel.

"Hey!" one of them yells when they finally see the Umbramanes. However, it's too late. A cascade of violent bullets come down on us and we are forced to jump into the side halls of this subway. Navin never expected the Umbramanes to be against him. Sassi, Kilon, Beck, Caynan, Lya, Daye, Geo, and I are surrounded by the best of the best. Alfonzo alone proves why he can teach these men and women what he knows. The GENOS and Rebellion have no chance. None.

Somehow in my chest and body, I know where Navin is. I can feel him deeply. As the others are busy with the multitudes within these small halls of the subway, there's something drawing me to a side passage.

Before long, we hear the twist and turn of heavy Irish accents. Gal and Diem run through. They look worn out and bloodied, but they love it. "You can't get this done without us," Gal smiles.

"Where's Daye?" Lya asks suddenly.

"What?" I throw my eyes around the underground brick station, searching for Daye. Geo is straddling a man with a black mask, and he rips it off before he punches him again and again.

"There!" Lya cries out and races toward a hall where I see the back of Daye disappear. "Daye!" Lya cries and takes off in a sprint after her sister.

"Lya!" I yell and instantly race after them, and many of the others follow me.

The back halls grow dimmer and dimmer. "Come on!" Daye yells from farther ahead. There is no way to catch her.

"Daye, wait!" Lya cries out to her sister.

That's when it happens.

That's when everything I have feared becomes reality.

That's when Navin reaches out from the shadows and grabs Daye in his arms.

"Daye!" Lya screams. "Let her go!"

I wish I was closer, but seconds are sometimes too long. Lya dives toward them, knocking Daye out of his arms as they all fall to the ground. Several of Navin's men come from the opposite direction, including Masey, but Lya and Navin's fight is so aggressive and so fast, that it's difficult to see what is happening. Daye cries out as she reaches for her gun, which flew across the old tracks. "Lya!"

One of Navin's men covers her gun with his boot.

The moments last too long, yet not long enough. "Lya!" I scream from the lowest part of my belly.

Navin raises his arm in the air, the shiny metal of his knife glistening under the dim lights. "Nooooo!!!" I scream.

I know other people are yelling, but all I can hear is my own voice. Navin brings the knife down and plunges it into Lya's head just behind the ear. Her body stops fighting. Time stops. While Daye screams for her sister, the first thought that comes to me is that I failed. I failed her again.

"Noooo!!" The only time I've ever heard the kind of anguish that comes from my body and soul as I cry out was the night I heard Sassi scream for Nayo. Yet something strange happens around me and within me. The air swirls about, creating a tornado of dust and leaves as Navin lowers Lya's lifeless body to the floor. The swirl in the air becomes bigger and bigger until it overwhelms my sight. Something is happening and it begins with my prickling skin and the warmth in my chest. Our hair rises with the swirling wind and my tears are blown from my cheeks. That's when I see the realms converging into one, like a double exposed photograph. More people appear within this subway, yet they step through things, instead of around. I slowly turn around, watching as apparitions fill in around us. Daye is crying and holding Lya within her arms. "I saw this! I should have known. I saw this in the hot springs. She died for me . . . I should have known." Her pain echoes through the passage.

The swirling gets faster and faster. These apparitions turn from ghosts to just as real as those within this fight. My eyes lock with Sassi's as she runs onto the scene from where she's just been. She notices my confusion and surprise, then when her eyes take in what has come, her feet slide across the dirt to a sudden halt.

That's when I see the blonde hair.

Beckah. Her eyes look up as she walks beside Geo, letting her hand glide along his shoulder, yet he can't feel her, nor does he see her. My knees are weak as the power of the wind fights against my stance. The dust and leaves are blinding Navin as he pulls his knife from Lya, forcing Daye to crawl away from him.

Something travels along my shoulders and when I turn, Nayo, with her beautiful eyes and smile, passes by me. I watch as Sassi's tears come faster and heavier. She is the only one who has this gift like me. She watches as her daughter glides toward her. Across the way, stepping between two of Navin's men, are Leigh and Holona.

Everyone within this other realm stands shoulder to shoulder, wrapping themselves in a circle around the underground subway. The thicker this line of men and women, the more my skin rises. They stand around us, their eyes concentrating, their hands reaching out to Lya.

Beckah and Nayo walk through everyone, not caring about the restraints of this world. They reach out and touch Lya on the chest and forehead. When they begin to step away, I see the energy pulled from her body, released as if her soul was trapped.

I can see the look in Daye's eyes as she climbs to her feet, wanting revenge. She races toward Navin, unarmed. "Daye!" I cry out. "Don't! Step back! Step back!"

"Daye!" Geo yells from just a few feet away. Daye stops, turns her red and tear-filled eyes to Geo. Beckah grins as she sees the connection. "Let us get this. I've got you; let us get this," Geo whispers to Daye. It seems a relief to her as she walks heavily toward Geo. He looks in her eyes for just a moment.

My knuckles are white around my weapon as I step toward Navin. His men raise their guns at me, but my only interest is him.

"Drop it!" Navin's men yell, including Covey. But I can't, this gun is glued to my skin like the promise to my child that I would protect her.

From the darkness behind Navin, comes Isaiah.

I hear footsteps running behind me—many of them. Arek has found us. "Remy?!" Arek says as he studies what has happened. He yells loudly and angrily when he sees Lya.

Navin and I are pointing our guns at each other. No one is weak enough to Trace. It's like looking for a needle in a haystack as every one of us are experts at protecting our minds. But they don't see what I see. They don't hear the chanting that I hear, the rhythms of those who are not in this world anymore.

Navin shoots me directly in the chest. I fall back, but that's when the circle of the other realm steps closer. Instantly I can feel the power. As blood drips down my shirt, I climb to my hands and knees. "Remy!" Arek yells as he hurries toward me. Sassi, Kilon, Arek, Gal, and Diem begin shooting.

Continuous rounds of fire fill the air all around Navin and me. Arek, Geo, Sassi, Gal, Diem, and Kilon shoot until they've taken down every last one of Navin's men. Even Isaiah, Masey, and Covey are soon bleeding. Isaiah is lying on the tracks—his breathing becomes shallow. Wheezes slip from Covey's throat as he holds on to the wall for a moment, then drops; and I watch as Masey takes her last breath. I'm desperate to keep my attention on Navin, to be one step ahead of him. My eyes burn with sadness and my chest is tight in desperation. The men and women of the other realm take another step closer until the circle is even tighter around us.

For the first time, there are no more mind games to play. No more Tracing. No more Tri Planum.

I can feel my body expand and contract just as it used to before I'd Travel, but it doesn't happen. Nothing happens and my body stays where it should.

"Surprise," I say quietly to Navin. "No more haunting me, no more Traveling. I found what you planted . . . I figured it out. You might actually remember . . . somewhere deep . . . as a little boy . . . I gave it to you. The curse you and Japha planted so long ago on a little girl who didn't understand . . . who didn't know any better. But I'm not her anymore . . . and you've never been good enough. Not without Dr. Karine. Listen . . . *Tre kilou neu fumen caretsiva sui.*"

Navin looks at me with confusion. Then he peers down at his body with surprise.

"Do you feel it? The expanding, the contracting . . . but mostly the stealing . . . the stealing of someone's control." It's obvious from the look on his face that something is happening that he's never experienced. "Beck?" I call out.

"Yeah?" I hear from somewhere behind me.

"Get ready."

"For what?"

"I promised," I say as a tear falls down my lip, then off my chin. The swirling wind has not died down and my tears never reach the ground. *"Tre kilou neu fumen caretsiva sui,"* I whisper again and again.

Navin's body becomes rigid and he convulses, just as my body used to, and his eyes roll back into his head.

Before long, Navin appears beside me. No weapon in his hands. He looks surprised that he's there. Then he looks down and sees his body convulsing and shaking.

"Are you ready?" I ask Navin as I turn my gun toward him.

"Ready for what?"

"Beck?"

Beck moves through the crowd and points his gun at Navin as he lies on the ground. "I'm here!"

Navin knows he has nowhere to run. "It's already started . . . the GENOS are strong and the Rebellion has already changed the world. There's nothing you can do," Navin says with fear in his eyes.

"This is what I *can* do. Sassi," I call out.

"Yeah?"

"Your phone . . . pull up Andrew. Pull up the Bryers."

Within moments Sassi lifts the screen. Together we watch as GENOS are battled all over the world. Andrew shares footage from streets all over. "We won't let him win. Not the Rebellion, not the Prophets, not the Powers that be. Look at this," Andrew says with a laugh as he shows more footage of vigilantes taking the black masks down. "The Rebels never thought we'd join forces, did they? They never thought the Velieri and Ephemes would rise above subjugation together."

"It doesn't matter Navin," I say. "Whatever you have set up, we will displace. You never thought we'd win."

"Wait!" Navin yells.

"Beck!" I yell.

In sync, we take our shots.

In seconds, the Traveling Navin has disappeared and his body lies on the tracks of the station, no longer moving, which means the Navin that traveled to me is no longer there.

"Remy!" Arek yells suddenly.

Someone grabs me from behind and pulls me back. I'm weak and in pain from the bullet in my chest. Isaiah presses a gun to my head.

Arek and Kilon are too fast for him. They unload their bullets— Kilon even sends an extra barrage of bullets into Covey, making sure it is done.

I cry out as Isaiah begins to fall to the ground and won't let go of me, but Arek is able to grab me in his arms before I fall. For several moments I breathe into his chest. Before long, Daye is at our side and he pulls her in too.

When I finally remember, I look around, but the others are gone. Those who petition for us, like Holona said, are also gone and so is the wind.

We are all silent for a moment.

"One will give up their life for the other," Geo whispers a passage from the prophecy. Lya did just that.

Before long we carry Lya out of the subway and into the morning light of the New York streets just as the sun peeks over the buildings, knowing that our job is not yet over. All this time and we still don't know what has happened to my father.

CHAPTER FIFTY-SIX

On the outskirts of New York, several military planes sit side by side. One that carried Sassi, Kilon, Arek, and me; another that transported Gal after she led her team on a successful mission to the Bryer in the Catskills; one for Diem, and so on. These are our lifeline. Without Briston's military connections that have remained on our side, we would never have been able to accomplish what we have. Yet we now find ourselves in a scramble to end this war, despite the damage that has already been done.

Several soldiers carry a stretcher with Lya's body wrapped in layers of blankets that we found within an abandoned store on our way out of the city. They hike up the rear ramp of the aircraft and secure her inside. Daye has not left her, and Geo has not left Daye, until Arek pulls Geo away and speaks quietly. "Take Daye home. We still have work to do, so I ask that you take care of her."

Geo nods. "I will." His eyes narrow with concern, "Listen . . . we've done Tri Planum and beyond," he looks at me when he says this, "and because of that you can handle anything and anyone within those borders."

"Thank you, Geo," I reach out and squeeze his shoulder.

"Don't worry about Daye, I'll take care of her." Normally the tension is obvious on Geo's face, but today his features are soft with confidence. "Be safe and I'll see you on the other side."

Daye makes her way to us and as she says goodbye, the tears fall softly.

"Be safe," I whisper to Daye.

She nods.

Arek pulls her in his arms. "You can do this." Then, he takes a moment once more to look in her eyes with his hands on each side of her face, "We'll be home soon."

"Do you promise?" These are her first words since leaving the subway. Arek knows he can't promise her—this mission is dangerous. But even though Arek can't tell her what she needs to hear, she understands. He holds her for a while, then she turns and climbs up the rear door of the military plane to sit in its belly beside Geo. I watch as they secure themselves, then he takes her hand in his. Before long they fly away, heading to Switzerland—heading home. I want nothing more than to be there with Arek.

When they are out of view, we board a waiting military plane to meet with Alfonzo and the rest of the Umbramanes before we separate. Sassi, Kilon, Gal, Diem, and Beck are all there as well.

We study maps of the Cellars with Alfonzo. "Several of my Umbramanes will be sent to each one." Alfonzo is cool and collected, even though he knows the intensity this undertaking will require.

"We appreciate it," Arek says, then he explains the plan in detail.

Beck returns after a phone call: "Mak is already en route to get Kenichi out."

"Really?" I ask with surprise.

"Yeah, the moment he heard, he and his team headed out."

Alfonzo nods, "Well then, we haven't much time."

"Beck will keep us updated and will help you with anything you need," Arek clarifies.

My heart races at the thought of entering a prison again. When we hear loud crashes and shattering glass from Beck's computer, the entire group turns. "What's happening?"

"They're trying to get in. Come now!" Briston cries out, then the sound goes dead.

"Briston!" Beck yells, but there is no answer. "We need to go." He jumps to his feet and begins packing his computers. "Get as many inmates back in their cells as you can, and when you do, I'll lock the doors."

"Let's go!" Arek yells.

Nine hours later we are driving through the modern gates of the Cellar in Switzerland. The last time I was here, I was the criminal. So much has happened, yet my body remembers. The tension starts small, then builds, until my head pounds and my muscles ache. Arek leans into me and whispers in my ear, "We can do this."

Caynan meets us out front. "They've gone wild inside. But we have them . . ." He points to an army of men and women in tactical gear, guarding the modern gate as well as surrounding the exterior. "If anyone gets out, this group will do their best."

"Thank you, Caynan," Arek says. "Did you bring what I asked?"

Caynan smiles, "I did." Together we walk to his van and he opens the back doors. Every weapon that Arek and I stowed at our home and the ruins is there and ready for us. For the first time as my fingers wrap around the cold steel, relief fills me. We pass out the heavy artillery. Clips upon clips are tossed around for reloads until every inch of us is armed. Even Caynan, whom I rarely see holding a gun, arms himself to the best of his ability. When I look at him, he shrugs, "I'm getting used to it."

"What about your suit?" I grin. "You might get dirty."

"I have three more at home in this color. I'm good," Caynan winks.

Beck must stay on the computer to open the doors for us as well as Alfonzo and his men. "Once I unlock the door, you will have one minute to get in before I lock them again," Beck explains. The monitors give us a clear view of what's happening inside. At nearly every exit and entrance the criminals are working tirelessly to get out. Throwing chairs at windows, using the dead guards' weapons, and pounding on the handles of every door until they break. "I'll unlock this door, since there are only a few, but the moment you walk in, be ready," Beck says.

I touch Beck's shoulder and he looks up at me. For the first time the pain of this place shows in his red eyes and tight lips. I am quite jealous that he will be in the van outside.

Finally, we wait outside the basement door, where they forced me to enter on the first day of my time at the Cellar. The count-down begins. Kilon, Sassi, Gal, Diem, Arek, and I, with several of the Umbramanes at our side, silently wait outside the door. Click by click.

One second at a time.

Three.

Two.

One.

Kilon kicks the doors open, which sends several of the inmates flying backward. This gives us just enough time to rush in.

Immediately the task of guarding our minds is first. Just as before, the air is so thick, it's like breathing rotten, foul-tasting liquid. The smell brings me back instantly—a strange combination of mildew, human waste, and rot. It's the doom and the intense oppression that infiltrates every ounce of our being that devours our thoughts the moment we are inside. We haven't even made it to the levels with the inmates. Sassi and I are the only ones who see the Unyielded, rather than just feeling them.

Sassi checks the door behind us and it is locked once again. We race through the halls. Several inmates come at us like madmen with weapons that they haven't the wherewithal to control. It is a fight to guard ourselves from their vile thoughts and emanations.

"We go together. One level at a time," Arek says.

As we climb two flights of stairs, we run into inmates who are searching and desperate for a way out. We have no choice but to kill them before they kill us. Finally, we reach the third floor where most of the inmates are locked in the halls. I know my father is on the fourth floor.

"Beck," Arek says with his earpiece in place, "we're at the first hall on the third floor. Unlock the doors." Arek raises his gun to his chin, and we follow. "Those we can save, do so."

The buzzer sounds, telling us that we can get in. When we do, dozens of inmates charge us with wide eyes of insanity. Their desire for freedom to do the darkest deeds is almost palpable. Without taking a shot, Kilon and Arek work together on the first man who angrily rips and claws at them. Then together, they twist and extend him until he has no fight left and throw him back in the cell. "Lock three-oh-one!" Arek calls out. Beck does as he's told.

One after the other we do this. There is nothing greater to watch than when Kilon can seep in and send many of them to sleep. We hurriedly push them into the cells. When I compare who I was before within these halls, it is nothing compared to today. I drag their fears to the surface, playing with them so that they are so afraid or confused that they run back into their cells. Some are gifted, so we fight them physically; some are dangerous beyond what we expect, and it takes several of us at a time to get them under our control.

There's nothing Sassi and I can do for the Unyielded within these walls. Most of them live in a state of confusion, experiencing neither this realm or another. At times they seem to know we are there and what we are doing, only to forget the next moment and go back to their angst. Staring at the wall just in front of me is the Unyielded man who laughed during the night of my torture. Only this time he pays no attention to me—he rubs his hands together until his skin is raw and tortured cries escape his lips—so I race past him and on to the next inmate.

421

By the time the first level is completed, we look back and see only two who lost their lives. The other inmates angrily stare at us through the rectangle slots of their metal doors.

The next level is much of the same. One at a time we wrestle the Cellar's inmates back into their cells. Beck is frantically working on his end with multiple Cellars and teams. When we get halfway through, I see the door that holds my father, and I run to it. It has been broken into and stands wide open. "Dad!" I yell.

I race inside the guards' room and there he is, his weapon raised to his nose, with blood seeping down his face, as he crouches in the corner waiting for the next person to enter. "It's me!" I yell to warn him. He drops his weapon to his side, and we crash into each other with gratefulness that he's still alive. "Are you okay?" I ask in his arms.

"Yes. I'm fine. My arm's broken, but it will heal," Briston says. Then he looks me over. "You're perfect."

Arek breathes out a sigh of relief when he comes around the door. "Okay we have two more floors, and the last floor is the most dangerous."

We do the same for the next floor, but this time we leave four dead. One more level remains. Before Arek asks Beck to unlock the hall, we check our weapons. Finally, we hear the squeal of the lock, then Arek twists the handle, and we rush inside. My mind is instantly attacked. Every fear, every doubt, every weakness that exists from my body to my soul is heightened. I drop my head in my hands and take a moment to find my rhythm again. Everyone does the same and this gives the inmates a chance at the upper hand. We try to fight, but our minds are instantly not our own. Even Briston cries out in anguish.

The last time I was here, this place stole from me. It stole my power, my energy, my mind, and ultimately preyed on my brokenness. The feeling of desolation was cruel and exactly what these inmates wanted from me. Why did they want this? Because within them, they experience it every minute of every day and the last thing that misery wants is to be alone. Since that time, all of us have changed by facing our most buried wounds. So why are we struggling? The truth is this: we hold on to pain and wrap it around ourselves like protection and joy is lost too quickly.

I reach across the hall and touch Arek's face. He turns to me and touches mine. The aloe sinks deep. I grin, feeling the darkness roll off me, no different than low tide pulling away from shore. Sassi grows tall once again, then Kilon, Briston, the Umbramanes, and Caynan. Sassi grabs the arm of one of the inmates as he swings it toward her head and, with a perfectly timed twist, he spins in the air falling heavily with a loud crack against the cement floor. Kilon and Sassi easily push him inside the nearest cell together and cry out to Beck to lock the door. Just as the click happens and the inmate is sealed within, a new convict dives toward them—Kilon stops him midair with his powerful arm against the attacker's head. One blow from Kilon is enough and Kilon tosses him into the nearest cell. Arek races forward: his strategy is his safety. He works three men at a time, using their own bodies and minds against them, then he calls out for Kilon to help him finish the job. Briston, his arm now gaining strength, hardly touches the man he fights. Every bit of authority and wisdom he has gathered over centuries overwhelms the evil in these men until they are moving slowly. Sassi, Kilon, and Arek help Briston gather up these men once they are weak and useless, and soon they are trapped behind the metal doors.

The Umbramanes are fast and precise.

And me—a surge springs forth, my body never far from the Void now. I strip them of their rhythm and ride their fear until the manipulation is easy. They panic at the sight of me—their monsters manifested. It's then that I take control and their shoes squeal along the floor as I reach out and a simple fingertip pushes them within the cells. When I look up, a familiar face is heading my way. Fredo, the inmate that Meryl hoped would kill me when he trapped me in the cafeteria, who nearly killed me when I wasn't strong enough to fight him off, is headed directly toward me. He's angry and determined to finish what he started. I stop, press my feet into the ground, and direct my power toward him. I slide right into his psyche, manipulating him by using his own demons, before he becomes aware. However, once he feels me in there, it is too late. When he is just an arm's length away, his eyes grow wide over the devil I have become, but I give him no time to back away. "Fredo." I say, just before I unleash everything with me. He is so much larger than I am, but it does not matter. He tries to fight my fast hands and perfectly placed strikes. He falls like a giant oak to the cement floor and I climb over him and force him to look at me. With panic on his face and blood coming from his bald head, he throws his arms over his face in fear because of what he sees in me. I grab his chin and force him to look me straight in the eye.

"Not how you thought this would go?" I ask. He cries out in fear. I stand up, close my eyes, directing my energy toward him. I listen to the scraping and clawing as I push him into the cell. When I open my eyes, his fingernail marks scrape the floor from my feet to the cell and he cries out as he fights to stay in the hallway. Fredo grabs the doorjamb on each side as though some invisible darkness is pulling him back into the shadows. Finally, his hands are ripped from the metal doorjam and he disappears into the black. "Close 510!" I cry into my earpiece, as I slam the metal door shut. In seconds I hear the clink and squeak of the internal lock, and Beck says, "Done."

We continue from one end of the massively long hallway, taking a quarter of it at a time. Kilon jumps ahead as we battle our own inmates, and three come racing toward him. Faster than I've seen before, their feet slow down and their eyes droop until every limb hangs like a rag doll and they fall to the floor, dead asleep. Whether we've come a long way and learned more from this last battle, or these men and women don't have the power that Navin, Leigh, Covey, Karine, and Isaiah had, it doesn't really matter. We beat them too.

Sassi runs fast toward them, uses one of their knees to step up and flip herself over his shoulder, then she takes him from the back with her forearm pressed to his neck, and pushes him inside the cell.

Inmate after inmate fail to take us down. Each one of us has our own way, and each one of us works together like the team we have become. Even Caynan has found his own way, and we gather around him to make sure that he is safe with each attacker. When there are three left, we only have to stare at them and they step back in fear. Without weapons, without violence, the last three walk into their cells of their own volition.

"Shut the last one down!" Arek yells at Beck.

"Done!" Beck hollers quickly.

We stop for the first time, out of breath and taking a moment to recoup. Yet it isn't long before Sassi catches my eye. She smiles, as do I. The wave of liberation floods us and we give ourselves a moment to celebrate. Arek pushes his way through the others and heads straight into my arms. He picks me up and the weight of the world is no longer in his eyes as he stares into mine.

By the time we reach Beck, Mak has found Kenichi, and we watch their cameras as he helps his father out. Alfonzo declares success for every Cellar within two hours. Now, we go home, prepare Lya's funeral, and everyone will meet again to find out who we lost and to celebrate what we've gained.

CHAPTER FIFTY-SEVEN

Back on our land, the snow has lifted, and the spring has begun. I hold the ashes of my daughter in my hand as I walk through the meadow in its fresh spring colors. I hear the low hum of vehicles, which draws my attention back to the driveway of our house.

Mak's handsome face appears as he steps from an SUV filled with others.

I run to him. He wraps me in his arms and we stay there for many moments. Soon, when I look up at him, I notice the sadness in his eyes. "What? Where's Kenichi?"

Mak clears his throat, "No, he's fine." Tears come to his eyes, "Aita is gone."

"I'm so sorry, Mak."

"And I'm sorry too. But she wanted to help and she stayed right by my side." He places a palm on my cheek and together our tears drop to the green grass below our feet.

More of our team arrive by evening. Peter, appearing much older than when he left, smiles when he sees Arek. I've never seen these brothers embrace with such strength and relief. Soon, Peter searches for Lily among the crowd. Through the glow of the fire, he catches sight of her. She runs to him and they hold each other. After a moment, he slips his hand down her hair and cheek, then leans in and kisses her.

I'm grateful when I see Jay walking past the fire toward me—his wife is at his side. He looks tired, but he's alive. "Jay."

"We made it and saved as many as we could." Jay lays an arm over his wife's shoulder and kisses her temple. Briston, Caynan, and Hok come as well. Briston holds a book in his hands—when he comes close, he takes my hand and presses it on the old leather.

"What is this?" I ask.

"One of the Manchester Books," he whispers.

"Where did you find it?" Arek asks with surprise.

"It was intercepted by Kinnie Brown, leader of the Reds," he said. "She knows where the others are, but it's going to be a fight to get them back."

Hok seems skeptical, "Can we trust her? After all we've found with the Reds?" Briston hands Hok a paper. "What's this?" Hok asks.

"Kinnie's list of every Red leader who was found out and has already been defeated. I would stake my life on Kinnie. She's one of the good ones," Briston assures everyone. "In fact, she's taken a liking to our guy Jay. He's going to help her get things back in order."

"Jay?" I smile at him.

Jay shrugs. "What can I say? It's time to get ourselves back in line and who better than the Panel Beaters to do it."

Briston looks at me with a raised eyebrow and I know what he's thinking.

"Find somebody else, Dad. I need a break," I grin. "We'll find the books after a long vacation."

Mak and Kenichi come to join us. Soon everyone is there. We all stare at the book, our history belonging within its pages.

"If we are rewriting our story, why do we need these?" Daye asks with Geo's arm around her.

Kenichi bows his head with his hands in prayer position. "There are more prophecies within this book. Ways to exist, what is to happen next, how to bring this world back to order. We learn from our history even if it's what not to do. If they get into the wrong hands—"

"No," I interrupt. "Nope. No more prophecies."

The others laugh, but deep within we know what needs to be done. Caynan, Prophet Jenner, and Thire join us. Thire hands me a mask that the GENOS wore with pride. The red Xs on its eyes still make my skin crawl. "Meryl was the first I ever saw wearing this," I say.

"Well, this is the one that was taken off Prophet Hawking," Thire explains.

"So, we don't need to worry about her?" I ask.

"Not anymore," Thire assures.

Beck speaks up, "Somehow Hawking ended up back at one of the Bryers and tried to hide behind that mask. But . . ." he takes a second to breathe, "Adam figured out where she was and killed her."

"Wait. Where's Adam?" I ask as I squeeze the rubbery mask between my fingers.

"He died leading the others to safety. He did well." Beck consoles me.

We take a moment, then I turn and throw Prophet Hawking's mask into the fire. It lands on a piece of wood and instantly begins to bubble and melt. I breathe out, thinking about all the time that has gone by.

"There are many more GENOS still out there," Peter says as he and Lily come near.

"I guess that all we can believe is that we've started the change." I say quietly as I watch the rest of the mask turn to ash.

This reminds me that I'm still carrying Lya's ashes. As everyone watches, I reach my hand into the urn and release some in the air. It is soft and light. Arek does the same, followed by everyone else.

Something feels different.

"Remy," Holona's soft voice whispers nearby.

Leaves pick up and pass before my eyes. Once again, the air is rich as though I am breathing in speckles of gold. Something divine visits me again, turning the sky several shades of purple and deep pink. A perfect breath passes through every molecule as if it's blowing a thick mist across the grass. Something more takes the space around us. Misshapen and jagged lines of shadow pass in front of my eyes and within the air. The two worlds mesh into one. The apparitions, although the others cannot see them, are walking around us and through us leaving their trail of luminescence. Holona is standing within them, and she smiles. She, too, is just a shadow.

I let another handful of ash release within this beautiful field.

"Look around. She's here," Holona says with her sweet and gentle voice.

"Who?" I ask.

She nods to my left.

I turn and not far from me is a woman. She's just a figment, a barely-there form of spirit, and even though she's difficult to make out, my eyes widen with shock. It is Ava, my Ephemeral mother whom I loved so much. She walks within us and around us as though there is work to constantly be done. While most of the time neither realm sees the other, for just a small moment, she turns to me as if she sees me. I take a couple of steps forward and Arek looks at me inquisitively.

"We are no different," Holona says. "Epheme or Velieri, we are human and we all rest within the same place." Soon, Ava is gone and our meadow is back to the nighttime party we created.

I release the rest of the urn within a cloud of ash, and all of us watch as it floats away. Daye wraps her arms around me, then Arek wraps his around us. We pass around drinks and raise our hands to the sky.

Kilon, with his deep and rich voice, lets out a battle cry, hitting his chest three times and everyone else follows. Kilon's voice is loud and clear, "To those who lost their lives, may they find peace on the other side."

CHAPTER FIFTY-EIGHT

The world no longer has order. Navin and Japha wanted chaos and they made it happen. Yet as the weeks pass, and we watch the world in its aftershock, we begin to realize that many Velieri have joined forces with many Ephemes to protect the weak. The GENOS still exist and are on a rampage to finish what Japha and Navin started.

Daye and Geo marry quickly in a small ceremony on our land; my father and Elizabeth finally get to experience the love that should have been theirs long ago.

Arek and I try to disappear. He takes me to our favorite beach, and we lie in the sand with his arms wrapped tightly around me. I've never felt so peaceful and safe. Until Andrew Vincent shows up on our doorstep one day and makes it clear that I won't be able to hide. My rest time won't happen until things are cleaned up and the world starts finding its rhythm again. People won't allow it. I am famous, both in the Velieri and Ephemeral world, and there are expectations of me.

So here I am, living with Arek at the peak of our rebuilding.

We travel for talks of treaties with the Reds and their leader, Kinnie Brown. Both sides are used to doing things their own way, based on lies, so it is now a time to learn and listen. What do we do now that many of the power seekers and the greediest leaders are gone? We're not naïve enough to believe that others won't try to take their place.

We force ourselves to look at what went wrong and how so many of our leaders were a part of our demise. One thing remains clear: the power of the few should never be able to control the lives of so many.

Prophet Jenner has become a voice for our new world. With a massive crew of people, she travels to the wounded and gives time to people who have lost everything. I believe, as I watch her, that she is the answer to our changes. However, she disagrees. To Prophet Jenner, people should be their own heroes, not rely on five Prophets and thirty-five Representatives of the Powers. In her speeches she insists this. "It is time for change. No longer should we allow just five men or women to dictate our lives. In fact, no longer do we allow only a few to exist in that power. Many of you are out there, you who swore loyalty to Navin and his Rebellion. You who wore the mask of the GENOS and killed those weaker than you. We know you are still out there, but many of us are ready to rebuild. And as we do, we will rise from the ashes. We will find those who still wish to do harm to our lives, to our freedom, to our democracy. It will no longer be. Trust me as I say it one more time . . . we are in the age of freedom. And no one will ever be allowed to steal our existence of both Ephemes and Velieri, ever again. No longer do we live separate. We exist together. We exist in freedom."

People still die daily because of the GENOS. When Kilon comes to the forefront of one of our meetings, I know there's something important he needs to share by the look in his eyes.

"I'd like to create an army with Alfonzo Geretzima. Together we will find every GENOS that's left. It doesn't matter how much progress we make, if there are still people in danger all over the world, it is not enough."

Prophet Jenner, Kinnie Brown, and many of us whisper for several minutes. Then they look up with soft eyes. "Anything you need, just let us know."

Kilon is almost surprised. "Thank you."

Jenner stops him, "Oh, and Kilon."

"Yes Prophet Jenner," he asks.

"Good luck to you."

Little by little we instate new policies and devise plans for the future. The damage is far and wide, but so is the hope.

I stare out the window at the newly fallen snow over the most beautiful meadow that I call home. From the trees comes a very familiar face and I smile. Vi runs to the middle of the open field and sits down, then looks at me as if she has something to say. I grab my coat and before long she and I walk beside each other, so close that her hip touches me. We hike together until we reach the lookout. With everything covered in white, just the treetops show and the beauty is mesmerizing. Vi sits beside me as we look out over something so large and so grand that it revives a knowledge that we are not alone.

I am startled when I feel a hand on my waist, then Arek quickly pulls me into him as Vi watches on. "How do you always know where I am?" I say quietly.

He kisses me and lingers just a moment as a sly smile slips across his face. "You and I are one . . . where you begin, I end, and where you end, I begin."

With nowhere to be today, he presses his lips onto mine until they burn and swell as the soft drops of snow wet our skin. I wrap my arms around his neck and his tall body lifts me until my feet dangle above the ground. After a moment he looks out, finally noticing the gorgeous view, and that's when I realize that his eyes are lighter than I've ever seen them. "Wow," he says as his hand takes mine. After several minutes he turns to me and whispers, "Let's go home."

Then together, with Vi at our side, we head home, hand in hand.

EPILOGUE

"You have to come now," my father says on the phone.

"Wait, what are you saying?"

"You need to see for yourself."

I hang up and grab my keys. "Arek! We have to go!"

It isn't long before I stand outside a chain-link fence. After the uprising, nothing is the same, but schools and daycares have now reopened, albeit under the pretense of careful security and safety. A schoolyard is beginning to look like a schoolyard again.

When the kids run out to play, that's when I see her. I know exactly which one she is. Daye pulls up in her car with Geo and they come to stand by us.

"Right there," I tell them.

The dark-haired little girl with deep green eyes looks up from the playground and stares directly at us. No more than three years old, this little girl holds our hearts in her hands. And while we don't know what will come, we know what is here now.

With the softest smile and no hard shell, Lya smiles.

THE END

ACKNOWLEDGMENTS

I want to thank my beautiful husband who has been with me for most of my life. You are my muse for every love story within my books. I thank my lucky stars that you are beyond supportive, and work so diligently at making OUR dreams come true. I'm obsessed with you and that will never change.

Thank you Evie and Georgia for becoming such loving, amazing, and determined women. It has been my greatest joy in life watching you grow to give people so much love, attention, and care. This world is a better place with both of you in it. And never forget, be the heroine of your own stories.

Thank you, Mom! There's never been a more positive voice at just the moment of breakdown, than yours. I can only imagine the puddles of tears on my bathroom floor that would still be there if I didn't have you to go to.